W9-CBZ-229

Mother Road

Books by Dorothy Garlock

After the Parade
Almost Eden
Annie Lash
Dream River
The Edge of Town
Forever Victoria
A Gentle Giving
Glorious Dawn
High on a Hill
Homeplace
Larkspur
The Listening Sky
Lonesome River
Love and Cherish
Midnight Blue
More than Memory
Nightrose
A Place Called Rainwater
Restless Wind
Ribbon in the Sky
River of Tomorrow
The Searching Hearts
Sins of Summer
Sweetwater
Tenderness
This Loving Land
Wayward Wind
Wild Sweet Wilderness
Wind of Promise
With Heart
With Hope
With Song
Yesteryear

DOROTHY GARLOCK

Mother Road

An AOL Time Warner Company

This book is a work of historical fiction. In order to give a sense of the times, some names of real people or places have been included in the book. However, the events depicted in this book are imaginary, and the names of nonhistorical persons or events are the product of the author's imagination or are used fictitiously. Any resemblance of such nonhistorical persons or events to actual ones is purely coincidental.

Warner Books, Inc., 1271 Avenue of the Americas, New York, NY 10020

Visit our Web site at www.twbookmark.com.

 An AOL Time Warner Company

Printed in the United States of America

First Printing: June 2003
10 9 8 7 6 5 4 3 2 1

Library of Congress Cataloging-in-Publication Data
Garlock, Dorothy.
Mother Road / Dorothy Garlock.
p. cm.
ISBN 0-446-53062-X
1. United States Highway 66—Fiction. 2. Automobile repair shops—Fiction. 3. Motherless families—Fiction. 4. Depressions—Fiction. 5. Oklahoma—Fiction. 6. Rabies—Fiction. I. Title.

PS3557.A71645 M66 2003
813'.54—dc21 2002191009

With love to my grandson
ADAM MIX,
whose claim to fame is that
he advertised *Larkspur*
on his underwear.

"Oklahoma Route 66"

Route 66. It is a symbol of American ingenuity, spirit and determination. For millions, it represents a treasure chest of memories, a direct link to the days of two-lane highways, family vacations, and picnic lunches at roadside tables. It brings up all the images of going somewhere, of souvenir shops, reptile pits, and cozy motor courts, of looking forward to the next stop—a slice of breezy shade, an Orange Crush, a two-cent deposit.

Route 66. It's a winding grade, a rusty steel bridge, and flickering neon at a late-night diner. It is mountains and desert, plains and forest. American's Mother Road, all of this and more, is today the world's most famous highway, even though officially it no longer exists. And it all began, simply enough, with the ordinary needs of a growing nation and in 1924 the vision of one man, Oklahoma Highway Commissioner Cyrus Avery.

Jim Ross, author of
Oklahoma Route 66

Mother Road

SONG OF THE ROAD

The dust took my land and nothing grew
I took off with my brood. Was all I could do.
On Route 66, some folks was kind.
Andy Connors is one who comes to my mind.

At his garage he gassed up my heap,
Gave me 'n my family somewheres to sleep.
Then that rabid skunk give him such a bite!
He needed them shots that could fix him up right.

A stranger drove in and took him to get 'em,
Then took over the place. Guess Andy let him.
Stranger tended the store, daughters and farm
And the woman who lived there; kept 'em from harm.

Quite a story begun there, something to tell.
You can read all about it if you set fer a spell.
Me—I'm off in the mornin', me and my kin,
On Route 66 where big dreams begin.

Mother Road, take me west.
Lead the way to where the chances are best.
Rough or smooth, paved or gravel,
You're the pathway to hope that I'm aimin' to travel.

—F.S.I.

Chapter 1

1932
Route 66
Sayre, Oklahoma

THE POWERFUL AUTOMOBILE, RACING ALONG the newly paved Route 66, slowed as it crossed the bridge over the north fork of the Red River, then picked up speed. At the top of the grade, the Hudson was pulled to the side of the road and stopped. For the last ten miles the driver had been reading signs attached to fence posts: CAR TROUBLE? NEED GAS? ANDY'S GARAGE AHEAD.

Close to the paved ribbon of highway were a small building with large doors folded back and a single gas pump at the side. In big black letters across the peaked roof of the building was another sign: ANDY'S GARAGE—GAS—CAMPING.

A short distance away, woods surrounded the campground on two sides. A dirty-white, low-pitched canvas tent flapped in the breeze, near it a stacked brick fireplace and a crude wooden table. A woman sat on a stool in front of the tent. A child played at her feet.

To the side of the garage and set slightly back was a small frame house with a sloped roof, which covered the porch that stretched across the front. Hanging from a branch of the tree that stood between the house and a garage was a child's swing. Flowers bloomed in beds beside the porch.

A woman wearing a sunbonnet worked in a large, neat vegetable garden. Behind the house were a privy, a chicken house and a small barn with a lean-to shed attached. Out from the barn a cow and a horse grazed in a pasture made green by the spring rains.

The buildings that sprawled along the highway were the only ones in sight. A mile down the road was the town of Sayre, Oklahoma. When the driver of the Hudson was last there, the town had hardly warranted the dot it made on the map. It had consisted of little more than a gas station, grocery store and a greasy-spoon diner. Now situated along the busy Route 66, it was likely, he thought, to have a café, a rooming house or a hotel.

Guilt had been eating a hole in Yates's gut for the last few years. He owed a debt to Andy Connors and had never as much as said "Thank you." He intended to do something about it, so that he could get on with his life and, when the time came, leave Oklahoma with nothing still to be done.

Yates pulled back onto the highway, newly paved with portland cement, and drove slowly down the hill. On reaching Andy's garage, he pulled in and stopped beside the gas pump.

The man who came out of the garage, wiping his hands on a greasy rag, walked easily on a peg belted to his upper leg. Beneath a soiled cap his hair was light, his eyes blue in a sun-tanned face. He had aged, but his face had been imprinted in Yates's memory. He would have been able to pick Andy Connors out in a crowd of a thousand, even though he was a smaller man than he remembered.

"Howdy. Need gas?" Andy's face was clean shaven, boyish and friendly. "Dumb question, huh? You do, or you wouldn't have stopped here next to the pump."

"I think it'll hold about ten gallons." Yates watched Andy pump the lever back and forth to fill the glass cylinder atop the pump. It was marked like a beaker to measure the gas.

"Warm day out there on the highway," Andy remarked as he unscrewed the cap from the gas tank. "But it'll get hotter," he added when the man nodded. "It's only June. By the Fourth it'll be hotter than a pistol around here."

Andy glanced at the man, who wore a handsome tan Stetson and custom-made boots. He'd hate to tangle with this *hombre*. Everything about the tall, broad-shouldered man was big and hard, quiet and serious. Andy had met people from all walks of life as they traveled Route 66, nicknamed the *Mother Road*, heading west to California—the promised land. This man looked as if he could plow his way through a batch of wildcats without breaking a sweat.

While the gas poured into the tank of his car, Yates's sober gaze drifted across the still and somber landscape to where a mean-looking black and brown dog lay in the shade of the garage eyeing him with skepticism.

Shiny tin signs advertising tires, tubes, spark plugs and NeHi soda pop were nailed to the side of the garage building alongside signs promoting Garret snuff and chewing tobacco. Clothes hung on a line in the space between the house and the barn. All was quiet except for the buzz of a june bug and the song of a mockingbird. Two cars passed each other on the highway not more than twenty feet away; their tires sang on the paving.

The laughter of a child caught his attention. The little girl in the campground had broken away, her chubby legs taking her toward the highway. The woman chased her, caught her up in her arms and tickled her until she squealed with laughter.

A family trying to make it to California and the promise of a better life.

"How's business?" Yates asked.

"Good enough to get by," Andy replied. "Most of the folks coming down this highway aren't out for a joyride. I fix them up as best I can and get them on their way." Andy removed the nozzle from the gas tank and, as he hung it back on the pump, noticed a Texas license plate on the black sedan. He didn't often see Hudsons along the highway. They were big, powerful and expensive cars. This one looked as if it had eaten up plenty of miles.

"Don't you hanker to take the road to greener pastures?" The Texan almost smiled when he asked the question.

"Naw." Andy chuckled. "As long as I can crank out a living here, I'm stayin'. How about you?"

"One place is pretty much like the other. It's what a fellow makes of it."

"I'm with you there. Ten gallons at fourteen cents. Pretty easy to figure, huh?" Andy tightened the cap on the gas tank of the car.

"I've been paying sixteen and eighteen cents all along."

"That so? Fourteen cents gives me a profit. Living out here on the highway, I get first crack at the gas customers going west. Some of them have rolled down the hill to get here," he said with a chuckle. "But I make most of my living in the garage. I don't pretend to be the best mechanic in the world, but I'm right handy at the small stuff." He jerked his head toward the campground. "Folks can rest over there while their car is being fixed. Traveling is hard on the women and kids."

"How about folks who can't pay?"

"Oh, they pay one way or the other. I've had my horse shod and the porch shingled." Andy chuckled. "See that big pile of stove-wood over by the house and the new privy? Most folks are pretty decent and want to pay their way. Of course, there are a few you've got to look out for. I've not been robbed yet. I think they figure I don't have enough to bother with."

Yates counted out the money. His silver-gray eyes homed in on Andy's face while he put the coins in his hand.

"Appreciate your business," Andy said. "Stop in again if you come this way."

Yates nodded, got into the car and watched Andy spin around on his peg and go back into the garage. When he was out of sight, Yates drove away slowly to avoid stirring up dust. As he passed the open doors of the garage, he could see Andy bending over a tub of water with an inflated tire tube, looking for bubbles that would indicate a hole, which needed to be patched. A man in overalls far too short for his long legs stood beside an old car with its backend jacked-up on one side.

Connors is just as I remember him—quick, smiling; I'm no longer the skinny, sick young kid I was back then, but somehow I had expected him to recognize me.

TWO DAYS LATER.

"Leooonaaa! Get the gun!"

Andy tried to evade the small attacking animal that continued to run at him. He balanced himself on his leg and knocked the skunk away with his peg. The crazed animal continued to come at him. Then it sank its teeth into the rubber on the end of his peg, causing him to lose his balance and almost topple to the ground.

"Leooonaaa!"

Hearing the commotion, a shaggy dog came running from the side of the house, barking furiously.

"No! Calvin! No!"

"Andy!"

"Get the gun!" Andy shouted, trying desperately to ward off the skunk with his wooden peg.

"Andy!" The shrill voice of the girl jumping off the porch and running out into the yard came seconds before the sound of a BOOM and the whiz of the traveling bullet, which hit the skunk and threw it a dozen feet from the man who had fallen on the ground. A putrid odor immediately filled the air.

"Did it bite you?" The girl reached Andy and helped him to stand.

"Keep Calvin away from it."

"Go, Calvin," she yelled angrily. "Go!" She stamped her foot.

The shaggy dog backed away and slunk under the porch. He didn't understand Leona's reason for being angry. *He knew better than to bite into a stinking skunk.*

"I've got to bury it."

"Did it bite you?" Leona's voice quivered with fear.

"I've got to bury it," Andy said again. "Calvin might take a notion to drag it off. Skunks don't come out in daylight unless they're sick."

"Rabies?"

"Could be. But there hasn't been any around here in a while."

"I'll get a shovel. Watch Calvin."

"I'll bury it after I get my . . ." His words trailed as the horror of what happened settled upon him. "That was a good shot, Lee." His trembling voice squeezed through his tightened throat.

"I didn't shoot. I didn't have time."

"Then who?"

"I don't know. I didn't see anyone."

"It came from the woods."

Andy scanned the edge of the timber from where the mysterious shot had come. As he watched, a man carrying a rifle rode out of the timber on a big buckskin horse. Andy squinted his eyes to get a better look at him. He was sure that he wasn't anyone he had seen before, nor was the horse familiar. The rider wore a dusty black Stetson and a blue shirt with sleeves rolled up to the elbows.

The horse reached the yard. The size of the man riding him struck a chord in Andy's memory. He looked into the dark, somber face and recognized him. A day or so ago, driving a big Hudson Super-Six, he had stopped for gas.

"Howdy. Thanks for killing the skunk." Andy choked out the words. "It's not goin' to smell very good around here for a while."

"Did it bite you?"

"It might have. I'll bury it so that the dog won't get to it. That was a damn good shot." Andy's voice trembled. He was obviously shaken.

"I didn't want to shoot between you and the woman, but I was afraid to wait." Yates shoved the rifle down in the scabbard, swung down from the saddle and walked over to look down at the skunk. "It's sure to be rabid. We'd better pour a little gas on it and set it on fire." He looked at Andy with narrowed, unblinking gray eyes. "What do you mean, 'it might have' bit you?"

"I'll get the gas. I . . . felt . . . something on my leg."

"Daddy!" A small girl with blond braids came off the porch and ran out into the yard, her long nightgown flapping around her legs.

"Stay back, honey. Go back to the porch." Andy started toward the child.

"I'll get her, Andy." The woman who had gone to fetch the shovel came out of the barn. She dropped it when she saw the little girl jump off the porch and head for the dead skunk. She ran to her and grabbed her up.

"Stinks," the child shouted. "Daddy, it stinks."

"Daddy will take care of it. We've got to stay out of the way."

"I smell skunk!" The door slammed behind another girl who stepped out onto the porch. She was older than the one who had run out into the yard.

"Stay there, Ruth Ann," the woman called.

"Did Calvin catch a skunk?"

The slim woman with the bare feet had thick mahogany-colored hair that tumbled in loose waves about her shoulders. Gripping the hand of the little girl, she pulled her up onto the porch and hugged both girls to her.

Yates's narrowed eyes took in the scene. Although crippled, Andy Connors had done all right for himself. He had a pretty wife and two pretty little girls and was apparently making a living for them.

Leona watched the strange man stride forward and take the gas can from Andy's hand.

"I'll do it. I found blood spots we'd better burn off."

His voice was deep and forceful, yet it wasn't harsh. It went with the strong planes of his face. He looked dangerous, dark, strong, yet graceful. He was a big man. Andy seemed small beside him.

"If the skunk bit you, you know what it means."

The stranger poured the gasoline on the body of the skunk and made a trail of it for several yards. He recapped the gas can, moved a short distance away and set it down on the ground. After striking a match on the bottom of his boot, he held the flame to the trail of gasoline. The low fire traveled to the dead animal, where it burst into flames. He watched the fire for a minute or two, giving Andy time to come to terms with what had just happened to him.

"Andy?"

Yates turned when he heard the woman call. Andy had reached the back door of the garage.

"Watch that the fire doesn't spread," Yates said to the anxious woman on the porch. He picked up the spade and, with one easy shove with his booted foot, sank it into the ground.

Inside the garage, Andy leaned on the hood of his '29 Ford coupe. *Dear God, on the way from the house to the garage his life and that of his kids had been changed—maybe forever.*

"Let's take a look at where it bit you." The stranger had followed him into the hot, semi-darkened garage. "If it didn't break the skin—"

"It did. I didn't want to scare Leona and the girls."

"They'll have to know sooner or later."

Andy leaned against the wall, then eased down onto a bench. He lifted the leg of his duck britches and looked down. His face paled, his hands shook, and he broke into a sweat when he saw the trickle of blood that ran from the puncture wound just above the top of his sock.

"Is there a doctor in Sayre?"

"New one. Hasn't been here long."

"You'll probably have to go to Oklahoma City."

"Oh, shit! I can't go and leave Leona and the girls out here by themselves. A lot of decent folks travel the highway, but robbers, bootleggers and murderers travel it, too. I sleep with a gun within reach every night."

"The skunk was sick. I'm sure of it. It was running around

in a circle when I first saw it in the woods. I followed it, hoping to get a shot at it."

"There's not been any rabies around here . . . that I know of."

"There is now. Without getting the inoculation shots you'll die of hydrophobia." The man's voice was as matter-of-fact as if he were talking about the weather.

Andy took a deep breath, trying to control his fear. The breath didn't help. His heart was pounding like the beat of a drum in a Fourth-of-July parade.

"They'll have to go with me. I can't leave them here by themselves."

"A series of shots might cover the span of a month or two. Can you keep them with you for that long?"

"Oh, Lord. I hadn't thought of that or how I'll ever pay the doctor."

"Main thing is to get you treatment. Then worry about that. I'll turn my horse into your pasture, bury the skunk and take you to the doctor. If you have to go to the city, I'll come back here before dark and bunk down in the garage until we see which way the wind blows."

Andy looked at the man standing over him for a long time.

"Mister, I don't even know your name."

"Yates."

"Name's Andy Connors. I'm obliged for your help. Hell, if you hadn't killed it, it might of got to Leona or the girls." Andy followed Yates out of the garage.

"I don't know much about rabies, but to be on the safe side, we should get you to the doctor as soon as possible." Yates pulled the spade out of the ground, probed the ashes where he had burned the skunk, then dug a hole and buried them. He came back, handed the spade to Andy and untied his horse.

"I still don't know why you're doing this, Yates."

"It's payback time, Andy."

Ignoring the woman and the children on the porch, Yates unsaddled his horse, turned it into the side pasture and carried his saddle to the barn.

"Andy, invite the . . . man in for breakfast," Leona called from the porch.

"We're going to town for a while."

"Can't you eat first?"

"No. I'll leave the key to the gas pump on the hook by the door. You know where I keep the sack of change. I'll be back as soon as I can. Behave while I'm gone, girls."

"We will, Daddy."

"Do you want your crutches?" Leona asked.

"No. I don't think so." Without another word Andy, feeling his world collapsing around him, went back into the garage and stood with clenched fists.

When the stranger came around the end of the porch, a single close-up look told Leona two things: She had never seen a more unapproachable man, and she had never seen one who oozed more confidence. If his size weren't enough to distinguish him, certainly the raven-black hair showing beneath the dusty Stetson and the steely gray eyes would have been. His face was still, absolutely expressionless, although his eyes, when they met hers, seemed to sink right into her.

"Ma'am." He put his fingers to his hat brim and continued on toward the garage without breaking his long-legged stride.

Leona's instincts whispered that something serious had

happened to Andy that he didn't want to talk about. *Oh, my God, don't let it be that the skunk has bitten him!*

With a feeling of fear and dread, she watched the tall stranger go through the small door in the back of the garage and close it behind him. Minutes later, Andy's car backed out of the garage and turned onto the highway toward town.

The stranger was at the wheel.

Chapter 2

WHEN IS DADDY COMIN' BACK?"

"He didn't say. Drink your milk, honey."

"He was goin' to fix the swing today. That old passerby kid broke it down."

"He didn't mean to break it, JoBeth. The rope was rotten."

"I don't care. I want Daddy."

"Shut up whinin'. You're just a . . . baby." Eight-year-old Ruth Ann kicked at her younger sister under the table.

"She kicked me! Make her stop," JoBeth demanded.

"That's enough," Leona said sternly. "Eat your lunch. I've got to go back to the garage. While you two are fighting, someone could drive in and steal us blind."

"When is that stink goin' away?"

"Yeah, when's that stink goin' away?" JoBeth echoed her sister.

"In a few days. When you finish eating, put your dishes in the dishpan and cover them with water."

"I'm not washing *her* dishes." Ruth Ann's mouth was turned down at the corners, and her blue eyes held the familiar look of rebellion.

"You'd better get that look off your face," Leona teased

lightly. "It may freeze like that, and the kids in school will think that you're just an old sourpuss."

"It won't freeze. It's not cold outside."

"When is Daddy comin' back?" JoBeth asked for the tenth time.

"He didn't say." Leona left the window and hurried to the door. "There's a car at the gas pump. Stay here and do the dishes, Ruth Ann. JoBeth, dry them," she called over her shoulder as she went down the well-worn path to the back door of the garage.

Leona was so worried about Andy that she hadn't been able to eat. The last glimpse she'd had of his face had told her what he and the stranger hadn't. *The skunk had bitten him.* People went mad when bitten by a rabid animal, didn't they? Please, God, don't let that happen to Andy. He's already had enough trouble in his life.

Passing through the garage, Leona came out into the bright sunshine to see a shiny black sedan parked beside the gas pump and a man in a white shirt and a black felt hat waiting beside it. He was almost as wide as he was tall and was sweating profusely.

"Hello," Leona said pleasantly. "Need gas?"

"Why else do you think I stopped here?"

Leona lifted her brows, pushed the lever back and forth and watched as the gas gushed into the round glass cylinder at the top of the pump.

"God, it stinks here. Somebody run over a skunk?"

"How much do you want?"

"How much is it?" the man asked.

"Fourteen cents," Leona replied and nodded toward the sign on the pump.

"Little high, but I guess by being out here on the highway you can sucker folks out of their money."

Leona's shoulders tensed. She stopped pumping the gas and turned to look into the man's eyes, made to look small by his fat cheeks. He had the blotchy red and gray complexion of an unfit, overweight . . . mess.

"What do you mean . . . sucker?"

"You know what I mean, sister. You've got 'em where the hair is short. Poor, miserable bastards are out of gas. You can charge whatever you want."

Leona's temper flared. "I don't have to take your insults. You saw the posted price. Why don't you go on down the road and try to chisel someone else out of a profit?" She hung the pump hose back on the hook and headed back toward the garage. She had never lost her patience with a customer before, but this one was a miserable . . . toad!

"You don't have to get in a huff," he called. "Is fourteen cents the best you can do?"

"Listen, mister." As Leona spun around, the skirt of her cotton dress danced against her bare, tanned calves. "We make five cents a gallon on gas. You saw the sign. You knew the price when you pulled in here. If you don't want to pay it, get on down the road and quit wasting my time."

"If I buy ten gallon, you've made a half a buck for about five minutes work."

"Yeah. We're getting so rich we plan to buy out Phillips 66 any day now."

"Being a smart-mouth won't get you many customers."

"Thank God they're not all like you!"

"A man's got to be careful. Money doesn't grow on trees, you know."

"Well, whatta ya know! All this time, I thought it did."

"I'll take two gallons."

"Are you sure you can afford it?" Leona spat the words as she returned to take the nozzle from the gas pump.

The man watched the cylinder to be sure he got the full measure. When the gas was in the car tank, Leona hung up the hose and held out her hand. After counting out two dimes and eight pennies, he dropped them in her hand. She put the change in her dress pocket and walked away. Customers like him were few and far between. Why did she have to get one on a day when her patience was thin from worry over Andy?

"Why didn't you bite him, Calvin?" Leona said to the brown dog stretched out on the hard-packed-dirt floor of the garage. The dog's tail swished back and forth, as he acknowledged her words and eyed the progress of the car moving out onto the smooth highway and disappearing down the road.

Leona sank down on the bench beside the double doors. Calvin crawled on his belly until he was near the toe of her shoe and sighed contentedly as she moved her foot to stroke him. She fanned her face with a folded newspaper that lay on the bench and lifted the heavy, damp hair off the back of her neck.

What if Andy didn't come back? The thought hit her like a blow in the stomach and robbed her of logical thought. Oh, Lord! What would she do? What would happen to the girls? He had always been there, steady and confident, even during the toughest times.

"Ruth Ann called me a runt!" JoBeth rushed from the back door of the garage, her fists balling the tears from her eyes.

"What's so bad about that?" Leona held out her arm, and the child nestled against her. "A runt is the smallest of a litter and often the prettiest. You should have thanked your sister for the compliment."

"She don't like me."

"Of course she does. You're her little sister. Now smile for me. Show me your dimples."

"She made me be quiet so she could hear that old *Ma Perkins*."

"Your daddy doesn't like for you girls to fight. He worked hard to get the money for the radio for you to enjoy."

"I don't hardly ever get to turn it on."

Leona's attention was drawn from the child to the highway. An old Model T car with belongings strapped to the top and on the back had coasted down the highway and was turning into the drive. It stopped well back from the gas pump. Inside the car were three adults and more children than she could imagine would fit.

Another dirt-poor Okie family full of hopes and dreams has pulled up roots and headed for California.

The tragic years of the Great Depression were leaving deep scars on the land and emotional wounds on the people who traveled the highway. Leona had watched the procession of refugees in single cars or caravans, carrying their furniture, kids, and modest aspirations, fleeing the choking dust storms and taking Route 66 to California.

A common saying along the highway was that you could tell a poor Okie family from others because they had only one mattress on top of the car. A family of mediocre wealth had two mattresses; and three mattresses strapped to the top of the car meant the Okies inside were rich.

A man in overalls, an old straw hat, and with a stubble of whiskers on his face got out of the Model T after it coasted to a stop. He lifted the hood. Steam rose from the radiator. With a heavy cloth wrapped around his hand, he removed the radiator cap and jumped back when boiling water spewed up. He went to the back of the car, unhooked a galvanized bucket and came toward Leona where she sat on the bench in front of the garage.

Calvin stood and growled. The hair stood up on the back of his neck. He wasn't sure if the man was friend or foe, but he wasn't taking any chances.

"Hush, Calvin. It's all right." Leona got to her feet.

"Howdy, ma'am. Could I trouble you for a bucket of water?"

"The well is behind the house. Help yourself."

"Thanky." He put his fingers to the brim of his hat.

"Mister," Leona called. "Your family is welcome to get out and rest over there in the shade." She motioned toward the campground.

"That'd be a blessin', ma'am." His tired face relaxed into a smile. "They been in the car two days, slept there. It would help a heap if they could get out and stretch their limbs."

"That's why we have the campground."

"Do . . . ah . . . folks spend the night there?"

"Some do."

"Ma'am, I'd be obliged if we could stay overnight here and rest up. If there's a charge I can't pay cash money, but I'm right handy with tools." The man moved his hat back from his dusty, whiskered face. He looked at her with tired, bloodshot eyes.

"There's no charge. The first traveler here is welcome to stay. All we ask is that you leave the place as clean as when you found it."

A thin smile spread his lips. "We'll be sure to do that. And I'm obliged, ma'am. The women and kids are gettin' all outta sorts from bein' cooped up."

He went back to the car and opened the door. Five children piled out. They stood grouped around him.

"The lady says we can stay the night. Go on over to the

campground. Show her we 'ppreciate stayin' by behavin' yourselves. And, kids, keep well back from the road. I'll bring a bucket of well water after I take care of the radiator and move the car over." He helped an older woman from the car, then a younger one carrying a baby.

When the group passed Leona and JoBeth, the younger woman paused. She was terribly thin and fatigue lined her face. "Thank you, ma'am."

"You're welcome to the water-well and to the use of the privy there beside the house."

"Thank you." With her hand behind the head of a small girl, she urged her on toward the campground.

Leona watched them pass and, just for a moment, the worry over Andy slipped from her mind. For the past year families had streamed down what was fast becoming known as the Mother Road. Leaving their homes in the dust bowl, drought-ruined farms or jobless cities, they were all looking for a better life in California. A few had stopped on the way back from that promised land to report that the soil was so fertile a man could make a living raising vegetables on a ten-acre plot.

At times Leona wished that Andy would get itchy feet, and they would leave here. But he was perfectly content right here on the highway halfway between Amarillo and Oklahoma City. He wanted roots for his girls—something he'd not had when he was a boy.

Dear, sweet Andy. Surely God wouldn't be so cruel as to let him come down with the dreaded rabies.

"Can I play with that little girl?" Five-year-old JoBeth whined and looked wistfully toward the children in the campground.

"Let's wait and see. She's helping her mama with the baby now."

The afternoon wore on. Several cars stopped for gas. A few travelers stopped to buy tire patch, a tube, a boot for a too-thin tire or one with a hole worn through. While they were there, a couple of customers bought soda pop. One bought chewing tobacco. The driver of a truck pulled in and asked to borrow a wrench. Leona was careful to watch that he didn't drive away without returning it.

The family in the campground had put up two small tents. The children played around the tents, never venturing over toward the garage or toward the highway. The women and children had trooped to the outhouse. They were a quiet family and Leona was glad for their presence. Andy would have been visiting with them by now. He would know their names, where they were from and where they were going.

Andy genuinely liked people.

By early evening Leona's nerves were frayed to the point where she snapped at the girls. When JoBeth began to cry, Leona apologized.

"I'm sorry, honey. But please stop nagging me. I don't know when your daddy will be home. He knows that we are here waiting for him and will come back as soon as he can."

"Will he bring us somethin'?"

"He may and he may not."

"He won't. He'll never come home." Ruth Ann stated firmly, and JoBeth burst into tears again.

"Of course he's coming home. Why would you say such a thing, Ruth Ann?"

" 'Cause he might not come."

"He will," JoBeth yelled. "She don't care if Daddy don't come home."

"Of course she does. We are all worried and saying things we'll be sorry for later."

"I won't be sorry," Ruth Ann said defiantly.

"It's time to close the garage. I think we should make some candy tonight after supper. What do you think?"

"Can we make fudge?"

"We don't have any cocoa, honey. How about pralines? We'll use the pecans we cracked the other night."

"Goody. I like pralines." JoBeth grabbed Leona's hand and jumped up and down.

"You mean it?" Ruth Ann asked.

"Would I suggest something like that and not mean it?" Leona put an arm around each girl. "Pen up the chickens while I lock up the garage. It'll be dark soon. I'll milk, then after supper we'll make the best batch of pralines we've ever had."

A small smile fluttered across Ruth Ann's face. Leona was relieved to see it. The child was serious far beyond her years and old enough to remember the sad times. Leona watched the girls scamper out of the garage and up the path to the house, before she turned to close the double doors of the garage.

She glanced down the highway as she had done a hundred times during the day in hopes of seeing Andy's Ford coupe, and there it was turning into the drive. Her heart hesitated, then settled down to a dull thud of dread when she saw that the only man in the car wore a big Stetson. He drove the car up to the doors of the garage, stopped and got out.

Calvin shot out of the garage and ran at the stranger with a vicious snarl.

"Calvin! No!"

Chapter 3

To Leona's surprise, the stranger knelt down and held out a hand to the dog. Calvin tilted his head; his tail made a half-hearted wave, then stilled. He seemed to be looking the man over and making a decision. Finally he went to him.

"You're a mighty fine dog. You run a good bluff. You're not as mean as you pretend." The man scratched Calvin behind the ears before he stood.

He was . . . so big . . . and his face looked as if it would crack if he smiled.

"Where is Andy?"

"Hospital. In the city." Yates opened the rumble seat of the car and pulled out a folded army cot.

"City? What city?"

"Oklahoma City. The skunk bit him." He carried the cot into the garage and came back for a leather suitcase.

"Well?" Leona said impatiently.

"He'll have to have a series of shots." The man walked away with the suitcase and a large paper sack.

"You took him all the way to the city?" Leona asked when he returned to the car.

"Yeah. St. Anthony Hospital. They'll treat him." He took a toolbox from the car and went back into the garage. When he returned, he ignored her and took another box from the car seat.

"Stop!" Leona said sharply. "What did the doctor say? How bad is he? When will he be back?" Their eyes met and held. Color tinged her cheeks, as his gaze traveled over her face, taking in the freckles on her nose, the wisps of wavy hair that stuck to her cheeks. She stared back at him, her eyes bright with a shimmer of defiance.

"The doctor said he'd die without the shots. He won't be back for at least six weeks," the man told her on his way back into the garage.

"Oh, Lord! I was afraid of that." Leona followed him inside. "Why can't he come home between the shots?"

"They want to keep him there. The doc said they'd find him a room near the hospital to save him from making the long trip twice a week."

"He'll need money."

"He's got money."

"From you?"

"My money's not dirty."

"Thank you for that very important information," she said as sarcastically as she could manage.

"You're welcome."

She flung her hand out toward where he had stacked bundles from the car. "What's all this?"

"My stuff. I'm moving in here until Andy comes back."

"Why?"

"Because I told him I would. Satisfied?"

"No, I'm not satisfied. How do I know Andy told you to move in?"

"You'll just have to take my word for it."

"I don't believe you took him to Oklahoma City. This car

wouldn't have made it. Andy's even afraid to take it to Elk City."

"You're right it wouldn't have made it. I left this car in Sayre and took him to the city in my car."

"Why are you doing this?"

"I owe Andy a debt from way back."

"I don't believe you."

He shrugged.

"I don't even know your name."

"Yates."

"Yates, what?"

"Yates will do, ma'am." His voice was low, raspy and impatient, as if it hadn't been used much.

Leona opened her mouth to ask first or last name, then changed her mind and glared at his back. He turned, saw the exasperated look she was giving him and became aware of two things. She was not a woman to be set aside and ignored, and she wasn't one of those females who would go all fluttery and swoon. Her feet were firmly planted on the ground, her back was straight, her head up. With eyes the color of sky, she looked at him as if she would like to cut out his gizzard. The thought almost made him smile.

"I'll move the car to the back. Andy said not to leave it sitting out front at night." He got into the car, backed it up and drove around the side of the building.

Leona was so frustrated she could scream. She and the girls had a right to know who was moving in, taking over Andy's garage. And she had to know more about Andy's condition. She waited until he returned to the garage.

He came into the back door with a guitar case, placed it well out of the way and began setting up the cot. Leona waited. He ignored her. She looked at him intently, trying to guess what kind of man lay beneath the stern demeanor. His shoulders were a yard wide; his back was a broad wedge tapering to narrow hips. He was long-legged, long-armed and well-muscled. He looked capable of fighting his way out of a sack of wildcats.

The mark of a loner was on him. Was he really a good man helping a friend or was he taking advantage of an opportunity to do . . . what?

Leona continued to study him. He was not the most handsome man she had ever seen, but he was far from the ugliest. He had a broad forehead and wide-set eyes thickly fringed with dark lashes. His high cheekbones were well defined beneath the black stubble of beard, and his jaw reflected the determination he had already exhibited. The hair that showed beneath the dusty Stetson was black and slightly curly. Leona could hardly hold back a nervous giggle; she hoped that he was bald as an egg beneath the hat. It would serve him right for being so darn high-handed!

"Well, what have you decided?" He spoke without looking at her.

"About what?"

"About me. You've been giving me the once-over for the last five minutes."

"Do you have eyes in the back of your head?"

"Sometimes."

"I've decided that you're big, and that you're probably bald under that hat."

"I can't deny the first, but I can give lie to the second." He snatched the hat off his head and flung it down on the cot. Atop his head was a mop of thick, black-as-midnight curls. "Disappointed?"

Light gray eyes squinted at her. Not even a hint of a smile or the suggestion of softness broke the blunt, hard, craggy lines of his face with its strong nose and jutting chin. It was a take-me-or-leave-me kind of face. Something that may have been amusement flickered in his eyes.

"Why should I care if you're bald or not? I'm just surprised that someone hasn't snatched every hair out of your head—you're so rude!" With that Leona flung her chin up, left the garage and walked up the path to the house.

With his head down, Yates glanced at her slim legs as she passed him. She was pretty and spunky. Obviously she cared about Andy, who hadn't said much about her on the trip to the city, only that she was capable, knew the prices of the items he sold and would be a help at the gas pump. Yates had not had a relationship with a woman that lasted over a week or two, and figured he didn't know much about them, but he knew this much: Mrs. Connors was a woman who had taken a few hard knocks and knew how to stand up to them.

Andy had been worried about leaving her and the girls alone out on the highway. Yates explained to him who he was and why he felt he owed him. A surprised Andy sputtered, shook his head and in the end had welcomed his help.

Yates arranged all of his belongings along the back wall of the garage. He didn't own anything that didn't fit easily in his car or that could not be disposed of when he took to the road again. He reasoned that if he owned things, they would eventually own him. Sooner or later he might accumulate so much that the weight of it all would hold him in one spot.

The previous owner of the horse and saddle had agreed to take them back when Yates was ready to leave. Wherever he stopped for a while he had usually been able to make such a deal. Nothing relaxed him or gave him more pleasure than to mount a good horse and ride out onto the prairie where he could look in any direction and not see another living soul or the evidence that one had been there.

The day after he bought the horse, he had ridden across

country to the place where he had met Andy for the first time. Yates considered that meeting the beginning of his adult life. Now, he looked out the garage doors to the highway and dragged his thoughts back to the reason he was here. He had come to pay a debt, a long overdue debt. As soon as Andy Connors returned and was on his feet, he'd hit the road and consider his debt paid.

"Daddy's home!" JoBeth jumped off the porch step.

"No, honey!" Leona caught the child before she could dash down the path to the garage.

"His car's here."

"The man who took him to the doctor brought it back. Daddy didn't come home. He's staying with the doctor for a while."

"I told you he wasn't comin' back," Ruth Ann announced from the doorway.

JoBeth burst into tears.

"We'll go in and talk about it." Holding the little girl firmly by the hand, Leona urged her toward the door. In the kitchen she sat down in a chair and pulled JoBeth to her.

Ruth Ann stood ramrod straight with her back turned.

"I'll tell you just what the man told me. The sick skunk bit your daddy on the leg. The doctor will have to give him shots for about six weeks, so that he won't get the sickness from the skunk. They want him to stay in the hospital where they can watch him and be sure that he will be all right." Leona paused, then added, "That's all I know."

"He'll die," Ruth Ann said bitterly.

"He'll not die," Leona replied forcefully. "They have inoculations for that sickness. Remember when you had the vaccination for smallpox? Your arm was sore and it made you sick for a while. The shots might make your daddy sick.

Maybe sicker than the smallpox vaccination. That's why they want him to stay in the hospital."

"So they can make him better?" JoBeth asked.

"So they can make him feel better. The only thing we can do for him now is take care of things here at home so that everything will be the same when he comes back."

"Can we go see him?" JoBeth asked.

"I don't know, honey. He's in Oklahoma City. That's a long way from here." Leona went to where Ruth Ann stood, gripped her shoulders and pulled the child back against her. "He'll be all right. You must believe that and not think the worst."

"He'll die. I know he will." Sobs broke loose. She turned and buried her face against Leona.

"No. Don't think that." Leona hugged the child to her and smoothed back her hair. "He'll come back and tell us all about it—about the big hospital and about being in the city. Maybe he'll even ride a streetcar."

"I'm scared he won't come back."

"He'll come back, honey. We'll write to him so he won't be lonesome up there in the city. You can draw a picture for him. He is so proud of the way you draw. JoBeth can make the ABC's and show him how she is learning to write her name. He'll write back and put lots of X's on the bottom of the page."

"What's X's?" JoBeth asked.

"Kisses. Here's one for each of you. MaryLou is out there waiting for me. I've got to go milk her. Did you gather eggs, Ruth Ann?"

"Not yet."

"Gracious me. We'd better get our chores done if we're going to make candy tonight."

Leona washed her hands in the basin in the dry sink, wet

a clean cloth to wash the cow's teats, then picked up the milk bucket and headed for the barn.

While she milked, she leaned her head against the side of the patient cow and thought how fortunate they were that MaryLou produced good rich milk. They had all the milk and butter they could use, a good garden spot close to the well so that she could water the plants if necessary, and a dozen good laying hens. They had a sound, dry storm cellar and almost fifty jars of canned food.

Andy had been looking to buy a couple of runt pigs to fatten on the extra milk. Even without money coming in from the garage, they would be all right for a while.

"Ma'am." The deep masculine voice behind Leona startled her so much that she almost overturned the milk bucket when she whirled around. "Is there a spot in here where I can store a few bales of hay for my horse?"

"You scared the fool out of me." Leona spoke more harshly than she intended.

"Sorry," he muttered with his back to her.

She had not yet admitted to herself that she was a little afraid of Yates and what his unexpected intrusion in their lives could mean. He was so quiet, so intensely male and alert. An odd feeling raced through her, making her shiver.

Leona blamed her reaction to him on the strange events of the day and on the fact that she'd not had to deal with an *unsociable* man before. All the men of her acquaintance would talk the leg off a mule.

Ignoring her outburst, Yates picked up his saddle, flung it over a sawhorse and reached for the rifle he had placed high on a beam that morning before he took Andy to the hospital.

"Thank you," he said as if she had spoken. "That spot in the corner will do just fine." With that he left the barn.

As she finished milking, Leona heard the scrape of the tin conduit, as Yates moved it to the lip of the pump so that he could fill the watering tank for the two horses and the cow. Then she heard the familiar squeak as he worked the pump handle.

When Leona came out of the barn, Yates was crossing the yard on his way to the garage. Calvin tagged along behind him. JoBeth and Ruth Ann were on the back porch with a basket of eggs, gawking at the strange man coming out of their barn.

"Why is he here?" Ruth Ann demanded when Leona reached the porch.

"He's going to work in the garage until your daddy comes back."

"What's his name?"

"Mr. Yates."

"I don't like him."

"You don't know him. Open the door for me."

Inside the kitchen, Leona set the bucket of milk on the counter and spread a cloth over it. She understood that Ruth Ann resented Mr. Yates for being here when her daddy wasn't. Leona admitted that she had felt resentment, too . . . at first. She excused herself by putting some of the blame on the man's stand-offish attitude and on his lack of communication.

She knew that in the dead of the night, she would be glad that he and his rifle were here.

The sheriff had told Andy repeatedly that by being out here in the country and on the highway that was used nightly by bootleggers, he was a "sitting duck" for robbers.

And they'd had a few scares.

Late one evening Pretty Boy Floyd had stopped for gas. Andy had recognized him immediately and passed the time of day with him as casually as he did with all his customers. He said the man couldn't have been nicer, but Andy had been shaken by the encounter.

A month ago one of the campers had recognized the notorious George (Machine Gun) Kelly and his partner Eddie Doll who, back in January, had kidnapped a banker's son in Indiana. Andy had put gas in their car and sold them a new set of spark plugs.

A couple of times a month, in the middle of the night, a bootlegger needing gas would pound on the door. Andy was always accommodating and, whether it was that or the fact that he was crippled, he had always been treated with respect by the "men of the night" as he called them.

It would be interesting to see how Mr. Yates dealt with them.

Chapter 4

WHY DOES CALVIN LIKE *THAT MAN*? I thought Calvin was *our* dog." Resentment made Ruth Ann's soft mouth turn down at the corners.

"He *is* our dog. I see you got . . . one, two, three, four, five . . . six eggs. Good. That makes ten today."

"If he's our dog, why is he following . . . him?" Ruth Ann demanded.

"He likes him. Maybe that should tell us that the man isn't so bad. You'll have to admit that Calvin is a good judge of men. Remember that bum that stopped here about a month ago? Calvin didn't like him, wouldn't make up to him no matter what he offered. And when the bum left, he took a pair of your daddy's pants off the clothesline."

"There's a sack on the porch, and I can't open the door. I want to get Calvin," JoBeth screeched and stamped her foot.

"She's in a snit," Ruth Ann said. "She's just a stupid baby. You've spoiled her," she added with a lofty air.

"I'm going to get into a snit myself," Leona threatened, "if you girls don't stop fighting."

"I want to go out," Jo Beth yelled.

"Then go."

"I can't 'cause of the sack."

Feeling her patience slipping, Leona went to the front door. Against the screendoor leaned a large paper sack. She recognized it as the bag Mr. Yates had carried into the garage from the car. Leona pushed gently on the door until it moved the sack enough for her to squeeze out onto the porch. JoBeth followed.

The bag was chock-full of groceries. Leona could see cans of peaches, salmon, corn and packages of dried beans, macaroni, apricots and raisins. There were a couple of packages wrapped in white butcher paper and tied with a string—one appeared to be meat, the other cheese.

"For goodness sake! Does he think we're destitute?" Leona glanced toward the garage, saw that the back door was open and headed for it. She rapped on the door frame and called, "Mr. Yates?" When there was no reply, she stuck her head inside the door. It was dim inside the garage with the two big doors closed, but light enough for her to see that he wasn't there.

JoBeth tugged on her hand. "He's with the campers."

Yates and the camper were working beneath the hood of the dilapidated car. Calvin stood beside him.

Grasping JoBeth's hand, Leona headed for the campground. The older woman sat on a folding chair holding the baby while the younger one supervised the children. Two of the bigger boys were feeding sticks into the campfire, where a blackened pot sat on the iron grate. They paused to watch Leona and JoBeth as they approached.

"Good evening," she said to the woman. "Are you having to scrounge for firewood? If you need it, take a few sticks from our woodpile."

"We have an ax, but Fred doesn't want the boys to use it. He'll go back in the woods and bring in firewood." The woman appeared to be exhausted, but the children were in high spirits. They were clean and well-mannered. Leona wondered how the work-worn woman managed.

"I came down to ask if you could use some milk. We have a real jim-dandy cow, and she produces more milk than we can use right now. We plan to get a couple of runt pigs to fatten for winter, but in the meanwhile, I just can't bear to pour out what we can't use."

"If you're sure you can't use it, ma'am, we'll take it off your hands."

"Milk sours fast in the summertime. I can use just so much sour milk. I'm from the old school, just can't stand for anything to go to waste. If you can use it, I'll bring it down."

"One of the boys will fetch it and save you a trip."

"There's at least two gallons. Do you have some sort of a container?"

"Yes, ma'am. We have a couple of pails with good tight lids." She motioned to one of the children, who ducked inside one of the tents and came out with two tin pails. "Paul, you and Edgar go with the lady."

"Well, if I don't see you again, have a safe trip. I wish you all the luck in the world."

"Thank you. We're goin' to need it."

Leona stopped beside the car. Yates's head was still bent over the motor.

"Mr. Yates, I would like to speak to you for a moment."

He turned, looked down at her and reached for a rag to wipe his hands. "Go ahead."

"In private, if you please." He nodded and moved away from the car. "JoBeth," Leona said, "take the boys to the house and tell Ruth Ann to fill the pails from the bucket of milk on the table."

Happy to be doing something important, the child ran toward the house. The boys followed at a slower pace. Leona didn't speak to the tall man beside her until the children were out of hearing distance.

"Come get your groceries off our porch, Mr. Yates. We're not so poor that we can't feed ourselves." Her icy-blue eyes met his unblinking gaze.

"You're not, huh?" His voice was low, husky and irritating.

"No, we're not!" Leona took a deep breath and when she released it, anger boiled up. "We have a cellar full of canned goods. We have a cow, chickens and a garden. If you want to impress someone with your generosity, I suggest that you give your sack of groceries to the campers."

"Crawl down off your high-horse, Mrs. Connors. I made a deal with Andy to stay here. While I'm here, I'll furnish my own grub. If you cook it I'll throw in some extras for your trouble. If that doesn't suit you, I'll cook it over a campfire."

"I'll cook your meals but—"

"Good. Then it's settled. I'd like the pork chops for supper. I have a fondness for pork chops, brown gravy and biscuits."

Leona's mouth opened, closed, then opened. "But you don't have to furnish our food. The girls and I will get along just fine. I'll cook your meals," she said for the second time. "I'll do it in exchange for the work you do for Andy."

"Tomorrow I'll hitch a ride into town and get my car. I'll bring back ice—"

"The ice man comes tomorrow. He'll fill the cooler with ice and soda pop. We don't need you to run errands. I can drive the car."

"Listen, lady." His voice was low and hard as his patience ran out. "You can be as unpleasant as a cow with her teat caught in the fence; but I'm here, and I'm staying until Andy gets back and is on his feet, whether you like it or not."

"I didn't say I didn't like you being here. I just don't like your . . . charity and your high-handed manner."

"Charity? What you just did was charity." He jerked his head toward the campers. "You trotted down here with your cock-'n'-bull story about having too much milk. That woman wasn't fooled, but she swallowed her pride and took it for her kids. That's what I call good, down-to-earth common sense."

Leona's face reddened. She breathed deeply to steady herself and spoke in a low, controlled voice.

"It's the truth. We have more milk than we can use."

"If you say so. Remember this, I pay my way wherever I go, whatever I do. I'll not be obligated to you or to anyone else. Is that understood?"

"Perfectly."

"If you don't want the groceries, you can throw them the hell out. But you're going to get them anyway. Make out a list of what you need, and I'll get it." He turned and walked rapidly toward the garage. Leona followed, hurrying to keep up with his long legs.

"I'm sorry. I appreciate what you are doing for Andy. It goes against the grain to accept anything more from you, especially since you've been so uncommunicative."

He turned. "Well, what the hell did you want me to tell you—that if Andy didn't get the shots he'd go mad within three to four weeks and have to be tied to a cot until he screamed himself to death? Or that the cost of the treatment was going to put him in debt for years?"

"I wanted the truth without having to drag every blasted word out of you. That's all I wanted!" When she met his eyes straight on, her breath stuck in her throat at what she saw in his face. At that moment he seemed dangerous . . . almost savage.

What kind of man was he, and where had he come from?

"All right, here it is. They'll give Andy the vaccine in the stomach over a four-to-seven-week period. It's very painful. The doctors are keeping him there because it's a hell of a long trip for him to make two or three times a week when he'll more than likely be as sick as a dog after the shots. Some don't survive the massive dose of vaccine. Is that what you wanted to hear?"

"Gracious me!" Leona's hand went to her throat. "I'm—" She started to say something else—what, she didn't know. Her voice suddenly dried up.

"That's the long shot, but it's still a possibility. The man is worried sick about leaving you and the girls alone out here on the highway, where not a night or a day goes by that someone between Oklahoma City and Elk City isn't robbed. I'm going to take *that* worry off his shoulders."

"I . . . know how to shoot the gun."

His eyes narrowed as he studied her face. It was framed with rich auburn hair: silky, shiny and wind-blown. Her lashes were dark, long and thick. And her eyes were the color of a blue-green stormy sky, shifting in hue to reflect her moods. They were compelling eyes that held a hint of mystery. As for the rest of her, she was long and slender and as supple as a willow switch.

"How old are you?" He voiced the question before he thought better of it.

"That is none of your business!"

"You're right, it isn't." Yates was unaware that he almost smiled on hearing her quick retort. "Andy is depending on me to take care of his family until he gets back. Come hell, high water or you, Mrs. Connors, I'm going to do it."

"I'll cook your pork chops and send one of the girls to get you when they are ready."

Yates watched her walking back toward the house. A puzzled frown wrinkled his brow. Her head was up, her shoulders straight. She was proud as a thoroughbred, pretty as a spring morning and stubborn as a mule.

A few stars had appeared in the darkening sky when Yates, sitting on a bench beside the garage door, heard his name called from the porch.

"Mr. Yates? Your supper is ready."

By the time he got off the bench and put down the brush he had used to polish a pair of his boots, the woman had gone back into the house. But as soon as he stepped up onto the porch, she was there opening the screendoor.

"Come in."

He followed her through a dimly lit room to get to the kitchen that was lighted by a single bulb hanging from an electric cord in the center of the room.

"You can wash there in the sink. The water in the basin is warm."

Yates's eyes swept the well-ordered, conveniently arranged room. A tall kitchen cabinet sat against one wall alongside a counter with a cloth curtain covering the shelves below. Next to that was a dry sink with a red iron pump. The supplies he had bought at the grocery store were stacked neatly on the counter.

A cookstove, probably used for heating as well as for cooking, dominated the opposite wall. Heat radiated from it as Leona bent to take a pan of biscuits from the oven.

He washed his hands in the basin, and while he dried them on the towel hanging above it, he watched her. Her face was flushed from the heat of the stove. She upturned the biscuits on a plate and took them to the table. The older of the two girls stood at the stove stirring something that smelled vaguely familiar. The little girl sat on the floor in the corner writing on a newspaper with a crayon.

Then he noticed that the table, covered with a white oilcloth printed with blue flowers, was set for one.

"Sit down, Mr. Yates. After this I'll serve your supper at six o'clock, that is if you're not busy in the garage."

"What time did Andy eat?"

"We had the big meal of the day at noon and a lighter supper at night, depending on when he closed the garage. I kept an eye on the gas pump while Andy ate at noon."

"I don't wish to disrupt your way of doing things. The big meal at noon will suit me fine."

"Well, sit down," she said again, looking up at him.

He was younger than she had first assumed. He was wearing a clean shirt. His damp hair was already rebelling against the brush. Something in the lazy negligent way he stood there with his hands on the back of the chair caused a sudden fear that he could, if he wished, reach out and swat her as he would a pesky fly.

Gracious. Outside he was big. Here in the kitchen he was as big as an oak tree. No wonder the girls were afraid of him.

"Have you and the girls had supper?" He continued to stand with his hands gripping the back of the chair.

"We ate earlier." She brought a platter of pork chops to the table, then returned with a bowl of gravy. "I would give you iced tea but we're out of ice until tomorrow."

Yates sat down and put a couple of biscuits on his plate, split them and covered them with the rich brown gravy. While he ate, the little girl in the corner sent shy glances in his direction. One time he caught her eye and winked at her. She lowered her head until it was just a couple inches from the paper and didn't look at him again.

Yates ate only two pork chops, but the entire plate of biscuits. They were the best he'd ever eaten. Andy was lucky his wife was a good cook.

It was strange to be sitting in this kitchen with Andy's family. Stranger yet that he liked being here. The only sounds in the still room were those made by iron clanking against iron as the woman moved the skillet to a cooler place on the top of the cookstove.

"Is it ready?" Ruth Ann whispered.

"Get a cup of cold water." Leona took the spoon from the girl's hand. "That's the only way we can tell." She dribbled some of the hot candy into the cup of water. "Roll it around in the water with your finger. See if it forms a soft ball."

"It does!"

"Then it's ready. Now we beat it until it gets thick and creamy. Go ahead and start beating. I'll butter the platter." Leona's eyes met those of the man at the table, who had finished eating and was sitting quietly. "We're making pralines, Andy's favorite candy." She wasn't sure why she needed to explain to him what they were doing.

"I thought that was what you were doing. It smells good. My mother made pralines at Christmas after she coaxed me into cracking the pecans."

This big, hard man had a mother somewhere! Leona shook her head wondering why that should surprise her and turned to take a platter from the shelf. Even a skunk had a mother, she thought irritably.

Then Ruth Ann screamed. "Oh . . . oh!"

Leona dropped the platter on the counter and grabbed the child's wrist so that she could see her palm.

"Oh, honey—"

"It hurts! It hurts!"

"I thought I had the rag wrapped around the handle."

"Oh, oh—"

"Hold it under the pump." Yates was suddenly urging the pair toward the tin sink.

"Butter . . . is best," Leona said.

"Water," Yates insisted. "It'll take away the sting."

Leona had to press against him in order to take the stopper from the sink and allow the water to drain through a pipe to the yard. JoBeth crowded in beside Leona, pushing her closer to the stranger, who stood behind Ruth Ann holding her small hand in one of his and working the pump handle with the other. After a minute he pulled her hand out from under the water and looked at it closely.

"I don't think you'll have a blister."

"It . . . hurts."

"Do you have any ointment?" Yates asked Leona.

"Nothing for burns but butter or lard."

"I have something. Here, hold her hand under the water and I'll get it."

Leona moved in behind Ruth Ann and took her hand. For a few seconds Yates's arms were around both of them. A wisp of Leona's hair dragged on his whiskered chin. Her woman's scent brought his maleness to full alert. His body jerked with a jolt of desire. He stepped away quickly.

"Be right back," he said and hurried out of the house.

For God's sake! What the hell is the matter with me? The woman is Andy's wife.

After pulling the chain to turn the light on in the garage, Yates rummaged around in his suitcase until he found a small bottle. Pulling the chain again to plunge the garage into darkness, he stood for a moment and wondered what the hell he was doing here, and why he had suddenly reacted to that woman like a stallion in heat. On the way back up the path, it occurred to him that staying here to pay the debt he owed Andy might just be the wrong thing to do. Maybe he should hire someone to look after them and move on.

At the kitchen door he paused when he heard what the younger of the two girls was saying.

"Aunt Leona." She was pulling on the woman's arm to get her attention. "Aunt Leona, Ruth Ann can't draw Daddy a picture now."

"Yes, she can. She burned her left hand. She draws with her right."

"I can draw Daddy a picture."

"Both of you can." Leona turned her head, suddenly aware of the big man who was filling the doorway and whose eyes were on her.

Aunt Leona? Andy's sister? Not his wife?

Chapter 5

YATES CAME INTO THE KITCHEN. His silvery-gray eyes held Leona's as if seeing her for the first time. He came up behind her and looked at Ruth Ann's hand over her shoulder. He reached around Leona and pulled it out from under the stream of water. Leona's hand dropped from the pump handle. She moved quickly to avoid contact with him.

"Did the cold water take away the sting?" His voice was soft when he spoke to Ruth Ann.

"Uh-huh, but my hand's cold."

Yates cupped the small hand in his. "Yeah, it is. I've got something here that will help the burn."

"What is it?" Ruth Ann looked up at the big man bending over her. It was strange having him here in their kitchen.

"It's the juice from an aloe plant. A Mexican woman down in Del Rio gave it to me when I burned my hand. People down there have a plant or two around the house. When they have a cut or a burn, they break off a leaf and squeeze the juice out onto it." Deliberately, he lifted his eyes to the woman standing beside them. "I'll see if I can get your *Aunt Leona* a plant."

Leona didn't like the look in his narrowed eyes. She

hadn't told him that she was Mrs. Connors. He had just assumed that she was, and she hadn't corrected him. Now she wondered why Andy hadn't mentioned that she was not the girls' mother.

Silence between them stretched, then snapped.

"I know about the aloe plant," Leona said calmly, deciding that she didn't care if he was miffed. If Andy had led him to believe she was his wife, he must have had a reason.

Yates poured two drops of the thick liquid from the bottle onto Ruth Ann's palm.

"Smooth it around with your finger," he said to Leona. "Your finger is much softer than mine." He stood back, corked the small bottle and set it on the table. "Let air get to the burn but keep the skin softened with the juice."

"Are you a doctor?" JoBeth asked.

"No. I'm just a wandering cowboy." Yates looked down into the earnest face of the child. She had Andy's blond hair and blue eyes.

"You know a lot of doctor stuff."

"While roaming around, I picked up a thing or two."

"Daddy says that people that roam around don't have roots. He said people are like trees. They have to stay in one place to grow roots. Then they'll be big and strong." Ruth Ann was warming up to the stranger. "Daddy says folks going down the highway are like seeds blowing in the wind, looking for a place to light."

"He's right about that."

"Do you have a little girl?" JoBeth asked.

"No." He reached out and gave her a hesitant pat on the head as if touching a child was a thing he'd not done before.

"Girls, let Mr. Yates finish his supper." Leona wrapped

a cloth around the hot handle on the iron skillet and began to beat the light tan mixture.

"You ate a whole pan of biscuits." Ruth Ann spoke with wonder in her voice and looked at the tall man still standing beside the table. "Daddy don't ever eat a whole pan of biscuits."

"I'm bigger than your daddy, and I was hungry for biscuits. Your Aunt Leona is a good cook."

The beating strokes hesitated for a second. Leona looked up to see his eyes on her, his black brows raised in silent query. She licked her dry lips and tore her gaze away from the hard face of the stranger, who was having an unsettling effect on her.

"My mama was a good cook," Ruth Ann's voice filled the void.

"A good cook," JoBeth echoed. "She cooked cookies and . . . ever'thin'."

"How do you know?" Ruth Ann retorted. "You don't even remember her."

"I do, too. I remember Mama, don't I, Aunt Lee? Ruth Ann's bein' mean again."

"She's always sayin' she remembers Mama when she don't. She was just a baby when Mama went away," Ruth Ann explained to Yates.

"That's enough, Ruth Ann. Get the platter and put a dab of butter on it." Leona tried to blame the shakiness in her voice on the exertion it took to beat the thickening mixture in the skillet, but she knew better. It was *that man* sitting there like a spider ready to jump!

"I can't with just one hand. Make JoBeth do it."

"One of you do it. As soon as I stir in the pecans, it'll be ready to pour."

Yates moved quickly and silently. He dipped into the

crock of butter, put a glob on the platter and moved it around with the knife blade.

"Aunt Leona does it with her fingers," Ruth Ann said.

"I don't think my fingers are clean enough for that," Yates replied.

"Are you going to stay and have some?" JoBeth had lost her shyness with Yates.

"I've not been invited."

"I'll invite you if you promise not to eat it all."

"Laws!" Ruth Ann cast Yates an apologetic look and rolled her eyes to the ceiling.

"You'd better think about it before you invite me. That'll be a hard promise to keep." Silent laughter crinkled the corners of Yates's eyes. His deep voice had a gentle drawl when he spoke to the girls, and his face softened, transforming it into less intimidating lines. "Let me," he said, as he saw Leona lifting the heavy skillet with both hands.

He carried the skillet to the table and tipped it over the platter. Leona scooped out the hardening candy and smoothed it.

"I get the skillet," Ruth Ann announced.

"You both can have it. Get two spoons, JoBeth."

Yates, followed by the two girls, took the pan back to the cool end of the cookstove. When he turned, Leona was taking his soiled dishes to the dishpan.

"You're welcome to stay, Mr. Yates. It will be a little while before the pralines are cool enough to cut. Meanwhile I'll do up these dishes."

"If you're sure you don't mind. It's been a long time since I've had a homemade praline." He pulled the chair back against the wall and sat down. He impaled her with his eyes. The message was clear. He was staying until he got answers to a few questions.

"I don't mind in the least."

You're not a good liar, Aunt Leona. You wish I'd get the hell out of here, but I'm not going until I know why you and Andy let me think you were his wife.

"You don't get home often." Leona made the statement, as she wrapped a clean cloth around the plate of uneaten pork chops.

"Not often," he admitted as the electric light flickered. "I'm surprised you have electricity out here."

"We haven't had it long. We're at the end of the line. It goes out sometimes. I keep a lamp handy." When the lights flickered again, she brought a glass oil lamp out of a cupboard and set it on the table. "Just in case," she said and went back to get the teakettle to pour water over the dishes in the pan.

"Will the lights go off, Aunt Lee?" JoBeth asked.

"I don't know, honey. They do sometimes when the wind comes up."

"I wanted to make my letters for Daddy."

"It's too late tonight. You can do it tomorrow. We can't mail him a letter until we know where to send it. I'll call when we go into town and get his address. I'll need to get some stamps, then we can leave letters in the mailbox for Mr. Wilkes to pick up when he delivers the mail."

"You'll have to call Oklahoma City. In order to save time, I took him directly there."

"I don't see why you didn't take him to the doctor in Elk City first?"

"The treatment center for rabies is in Amarillo or Oklahoma City. The city was closer and they have a good hospital."

"We'll send him a letter in care of the hospital," Leona said to the girls.

"I'll ride along with you in the morning and bring my car back."

Leona turned to look at him. "We never go and leave the garage unattended."

"Even on Sunday?"

"If people need gas on Sunday, we pump gas. We don't leave them stranded. If Andy isn't here, I am. That's why he taught me to drive."

"I want to bring my car out here. Did Andy have someone to help him out on occasion?"

"Deke Bales helped him sometimes when he had a job he couldn't handle. Deke stayed here the few times when both of us were away."

"Tell me about him." Yates saw her lips tighten. She had no intention of telling him any more than she had to.

"Andy thought him . . . trustworthy."

"He likes Aunt Leona. He wants to take her to Elk City to a picture show." JoBeth made the announcement, proud that she could contribute to the conversation.

After a silence, Ruth Ann hissed, "Do you have to tell everything you know?" She scowled at her sister. "Aunt Leona don't like for us to . . . tell things."

"Mr. Bales likes her. Daddy said so!"

"She don't like him. She won't leave us to go—"

"That's enough, girls," Leona said sharply.

"Make her go to bed, Aunt Lee. She's just a baby."

"The candy will be done in a minute. You can each have two pieces, then off to bed with you. We've all had a trying day."

"See what you've done?" Ruth Ann said to her sister.

"For that you can't use my crayons . . . ever! You break them anyway."

"I do not! She's tellin' a story, Aunt Lee."

Leona dried her hands on a towel and, ignoring the silent man in the corner of the kitchen, went to the table and pressed a finger to the candy in the platter.

"It's set enough to cut." With the girls crowding against her, Leona cut the hardening brown candy into squares, then scooped out a piece for each girl. "Mr. Yates?" Her gaze met that of the quiet man. Caught suddenly once again by the color of his eyes, a light, light gray that shimmered between thick black lashes. They were a startling contrast against the sun-browned skin of his face.

"I'll wait until you can sit down."

"I'll not be sitting down for a while. After the girls go to bed I've things . . . to do."

"I'm in no hurry. I'll wait."

Damn! Why doesn't he take the candy and get the heck out of here?

"Will there be some left for tomorrow?" JoBeth pulled Leona down to whisper in her ear.

The whisper was loud enough to reach the sharp ears of the big man sitting against the wall. The corners of his lips quirked upward.

"If it's all gone in the morning, don't blame me. Blame your aunt."

"Promise?" JoBeth peeked at him from under her aunt's arm.

Yates held up his hand. "Cross my heart and hope to die."

"Punch a needle in your eye?" JoBeth giggled.

"Cut my throat if I tell a lie."

The little rhyme jumped out of Yates's memory, surprising him. What surprised him even more, was when the child came to lean against his thigh.

"You can have three pieces 'cause you're big." She stood on her toes so she could whisper in his ear.

"Thank you," he whispered back. "I'll get by with my two pieces the same as you."

"I like you."

"I like you, too."

"If Daddy can't be here, I'm glad you are."

"He'll be back before you know it."

"Daddy was goin' to fix our swing. Can you do it?"

"What the matter with it?" Yates discovered that he was thoroughly enjoying himself with the little girl, who leaned against his knee.

"A passerby kid broke the rope."

"I'll take a look at it tomorrow."

"JoBeth," Leona's voice broke into the whispered conversation. "Come over here so that I can wash you. It's bedtime." After washing the child's face and hands, she sat her down on a chair and wiped off her bare feet.

"Seems funny without Daddy here." Ruth Ann leaned against the table, one bare foot atop the other.

"Yes, it does," Leona agreed.

"I miss him."

"I know you do, but let's be glad he's where the doctors can take care of him. Sit, honey," Leona said to Ruth Ann after she finished with JoBeth. "I'll wipe off your feet."

"'Night, Mr. Yates." JoBeth paused when she passed him, reached up and placed a wet kiss on his cheek.

He was so startled he barely croaked out, "Goodnight."

Ruth Ann shook her head showing her annoyance with her sister and said, "Thank you for the . . . bottle of stuff."

"You're welcome. Goodnight."

Leona lingered in the bedroom a few minutes stalling for time after the two girls were settled in the double bed. She picked up clothes and then, with the light turned off, she reached for the hairbrush and ran it through her hair.

Finally, knowing that she could put it off no longer, and with heart pounding so hard she could hardly breathe, she straightened her shoulders and went back to the kitchen.

Chapter 6

LEONA GLANCED AT THE MAN SITTING AGAINST THE WALL. The only movement he made was when his eyes turned to meet hers. She looked away, went to the table, slid two pieces of candy onto a saucer and reluctantly took the steps necessary to reach him.

"Thank you." His eyes held hers when he took the saucer from her hand. "Are you going to have some?"

"Not now." She stepped back and stuffed a strand of unruly hair behind her ear.

"Trying to get rid of me, huh?"

"It's been a long day."

"Why didn't you correct me when I called you Mrs. Connors?"

"I didn't think it important."

"Are you Andy's sister?"

"No."

"Any kin to Andy?"

"Why do you want to know?" she asked again.

"Partly because I don't like to get into a game without knowing who is playing. The other part is curiosity."

"Well, at least you admit to being curious." She went to the dishpan and brought a rag to wipe the table.

"Now that I think about it, Andy didn't tell me that you were his wife, but he didn't tell me that you weren't."

She shrugged and continued wiping the table.

"Well?"

"Well, what? You want me to satisfy your curiosity about something that doesn't concern you? I'm not going to."

Leona's stomach stirred restlessly. She tried to ignore him and washed the dishes. Silent minutes passed while her nerves stretched taut. When she heard him cross the room and felt his presence behind her, she held herself tightly for fear that if he touched her she would turn and hit him with the pan she was washing. He reached over her shoulder without touching her and slipped the saucer into the dish-pan.

"Did you think that you'd be safe from me if I believed that you were Andy's wife?" The low husky voice came close to her ear. When she didn't answer, he continued. "Don't worry, lady. Your virtue is in no danger from me."

She moved away from him, her back ramrod straight. When she turned to look at him, indignation was in every line of her face.

"I never for a minute thought it was." Her voice was calm, but her stomach was about to revolt, and her heart was racing like a wild mustang.

"Then why are you as jumpy as a cat on a hot stove whenever I'm near you?"

"I'm not! Please leave, Mr. Yates." Her voice was quiet and cold.

He studied her in silence. His thumbs were hooked in the front pockets of his jeans, his head tilted to one side, his eyes holding hers and his expression revealing nothing of his thoughts.

"What's between you and Andy? You're more than hired help."

His blunt questions irritated her. She drew in a quick breath. "That's none of your business. Andy is the most decent man I've ever known."

"Is he in love with you?"

"He's fond of me."

"Where's his wife?"

"Ask him."

"I'm asking you." Yates reached out and put his fingers beneath her chin to lift it. His eyes bored into hers.

"You've got all the answer you're going to get from me." Leona jerked her chin loose from his fingers.

He went to the door and turned. "What time are you going to town tomorrow?"

"Early."

He nodded. "Goodnight, Leona."

Unaware that she was holding her breath, Leona didn't move until she heard the squeak of the screendoor closing. Then the air went out of her lungs with a puff and her shoulders slumped.

Damn the man! He had set her nerves tingling and made her as jumpy as an ant on a hot griddle. The strange part of it was that she wasn't afraid of him in the physical sense; but in a small part of her mind, she knew that having known him, she would now be looking at men in a different light.

Yates hadn't been aware that he was tired until he pulled the cot over to the open doorway at the back of the garage, and with his revolver on the floor beside him, lay down and stretched his long limbs. With his hands stacked beneath his head, he looked out the door at the dark sky now crowned with millions of stars. He liked the stillness of night; it was when he did his best thinking.

He listened to the sounds made by the cars that passed on the highway. Not many people traveled at night here in Oklahoma. When they got over into Arizona and eastern California many of them would rather stop during the heat of the day and continue after the sun went down.

Yates's mind wandered over the events of the day. This morning when he saddled his horse at first light to take a ride over the countryside, he couldn't have imagined that he'd be sleeping tonight in Andy Connors's garage thinking about the woman in Andy Connors's house.

Hell, he couldn't blame her for being nervous. She didn't know him, so how would she know that he'd no more force himself on a woman who didn't want him than he'd take wings and fly?

While roaming the country he had come in contact with women of all kinds. They were the same as men; some good, some bad, some so nondescript that he was only barely aware of their existence.

He'd never met a woman quite like Leona. She had a sort of inborn breeding, like a wild mustang that had a thoroughbred somewhere in its lineage. She was so willowy that she seemed fragile, but she was wiry, like a cat who would fight if cornered. The way she moved made him think this—an unconscious mixture of caution and alertness.

The plain fact, he admitted now, was that he had wanted to touch her and he had liked what he had touched. He could still feel the softness of her chin between his fingers, feel her warm breath on his hand and smell the warm womanly scent of her.

Something had happened to her to make her leery. He wondered what the relationship was between her and Andy.

What was she to him? She appeared to be more than a nursemaid he'd hired to look after his girls.

It had been a good while since he'd been interested enough in a woman to give her this much thought. Leona was proud and plucky and out of his reach, because she was living with Andy, giving Andy's children a mother's care. Yates knew from first-hand experience that the love of a mother and father was the most important factor in a child's life.

His early childhood years had forged him into the man he was today. No one had ever loved him but his mother and his grandparents during the first few years of his life. He didn't even know if he was capable of love. He'd lived most of his life without it.

Yates didn't like to think about his own childhood. From an early age he had wondered why the man he called "Papa" had no time for him and why he was the cause of long and loud arguments between his parents.

It wasn't until he was fourteen years old that his mother thought he was mature enough to understand the circumstances of his birth, the reason she had married Arnold Taylor and why the ranch would be Arnold's for as long as he lived. She explained to Yates that the ranch would remain intact and on Arnold's death it would go to him.

Holly Louise Yates had been a young, lonely sixteen-year-old girl living on an isolated ranch when she fell in love with a young man who had come with a party from Virginia to hunt on her father's land. He had amused himself by flirting with the naive young girl. She had been in heaven, reveling in his attention, willing to give him anything he wanted. When he left to go back east to his fancy school, she had given him her virginity and was pregnant.

She never told Yates how devastating it was to her parents; nor did she tell him the name of the young man who had fathered him, and he never asked.

Holly Louise lost her parents when she was twenty. Feeling alone and frightened of the responsibility of raising a child alone and running a large ranch even with trusted help, she had married Arnold Taylor, the son of the local banker, on the condition that he adopt her son and give him his name.

The Yates Ranch, south and west of San Angelo, was one of the largest in southwest Texas. Less than a year after the death of Holly Louise, Arnold Taylor remarried. His new wife demanded that the ranch be renamed the Taylor Ranch and was furious that Arnold couldn't sell an acre of it without Yates's signature. Arnold and his new wife had made life miserable for the boy. He left home without a dime in his pocket as soon as he finished school. He worked on ranches or at any job he could get for a year and spent a month in jail before he joined a bridge-building crew.

On his twenty-first birthday, he contacted his mother's lawyer and returned to San Angelo to confront his adopted father and demand the money left to him by his mother and his grandparents.

After a vicious round of arguments, Arnold had gone to the bank with Yates. When the banker handed Yates the check, he had put it in his pocket, walked away and had not looked back. He immediately went to the courthouse and had his name legally changed back to the one that was on his birth certificate. H. L. Yates. The initials were from his mother's name, Holly Louise.

Yates considered himself lucky to have had friends who had advised him to diversify his investments so that he hadn't been hurt bad in the crash of '29. He still had the bulk of his inheritance and was able to keep loose, free and unfettered, to go when he pleased.

When the time came to return to the place of his birth and take up the responsibility of preserving his heritage, he would choose a strong young woman to bear his sons to carry on the Yates name. He didn't expect to love her, but he would respect her as the mother of his children.

His thoughts went to the last report he'd had from the lawyer who was looking after his affairs. Arnold Taylor was a piss-poor manager, the lawyer had written, but the bastard was lucky. There had been decent rainfall in the area, and in spite of low cattle prices the ranch was holding its own. The other news he'd had to offer Yates was at the end of the letter.

Arnold has lost a lot of weight lately and is looking rather peaked.

Leona put in a restless night. She was up at dawn doing the morning chores. When she came out of the barn after milking she saw that the campers were cooking breakfast over the campfire. She lifted her hand in greeting. The woman waved back.

In the kitchen, Leona put the coffeepot on the small two-burner kerosene stove. On the other burner, she placed the skillet for the bacon. She didn't fire up the cookstove in the summer unless she needed to use the oven. Determined to have as little to do with the man called Yates as possible, she had decided to serve his breakfast on the front porch. Andy liked to eat out there, so that he would be able to see if anyone stopped at the gas pump.

Leona was breaking eggs into a bowl when she heard Calvin barking. She looked out the back window to see Yates at the pump and Calvin frolicking around him. The dog was in heaven. Yates was holding a stick out of his reach and Calvin was jumping to get it.

Leona watched as the man played with the dog. Laughter reached her when Calvin grasped the stick and he tried to wrestle it from him. It was the first hearty laughter she'd heard from Yates. Then he was down on one knee scratching the dog behind the ears and dodging Calvin's licks of affection.

He seemed to be more . . . approachable this morning. But still, she reminded herself, she'd better not let her guard down. He was what some folks would call a "rounder" and far too hard, too ruthless and too worldly wise for her.

It irked her that he could fluster her.

She had decided during the night that the best course of action would be for her to treat him the same as she would if Andy were here—fix his meals, answer only his questions about the garage, keep a distance between them.

She was pouring the eggs into the skillet when the knock sounded on the back door.

"Come in," Leona said without turning around. "Coffee is ready. Fill one of the cups on the counter and take it to the front porch. I'll bring your breakfast in a minute."

"Good morning." It irritated Yates that she kept her back to him.

"Morning," she said, stirring the eggs in the skillet. "We don't have biscuits this morning. I didn't want to fire up the stove because I'm going to town. I'll make them for dinner."

After a lengthy quiet, she looked over her shoulder to see him lounging in the doorway, his shoulder against the jamb. His silence mangled her nerves. Aware that he watched her, she tilted the skillet over a plate and scooped out the scrambled eggs and forked several strips of crisp bacon onto the plate. Then, ignoring him, she carried the plate and eating utensils through the front room to the porch and placed them on the small table beside the chair.

He was still standing in the doorway when she returned to the kitchen. Ignoring him, she poured a cup of coffee and turned to find that Yates had moved from the back door to the one leading through the house, blocking her way to the front porch. Without hesitation she thrust the cup of hot coffee in his hands.

"I hope you like scrambled eggs," she said with all the poise and self-control she could muster.

"I like them any way as long as they're not raw." His eyes clung to her face. A dimple he hadn't noticed before appeared in her cheek. She was so confident, so calm and so damn pretty. She turned back to the stove and he spoke to her back.

"The camper wants to stay another day so the women can wash some clothes. He'll keep an eye on things while I go get my car."

"You're taking the responsibility for leaving a stranger in charge of the garage?"

"Mr. Oliver seems a decent sort. He tried to give me a five-dollar bill he found by the gas pump."

"*Found* by the gas pump? Were you testing him?"

"It's a good way to tell if a man is honest."

"The girls and I will be ready to go as soon as they have their breakfast."

"What about you?"

"What about me?"

"Have you had breakfast?"

"I'll eat with the girls. You'd better get to yours before it gets cold." With that she dismissed him and turned back to break more eggs into the bowl.

Chapter 7

YATES DROVE ANDY'S CAR INTO TOWN. Ruth Ann sat between him and Leona. JoBeth sat on Leona's lap. For once, Leona was grateful for the child's excited chatter, so that she didn't have to make polite conversation with the stony-faced man.

As soon as Yates parked the car in front of the post office, they got out. He came around the car and handed the keys to Leona.

"Are you goin' with us to buy stamps for Daddy?" JoBeth had wiggled her small hand into Yates's big one.

"No. I'm going to the hotel and check out of my room, then to the store."

"I've not been in a hotel. What's it like?"

"It's a place people stay all night when they are traveling."

"Don't they stay in campgrounds?"

"Sometimes."

"Don't you know anything?" Ruth Ann said impatiently. "Stop asking so many questions."

Ignoring her sister, JoBeth continued. "Whatter you goin' to buy, Mr. Yates?"

"I haven't decided yet. Any suggestions?"

"Come on, girls," Leona said quickly, pulling on JoBeth's

other hand. "We'll be back in time to fix your dinner, Mr. Yates."

"I didn't doubt it, Miss . . . Leona." He watched her and the two girls until they entered the post office, then walked on down the street to the hotel.

Leona had put up a thicker wall since last night, he mused. Hell, he'd only touched her chin. What would she have done if he'd kissed her? Gone up in blue smoke? He found himself chuckling. It surprised him. He had chuckled, smiled, laughed more since he'd met Leona and the girls than he'd done in a month. He decided that he liked kids, especially that little one. She was a ring-tailed tooter.

When he came out of the hotel, he paused on the steps and looked up and down the street. Downtown Sayre consisted of a dozen or so business buildings strung down both sides of a poorly paved street. It looked much like other small towns he had been in. All had suffered from the Depression. A fourth of the buildings along the main street were vacant. If not for trade from the highway the town probably would have dried up and blown away long ago.

Andy's car was still parked at the post office, but Leona and the girls were not in sight. The postmaster was sorting mail when Yates walked in.

"Morning. Anything for H. L. Yates?"

"Yup. Got a general delivery that come in this morning from"—the man squinted at the postmark—"San Angelo, Texas. That's a long way from here."

"Yeah it is." Yates took the letter and put it in his pocket. "Thanks."

"You going to be around for a spell?"

"Thinking about it." Yates walked out, leaned against Andy's car and opened his letter. He scanned the contents and muttered, "Shit! Why now?"

He returned the letter to the envelope, walked down the street and into the grocery store.

"Howdy." The friendly greeting came from the man behind the counter as soon as Yates stepped inside the door. The shopkeeper remembered the big dark man and the bill of groceries he'd bought the day before.

"Howdy. Are you in charge here?"

"Wayne White." The white-aproned man stepped out from behind the counter and extended his hand.

"Name's Yates." The two men shook hands.

"Glad to make your acquaintance."

"Does Andy Connors have a bill here?"

The question took Mr. White by surprise. He blinked, cocked his head to one side and went back behind the counter.

"Most folks 'round here run a bill."

"Andy is in the hospital in Oklahoma City—"

"Ah law! I didn't know that."

"He was bit by a sick skunk and will be there for some time, taking the vaccine. I'm his cousin. I told him that I'd take care of his bills and stay at the garage until he's on his feet again." While lying he looked the man in the eyes.

"That's mighty decent of ya, Mr. Yates."

"Not at all. Andy would do the same for me."

"I never knew Andy had any folks around here."

"I'm from Texas and just happened to be passing through. Good timing, huh?"

"I'll say. Good for Andy. He's had a heap of trouble. Will he be all right?"

"The doctors won't know for a while if he's going to take to the vaccine. Some folks are allergic to it. I'll be taking Leona and the girls to see him in a few days."

"Rabies, huh? There's been a little around here off and on for years."

"You might want to put up a warning for folks to take special notice of their animals."

"I'll do that and I'll spread the word about Andy. We'll hold a prayer vigil for him."

"He would appreciate it. What does he owe you?"

Mr. White pulled a tin box from under the counter, thumbed through the tabs and pulled out one of them.

"Andy's good pay. Never lets his bill go over a couple months. Right now it's nineteen dollars and sixty-two cents. That's as high as it usually gets."

"This will cover his back tab." Yates pulled a roll of bills from his pocket and peeled off two ten-dollar bills. He then placed two more bills on the counter. "Leona will be in soon to buy some supplies. Cover it with this and put whatever is left over on an account for when she comes in again."

Mr. White eyed the bills. "Why, that's mighty decent of ya, Mr. Yates."

"Not at all. I owe Andy more than this. Oh, by the way. Don't tell Leona about the money on account until you fill her bill. Women can be pretty stiff-necked at times. If you know what I mean."

"Yes, sir. I know what you mean." Mr. White turned to place a can on the shelf behind him. "Miss Dawson charges very little to Andy's account. Andy and his girls usually come in with a list."

Miss Dawson. So that's her name.

"How long has she been out there with Andy?"

"Let me see. It must be 'bout three years now. I don't rightly remember." He reached for a paper sack, folded it and placed it in the holder.

Yates waited. It was obvious the man didn't want to discuss Leona Dawson. When it became apparent Mr. White would say no more, Yates picked up a pack of chewing gum and placed it on the counter.

"I'll take this and a dozen peppermint sticks." After the candy was put in a sack, he paid Mr. White, thanked him and headed for the door. Before he reached it, Leona and the girls came into the store.

"Mr. Yates," JoBeth yelled and ran to him. "What did you buy?"

"JoBeth!" Leona hissed. "That's not polite."

"I bought chewing gum," Yates said, ignoring Leona. "Want some?" He opened the package and offered it to each of the girls, who took a stick, then offered it to Leona, who shook her head.

He watched her chin lift and her eyes move away from him as he put the rest of the package in his shirt pocket. Today she wore a blue checked dress with puffed sleeves. It hugged her breasts and narrow waist. He didn't like the small-brimmed straw hat that sat at an angle on her head. It covered too much of her hair and offered practically no shade. He noticed a few freckles on her nose and that she had added a faint color to her lips, which were pressed so tightly together that the dimple in her cheek flirted with him.

"Where'er you goin' now, Mr. Yates?" JoBeth was again pulling on his hand while Ruth Ann looked out the door, embarrassed by her sister's questions.

"I think I'll go back to the house and eat all the pralines that are left." His twinkling eyes reluctantly left Leona to look down at the child. He saw that the smile had faded from her small face. "I'm kidding, honey. I'll not eat a bite of it until you get back."

"Promise?"

"Promise. But don't tarry long. Your aunt promised me biscuits for dinner."

"Don't worry. You'll have them," Leona gritted between clenched teeth.

"See you back at the house, ladies." Yates tipped his hat to Leona even though she had her face turned away.

Yates left the store wondering why the smile had left Mr. White's small pinched features when he spoke about Leona, and why she had looked like she had rather be any place in the world but where she was.

On the way down the street to his car he passed the hardware store, paused and wondered what she would say if he bought a tin oven to set on top of the kerosene burner she was using this morning. He stood looking into the window balancing the pros and cons.

When she built a fire in the cookstove and the temperature outside was in the nineties, the heat in the kitchen would be almost unbearable. She would be sure to bake biscuits every day because he had expressed a liking for them. He didn't like to think about her sweating over a hot cookstove. On the other hand, she would resent his buying the oven, not wanting to be further obligated to him.

What the hell. Yates went into the hardware store. She was going to be mad as a wet hen anyway when Mr. White told her the grocery bill was paid. She might as well be mad about two things while she was at it.

Yates was changing a tire, and Mr. Oliver was putting gas in a car when Leona and the girls returned from town. In order to avoid Yates, Leona drove past the house and parked the car beside the barn. She and the girls went into the house by the back door.

"What's that?" The first thing Ruth Ann saw on entering

the kitchen was the shiny portable oven sitting on the kerosene stove. She opened the door, peered inside, then answered her own question. "It's an oven, Aunt Lee."

Leona, taking off her hat, didn't answer. She was hammering down the anger that had bubbled up because she knew what it was and who had put it there.

"Where'd it come from?" JoBeth opened the door to the oven and closed it with a bang.

"Stop! You'll break it," Ruth Ann said irritably. "Where'd it come from?" She repeated her sister's question.

"Maybe the tooth fairy left it?"

Leona's sarcasm didn't register with the girls. She was already so mad she could chew nails over the way Mr. White, with a sly smile, told her that Andy's *cousin* had left money on account at the store and how pleased she must be to have a man there to look after *her* while Andy was gone.

"Maybe Daddy came home!" JoBeth ran toward the front door.

"No, honey. Daddy didn't come home," Leona said hurriedly. "It probably belongs to Mr. Yates, and he's going to let us use it for a while."

"He's nice. I like him."

"'Cause he gave her gum," Ruth Ann said knowingly to her aunt.

"He didn't eat all the candy," JoBeth said in Yates's defense after she peered beneath the cloth covering the platter.

"You can't have any now. It will spoil your dinner. Now change your dress and go out and play while I get it ready."

"Do I have to change my dress?"

"Of course you do. That's your Sunday dress."

Leona desperately wanted to be alone. Her nerves were usually strung tight after a trip into town. She would never get over the hurt and the humiliation of being shunned by people she had known all her life. Now that the news was out about Andy being in the hospital and a *cousin* staying with them, the gossips would have a heyday. They would be sure that she was sleeping with him, just as they were sure she had been sleeping with Andy.

She stood in the middle of the kitchen after the girls went out and pressed her palms to her hot cheeks. Heat had come up her neck to cover her face when she recalled that Mr. White had raised his brows when he told her that Andy's *cousin* had already paid for her purchases. Then, with his back to her, he had informed her that the *cousin* had wanted to know how long she had been *living* with Andy.

After she set the few items that she had chosen to buy back on the shelves, she squared her shoulders, looked him in the eye and told him that Andy's *cousin* would be taking them to Oklahoma City to see Andy, and that they would stop on their way back and do their grocery buying in Elk City.

She had been pleased to see that her words had shaken the narrow-minded, opinionated man. She hoped he stewed all day about what his loose words might have cost him. It had taken all the willpower Leona possessed to leave the store with her head up. Now, alone, she couldn't keep the tears from her eyes.

It was too much! *Cousin* had bought an oven to go on the kerosene stove.

"Aunt Lee! Aunt Lee!" The front door slammed behind JoBeth. "Mr. Yates fixed the swing. I'm playin' with the camper kids."

"That's good, honey." Leona bent over the washdish in the dry sink. "Run along. I'll call you for dinner."

Leona dabbed at her eyes with the towel, but the tears would not stop coming. Through a blur, she built a fire in the cookstove. Damned if she would use his darned old oven! She didn't know how to use it anyhow. Standing at the tin sink, she peeled several potatoes then sliced them into the iron skillet she had set directly over the flame after she had removed the round stove lid.

Cousin would get the warmed-over pork chops he hadn't eaten last night, and she would make his damn biscuits.

In the large granite bowl, she made a well in the flour and added salt, baking powder and a lump of lard. After adding the buttermilk, she wiped her eyes before she began mixing in the flour with her hand. She had done this a million times and didn't even have to think about what she was doing. The dough was about ready to pinch off and put in the baking pan when Yates's voice came from the doorway.

"Leona?"

She straightened her shoulders quickly and made a hasty swipe at her cheeks with the back of her hand.

"What?" Thank God, her back was to him.

"The ice man is here."

"He knows what to do."

"Do I pay him?"

"Pay him out of what you've taken in and write it down." She pinched off dabs of dough and formed them with her hands before putting them in the pan. "I'll call you when dinner is ready."

Silence. Her nerves screamed when she heard him leave the doorway and come toward her. He didn't stop until he was standing over her. She kept her head bent over the dough.

"Why aren't you using the oven I bought?"

"Because I don't want to!" she snapped.

He reached out and cupped her chin in his palm and turned her face to him. "Why are you crying?"

"That's none of your damn business!" She spoke from between clenched teeth because of his grasp on her jaw. Dammit, she wished she could deny that she was crying, but she couldn't with tears rolling down her cheeks.

"Are you crying over the oven?"

"Get out of this kitchen, *Cousin.*" Her eyes, bright with tears and anger, glared at him. Tears had spiked her lashes.

"It's just a loan. I'll take it when I go."

"You just had to impress Mr. White, didn't you, *Cousin?* I'm sure you did the same when you bought that *thing* from Mr. Hayes at the hardware."

"I thought claiming to be Andy's cousin would give some legitimacy to my being here."

"Oh, yeah! That helped *me* a lot. Now . . . get the hell away from me or . . . or I'll hit you with this dough!" She lifted the ball of dough she was holding.

"You don't seem the type of woman to swear." His voice was barely above a whisper. His eyes stared into hers, because she was too proud to look away.

"You don't know anything about me, but if you hang around long enough you'll find out. Turn loose of me and don't put your hands on me again!" Tears that rolled down her cheeks now rolled over the hand beneath her chin. She was so humiliated she wanted to die.

"I only wanted to make things easier for you." He released her chin and walked quickly out of the room.

Leona dropped the dough back in the bowl and grabbed a towel to wipe her face. She was disgusted with herself for crying and hated herself for doing it in front of *him.* With worry over Andy and having to deal with that exasperating man, the trip to the grocery store had been too much for Leona.

Long ago she had stopped going to church. She took the

girls, dropped them off, then returned for them. If they were ever questioned about their daddy living in "sin" with *that* woman, they never mentioned it.

Maybe she should have married Andy when he asked her a couple of years ago. She cared for Andy as she cared for his children. He was the best friend she'd had since her sister died. She was sure that he felt the same about her. He had asked her to marry him when they first heard the gossip about them although they both knew that they didn't love each other like a man and woman who wanted to marry. He was trying to protect her reputation, but it was already too late.

She had urged him to wait and see what happened. Most folks didn't treat Andy any differently. They realized that he needed someone to take care of his girls. So as time passed, with Virgil's constant harping on her living here with an unmarried man, she had become the "scarlet woman" of Sayre, Oklahoma.

Working automatically, she put the biscuits in the oven and, with her tin-can chopper, chopped an onion in with the potatoes frying in the skillet. While they cooked, she set the table for Yates and the two girls. When the biscuits were almost ready to take from the oven, she went to the door and called to the girls.

"Tell Mr. Yates his dinner is ready, then come in and wash."

The girls were all smiles. They had been playing on the swing with the camper's children. They went to the basin in the tin sink. A little later, as Leona was putting the last of the food on the table, she looked out the window to see that Yates was at the wash bench on the back porch. Just as she had done for Andy, she had put warm water in the basin, a cake of lye soap in the soap dish and a towel nearby.

Leona was leaving the room when Yates came in the back door. "I'll tend the gas pump while you're eating."

"Mr. Oliver is out there."

"Mr. Oliver doesn't work here. We don't even know him."

When she left the room he was still standing in the doorway. The girls were standing behind their places at the table, wide-eyed and silent.

Leona went down the path and into the back door of the garage and out the big double doors. Mr. Oliver was pumping air in a tire tube.

"Howdy, ma'am." He put his fingers to his hat brim.

"Hello. This breeze feels good. I'm glad to get out of that hot kitchen for a while."

"Yes, ma'am."

"I see that Mrs. Oliver got her washing done." She nodded toward the campground, where the woman was taking dried clothes from the bushes where she had spread them to dry.

"Yes, ma'am. Don't take long to dry on a day like this." Mr. Oliver came to Leona and held out a folded bill he took from a pocket in his overalls. "I found this over by the gas pump this mornin', ma'am. Mr. Yates said it weren't his. He counted his money to be sure then told me to keep it, but I don't feel right about it."

"It isn't mine, Mr. Oliver. And it couldn't belong to the garage. Believe me, if we'd lost five dollars we'd know it. It was probably lost by one of the gas customers and belongs to whoever found it."

"It's what Mr. Yates said. I'd hate to keep it if somebody needs it worse than me." He put the bill back in the bib pocket of his overalls.

"Maybe you were meant to have it."

Leona took a piece of dried cornbread from her pocket, crumbled it, threw it out on the drive and waited for the sparrows to come down off the electric line. The swarm of small birds settled near where Leona stood and began eating the crumbs.

"Were you waiting for me?" she asked the fluttery little birds. "I bring them a few crumbs each day about this time," she explained to Mr. Oliver.

Leona stood still, and the little birds came closer and closer to her feet. Watching small wild creatures gave her a great deal of pleasure.

"They aren't shy. They can't afford to be or the bigger birds will swoop down and gobble up the food." She spoke with a tinge of regret in her voice.

"Yes, ma'am. It's the way of things—the big swallow up the little."

Chapter 8

STAY ON THE PORCH OR UNDER THE SHADE TREE," Leona said to JoBeth. "It's too hot for you out here in the garden."

"Mr. Yates gave me a chip of ice. He gave some to the camper kids, too."

Leona grunted a reply and continued to chop weeds from between the rows of green beans.

"He gave us all a peppermint stick." JoBeth was dancing up and down to keep the hot dirt from burning her bare feet.

"Go back to the porch," Leona said again. "You don't have anything on your head."

"If I put on my sunbonnet can I play on the swing?"

"Why don't you spread a quilt on the porch and look at your books?"

"I don't want to. Can I take the camper kids in to hear the radio?"

"I'd rather you didn't. You can ask them when I come in. I'll be in as soon as I pick beans."

"Can I go talk to Mr. Yates?" JoBeth whined.

"No." Leona spoke sharply. "Mind me, JoBeth, and go to the porch."

"You don't let me do anythin'." The child ran toward the porch.

Leona went down the row of beans being careful not to knock off any blooms and to pick only the ones that were three inches or longer. Her bucket was full by the time she reached the end of the first row. She stood to ease her back and looked over the two additional rows to be picked. This was the best garden she'd ever had, and she was proud of it. At this rate they would have all the beans they could eat and all that she could possibly can.

Picking up the bucket, she went to the house. After setting the bucket on the porch she headed for the campground. She removed her sunbonnet when she reached the shade, where Mrs. Oliver was nursing her baby.

"It's cooler here in the shade," she said and fanned her face with the brim of the bonnet.

"I saw you working in your garden." The woman stood and lifted her baby to her shoulder. "Made me homesick."

"I'm hoping for some rain, so that I don't have to water again soon."

"It's a pretty garden," Mrs. Oliver said wistfully.

"I just picked a row of beans. You are welcome to pick the other two rows. According to the blooms still coming on, we are going to have plenty."

"Ah . . . ma'am—"

"I only pick them if they're three inches long," Leona rushed on. "I'll not get to the other two rows this week. By then they'll be old and tough."

"I sure do thank ya."

"No thanks are necessary, Mrs. Oliver. There's some green onions and radishes on the end of the rows. I planted them as an afterthought. Take some of those, too. My, I don't know why I get so carried away when I plant a garden."

"I'll take the boys. They'll pull weeds while I pick the beans. We'll be careful of the plants."

"If there's anything I hate to do it's pull or chop weeds, and the girls are too young yet to turn loose in the garden. I'd better get back to the house and snap the beans I picked if we're going to have them for supper." Leona lifted her hand in farewell and hurried away.

She went through the house to the washstand on the back porch, splashed water on her face and blotted it with the slightly damp towel that hung on the nail above the stand. She held it to her face for a hazy, unreal moment, inhaling the sharp, unfamiliar masculine scent, and couldn't really define how it made her feel.

"Aunt Lee, Uncle Virgil is here."

Leona froze. Guilt at being caught smelling the towel Yates had used was replaced quickly by apprehension.

Oh, no! Not today! A confrontation with her brother was always unpleasant.

"Uncle Virgil is here," JoBeth said again.

"I heard you, honey."

Trying her best to prepare herself for the scene that was sure to follow, Leona hurried through the house to the porch to make sure her brother didn't come into the house. Virgil's friend Abe Patton had driven around the garage and had stopped his car just a few feet from the porch. He and Abe were getting out when Leona came through the door.

"What's goin' on out here?" Virgil demanded the instant he saw her. He was a tall, thin man with stooped shoulders and thinning hair. The voice coming from the thin, bony face was loud and belligerent. For the hundredth time Leona wondered why he never spoke in a normal tone of voice.

"Hello to you, too, Virgil. I'm fine, thank you." Leona's voice was heavy with sarcasm.

She stepped out into the yard, not wanting to give him an excuse to even come up onto the porch. She knew why he was here. He'd been to town and heard the news about Andy, and no doubt Mr. White had spread the news about Andy's *cousin.*

"What's this about Andy bein' bit by a skunk?"

"It's true. He's in Oklahoma City getting the rabies shots."

"The Lord works in mysterious ways to punish the doers of evil." He lifted his eyes to the heavens, then turned them on his sister, who stood with her arms crossed over her chest. "Get yore thin's. Yo're comin' home. Abe'll make ya a good man. Yo're long past marryin'."

"I'll . . . not . . . go." Leona spaced the words for emphasis.

"Mind me now. I ain't takin' no sass from ya."

"I'm not going, Virgil. I'm staying right here. You might as well go crawl back into the hole you crawled out of and take that poor excuse for a man with you."

"Hush yore mouth! Hazel is willin' to take the girls in—"

"That's good of her . . . considering she's living in my mama's house and refused to even give me or Irene a picture of her or our father."

"That's enough out of ya! I ain't havin' no backtalk from no split-tail gal who fornicates with every man that comes down the highway!" Virgil shouted. "Hazel's a good Christian woman while you're nothin' but a Jezebel livin' in sin first with that heathen and now spreadin' your legs for some other jaybird."

Leona's temper flared. "Don't you dare say those things to me, you dirty-minded, sanctimonious pile of horse manure! You and Hazel are the heathens. Neither one of you have an ounce of compassion in your damn miserable hearts. You didn't even come to see your dying sister because she was married to Andy, who loved her with all his heart. Something you'd not understand. You hated him because he refused to be a religious fanatic like you."

"God will strike you down for your blasphemy!" Virgil shouted.

"Maybe. But I'll tell you this—Andy is the most decent man I've ever known. Irene never regretted marrying him. He was her savior. He saved both of us from *you!*"

Leona regretted that JoBeth and Ruth Ann were on the porch listening to every word that passed between her and Virgil, but they had heard most of it before. After he left she would have to assure them over and over that she would not leave them. Ruth Ann, being the older, was affected the most by Virgil's visits.

He had come periodically since Irene died to preach at Leona and demand that she give up her life of sin and return to the family home. Virgil believed that as the head of the family, he ruled all unmarried women in that family, even the disgraced ones, and it was his duty to set her feet on the path of *righteousness*. Leona was well-aware of how he enforced his rules. His own children were afraid to take a deep breath in his presence.

Leona had been ten, her sister thirteen, when their parents died within a year of each other, leaving Virgil, a religious zealot, married with two children, the head of the family. He moved into the family home and immediately took charge. It was prayer morning and night, church three times a week with prayer meetings in between and all day on Sunday. The girls spent long hours on their knees and were punished with the strop for the slightest infraction of his rules.

When Irene had run off and married Andy, Leona was forbidden even to speak to her. The last time Virgil whipped Leona was when she was fifteen. He had caught her putting her meager belongings in a pillowcase. He said it was God's punishment that Andy had lost his foot and forbade her to go to her sister. He and Hazel had overpowered her. Virgil had whipped her bare buttocks with the razor strop and locked her in a shed without her shoes. She had pried off a loose board, slipped out and walked barefoot five miles to Irene's house, crying and swearing never to return. She never did.

"Get yore thin's together," Virgil shouted to JoBeth and Ruth Ann. "I'm takin' ya outta this den of sin 'n' shame."

The little girls looked thunderstruck. The younger girl cowered behind her sister.

"You're not taking them anywhere." Leona's shout was equally as loud. "I'll . . . kill you before I let you get your hands on *my* girls."

"Yore girls?"

"*My* girls! Make a move toward them and I'll . . . I'll scratch your eyes out!" Leona looked into the bright, fevered eyes of her brother and wondered how her gentle mother could have given birth to such a poor excuse for a human being.

"I'll go to the law."

"You do that, Virgil, and I'll tell everyone in this county about the time my *God-fearing self-righteous* brother whipped his own little boy with a switch until the blood ran down his little legs and that his stupid cow-of-a-wife didn't lift a hand to help her child. Then I'll show them the scars you put on my back when I tried to stop you. They are still there, reminding me every day of how much I hate you."

"The Lord says spare the rod and spoil the child. Pa spared the rod and . . . look at what ya are! Yo're a disgrace to the Dawson name. Abe'll straighten ya out."

"Get the hell away from here, Virgil, and take that hypercritical jackass with you." She nodded toward Abe leaning against the car.

"God is not pleased with ya. Yo're greasin' yore path to the fiery furnace. Abe is a good Christian man willin' to overlook yore swearin' and whorin' and make a decent God-fearin' woman of ya."

"Ha! That's a laugh. You wouldn't know what was decent if it jumped up and bit you." Leona looked at Abe Patton as if he were a cowpie covered with maggots. He was a fleshier version of her brother and about the same age.

There was a fifteen-year spread between Virgil's age and Leona's. Virgil was the oldest of their parents' living children, and Leona the youngest. Her brother had been trying to force Leona to marry Abe since she was in grade school. She didn't doubt that had she not escaped his domination, Virgil would have let Abe rape her.

"I'd rather be burned at the stake than to marry that pious mule's ass. He's cowshit, Virgil. Cowshit! Both of you are." Leona's eyes flicked over them contemptuously.

"God ain't goin' to keep on forgivin' ya. I've had enough of yore backtalk! You're headed straight for hell." Virgil's anger had carried him several steps forward. He drew back his hand to strike her.

"So are you if you touch her!" The voice came from behind her. Leona turned her head quickly to see Yates, his steely eyes on Virgil, come from around the car parked by the back door of the garage. Her brother stood frozen, his hand still raised.

"Who er you?" Virgil demanded in a tight, screeching voice, a look of pure indignation on his bony face.

"You'll pray to die if you hit her." Yates came to stand beside Leona.

"Ya must be the so-called *cousin* I heared about. Stay out

of this. It ain't no business of yores." Virgil spoke belligerently, but lowered his hand.

Yates endured Virgil's sneering appraisal with no betrayal of the fury swirling through him.

"Keep that clap-trap going and you'll find out if it's my business or not."

"I come to take my sister and them girls outta here."

"And if they don't want to go?"

"They's women folks. They ain't got no say-so."

"Are you of age, Leona?" Yates asked.

"Long past," she answered without looking at him.

"Does he have a legal claim on you?"

"Absolutely not," she said tersely.

"That settles the matter." Cold gray eyes stared unblinkingly at the tall scarecrow of a man with thinning hair on top. "Get the hell out of here while you're able."

"Yo're a sinful harlot!" Virgil turned his hate-filled eyes on his sister. "There ain't no redemption for ya. God will strike ya down as he struck down that son of Satan for leadin' Irene astray." Hatred lifted his voice to a shout, spittle leaking from the corners of his mouth. "Yo're the dung of creation! A whore, a slut, a vile sinner! Yo're the filthiest scum this side of hell, is what ya are. God hates—"

"Enough!" With lightning speed Yates's hand lashed out. Powerful fingers clamped around Virgil's throat cutting off his words. Jerking the man close to him, he grabbed the soft sack between Virgil's legs with his other hand. "Say one more word, you pious son-of-a-bitch, and I'll crush these like they were paper."

A gurgling scream came from Virgil. He grabbed Yates's wrist to pull his hand away from his privates. For a long painful minute his feet danced in place as he attempted to get away from the punishing hands holding him.

"Hurts, doesn't it?" Yates snarled. "It would hurt more if I twisted them off." He emphasized his words with a twist of his wrist. Virgil screeched, his eyes rolled back in his head. "I should do it, not only for what you just called Leona, but for what you did to her and that little boy."

Strangled sounds came from Virgil's open mouth. His eyes bulged; he gasped for breath. Yates shoved him back toward the car.

"Open the door or I'll throw him through the window," Yates snarled at Virgil's friend, who stood stupefied.

Abe hurried to fling open the car door on the passenger side. Yates shoved Virgil down onto the seat, releasing his throat and the hold on his genitals at the same time. He quickly shoved the car door against Virgil's bony legs and held it there.

"That's just a little taste of what's in store for you if you come here again. I never want to hear of you talking to your sister the way you talked to her today and . . . if you ever strike her, or threaten to take the girls away from her, I'll hang you from a tree and skin you like a rabbit. Do you understand me?" Yates spoke in a hard, unyielding voice.

When Virgil didn't answer, Yates tromped hard on his foot with the heel of his boot. Virgil let out a strangled scream.

"Answer me, damn you!"

"Yes! Yes!" Virgil's face was crimson. His mouth worked to spit out the words.

Yates opened the door and released his legs. "That's a good boy." He helped Virgil get his legs inside the car, patted him on the shoulder like he was a small boy and slammed the car door.

Yates waited beside the car. Abe had some difficulty in getting it started, but when he did, he drove out of the yard as if a gang of outlaws were after him. Yates watched the car until it reached the highway. When he turned to speak to Leona, she wasn't anywhere in sight. Nor were the girls.

The humiliation was almost more than Leona could endure.

A yelling match with her brother always left her shaken. To have Yates witness it was the most demeaning experience of her life. As soon as Virgil was in the car, she hurried into the house and on to the bedroom fearing that Yates would follow.

How would she ever be able to face him?

"Aunt Lee"—Ruth Ann came to where Leona sat on her narrow bed—"don't cry, Aunt Lee."

"I . . . I'm trying . . . not to."

"Why does Uncle Virgil say . . . those mean things?" Ruth Ann came to her aunt and put her arms around her.

"I don't know, honey."

"Uncle Virgil said you're a whore. What's that, Aunt Lee?"

"It's a . . . woman who's not very nice."

"You're nice, Aunt Lee. I hate Uncle Virgil."

"I don't want to go live with him." JoBeth's voice quivered as she rushed into the room.

"You're staying right here." Leona held out her arm. The child rushed to her and buried her tear-wet face against her shoulder.

"You'll not let him take us?"

"No! I'll take you and run away to China before I let that happen," Leona said in a choked voice and hugged the girls fiercely.

"Don't worry, JoBeth," Ruth Ann said with the confidence of an eight-year-old. "Mr. Yates won't let him take us."

"I wish Daddy was here."

"He'll be back soon." Leona spoke without much conviction and wiped her face on the end of her skirt.

"Will Mr. Yates stay till Daddy comes home?"

"I . . . think so."

"He's going to take us to see Daddy."

"When did he say that?"

"You said it, Aunt Lee. You told Mr. White he was going to take us." Ruth Ann looked up at her aunt pleadingly. "He will, won't he?"

"I'll ask him," JoBeth said.

"No, don't do that." Leona spoke over the lump that came up in her throat. "Let's just wait and see how long your daddy will be there."

"Maybe we'll get a letter tomorrow," Ruth Ann said hopefully.

"Tonight we'll all write him a letter and put it out for Mr. Wilkes to pick up in the morning."

"But we won't tell him Uncle Virgil was here," Ruth Ann said. "It'd worry him."

"Ah, honey." Leona hugged the child to her. "Your mama would be so proud of you."

Chapter 9

SON-OF-A-BITCH!"

Yates cursed as he went back to the garage. It was hard for him to believe the pious windbag who he'd just managed to keep himself from gelding was Leona's brother. It cleared up one thing in his mind—Leona was the sister of Andy's dead wife, the girls' aunt. Why hadn't he thought of that? Her brother, and possibly others of his ilk, considered her a fallen woman because she was living out here with Andy and the girls without the benefit of marriage.

Curious when he had heard the raised voices, Yates had paused to listen. Leona had spunk. She was standing up to the loud-mouthed, overbearing bully. Yates hadn't meant to get involved in the squabble until the bastard lifted his hand to hit her. If that had happened, he would have swept the ground with him. There was nothing that got his temper up and rolling like seeing a woman or a child mistreated. Later he had wanted to kill him . . . instead, he thought with satisfaction, he had hurt the bastard plenty.

There were things about Leona Dawson that he didn't understand, and he wasn't sure why he was even interested, but he was . . . definitely. He couldn't help but to wonder if there was more between her and Andy than what appeared on the surface.

Why hadn't Andy explained to him who she was? And why had she cried when she returned from town?

Yates had expected her to be angry over the oven, but not to cry about it, for God's sake! What he had seen on her tear-streaked face was not only defiance, but hurt and embarrassment, too.

Yates's thoughts were interrupted when a car drove in and stopped at the gas pump. The man who got out wore tan trousers tucked into custom-made boots, a white shirt and a five-dollar Stetson. Yates was a good judge of men. This one would stand out in a crowd, not only because of his dress, but because he was tall, broad-shouldered and carried himself like someone who knew where he was going. Well-dressed Indians were not uncommon in Oklahoma. Oil had made some of them wealthy.

"Howdy." Yates moved the pump lever back and forth to fill the glass cylinder.

"It should hold ten gallon. Andy here?"

"No." Then Yates repeated the words he'd said several times today. "Andy had a little run-in with a sick skunk. He'll be in the hospital for a while taking the vaccine."

"Laws! I'm sorry to hear that. I always enjoy my visits with him when I pass this way. Name's Fleming, by the way. Barker Fleming from over near Elk City."

"Yates." Yates held out his hand.

"What do the doctors say about Andy?" Fleming asked with a worried frown.

"They'll give him the vaccine. The success rate is good, but there's nothing for sure."

"God, I hope he makes it. Life has given him some hard knocks."

"That it has," Yates agreed. "Are you one of the Flemings that ranch south and east of here?"

"If it's a Fleming, we're related. My father has been ranching here for forty years. He has five sons, but not all of us are ranchers."

"I bought a horse from a fellow who said he'd got it from the Fleming ranch."

"We raise and train our stock animals and a few others." Barker Fleming glanced toward the house. "Are you from around here?"

"No, I'm from Texas."

"Pardon the questions, but it lays heavy on Andy that he has no relatives to care for his girls if something should happen to him."

"I'll be here until he's back and able to work." Yates was watching the cylinder and shut off the flow of gasoline.

"He knew the danger of being here on the highway, but he had a good attitude about it. His only worry was for his girls and Miss Dawson."

"I'm not a relative, but if something happens to Andy, I'll see to it that they're cared for."

"It must be a hell of a relief to Andy to know that."

"Have you known him long?" Yates tightened the cap on the sedan's gas tank.

"I met him seven or eight years ago, just before he lost his foot. Where's he taking the vaccine?"

"St. Anthony Hospital in Oklahoma City."

"I'll be going to the city in a day or two. I'll go by and see him."

"Check with Dr. Harris."

"I'll do that." Barker handed Yates a couple of bills.

Yates took the bills and dug in his pocket for the change.

"Tell him that I'll bring Miss Dawson and the girls as soon as I can find someone to stay here at the garage."

"Deke Bales has stayed here a few times."

"Miss Dawson told me that. Do you know how I can get in touch with him?"

"Deke works for me. Do you want me to send him around?"

"Well, yeah, but if he works for you—"

"He works at the ranch. I can spare him for a day or two."

"Does he work on Sunday? I told Andy that I'd bring him a change of clothes, his shaving things and his crutches by the end of the week."

"Sunday is like any other day to Deke."

"It's important to Andy that someone be here to get gas for folks if they need it."

"I'll see to it that he's here."

"I'm obliged. If you see Andy before Sunday, tell him that everything is all right here."

"I'll do that. Nice meeting you."

"Same here."

Fleming was a familiar name in this part of the country, Yates thought, as he watched the car leave the drive. The family, respected by both Indians and whites, was involved in ranching and meat processing among other things. The hides from Fleming packing plants supplied their tanneries. Fleming leather was used in making some of the finest custom-made shoes and boots sold in the United States. And surely, Yates mused, with all the land they own there must be oil on some of it.

When he went back into the garage, JoBeth was sitting on the bench beside the back door.

"I come out to see Mr. Fleming, but—he was goin'—"

Her lips trembled and her eyes filled with tears. "I was goin' to tell him about Daddy."

"I told him. He's going to stop by the hospital and see him."

"Sometimes he brings Marie to play."

"Marie?"

"His little girl. Marie saves the funny papers for Ruth Ann. Her favorite is Little Orphan Annie, but I like Tarzan."

"Dick Tracy is my favorite."

"He was Daddy's, too. Mr. Yates? Can I stay here a while?" The five-year-old clutched a rag doll with yellow yarn hair. "Daddy let me if I didn't get in the way."

"Does your aunt know you're here?"

"Uh-uh."

"You'd better go tell her. She'll be looking for you."

"She won't. She's not done cryin' yet."

Yates didn't know how to reply to that and evidently JoBeth didn't expect a reply.

She said, "Ruth Ann said you'd not let Uncle Virgil take us."

"Are you worried about that?"

"Uh-huh. I wish Daddy was here."

Yates squatted down until his face was level with that of the child. He had no experience with children, but he knew that this one was suffering from anxiety.

"Your uncle won't take you away from here, honey, unless you and your aunt want to go."

"Promise?"

"Cross my heart and hope to die."

JoBeth dropped her doll and flung both arms around his neck. The action so surprised Yates, that he didn't know what to do. Awkwardly, he patted the child's back.

"There, there," he murmured.

"Aunt Lee told Mr. White you was goin' to take us to see Daddy."

"I'm planning on it." Yates set the little girl back on the bench and stood.

"We're saving some of the candy to take to Daddy. Ruth Ann said maybe we'd buy our dinner at a eatin' place, but Aunt Lee said we'd take a picnic."

"Would you like to do that?"

"Eat at a eatin' place?"

"Both."

"Uh-huh. Are we goin' to the store in Elk City? Aunt Lee told Mr. White we was."

"Didn't she get what she needed from Mr. White?"

"Uh-uh. Aunt Lee put it all back and we went out."

"Maybe it wasn't what she wanted."

"Uh-uh. She was mad."

"How could you tell?"

"She set the baking powder can down real hard and walked fast."

"JoBeth!"

The little girl dashed for the door when she heard her sister call from the porch.

"Can I tell Ruth Ann we're goin'?"

"I'd better talk to your aunt first."

"She'll want to go. She likes Daddy," she said over her shoulder.

She likes Daddy. The words played over and over in Yates's mind. It bothered him that he was so curious about the relationship between Leona and Andy. Did Andy feel guilty about his feelings for her because she was his wife's sister? If they had married it would put Leona out of the reach of that crazy brother of hers.

The little girl had given him something to think about—

the damn grocer. Had White insinuated that he'd had an ulterior motive for establishing a credit for her at the store? If he had, he'd be set straight about it damn quick—after he rearranged his face.

He was still thinking about it and hoping to find Leona in the barn when he went there to feed the horses. He seldom felt the need to explain his actions. It surprised him that he wanted to tell her that he owed Andy and that the credit at the store was just one way he could pay back.

Yates was disappointed to find that Leona had already milked the cow. She stood patiently in her stall chewing her cud.

"Aunt Lee's makin' bread puddin' for supper," JoBeth called when he went out to move the tin conduit, so that he could fill the stock tank. "It's got raisins in it." The little girl was scattering grain, enticing the chickens into the pen for the night.

"My favorite," Yates replied while rapidly working the pump handle until the water began to gush, then slower as it flowed into the conduit.

"Come on, JoBeth." Ruth Ann, carrying the egg basket, walked past Yates. Her head was down and a mutinous look darkened her young face.

Yates watched her. Damn that uncle of theirs. Little girls shouldn't have to worry that some religious fanatic was going to come and take them. Hell. Now he wished he'd twisted his damn nuts off. That would've given the bastard something to think about besides snatching little girls out of their home.

Leona glanced out the kitchen window, saw Yates at the well and hurried to get the light supper on the table. She had to be out of here by the time he came in.

She needed more time before she could face him.

"Where's your aunt?" Yates asked when he went in for supper. Leona had yet to sit down at the table and eat a meal when he was there.

"She went . . . somewhere," Ruth Ann mumbled with her back to him. "Want tea?"

"I can get it."

"No. I will." The little girl lifted the lid on the icebox and carefully chipped chunks from the block of ice, put them in the pitcher and returned the pick to the leather holder on the side of the icebox. She stirred the tea with a long-handled spoon, filled a glass and carried it to the table.

"If Deke Bales comes on Sunday, we'll go to the city to see your daddy." Yates waited to see the little girl's face brighten. It didn't. She sat looking down at her plate. "Don't you want to go?" he asked.

"I'm not gettin' my hopes up. Mr. Bales will probably take off like a herd of buffalo when he finds out Aunt Lee won't be here."

"Mr. Fleming said he'd be here."

"He did?" Ruth Ann lifted her eyes. He could see the hope in her face.

"He did. He's reliable, isn't he?"

She nodded. "Aunt Lee will go. She won't let us go without her."

"I'm planning on her going. We'll stop at the store in Elk City on the way back."

"Store isn't open on Sunday." Ruth Ann imparted the news as if Yates should have known.

"You're right. I didn't think about that. We'll have to go another time."

"Will Daddy be in bed?" JoBeth crumbled cornbread into her glass of milk.

"I don't know. He'll either be in the hospital or a room nearby. We'll find him."

Yates helped himself to a couple of deviled eggs and a slice of cornbread. If not for the breeze coming in through the wide open doors and windows the kitchen would be as hot as the bread pudding and the oven Leona used to bake it in. He glanced at the small, shiny portable oven still sitting on the kerosene stove.

"Mr. Yates said maybe we can buy our dinner when we go to see Daddy," JoBeth said to her sister.

"You've told me that six times already," Ruth Ann replied impatiently. "Aunt Lee said we'll pack a picnic."

"We can do both." Yates put a spoonful of sugar in his tea. "We'll have to leave early, and it'll be late when we get back."

A few weeks ago if anyone had told Yates that he would be sitting in a kitchen carrying on a conversation with the two little girls and enjoying it, he would have told them that they were crazy as a bed bug.

"I need to talk to your aunt."

"'Bout buyin' our dinner?" JoBeth was spooning the cornbread from the glass and milk was running down her chin.

"No. I need to find out what your daddy did with the money he took in."

"He had a hidey-hole," Ruth Ann said.

"Humm. Smart of him. The banks aren't too reliable nowadays."

"Daddy said he wasn't going to be caught with his pants down."

"Why'd he say that, Ruth Ann?"

"You're too young to understand." Ruth Ann answered

her sister in a superior tone. Then she asked Yates, "Are you ready for the bread pudding?"

Reluctant to leave when the meal was over, Yates helped the girls clear the table. When Ruth Ann would have left the dishes in the pan, he suggested that they wash them.

"You'll have to tell me what to do. I've not washed many dishes."

"Then I'd better wash. You can dry and JoBeth can put away."

The task took less than a quarter of an hour and when they finished, Yates no longer had an excuse to linger until Leona returned.

"Where can I find your aunt?" He hung the wet tea towel on a line over the cookstove.

"She don't want ya to find her," Ruth Ann said bluntly.

"Why not?"

The little girl turned and glared at him. "Don't ya know anythin'?"

"Evidently not *that* or I'd not have asked. Why doesn't she want me to find her?"

"She's shamed!"

"Shamed?" he repeated.

"Shamed . . . 'bout what Uncle Virgil said. I hate him. I wish he'd die!"

"Mr. Yates, will you kill him for us?" JoBeth looked up at Yates. "So we won't have to ever go with him, and he won't come and make Aunt Lee cry. Will ya?"

"Ah, sweetheart." Totally stunned by the request, Yates sat down in the kitchen chair and lifted the child up onto his lap. "Killing is something we should never even consider. If we did something like that we'd be even worse than your Uncle Virgil."

"Ya hurt him and he went away."

"I wouldn't have, but I didn't think that he'd go unless I did."

"Could ya hurt him worser?"

"I might have to if he comes back here and talks mean to your aunt and tries to take you from your home."

JoBeth threw her arms around his neck. "I wish you was my uncle, 'stead of that old Uncle Virgil."

Chapter 10

After the girls had gone to bed, Leona sat on the back porch and rhythmically moved the wooden dasher up and down through the milk in the churn. She was so keyed up from the events of the day that she knew she wouldn't sleep and decided to get this morning chore out of the way.

Today had been the worst day of her life!

Calvin came out from under the porch, flopped down beside her and placed his jowls on her foot.

"You miss Andy, don't you, boy?"

Calvin's answer was a deep sigh.

Leona tied back her thick, wavy hair with a piece of twine and gazed at the bright, silent stars that blanketed the sky. She enjoyed the feel of the breeze coming from the south while listening to the fluttering of birds in the branches that extended over the roof of the porch. She also heard the faint stirrings of the horses in the corral beside the barn. At times one of them would stamp or blow dust from his nostrils. Occasionally the sound of a car going by on the highway reached her ears.

Where was it going, guided only by the headlights forging a path on the ribbon of paving? And where had it come from?

The first hours of darkness were the lonely hours for

Leona. When there was no longer work to be done and her mind was free to wander, she dreamed her secret dreams of finding a man who would love her as Andy had loved her sister. He had adored her with all his heart and soul, and it had almost killed him when he lost her.

Realistically Leona knew that she would never find her life's mate in this town where ninety-eight percent of the people thought that a man could fornicate with a number of women and still be respectable; but because she, an unmarried woman, lived in this house with Andy and took care of his girls, she was considered immoral.

She would have to go away from here, but how could she leave this little family she loved? It would be hard to leave the girls even if Andy remarried. But so far he hadn't seemed to have the slightest interest in marrying again. As far as Leona knew, he had not even looked at another woman since his Irene's death almost three years before.

Her thoughts turned now and fixed firmly on Yates, as they had done at odd intervals throughout the day. She reluctantly admitted to herself that she had been unreasonable about the portable oven. Her excuse was that after being so thoroughly mortified by the things Mr. White said at the store, as well as what he implied, finding the oven sitting on the kerosene stove had seemed to her to be the final humiliation.

Through the darkness, the stern, expressionless face of the stranger who had come so suddenly into their lives emerged and hung suspended before her—so close that she could see every silver fleck in his incredible eyes and the lines that bracketed his firm unsmiling mouth. His size alone intimidated her—she was not used to such big men. That wasn't exactly true. Most of the men who stopped at the garage were larger than Andy. Some of them intimidated her, while Yates intrigued her.

She would never forget the questioning look in Yates's eyes as he listened to Virgil spewing out his vile words of abuse and hatred. She was sure the word *trash* flashed before his eyes like an electric sign on the front of a honky-tonk. Just thinking about it caused a flood of scarlet to wash up her neck and heat her face.

One thing that puzzled her greatly was that Andy had never mentioned knowing anyone named Yates. It seemed to Leona that he hadn't even known him that morning when he rode in and killed the skunk. The only reason he gave for being here was that he owed Andy. What had Andy ever done for a man like Yates that would warrant all that he was willing to do for him?

What to do? What to do with the rest of her life was the question. *Is this all I'll ever have—caring for someone else's children?*

To still her thoughts she began to sing in a voice just above a whisper as she did sometimes to accompany the slush, slush, slush sound as the dasher moved up and down through the milk.

> *"O bury me not on the lone prairie,*
> *The words came low and mournfully*
> *From the pallid lips of a youth who lay*
> *on his dying bed at the close of day."*

It was comforting to Leona to sing the sad old songs her mother used to sing while working around the house. She intended, someday, to write down the words in order to preserve them for the girls.

"In a little rosewood casket,
setting on a marble stand
Was a package of love letters—
written by her true-love's hand."

Leona wasn't sure when she became aware that Calvin was sitting very still, staring at the corner of the house. She reached down and patted his head. He remained stiff and alert. She ceased the movement of the dasher so that she could listen.

"What is it, boy?"

The dog's tail began to wag. Leona stood. In the next instant Calvin was off the porch and running. He was clearly visible in the moonlight. She heard his whine of welcome as Yates came around the corner of the porch. Her first thought was to go into the house, her second thought was not to give him the satisfaction of knowing that she ran from him.

She sat back down. Her hand sought the dasher, and she began to move it rapidly up and down, subconsciously providing a reason for being there.

"Evenin'."

"Evening," she muttered.

"I need to speak to you."

"What about?" she asked sharply. Her voice cold and flat.

"What does Andy do with the money he takes in?"

Leona took a long time answering, then said, "He hides it."

"He doesn't bank it?"

"No."

"Do you know where he hides it?"

"Yes."

After a long pause, he said, "But you don't want to tell me."

"No. Find your own hiding place."

"Does he keep a list of what he sells?"

"Didn't you see it? There's a Red Chief tablet on the shelf in the garage."

"Yes, I saw it, and I've been writing down what was sold."

"Then why did you ask me?" she retorted testily. She could feel his eyes on her, but she refused to look at him.

"Mind if I sit down?"

"Why ask me?" she muttered. "You'll do as you please."

He sat down on the edge of the porch. Calvin went to lean against him. Yates scratched the dog's ears. Calvin whined contentedly.

Leona felt as if the air was being squeezed from her chest. She debated about getting up and going into the house without saying another word. But damned if she'd let him run her off. She had more right here than he did, she thought childishly. She continued to churn although she was sure the milk had made all the butter it was going to make.

"My mother used to sing one of the songs you were singing."

"Eavesdropping?"

"Yeah, guess I was. I thought if I showed myself you'd stop singing."

"You were right, I would have." Her mouth clamped shut. Being alone with him in the dark made her nerves tingle and goose pimples swarm over her flesh.

"Could I persuade you to sing some more?"

"No. I sing only for my own pleasure."

"I can understand that. It's the same reason I play my guitar."

The next few minutes were filled with a strange quiet; the only sound made was by the dasher as Leona continued to move it up and down through the milk.

"What did the grocer say to you about the credit at the store?"

"Nothing much."

"He must have said something to cause you to put down the things you were going to buy."

For a full minute she looked at the blur that was his face while she sought to control her temper. Then she stood and reached to pick up the churn. His hand clamped down on the top and held it to the floor of the porch.

"Don't run," he said softly. "Talk to me."

"I'm not running, and I've nothing to say to you."

"Sit down . . . please. I'm not your enemy, Leona."

"All I've got to say to you is that I think it's rotten of you to pick information from a child." Pride kept Leona rooted to where she stood.

"I didn't ask. She volunteered. Sit down for just a little while."

"And you soaked up every word." She sank down on the edge of the bench.

"Did he insult you?"

"He didn't think so."

"Did you?"

"I'm used to it."

"What do you mean by that?"

"You can't insult a strumpet, Mr. Yates, or an immoral woman who lives out in the country with a man who isn't her husband. To make matters worse she fornicates with him with his two children in the house."

"Is that what folks think of you?"

"You heard what Virgil had to say."

"What do they say about Andy?"

"Andy is a man. He can't be blamed for taking what's handy."

"Your brother is warped. I've seen fanatics like him before. There's no reasoning with them."

"You hurt him. He won't forget it."

"I didn't hurt him enough. I hope he gives me another chance at him."

"He's big in the church. Half of Sayre is holy roller. You won't be so welcome the next time you go to town."

"I've met some fine people who are holy rollers; not all of them are like your brother. Leona"—his voice was set; his eyes peering at her through the semi-darkness—"do you consider yourself a decent woman?"

"Of course!" she blurted through stiff lips.

"Because some people think otherwise, does it change you?"

"Of course not! I know what I am."

"Then why care what they think?"

"I care because of . . . myself and what it does to the girls."

"Why didn't Andy marry you if he wanted you to stay here and take care of his children? My God, he should have known that it would make things difficult for you."

"Don't you dare criticize Andy! He's the best man I've ever known. My sister loved him dearly."

"How about you? Do you love him?"

"Yes, I love him. He and the girls are the only people in this whole wide world that I love and who love me. Satisfied?"

"Yeah. I guess that says it all except why he lets your brother treat you the way he treated you today."

"You ask a lot of questions that are none of your business."

He was quiet for so long Leona thought maybe he was going to leave. Then suddenly, he said, "If Deke Bales shows up on Sunday, we can go to the city to see Andy."

"Why are you bothering with us?"

"I told you that I owed Andy, and this is one way I can pay my debt."

"You told me that, but you didn't say why you owe him."

"And you are wondering what a nice, gentle man like Andy would do for a hard case like me. Is that it?"

"You said it."

"A long time ago Andy helped me out of a tight spot."

Time ticked away as silence fell after his words. They looked at each other openly from across the churn. Finally Leona spoke.

"Andy is always willing to give a helping hand."

He looked at her quietly, trying to read her thoughts. The silence stretched between them like a taut thread. The moment came to an end when she drew in a ragged breath and stood.

"I've got to take the churn in."

Yates got to his feet. "Leona? Wait. I came to tell you that . . . well—" He hesitated. It had been years since he'd been so unsure of himself. He felt awkward and tongue-tied and he didn't like it.

"Well, what, Mr. Yates?"

"I just wanted to say there was no need for you to be embarrassed because I heard what your brother said."

"I wasn't just embarrassed by what he said, Mr. Yates. I was mortified, and I've heard that same sermon a hundred times since I was fifteen years old. I knew what to expect when he drove into the yard."

"You were embarrassed because I was there."

"Well, of course. Wouldn't you have been if the situation were reversed? Few people want their family's dirty secrets aired in public."

"It didn't seem to bother your brother."

"Virgil is an exception to the rule. But then again, he's an exception to a lot of rules."

"Don't be embarrassed. I never for a minute believed what he said."

"Maybe not now, but as more accusations pile up, you will start to wonder if there isn't some truth in it. That's just a natural reaction." Leona was rather proud that she could speak logically in spite of her shortness of breath and the heavy pounding of her heart.

"How does Virgil justify taking Andy's girls?"

"He's convinced himself that he'll be saving their souls, but it's really for spite. Andy took Irene out from under his thumb and then he lost me to Andy. I came to stay with her when he lost his foot, then stayed on when she took sick."

"And that's why he hates Andy."

"He thinks he lost face with some of his cohorts because he can't control the women in his family. And he enjoys a confrontation. It keeps him in the limelight. What you did to him will be told time and again to his fellow fanatics. He'll squeeze out every drop of sympathy he can get."

"Now, I wish I'd really given him something to tell about."

"You did enough." She bent to pick up the churn.

"I'll carry it in for you."

"I can do it. I brought it out."

"I wasn't here then. I am now." Yates lifted the churn and waited for her to open the door. "Will we have fresh butter for the biscuits in the morning?"

"If I get around to working the milk out of it." They entered the darkened house. Leona caught the screendoor to keep it from slamming and waking the girls. "Set it on the table," she whispered. "And thank you."

Leona's heart stopped in her chest while she waited for

him to leave after he'd eased the churn down onto the table. She gave a silent prayer for the darkness, so that he couldn't see how nervous she was being here in the dark with him. Seconds ticked by. He moved a step closer to her. His breath smelled of tobacco and mint. She attempted to move back and came up against the kitchen cabinet.

His hand, warm and firm, clasped her shoulder. He left it there for a minute, then moved it up to stroke her hair.

"You have pretty hair." He moved his face closer to hers. "Open your eyes," he whispered.

"Well, I don't . . ." It was all she managed to say.

"They're pretty, too. You're trembling. Are you afraid of me?"

"Yes."

"Why?"

"You . . . make me nervous."

"In what way?"

"Well . . ." She leaned her head back, but didn't tilt it to look up at him. "You're awfully big and . . . I don't know you," she finished in a rush.

His hand moved from her hair to cup her cheek. His thumb rubbed back and forth across her lips.

"I won't hurt you. And as long as I'm here I'll not let anyone else hurt you . . . or the girls." His fingers moved down beneath her chin to tilt her face up toward his. "Will your brother come back?"

"Oh, yes. He'll come back . . . sometime."

"You're worried that he'll bring the law and try to get the girls, aren't you?"

"Yes." Her voice was a breath of a whisper.

"Don't worry about it. I won't let it happen."

His fingers caressed the skin beneath her chin. It seemed inevitable that he would kiss her. With the logical part of his mind screaming *don't do it,* Yates bent his head and gently kissed her. Her lips were parted in surprise, and for a moment he tasted the sweetness of her mouth. It produced an almost overwhelming ache deep inside him; one that jarred his emotions as well as his body.

He kissed her again, deeper this time. An intimate man-hungry kiss. He felt the wetness of her mouth, the sharp edges of her teeth and the softness of her breasts pressed to his chest. She whimpered softly into his mouth.

He wanted more.

But before he gave in to that impulse, he came to his senses. With a muttered obscenity, his arms dropped from around her, and he backed away from her as if he had touched a hot stove. Without giving her a second look, he quickly left the kitchen.

All the way back to the garage, Yates cursed himself for giving in to the impulse to kiss her. Lord, what was the matter with him? He didn't have a lick of sense when he was around her! By kissing her he had probably given her the crazy idea that he had some romantic interest in her. Didn't she know that a man hungered for a female without the problems of an engagement or marriage?

He'd sure as hell be careful from now on. He had made up his mind long ago that he'd not take on the responsibility of a woman until the way was clear for him to go back home. Then and only then, he would choose a woman to keep his house, take care of his kids and keep out of his way, so that he would be free to come and go as he pleased.

Standing in the dark kitchen after the door closed behind Yates, Leona held her hands to her flushed cheeks. An engagement and marriage were the furthest things from her mind. She had been completely seduced by his soft, sympathetic words of reassurance and her own longing to have someone to lean on, to care about her.

He had taken the liberty of kissing her because he believed she was what Mr. White and Virgil claimed her to be . . . and she had stood there like a dumb ox and let him.

She didn't know if she was more angry with Yates, because he'd had the audacity to kiss her, or at herself for . . . liking it.

Chapter 11

DAWN WAS STREAKING THE SKY when Leona came from the barn and saw that the Olivers were loaded and ready to pull out of the campground. She set the bucket of milk on the porch, stood beside the house and waved to them. The old car filled with children, with hope and with perseverance, turned onto the highway and headed west. Leona hoped that whatever awaited them in California was better than what they'd had here.

She stood for just a moment and looked longingly down the long ribbon of highway that was Route 66. Leona wished with all her heart that she could take to the road and visit the far-off places she'd heard about: Amarillo, Santa Fe, the Painted Desert, Carlsbad Caverns and the Grand Canyon. She would like to see the orange groves in California and stand on a sandy beach and look out over the vast ocean.

At times the hopelessness of her future was almost more than she could bear. Leona refused to recognize the tears that for an instant dimmed her eyes. She was done with crying. It accomplished nothing.

"Leona."

Yates's voice brought her head up and straightened her back. She turned to see him standing close to the milk bucket on the porch. She nodded to him, stepped up onto the porch and picked up the bucket.

"There's a man out front who wants to know if there's a bit of work he can do for a bite to eat."

"Tell him to come around to the back porch, and I will fix him something."

"Do you feed every hobo who comes along?"

"If they are decent, I do. I'll ask him to shovel out Mary-Lou's stall. If he goes right to it, I'll make him up a food pack."

"You're a wonder."

"No, I'm not. I'm a human being, no better or no worse than anyone else. It could be me walking down the highway, hungry and not a soul in the world caring."

"I can't see that. I'll send him around and stay until he goes. I'm going into town this morning and get a tub, a tank or something to take a bath in. I'll put it there beside the barn where I can use the conduit to fill it from the pump."

She turned to face him. "You'll take a bath . . . right out in the open? I hear there's a nudist colony in New Jersey in case you want to join."

He laughed. "I'd consider it, if it wasn't so far away. Don't worry, little prude, I'll bathe at night." It was so unusual to see him smiling that she stared. "I'll fill the tank in the afternoon and let the sun take the chill off the water. The girls will enjoy it."

She lifted her shoulders in a shrug. "Suit yourself."

"Leona—"

"What now?" she barked impatiently.

"I'm not going to apologize for kissing you."

"I never expected you to. I doubt you've ever apologized in your life." She went into the kitchen and set the milk on the table. Much to her chagrin, he followed and stood just inside the door. She wanted to scream, to kick him, to . . . cry.

"A kiss between two adults doesn't mean much these days."

"You don't need to tell me that."

"I don't want you to think—"

"Think what, Mr. Yates? That I thought you might be interested in carrying on an affair with me? Don't worry, I understand that it meant absolutely nothing to you . . . or to me." She began to dip the chunks of butter from the milk she had churned the night before.

"It meant something. It was very pleasant."

"Pleasant?"

"Yes, pleasant."

"And handy, too, wasn't it?"

"What do you mean by that?"

"I may be a country woman with a less than lily-white reputation, but I'm not stupid."

"What's your reputation got to do with it? Oh, I get it. You think that I kissed you because Virgil said you were a woman who would welcome a man's advances, is that it?"

"And because of what Mr. White implied. But I want to set you straight about something while we're on the subject—from now on keep your hands to yourself or—you'll be cooking your meals over the campfire—while nursing a busted head. You may be bigger than I am, but you've got to sleep sometime." She kept her voice steady.

"I never gave a thought to what Virgil said. You're a pretty woman. I wanted to kiss you and I did."

"It must be nice to be big and strong and take what you want."

"You didn't exactly fight me off," he snapped.

The accusation whipped her pride and robbed her of

speech for a timeless moment. When she spoke it was in the tone a schoolteacher would use to dismiss a student.

"Excuse me. Go tell the man to come to the back. I'll call you when breakfast is ready."

Her dismissal irked him. He took the hobo to the barn, showed him the stall and the shovel, then stomped off toward the woodpile where he picked up the ax and began to split stove-wood.

And handy, too.

Her words stuck in his mind like a burr. Damn. She considered his kiss an insult, and all night he had worried that she might think it meant that he had romantic feelings for her. Horseshit! She needn't worry that it would happen again. He sank the ax into a stump and went to wait on a customer who had stopped at the gas pump.

Later Yates ate his breakfast alone on the front porch. When he finished he carried his plate and cup to the kitchen, where Leona sat with the girls at the table.

"I'm going to town when he leaves." He jerked his head toward the hobo on the back porch. "Need anything?" He placed the soiled dishes in the dishpan.

"No, thank you."

"Can I go, Mr. Yates?" JoBeth asked.

Leona answered. "No, honey, you can't go. I'm going to wash your hair this morning."

"Can't ya do it later?"

"No, I can't." Leona gathered biscuits, meat and cheese into a bread wrapper and took it to the man on the porch.

"Thank you, ma'am."

"You're welcome and good luck to you."

When she returned to the kitchen JoBeth was still grumbling. Leona was getting irritated.

"Don't you want to be here when the postman comes? He may have a letter from your daddy."

"You can go another time, sugar." Yates patted the child's head as he passed her. "I'll not be gone long," he said over his shoulder as he went out the door.

"Why er ya mad at him?" Ruth Ann asked.

Leona forced a smile. The question surprised her. "What makes you think I'm mad at him?"

"Because your mouth gets all tight and you don't look at him. I don't want him to go away till Daddy comes back."

"He won't let Uncle Virgil take us. He told me." JoBeth's little mouth turned down to cry. "If you're mad at him, he'll go away and . . . Uncle Virgil will come back."

"I'm not mad at him and he'll not go away. He promised your daddy that he would stay. He seems to be a man of his word." Leona got up from the table. "We have a lot to do if we're going to go to the city tomorrow. I want to wash your good dresses and white socks. We have to take your daddy clean clothes, his shaving things and his crutches."

Feeling the need to get out from under the eyes of the two children while she got her emotions under control, Leona went through the house to the front door and saw Yates's car leaving the yard with the hobo in the front seat beside him. A feeling of almost panic came over her.

What if Virgil came while he was gone?

She went into Andy's bedroom to check to see if the shotgun standing in the corner was loaded. Andy had insisted that she learn how to shoot the gun, and she was glad now that he had. She wasn't a great shot, but she knew how to load, point the barrel and pull the trigger, which in most cases would be enough.

Leona stood for a moment in the quiet bedroom after she returned the shotgun to the corner. There was not a doubt in her mind but that she would pull the trigger to keep Virgil from taking JoBeth and Ruth Ann. It would mean that she would spend the rest of her life in prison if she wasn't put in the electric chair. But it would be worth the price she had to pay to keep them out of her brother's hands should Andy not come back.

The next hour went fast. Leona heated water on the cookstove for her washing while keeping an eye on the gas pump. She pumped a couple of gallons of gas in one car and was collecting from her next customer when Yates returned with an oblong tank tied to the top of his car. He drove around the garage to the back of the house.

Leona was debating whether or not to go help him with the tank when Deke Bales arrived in his old Model T truck. Leona groaned.

Deke stopped beside the gas pump.

"Waitin' fer me, darlin'?" He got out of the truck and hurried around to work the handle to fill the globe on top of the pump. "You don't have to do that when I'm here."

Deke was so ugly he was pitiful—buck teeth, small pug nose, hair like a straw stack and practically no chin. He was younger than Leona and several inches shorter. She had known him all her life and couldn't remember a time when he hadn't been devoted to her. He had been her champion even in grade school, chasing away her tormentors like a small vicious bull dog.

"I'm needin' a couple gallons a gas, but it ain't why I come by."

"Why did you come by, Deke?" Leona asked the question knowing that he expected her to ask it, and knowing his answer would be the same as he had given a hundred times. It was a conversation that was repeated each time he came to the garage.

"To see if ya was all right."

"I'm fine, Deke." Leona smiled at him. "Right as rain."

At times his dogged devotion irritated her to the point where she wanted to scream at him. Poor Deke. He would lie down and let her walk on him if that was what she wanted to do. As small as he was, she knew that he would jump to her defense regardless of the odds against him. *How could she belittle such loyalty even if he did irritate her?*

"Mr. Fleming told me to come here tomorrow and look after things so you can go see Andy. Are you goin' with that cousin of Andy's?"

"He's not a cousin. He's a friend of Andy's."

"I heard that he was Andy's kin."

"It isn't true."

"He doin' right by ya and the girls? Bein' respectful, is he? If he ain't just let me know 'n' I'll put him in his place."

"He's treating us fine. But thanks." Leona spoke while a vision of Deke trying to put Yates "in his place" floated in her mind. *It would be like a determined kitten going against a wildcat.*

"I'll not stand by and let anybody hurt ya, darlin'. Ya know that, don't ya." Deke hung the hose back on the pump and counted out the change for his gas.

"I know that and I appreciate it." Leona accepted the money and turned to see Yates coming out of the garage.

"This is Mr. Yates, Deke."

"Pleased to meet ya." Like a friendly puppy, Deke moved forward on his short, bowed legs with his hand outstretched.

"Howdy." Yates accepted the hand and looked down at the little man in the big hat.

"Deke Bales? I've been wanting to meet you."

"Well now's yore chance."

"Bye, Deke." Leona wrote down the sale, left the money on the tablet and headed for the house.

"Bye, darlin'," he called.

Leona looked back to see that the two men had turned to watch her. Even though Deke was in his high-heeled cowboy boots, the top of his hat came to just above the other man's shoulder. They were a comical looking pair.

Deke had never showed anything but kindness and concern for her. He was boring and dumb and, Lord, how she wished he wouldn't call her "darlin' "! But she wouldn't hurt his feelings for the world and she wouldn't allow anyone else to hurt him. That included the almighty Mr. Yates.

Before preparing the noon meal, Leona washed the girls' hair, their good dresses and socks. The dresses were on the clothesline, and the girls were on the porch with their hair spread out on their shoulders to dry. They were excited about the tank Yates had brought to use as a bathtub.

"He's goin' to put the water in. Me and Ruth Ann can get in at the same time." JoBeth had talked of nothing else since Yates had placed the tank beside the barn. "Mr. Yates is goin' to put up a string or somethin' so we can hang a blanket and nobody'd see us when we take a bath."

"I'm going to cut my hair off," Ruth Ann announced. "A lot of the girls at school have bobbed their hair."

"We've been through that. Your daddy said no."

"It's not his hair. It's mine and I hate it."

"That may be, but right now sit here on the porch and let *your hair* dry. Tonight I'll put it up in rags so it'll be curls for tomorrow."

"I hate sleeping on rag curls."

"I could put it up now."

"No! You know I'll not let anyone see me with those things sticking out all over my head."

"Can I go see Mr. Yates?" JoBeth whined.

"No. He's busy. Deke is still here, and a car pulled into the garage."

"Why don't you like Deke?" Ruth Ann was in one of her contrary moods.

Leona frowned. "Where did you get that idea? I've never said that I didn't like Deke."

"Then why don't you go to the picture show with him?"

"Because I like him as a friend and not as a boyfriend. There's a difference. Now hush up about it."

"He's ugly," JoBeth stated emphatically.

"I don't want to hear you ever say that again." Leona's frown turned on the younger girl. "When you were born you had no control on how you would look, but now you can control how you act. Deke may not look so good on the outside, but inside he's a good, honest person who would be the first to help you if you were in trouble."

"But . . . he's ugly," Ruth Ann said belligerently, echoing her sister.

"Maybe to you he is, because you haven't bothered to look beyond his face."

Leona stormed back into the house before she said something she would regret later. Even little children didn't understand that what was on the outside of a person didn't necessarily reflect what was on the inside. When she looked at Deke she didn't even notice his looks anymore.

It was terribly hot in the kitchen, which only added to her irritation. The cookstove had been going since breakfast while she heated water for the washing. Green beans were cooking in a pot with chunks of potatoes and bacon for the noon meal. When Leona placed a pan of cornbread in the oven, the heat hit her face.

Glad to leave the hot kitchen for a while, Leona set up a small table on the back porch where there was a slight breeze, covered it with an oiled cloth and set places for Yates and the girls.

When the meal was ready, Leona wiped the perspiration from her face with the end of her apron and then headed for the garage to invite Deke to stay for dinner. His truck was gone, and Yates was accepting money from a man who was buying a tire tube. When the man left, Yates came into the garage to write the sale down on the tablet.

"Dinner will be ready in about ten minutes." Then after a pause, Leona added, "I was going to ask Deke to stay." She felt a need to give him a reason why she hadn't sent one of the girls with the message.

"The man is head over heels in love with you," Yates said without looking at her.

His words shocked her and her hackles began to rise.

"I don't know about that. He likes me. He feels protective of me because he knows . . . Virgil."

"It's more than that." Yates turned. His smile flickered and vanished when he saw the look of resentment on her face. "He warned me to be respectful and to watch my p's and q's around you." His chuckle was as dry as corn husks. "The little dickens said if I didn't, I'd answer to him."

"I'm sure you got a laugh out of that."

"No. He was sincere. He thinks that you're right up there next to the Virgin Mary."

"It isn't any business of yours, but I've known Deke all my life. He's always been . . . kind to me."

"He told me that the kids in school made fun of you because of the way Virgil made you dress. Your brother wouldn't allow you to be in the school choir because the songs they sang were sinful. He wouldn't even let you be in the Christmas play. Deke said the two of you were a pair and took up for each other. He was very open about it."

"I suppose you picked him for as much information as you could get."

"Yeah, I did," Yates admitted unashamedly. "He lives with his mother on Fleming's ranch. He's a good mechanic. Keeps all of Fleming's machinery going. He likes motorcycles. He'd like to race them someday. He hates Virgil and all he stands for. He says it's untrue and unfair what people in town say about you. He said that you were just a kid when you broke out of the shed Virgil had locked you in and walked five miles barefoot to be with your sister when Andy lost his foot. He swears that someday he'll kill Virgil for the way he's treated you."

"My, my. You didn't waste much time, did you?"

"Wasting time isn't my style."

The eyes that looked into hers were clear and remote. Like the sun, they were relentless. Nothing she saw in his expression reassured her or was sympathetic to the childhood torment she and Deke had endured. A chill went over her that even the hot June sun couldn't touch.

"I'll put your dinner on the table." Leona walked quickly out of the garage before she cried and disgraced herself. Deke had unwittingly laid her life bare to be scrutinized by this arrogant, unfeeling man.

"Leona."

She turned, keeping her irritation under control.

Dammit, what now? Hadn't he ground her pride in the dirt enough?

"What?"

"I liked Deke. I wasn't making fun of him."

"No? But you thought him a fool for having feelings for me," she murmured and went on toward the house.

The only bright spot in the day was the letter from Andy. It was delivered while Yates was eating dinner with the girls. Leona was in the garage when the postman arrived. She went out to the car.

"Hello, Mr. Wilkes."

"You've got a letter from Andy. I hope he's getting along all right."

"I'll find out when I open the letter."

"Tell him we had a prayer vigil for him at the church."

"I'll tell him. Thanks, Mr. Wilkes."

Leona went back into the garage and sat down on the bench. The letter was addressed to her in care of Andy's Garage on Route 66, Sayre, Oklahoma. She looked at it for a minute before she carefully tore off the end and pulled out two sheets from a tablet.

Dear Ruthy, Bethy and Leona,

How are my girls? I miss you. But I feel sure you will be all right with Yates. I guess he's told you who he is by now. I was sure surprised to see him again after all these years. I'm staying in a rooming house across the street from the hospital. The lady here is real nice and the days I had the shots she brought me my supper, but I was too sick to eat it until the next day. Barker Fleming was here this morning and will be back to get this letter to mail. He said you'd be here Sunday and that Deke would stay at the garage anytime you could come. Yates bought me a change of clothes before he left, but I need under drawers and a sock to go over my stump. Bring a couple of shirts and my crutches as my stump is sore. Bring my *razor and shaving mug. I'm using what the lady here loaned me. I don't know how I will repay Yates. He talked to the doctor, found my room and loaned me $10. The clothes he bought must have cost another $5. Take money from the hiding place and pay him. I don't know how long I will be here. The doctor tells me that I am not as sick as some who have to take the shots. I am so glad the skunk bit me instead of one of you. Yates will be on the lookout for another sick one. Don't worry about me. I'm doing all right. I'll be looking for you Sunday. Leona kiss the girls for me.*

Yours truly,
Andy

P.S. Tell Yates about Virgil. I forgot to tell him to watch out for him. Bring money for me to pay for the room.

Chapter 12

ANDY WAS DOING ALL RIGHT.

Leona reread the letter. Thank God for the vaccine and thank God Yates was here to get him to the hospital where he could be treated. Dear, trusting Andy. He had placed her and his girls, his most precious possessions, at the mercy of a man who just drove in off the highway. A puzzled frown wrinkled Leona's brow. What had the man said to inspire such confidence? She knew Andy well enough to know that a team of mules couldn't have pulled him away from them if he'd had the slightest doubt that Yates would let harm come to them.

Yates was taking his task seriously, there was no doubt about that. *But . . . oh, how his take-over, know-it-all attitude irritated her!*

Leona handed the letter to Yates when he returned to the garage after finishing his meal. She waited while he read it, then scanned the contents again. When he finished he folded the letter and returned it to the envelope. His squinted eyes glinted down at her.

"You don't need to pay me back the money now. I'll settle with Andy later."

"He said to pay you now and I will."

He ignored her reply and said, "We should leave before sun-up in the morning so you and the girls will have a few hours to spend with him. We'll start back after sundown. It'll be cooler then."

"How far is it to the city?"

"A little over a hundred miles. I figure it will take four hours with you and the girls along. They'll need to get out once in a while and stretch their legs. If I was driving alone I'd do it in three."

"We'll be ready."

"I filled the water tank I got this morning. The water is cold coming out of the well, but should warm up in a couple of hours. The girls want to bathe in it. I warned them not to get in the tank unless one of us was with them. It's deep enough for one of them to drown if they couldn't get to their feet."

"They're excited about tomorrow."

"And you? Are you anxious to see Andy?"

"Of course," she said, looking him straight in the eyes, then turned to look at the heavy black sedan with the gleaming hood ornament pulling into the drive.

A woman was driving. The ends of the bright red scarf holding back her hair were flying out the window. A man got out after she stopped the car a dozen feet from the door. He wore a soft tan shirt, duck trousers and Indian moccasins. He was approaching the door of the garage when Yates stepped out in view. Both men stopped and stared at each other.

"Hell, damn! That you, Yates?"

"Hell, damn! That you, Blue?"

"It's not Christ on a horse, you ugly son-of-a-gun!"

"Blue and Radna Bluefeather as I live and breathe," Yates exclaimed. "Who opened the gate and let you two out?"

The two men met, clasped hands and pounded on each other.

"Yates!"

Leona heard the screech. The woman who jumped out of the car and launched herself at Yates was small with long, thick, black hair. He grabbed her up and lifted her off her feet. Her arms encircled his neck and she planted a firm kiss on his mouth. Her long full skirt floated around her slender legs and booted feet as he twirled her around.

The man who watched them was rather short when compared to Yates, but he was thick in the shoulders and chest. The skin on his face was smooth and copper colored; tiny lines shadowed the corners of his dark-as-midnight eyes. The black silver-streaked hair that framed his Indian features, etched by time, was brushed straight back and tied at the nape of his neck. He was a handsome, unforgettable-looking man.

"Still poaching on another man's territory, huh, Yates? Unhand my wife or I'll put my fist through your ugly face." The Indian's tone was conversational. He reached out to take her from him.

"You always were a stingy cuss." Yates spun the tiny woman out of his reach and deliberately kissed her on the mouth before he set her on her feet. "Is he treating you all right? If not, I'll scalp him for you."

"Thanks, but I'm reserving that privilege for myself." She tilted her head toward her husband and grinned at him. "Yates isn't ugly, Randolph. He's beautiful." Her small hands reached up to caress Yates's cheeks. "Don't pay any attention to him," she crooned in a soft melodious voice. "He's put out because I won't let him drive."

"Smart of you. That wild Indian couldn't steer a wheelbarrow through a barn door." Yates's face was creased with smiles, his silver eyes glittered with pleasure.

"He knocked down a barbed-wire fence over by Lone Wolf takin' a short-cut across a pasture. After we blew a tire, I said, that's it, Randolph, get your sorry rump out from under the wheel. I'm drivin'."

"She's still feisty as ever, huh, Blue? Still calls you Randolph when she wants to rile you."

"Yeah. I'm going to whip her butt when we leave here." The Indian's twinkling eyes seldom left his wife. A smile tugged at the corner of his mouth. The small vivacious woman was obviously his pride and joy.

"Ask him what happened the last time he tried that."

"I don't want to know. I might have to get out my hunting knife and slice him up a bit."

"What are you doing here, Yates? Who was the woman who skeedaddled out the back?"

"Nosy, isn't she?" Blue threw an arm around his wife and drew her to him.

Yates laughed. "She can't be accused of beating around the bush, that's true. Come sit down in the shade. How about a cold soda pop?"

"It's what we stopped for."

Without going into details, Yates explained to Blue and Radna that he was helping out a friend who was in the hospital in Oklahoma City after being bitten by a rabid skunk.

"And you're staying here looking out for his woman and kids. How does that sit, having to stay in one place for a while?" Blue took a drink from the bottle of orange pop he was sharing with his wife.

"Not bad, so far. I'm taking them to Oklahoma City tomorrow to see him."

"We just came from there," Radna said. "We went in to see Jelly Bryce. You remember him, don't you?"

"I've never met him, but I've heard plenty. He was the sharp-shooter who took out the fellow who killed and butchered a woman in Rainwater."

"Jelly has taken out several notorious killers," Blue added. "He's still with the Oklahoma City police, but the FBI wants him to join up. He's not decided yet."

"He's really a nice man." Radna grinned at her husband. "Even if he is a jelly bean and handsome as sin. Blue"—she said to Yates—"has known him and his folks for a long time."

"I'm thinkin' of gettin' me a pair of those spats like he wears sometimes over his shoes, a string tie with tassels on it and a white Panama hat," Blue said seriously. "Think I'd look good?"

"You'd look like a bull in a hula skirt." Radna snorted and dug her elbow into her husband's ribs. "Stay as you are or I'll trade you in on a couple of twenty-year-olds."

"How's things up around Rainwater?" Yates asked.

"Oil wells are drying up," Blue said. "Rainwater will be dried up, too, before long. We're dickering to buy a little ranch south of here near Mountain View."

"Aren't you ready to settle down, Yates?" Radna asked with a flirtatious smile. "That red-haired girl in Rainwater was hankerin' to tie you down."

"That's why I left in such a hurry."

"Shame on you!"

Yates went to wait on a customer who had stopped at the gas pump. When he returned the Bluefeathers were preparing to leave.

"We're going to Santa Fe to see my brother. We'll stop in

a couple of weeks on our way back to Mountain View. Will you still be here?" Radna's smiling eyes peered up at him.

"I'm sure I will. I can't see Andy getting out of the hospital for another four weeks and he'll need another week or two before he's fit to take over the garage."

"Are you sure it isn't a woman that's keeping you here? From what I saw of her . . . she's pretty."

"Yeah, she's pretty, prouder than a game rooster and can't stand the sight of me." Yates's grin didn't quite reach his eyes. Radna noticed.

"You like her?"

Yates shrugged. "She's . . . all right—"

"Come on, thorny rose." Blue grabbed his wife's arm and urged her toward the car. "Since she chased me down and got the bit in my mouth she isn't happy to see any man without a rope around his neck."

"I don't see you puttin' up much of a fuss." Yates slapped Blue on the back, then spoke to his wife. "When you get tired of this dumb Indian, Radna, I'll be waiting in the wings."

"Waiting in the wings? Hell! Damn! What does that mean?"

"Come on." Radna tugged on her husband's arm. "I don't know if I'll have enough time to explain it to you before we get to New Mexico, but I'll try."

Yates stood in the drive and waved to his friends as Radna drove the powerful car out onto the highway. Although this was only his third encounter with the pair, he was very fond of them and felt as if he had known them forever.

He had spent a month in the oil boom town of Rainwater where he first met the Bluefeathers. They had just been married. The next time he met them was while he was working on an oil rig, in Bartlesville, Oklahoma. They were always the same . . . crazy about each other and taking life one day at a time.

Leona was dead tired.

She sat in the dark on the back porch toweling her hair dry before going to bed. It was good to allow her shoulders to slump, relax, and let her mind travel over the events of the long and tiring day.

After washing and ironing dresses for the girls, she had pressed one for herself. The chicken she had killed and dressed for tomorrow's picnic with Andy had fried in the big iron skillet on the kerosene stove, while she was bathing in the big washtub she had dragged in off the porch.

The girls had been in rare form; they were so excited about tomorrow's trip that she didn't think they would ever settle down and go to sleep. Ruth Ann had fidgeted, but had not protested over much, while Leona wrapped strands of her hair around the rag strings to make the long, bouncy curls her daddy liked. JoBeth had complained because her hair was too short for rag curls. Leona trimmed her bangs and convinced her that it would have to do until her daddy came home to give her a proper haircut.

She had not spoken to Yates since shortly after noon when she left him with his friends. She had been laying out a cold supper when he came around to feed the horses and fill the stock tank. She went out to milk when he came in to eat. Leona thought that he probably bathed in the tank while she bathed in the tub in the kitchen. It bothered her that she was constantly aware of where he was at any given time.

Yates was a man with many different facets to his personality. He had been genuinely glad to see his friends. They had certainly been glad to see him—especially the woman.

At times, Leona admitted, Yates excited her. But at other times he irritated her, until she was sure that she hated him and would be glad to see the last of him.

While she sat musing, she suddenly heard the soft sounds of music coming out of the darkness. Stone-still, she listened. Someone was playing the guitar. It had to be Yates. He didn't have a radio and there were no campers tonight. Quietly she got up and went back through the house to the front door.

All was dark except for the glow from the faint light that came from the small bulb in front of the garage. Leona eased out onto the front porch and sat down in the porch swing. Her eyes scanned the darkness. The sound was coming from the far end of the campground. The night he had heard her singing, Yates had said that he played for his own enjoyment. It was probably why he was as far from the house as he could get without going into the woods.

The fact that he was a talented musician was another surprising facet of the Yates character. The familiar strains of "The Missouri Waltz" came from the campground. Leona recognized the next tune but couldn't name it. Then "The Yellow Rose of Texas," and after that a series of country songs she had heard on the *Grand Ole Opry*, the Saturday night radio program from Tennessee.

Leona sat very still to eliminate the squeaking of the chains holding the swing. Time passed as she absorbed the music. The moon rose high in the sky. The only thing to interrupt her enjoyment of the unexpected treat was the occasional sound of a car passing on the highway.

Each time Yates finished a song, she thought sure it would be his last and readied herself to dash into the house for fear that he would see her when he went into the garage.

She leaned her head against the back of the swing and let the music wash over her, soothe her.

It was suddenly quiet. She sat up so fast the chains on the swing squeaked. She peered into the black night and cocked her head to listen. Then Yates's voice came out of darkness.

"Leona. It's me, Yates," he said quickly when she jumped to her feet.

"How did you know I was here?"

"I heard the squeak of the porch swing. Are you going in?"

"Ah . . . yes. My hair is almost dry."

He carefully placed his guitar on the edge of the porch and came up the steps. Calvin followed him and sank down on the porch with a deep sigh.

"It's nice out tonight. There's a good breeze from the south. Stay out a while." He eased down on the porch swing beside her.

"My hair is almost dry." She repeated the words lamely, then moved as far from him as possible.

His arm arched over her head and rested on the back of the swing. His fingers slid into the hair that touched her shoulders.

"It's still wet. Don't you do it up on bobby pins or something?"

"No. I let it hang until it's dry. My mother used to roll it around her finger and put a bobby pin in it. My sister Irene's hair was—curlier than Ruth Ann's." Leona tried desperately to keep from sounding breathless. *I'm babbling like an idiot!*

"Was your sister's hair this color?" His fingers were still in her hair.

"It was lighter—like my mother's. My father had the dark hair."

"Tell me about when you were little and your parents were alive."

"Why?"

"Curiosity. It's hard for me to think of you being related to Virgil. He's different and so much older than you."

"I was the youngest. A brother and sister between Virgil and Irene died—the brother when he was a tiny baby. The sister died of diphtheria."

"Has Virgil always been so obsessed with religion?"

"I hardly remember him at home. He was already married by the time I started to school."

"Were your parents religious fanatics like Virgil?"

"Heavens no! They would be heartsick if they knew how Virgil treated me and Irene."

Yates moved the swing gently. "When we get back from the city, I'll put some axle grease on the chain and get rid of this squeak."

They were silent for a long while. Leona was intensely aware of all the sounds that came through the hush of the night—the squeak of the porch swing, the far away call of an owl. She was also all too aware of Yates sitting close beside her, his strength and the hardness of his body. She finally got up the courage to speak.

"Do you have brothers and sisters?"

"No. My mother was seventeen when she had me. I was doted on by my mother and my grandparents. I had a happy childhood."

"Humm—"

"What do you mean, *humm?*"

"I was wondering why are you so aloof." The words were out before Leona could hold them back.

"Aloof? I've not thought of myself as being that way."

"I shouldn't have said that. I'm sorry."

"No. It's all right. I've been alone for a long time. I've lost touch with how I must appear to people. It's a habit with me to plow ahead doing what I think is right without consulting anyone else. You've already bit a couple of chunks out of me." His soft chuckle came out of the darkness.

In spite of not wanting to, Leona laughed. "At times you've irritated me."

"I never meant to—I take that back: A couple of times I did." His hand had moved to cup and squeeze her shoulder.

"Why?" She tried to hold herself away from him, but it was impossible with his hand grasping her shoulder.

"Meanness, I guess." He laughed. "I knew you'd get your back up. I'd rather have you spitting and sputtering at me like a little cat than ignoring me."

"I don't spit and sputter!"

"You got my attention that day when you thought I was bald under my hat."

"I didn't think it . . . I hoped it." Leona laughed and turned to look at him. She turned back quickly when she found his face so close to hers.

"Fooled you, though. Didn't I?"

During the silence that followed, Leona knew that it was time for her to go into the house. She didn't want to go . . . just yet. It was pleasant sitting here with him, his hand on her shoulder. She didn't feel in the least threatened even when his hand moved from her shoulder to the nape of her neck and he bent to hold a handful of her hair to his face.

"Vinegar. I thought I could smell vinegar."

"I use it in the rinse water. It keeps my hair from being so tangled."

"Tell me something. Is Deke the only fellow coming around here that wants to keep company with you?"

Leona was still for a long while. Suddenly his face was

too close to hers, she felt his breath on her cheek. Her heart pounded in her ears. Her poise vanished. She croaked out an answer.

"Oh, no. From time to time a traveling man or a rowdy hears about the strumpet of Beckman County, Oklahoma, and comes calling."

Leona sat in rigid silence after her outburst. Yates's arm tightened over her shoulders. He pulled her protectively close to him. For a moment she couldn't breathe. Her hip and thigh were against his, her shoulder beneath his arm. To her utter shame, she had to sniff to hold back tears.

"They better not show up while I'm here." The hoarsely whispered words came against her ear. "You're not like that."

"How do you know what I'm like?"

"I don't know what's between you and Andy. But I know you're not the kind of woman who would consort with just any Tom, Dick or Harry."

"You've only been here a week. You heard what Virgil called me."

"He'll not do it again in my presence or he'll wish to God I had killed him." Yates paused, then said, "Why don't you leave here? Do you have any relatives other than Virgil?"

"I have an aunt somewhere in Kansas. But I'll not leave my sister's children unless Andy marries again and I'm sure the woman would be a good mother to them. I'm the only mother they know now. Andy works hard. He needs someone to cook, wash and do all the things a woman does."

"Why didn't you and Andy marry?"

"To keep the tongues from wagging? No thank you. Andy is an honorable man. He offered when he heard the talk. I think the world of him, and I'll not tie him to me for the rest of his life. He may meet someone someday who will love him the way he deserves to be loved."

"What will you do then?"

"I haven't thought that far ahead."

They sat in companionable silence while several minutes passed. Calvin got up, stretched and came to Yates. A whining sound came from his throat.

"He wants to go to bed. He's been sleeping beside my cot in the garage."

"I thought he was here under the porch."

"He's one member of the family who likes me."

"The girls like you."

"And you, Lee?"

In lieu of an answer, she said, "Andy trusts you or he'd not have left us here with you."

"Andy didn't have much choice. You're lucky that I'm such a nice fellow."

Leona laughed softly. "Nice, my hind leg!"

"You're thinking I'm not nice because I kissed you. Would I be a down-right cad if I did it again?" He picked up her hand and laced his fingers through hers.

Leona jumped to her feet. "I've got to go in."

Yates stood. "I wouldn't force you, Lee." He refused to release her hand when she tugged on it.

"You did before."

"It just happened. I didn't plan it."

"Of course, it just happened. It's what a man does when he's with a promiscuous woman. He thinks she expects it."

"You think that's why I kissed you?" His hands gripped her shoulders. "I'm more particular than that. I kissed you because you're sweet and pretty, and I wanted to kiss you. That's all there was to it."

"You explained that. You said, 'a kiss between adults doesn't mean much these days.' I can't agree more."

"Well, then?"

"You may be surprised to know that I don't want to kiss you, Mr. Yates. Goodnight." Leona slipped out from under his hands and headed for the door.

"You liked it, Leona. You liked it as much as I did," he said irritably, before picking up his guitar and stepping off the porch.

Yates cursed himself on the way to the garage. When he went to the porch he hadn't intended to sit down, much less touch her. Something in her tugged at him. She wasn't really beautiful, just quietly pretty and invitingly feminine, steady and capable. Added to that, he liked to be with her, liked her as a person. He liked to talk to her even when she was peevish. She'd had it rough, but through it all she had kept her pride.

His next thought jolted him. If he were ready to settle down, he'd think seriously of considering a life with her. He never expected to have with a woman what Blue had with Radna.

You stupid son-of-a-bitch! Forget it. In spite of what she says, she's probably in love with Andy, or she wouldn't have stuck it out here. She would have put as much distance as possible between herself and that crazy brother of hers.

Chapter 13

A LIGHT WAS ON IN THE KITCHEN when Yates stepped out of the garage in the pre-dawn darkness to move his car up to the gas pump. The bobbing light of a lantern coming from the barn told him that Leona had been out to milk the cow. While Yates was filling the gas tank on his car, Deke drove his old Model T truck into the space beside the garage.

"Mornin'." Yates greeted him as he came around the end of the car.

"Mornin'. Ready to go?"

"Not yet. Leona just finished milking."

"Looks to be a fair day. Not much wind."

"That's good. This car is a gas guzzler bucking the wind."

"Listen here, Yates." Deke crossed his arms over his chest and leaned back against the fender of the car. "Leona's not been to the city before. I'm trustin' you keep an eye on her. Hear?" Deke had a serious look on his face. The brim of the big hat shading it was almost as wide as his shoulders.

"I'll do my best."

"Even if she's scared to death of the traffic, the streetcars and all, she'll not let on. That girl's got pride she ain't used yet. She won't want ya to think she's a country clod not used to the goin's-on in the city." Deke dug in his pocket and pulled out a couple of bills. "Take her to eat at one of them places that has chili and hot tamales. She's real fond of hot tamales that's been rolled up in a corn shuck."

"I'll take her if she's willing to go. You don't need to pay for it, Deke."

"I want her to have a good time. She's not had many trips like this. Always havin' to watch out for that crackpot Virgil. I'm goin' to have to kill that Bible-thumpin' son-of-a-bitch someday." He waved the bills. "Take the money and tell her the treat is on me."

"All right." Yates, realizing how important it was to the man, stuffed the bills in his pocket.

"Keep your eye on her. Some of them city people drive like they didn't have a lick of sense. She could step right out in front of a car and get run down by some boozed-up clabber-head. Watch that one of them jake-leg bums don't grab hold of her."

"I'll watch her." Yates hung the hose back on the pump and screwed the cap back on his gas tank. "Come on up to the house. Leona will have made coffee by now."

Later while Yates was stowing the picnic basket and the box they were taking to Andy in the car, Deke stood beside Leona.

"You look mighty pretty, darlin'."

"Thanks, Deke."

"Is that a new dress?"

"No. It's one I made last summer."

"It's pretty as a buttercup, darlin'. I've told Yates to keep an eye on you. Things move pretty fast in the city. You be careful, now."

"We'll be careful. The girls are excited—"

"Another thing, darlin'. Don't you and the girls be wanderin' off by yoreselves. There's roughnecks, bums, drunks and crooks of all kinds loose in the city. Stay close to Yates. He gave me his word that he'll look after you."

"Deke! I'm not an idiot!" Leona's face was red with embarrassment. She didn't dare look at Yates for fear he would be laughing.

"I know you ain't, darlin'. But I'll worry 'bout you till you get back."

"We'll be fine."

"If I didn't think Yates could take care of you, I'd take you myself." Leona turned her head away lest Deke see how irritated she was. His voice droned on. "You have a good time, darlin'. Eat lots of hot tamales and tell Andy to not worry about things here. 'Tween me and Yates we'll run things till he gets back and look after you and the girls, too."

"There's fried chicken and deviled eggs for you in the icebox. I made an extra large batch of biscuits this morning. I left some of them wrapped in a cloth on the table along with a jar of tomato preserves and one of pickled peaches."

"Thank you, darlin'. Your pickled peaches are even better than Mama's."

Leona looked down at the shaggy dog, who seemed to know that something was going on that he didn't like.

"You can't go, Calvin. Stay here with Deke. We'll be back tonight."

"Can I sit up front with you?" JoBeth, in her freshly ironed dress and white knee socks, tugged on Yates's hand.

"There'll be more room in the back. Your Aunt Lee will sit up front." He lifted the child up and set her on the seat.

"Oh, it's all right," Leona protested. "I'll sit back there with Ruth Ann."

"You'd better sit up front, darlin'," Deke said and opened the car door. "You can help Yates watch for cars coming off the side roads."

Leona glanced at Yates. The corners of his mouth were twitching. He was trying hard to keep from smiling. It raised her hackles. *How dare he laugh at Deke?* Other than Andy and the girls, Deke was the only other person in the world who cared if she lived or died. She felt a rush of affection for the little man who had been her loyal friend for so many years.

"Bye, Deke." She reached for his hand. Surprised that she had touched him, he squeezed her hand tightly and was reluctant to let it go. "You be careful. If a load of toughs come in, you know where we keep that old shotgun."

"Don't worry, darlin'. I'll be all right. Have a good time and give Andy a hello."

Yates started the car.

Deke released Leona's hand and stepped back.

Leona waved.

The sun was a red glow just beneath the horizon as they headed east toward the city.

"When will we get there?" JoBeth stood and leaned over the back of the seat.

"Before dinner time."

"The wind is blowing my hair."

"I brought a comb so we can comb it. Sit down and don't lean against the door."

Leona glanced at Yates. She could tell nothing of what he was thinking by his expression. She hoped the girls would behave. Yates wasn't used to being cooped up in a car with children. His car suited him and he handled it effortlessly with his elbow propped on the open window of the door. There was plenty of room for his long legs, and the seats were as comfortable as a rocking chair.

Who was he anyway? Where had he come from? There was a Texas license plate on his car, but that didn't mean he was from Texas. She didn't know any more about him or his connection to Andy than she had the day he arrived. Had she put herself and the girls at risk by going away with him into the unknown? What if they were not even headed for Oklahoma City? She had heard of men selling women into something called *white slavery.* She wasn't sure what it was, but she knew that it was something terrible.

Suddenly she wished for Deke—loyal, always the same Deke. Although he irritated her at times, she knew that if she ever needed a friend she could count on Deke. Lord, she wished that he could find someone to love him.

"Aunt Lee! JoBeth kicked me and put dirt on my stockings."

"I didn't mean to."

"You did so."

"All right. Settle down." Leona glanced at Yates to see if the girls were bothering him. He was looking straight ahead, and she would have been surprised to know his thoughts.

Lord, I've got to be careful. This is the first time I've had a woman and little kids in my car.

It was kind of scary being responsible for this family, but nice, too. Even now, with his attention on driving and the girls in the backseat, he was deeply aware of the woman beside him—of the way she sat with her legs demurely together and one hand in her lap, the other holding onto her small brimmed hat.

"Take off your hat," he said.

"I may have to. I can't hold it all the way to the city. But my hair will be a mess."

"Didn't you just tell the girls you'd brought a comb?"

He glanced at her again She removed her hat and placed it on the seat between them.

"We're going awfully fast."

"Only forty miles an hour. This car will sail along at eighty without any trouble at all."

"But you won't—"

"No, I won't. Relax," he said softly. "You'll scare the girls. I won't go any faster than this."

"Thank you." Leona looked out the window and watched the fence posts flying by.

"Did you ever hear of Barney Oldfield?" he asked after a short pause, then continued when Leona turned toward him and shook her head. "Back in 1910 he drove a car 131 miles an hour."

"No! That's hard to believe."

"It was a special racing car. Thirty years ago in 1902 he drove one a mile a minute."

"I don't know why anyone would want to go that fast."

"There's a spot over in New Mexico where it's level and smooth. I like to open up and see how fast I can go." Yates was grinning like a schoolboy.

"Why, that's foolish," she exclaimed. "You'll get yourself killed."

"Not if I'm careful." He was still grinning. Her breath caught. The stern lines on his face shifted and left him looking exceedingly young and handsome. Their smiling eyes caught and held for just a second or two.

"You're a daredevil," she accused.

He laughed. While he watched the road, she watched him. His large hands were relaxed on the wheel, his long legs sprawled as much as the space would allow. He was at home in the car.

"Have you ever seen a barnstorming show?" he asked.

Leona shook her head, then said, "No, but I've heard of them."

"Barnstormers usually appear at county fairs and carnivals. They give exhibitions of stunt flying and parachute jumping. Sometimes they have a daredevil wing-walker."

"While the airplane is in the air?"

Yates nodded. "And without a parachute."

"What in the world would possess a person to do such a dangerous thing?"

"The thrill of it, I guess. If he's smart, he stays on the good side of the pilot. One little dip of the wings and he'd be a goner." Yates shot her a teasing glance.

"I don't want to see anyone doing anything as foolish as that. My stomach would be tied in knots," Leona said in a positive tone.

Yates laughed. "If I hear of a show nearby, I'll take you and the girls. It's a sight to see."

"Aunt Lee, are we there yet?" JoBeth asked.

"Honey, we're not even to Elk City yet."

"I want a drink of water."

"You had one just before we left."

"But I'm thirsty."

"Wait until we get to Elk City," Yates said. "There's a schoolhouse on the other side of town with good, cold well water. I've stopped there a time or two."

Leona met his eyes straight on. As cold and remote as he usually was, he was remarkably patient with the girls. It suddenly occurred to her that he would be a good father: stern, but fair and protective. Did he have children somewhere? No, of course not. If he had them, he's the kind of man who would be with them. *Now why did she think this?*

Yates stopped the car beside the square brick schoolhouse. A black iron pump sat on a concrete platform in the school yard. Nearby were swings and a slide.

"Don't get your dresses dirty," Leona called when the

girls left the car. She followed the trio after she had given Yates a tin cup from the picnic box.

"Stand back and let me pump. The water will splash," Yates cautioned. He worked the pump handle, then filled the cup when the water flowed. After the girls had had a drink, he filled the cup, handed it to Leona and watched her while she took a few swallows, then took the cup and drained it.

Yates spoke to the girls. "We'll not stop again until we get to Weatherford. That's a little more than half way to the city. If you feel the need, use the outhouse over there." He pointed to two small wooden structures with a big *B* on one and *G* on the other.

"I don't have to go. Can I swing? Pleeease—" JoBeth caught Yates's hand in both of hers and looked up at him with pleading eyes.

"You'll get your dress dirty," Ruth Ann scolded, then to Yates with disgust, "She's just a baby. I want to go on and see Daddy."

"We shouldn't take the time now. Your daddy will be looking for us." Yates lifted the child up to sit on his arm and carried her back to the car.

On the road again, Ruth Ann read aloud a Burma Shave sign attached to fence post. *"Car in ditch, driver in tree, moon is full, and so is he. Burma Shave."*

"Why is the driver in a tree, Aunt Lee?" JoBeth stood leaning over the back of the front seat.

"He bounced out of the car when it hit the ditch. Sit down and try not to get your stockings dirty." The wind coming in the open window was scrambling Leona's hair. Yates placed his hand on her arm.

"Move over to the middle of the seat and the wind won't be so strong." Leona hesitated, then moved leaving a foot of space between them. "Isn't that better?" Yates's eyes left the road to glance at her.

"Much. I'll never get the tangles out of my hair."

"I'll help you."

Surprised by his words, Leona looked up to find him pondering her quietly. Suddenly terribly aware of him, she felt very young, unsure of herself and couldn't think of a single word to say.

"Can I get up there, Aunt Lee?" JoBeth stuck her head between Leona's and Yates's.

"It's windy up here, honey."

"It's windy back here, too," JoBeth whined.

"Let her get up here," Yates said. "Ruth Ann can stretch out back there and take a nap." When Leona stirred to move so that the child could sit between them, his big hand shot out and took her arm. "Let her sit on the outside. She's short. The wind won't hit her so hard."

Leona was forced to move closer to Yates when JoBeth climbed over the seat and settled down beside her. Her hip and thigh came in contact with his. She moved as if she had touched a hot stove. Now there were only inches between them. She was careful to keep her arm close to her side and her knees away from the gear shift.

"Deke told me that you were fond of hot tamales," Yates said, after miles of silence.

"He brings me some when he goes to Amarillo."

"He wants me to take you out for tamales and chili."

"He asked you to do that?"

"He wants you to have a good time."

"He can make me so . . . mad—"

"The man is crazy about you."

"He is not! We've been friends since the fourth grade and

that is all. Most folks overlook the fact that he's a good and decent man just because he . . . he—"

"Because he doesn't look the part?"

"Exactly. Deke has feelings just like anyone else."

"And you've been defending him since the fourth grade."

"We've been defending each other. And . . . I'd better not hear of anyone making fun of him." From Leona's tone of voice it was clear that she would brook no argument on the subject.

"I'd not do that. I admire his attitude."

"You do?" She dared to peek up at him and saw that he was smiling down at her and was suddenly reminded of the kiss they'd shared in the dark kitchen.

"Yes, I do."

"Andy says that he's the best mechanic he's ever known. If it's a motor he can fix it. Mr. Fleming depends on him to keep their machinery going."

"Deke told me about the motorcycle he built out of spare parts."

"He brought it to the garage a few times. He likes to race it against anything that moves. He'll get himself killed one of these days."

Leona looked down to see that JoBeth had fallen asleep. She eased the child's head down onto her lap.

"You can move closer to me. I won't bite you," Yates said with amusement in his voice. "Come on, move over. It'll give her more room." Leona had barely moved when her hip and thigh were touching his.

"She was too excited to sleep last night and was up early this morning." Leona rushed into speech to keep from remembering the brief moment when she had been pressed tightly to him. She smoothed the hair back from the child's face.

"Have you been to the city?" Yates asked, knowing that Deke had told him she hadn't been, but he wanted to keep her talking to him.

"No. But I've been as far as Weatherford."

"How did that come about?"

"I went with Andy to take Irene to a doctor there."

"Did the doctor help her?"

"No. Andy was frantic to find someone to make her well. He loved her desperately. I don't think he'll ever get over losing her."

"Does Andy have relatives nearby?"

"He ran away from an orphans' home when he was twelve. The only home he ever had was with Irene. He has no one now but me and the girls."

Yates was quiet while they passed through the small town of Clinton. Leona admired the way he handled the big car. His fingers were curled loosely around the steering wheel. He was a relaxed driver. They didn't speak again until they were out on the open road. They passed a caravan of cars and trucks headed west.

"So many people on the road," Leona said as if talking to herself. "All going west."

"This area was hit hard, not only by the Depression, but by the dust storms brought on by the drought."

"Mr. Fleming said that they should never have plowed the prairie north of here hoping for a wheat crop. Some of the soil is in Canada by now."

"Have you known Mr. Fleming long?"

"He's been stopping at the garage for several years. He's well liked even if he is—"

"Rich?" Yates glanced down at Leona.

"Because he's rich and an Indian, some people hunt for a reason to despise him."

"Like Virgil?"

"He doesn't have a good word to say for him in spite of the fact that Mr. Fleming has given money to the school and is almost the sole supporter of the soup kitchen in town."

"I'm thinking Virgil doesn't throw out his good words very often."

"Oh, he has friends. The radicals who go to his church are chummy with him. Some hang on to his every word. The deputy sheriff is one of them."

They lapsed into silence and the miles sped by. At first Leona tried to avoid touching the man beside her. Now she seemed to be relaxed and Yates could feel the warmth of her thigh against his. He was completely unaware that in this unusual situation in which he found himself, he was feeling a happy contentment he'd not felt for a long, long time.

Chapter 14

YATES PULLED THE CAR CLOSE TO THE CURB in front of a two-story house and stopped beneath a large elm tree.

"Is this it, Mr. Yates? Is this where Daddy is?"

Ruth Ann was so anxious, Leona feared she would be sick. She had insisted that Leona comb her bangs and smooth her curls. After the trauma of losing her mother, the child lived in constant fear that something would happen to her daddy.

"This is it. Your daddy is on the porch."

Yates got out of the car and hurried around to open the door Ruth Ann couldn't seem to manage. She jumped out of the car and ran up the walk to the porch. At the top of the steps she grabbed Andy about the waist and almost toppled him over.

"Daddy! Daddy! Are you all right?"

"I'm fine, honey. How's my girls?"

Hugging both his girls, Andy, with bright teary eyes, looked at Leona and Yates over the tops of their heads.

"This has been the longest ten days of my life," he said in a husky whisper.

After Andy introduced his family to his landlady they gathered around him on the end of the porch.

"The shots are not as bad as I thought they'd be," he explained. "They are painful for the moment but, thank goodness, I'm not now sick afterward."

"You'll get well?" Ruth Ann asked for the third time.

"The doctors tell me that I'll be as good as new after the shots. I'll come home as soon as they give me the last one. Barker Fleming comes to the city about once a week. He said he'd keep in touch and would bring me home."

Yates brought Andy's crutches from the car and the box of clothes Leona had packed. Then, wanting to give her and the girls time alone with Andy, he prepared to leave them, saying that he had a few things to do.

"You'll be back for the picnic?" Leona asked.

"You bet. I don't intend to miss out on that chicken and the deviled eggs. When I come back, we can go to the park we passed for the picnic." He looked down at JoBeth. "They have swings there, sugarfoot."

Andy's eyes followed Yates back to the car, then turned to Leona. "Are things all right at home?"

"Fine. But we miss you."

"I had to put my trust in Yates. I couldn't leave you out there alone. Deke would have quit at Fleming's and come to stay, but I didn't have time to ask him." Touched by the misery in his voice, Leona smiled and covered his hand with hers.

"You made the right decision." Her smile widened. "Mr. Yates didn't talk much at first, but I knew right away that he would take good care of the garage. And at night we felt safe with him there."

"It had been a long time since I'd seen him. Sometimes you have to go on gut instinct."

Leona opened her mouth to ask about his acquaintance

with Yates when JoBeth, snuggled against Andy, blurted, "Uncle Virgil come, Daddy. Mr. Yates hurt him."

"Oh, Lord. I forgot to tell him about Virgil."

"The news that you'd been bit by a skunk and were in the hospital spread around town like wildfire," Leona said. "Naturally Virgil took the opportunity to come out and rant and rave. He figured that we were alone out there. He got a surprise."

"He was saying mean things to Aunt Lee and was goin' to hit her, but Mr. Yates hurt him. Uncle Virgil yelled loud," JoBeth said with a broad smile.

"He told us to get our things and come home with him. Aunt Lee said she'd kill him before she'd let him take us," Ruth Ann added.

"Mr. Yates throwed him in the car. Then Aunt Lee cried 'cause she was . . . mad. I like Mr. Yates. He said he'd hurt Uncle Virgil again if he tried to take us away from Aunt Lee."

Andy's eyes went from one girl to the other while they were telling about Virgil's visit. It occurred to him then that he should take his girls and move to where they didn't have to worry about their crazy uncle. His troubled glance sought Leona's.

"They held up just fine, Andy. You would have been proud of them."

"I am proud of them and you, too, Leona. I don't know what we would have done without you."

"Mr. White made Aunt Lee mad, too. She put the bakin' powder can down hard on the counter and we went out."

"JoBeth!" Leona moaned.

"She tells everything. Aunt Lee said not to tell you that. You'd worry." Ruth Ann's voice was heavy with disgust.

"I want to hear everything. What happened at the store, Leona?"

"Nothing much. You know how nosy Mr. White can be. He said something that struck me the wrong way. I don't even remember what it was. Everyone asks about you, Andy: the postman, the ice man and many of your gas customers. Deke said to tell you hello."

"Here comes Mr. Yates." JoBeth climbed out of the porch swing and went to the steps. "Can we go on the picnic now? Huh? Can we?"

Yates grasped the hands she held up to him and swung her around. "If your daddy and Leona are ready."

"I'll be ready as soon as I get off this peg," Andy said. "I welcome the crutches for a change."

The afternoon was so pleasant that Leona hated for it to end. After they ate, she and the girls went to the playground where there were swings and a slide. They walked around a fountain that shot water ten feet into the air.

Andy noticed Yates watching Leona and the girls sitting on the ledge around the fountain.

"She's a damn good woman, Yates. And because of me, folks treat her like she was trash."

"Why didn't you marry her?"

"I asked her but she turned me down. She's smart enough to know that we don't love each other like married folks ought to, like I loved Irene. Leona is like a sister to me. I worry that life is passing her by while she takes care of my girls."

"It's her choice."

"No. She's stuck in a rut. She won't leave us to flounder about by ourselves. But if she did, she'd have to leave Sayre. Where could she go where she could make a living for herself?"

"Hasn't anyone come calling on her?"

Andy snorted. "No one decent. Virgil has seen to that."

"How about Deke?"

"Deke? Can you honestly see them together?"

"No. But he thinks the world of her."

"Yeah, he does, but he knows that her friendship is all he'll ever have." Andy looked intently at the man sprawled beside him. "I'll never be able to repay you for staying and looking after my family."

"You already have."

Andy shrugged. "I did what had to be done at the time."

"There were a dozen men there, and *you* were the only one who cared if I lived or died. I like to think that my life began anew that day."

"Lord, you can't know how grateful I am that you came along when you did. When I think of Virgil stealing the girls, my heart almost stops. He's got connections. Don't trust Deputy Ham. Wayne is one of the fanatics who hangs around with Virgil."

"What about the sheriff?"

"He's fairly decent, but he's out running up and down the highway looking for bootleggers."

"Don't worry about it. Virgil won't get close to the girls or Leona while I'm there. I almost wish he would. It would give me an excuse to tear into him."

Yates watched Leona and the girls coming toward them. She was neat and trim and the sun made the lights in her hair shimmer. As they neared, he could see that she was laughing and talking excitedly. She appeared to be as happy as a kid on Christmas morning. How could Andy not be in love with her? Leona, with her sweet body and pretty face, was a woman any man would cherish.

Now where in hell had that thought come from?

"Do we have to go?" JoBeth ran to stand in front of Yates.

"In a little while. Calvin will think you've run off to the city and are not coming back."

"No, he won't. I told him we were comin' to see Daddy."

"She got her dress wet," Ruth Ann announced.

"Not enough to matter," Leona hastened to say.

They took Andy back to the rooming house. The girls clung to him and Ruth Ann cried when they told him good-bye.

"I'll be home soon, honey. Yates and Leona will take good care of you until I get there."

"What if Uncle Virgil comes?" Ruth Ann was dragging out the goodbye as long as possible.

"Yates will take care of him," Andy said patiently.

"Yeah," JoBeth said. "Mr. Yates will hurt him."

"Oh, what do you know?" Ruth Ann spoke irritably to her sister and got in the car.

"If you're still here a couple weeks from now and Deke will stay at the garage, I'll bring them back." Yates murmured to Andy, then closed the car door and went around to get under the wheel. They drove away leaving Andy, looking sad and alone, standing on the sidewalk leaning on his crutches.

Dusk had settled over the city, and it was quiet inside the car as they drove away from the rooming house. Yates glanced at Leona from time to time. She sat looking straight ahead with her hands folded in her lap.

"Deke insisted on giving me money to take you out for chili and hot tamales."

"I couldn't eat a bite. We'd better go on home. It'll be late when we get there as it is."

"I know a place out on the edge of town where they sell tamales wrapped in corn shucks. I'll get some to take with us. We don't want to disappoint Deke."

While Yates was in the small café, he looked out the window to see that JoBeth had crawled over the back of the seat to sit beside Leona, forcing her to move to the middle. The pleasure of being responsible for her and Andy's girls was a feeling he hadn't expected.

For the past seven years he'd been moving, drifting. This was the first in all that time that he had been responsible for anyone but himself. Unbidden, an image of home flashed in his mind. Not the Texas ranch house occupied by his adopted father and his wife, but a cozy place with clean sheets, good meals, quiet laughter and a soft, sweet woman with loving arms waiting for him. He'd had lots of places to hang his hat during the past seven years, but there had been no place that he'd missed when he left it.

These were precisely the types of thoughts floating through his mind as he left the café and returned to the car.

"Is the little one wanting to go to sleep?" he asked as soon as he opened the door.

"She's tired out." Leona settled JoBeth across her lap.

"Move over a little more and give her room to put her feet on the seat."

"I don't want to crowd you."

"Maybe I like it when you sit close to me."

Leona's head swiveled around. "And maybe you're just being polite."

"Being polite isn't my long suit." Before he started the car he took off his hat and, leaning over her knees, placed it on the floor. "Not that my mother didn't teach me manners," he said when they were on the way. "She and my grandmother were sticklers for them."

It was almost dark by the time they left the lights of the city behind. On the western horizon was a rapidly fading ribbon of crimson, all that was left of the sinking sun. Inside the car the silence was comfortable. Yates glanced at the woman beside him then returned his attention to his driving.

Leona, lost in thought, was remembering how forlorn Andy had looked when they left. She could still see him standing on the walk, leaning on his crutches. The question that had haunted her for the past few years suddenly sprang into her mind. Should she marry him, settle for a sheltered life as his wife, denying both of them the chance of finding a deep and abiding love such as he'd had with Irene? She cared for him, he cared for her, and they both loved the girls.

When she thought of going to bed with Andy, a shudder passed through her. She would always see, in her mind's eye, Andy holding Irene in his arms, tears of grief streaming down his face.

"Are you going to sleep?"

The sound of Yates's voice jarred her back to the present. It was dark now, the car's headlights marking the path on the newly paved ribbon of highway.

"No. I was daydreaming."

"Worrying about Andy? He seems to be doing all right."

"He's doing the best he can. He's never been away from the girls before. I know that troubles him."

"We can come back next Sunday if Deke can take care of the garage."

"I meant to tell you to take the money for gasoline out of the garage money."

"Now you've told me." He smiled at her. She was looking at him and it seemed only natural that his fingers searched for her hand where it lay on her thigh. She didn't pull her hand away, but welcomed the warmth and the strength of his. For a brief moment they were the only two people in the world.

Wanting to keep him talking, she dared to ask, "How did

you know Andy? I've known him for a long time and he never mentioned you."

"I knew him for only a day or two, but they were the most important days of my life." When she made no comment, he continued. "He saved my life and lost his foot in the process."

Leona waited, afraid that he would stop talking. She said, "He never said anything to me about saving someone's life."

After a minute or two, he said, "I'd like to tell you about it so you'll know why I feel about Andy like I do." She tightened her hand on his and he began.

The dawn was drab and gray, the air cool and damp. The crew, waiting to go to work, stood on the ramp leading to the span section of the bridge. The foreman was assessing the damage done to the understructure by two days of continuous rain.

The construction of the bridge across the North Fork of the Red River was behind schedule. The foreman for the contractor who had won the bid to put in the foundations had been working his crew twelve-hour days on the highway project that would later be known as Route 66.

"Dad-blasted rain caused us to lose two days work—"

"Hey. Don't cuss the rain. It's the first that's amounted to a hill of beans in six months." The man who spoke was one of the men who drove a tractor pulling a slip-scoop. He was also a rancher who needed grass for his livestock.

"We been camped here two days." This came from the man who worked the crane that lifted the heavy beams in place.

"Darn river is either runnin' full or dry as an old maid's twat," another man grumbled.

"Fire up the steam engine," the foreman yelled as he pulled himself up and onto the ramp deck. He looked at

his watch, flipped a card from his pocket and wrote down the time.

The men cheered.

It was mid-morning when the foreman yelled, "Yates, shimmy down and fasten a line to the choker on that beam. The hook is coming down."

Yates, tall and lanky, swung himself down off the ramp and dropped to the red clay bank beneath it. Sliding on the slick mud he began to make his way to the steel beam lying half-in and half-out of the water. He was looking up at the lowering hook he was to attach to the choker on the beam when the bank beneath the ramp trembled, then gave way with a loud swishing sound.

One second he was standing beside the piling. The next he was pinned to it by the red mud that reached to his hips. Overhead the ramp deck creaked, tilted and loose deck boards slid off and slammed onto the wet bank when a support post collapsed.

"Back off! Back off! The whole goddamn thing could go!"

Yates heard the yelling and swearing and the creaking of the timbers above him. Sure that he would die when the rest of the bridge collapsed and slid into the muddy red water, he was too scared to let out a sound. But he was not too scared to realize that not a person on the face of God's earth gave a damn if he lived or died. He closed his eyes and waited for the mud bank to cover him.

Mother, why did you ever let me be born?

"Goddammit, Andy. Get off that hook!"

Yates opened his eyes to see a small, blond man only a few years older than himself, riding down on the iron hook at the end of the steel cable. One of his booted feet was firmly anchored in the crook of the hook, the other swung free to push himself away from the piling. He had a coil of rope on his shoulder, one end of it fastened to the hook.

"Grab the rope," he shouted and threw the coil.

Yates eagerly grabbed the rope and twisted it around his wrists. "Ready," he shouted.

"Haul away."

The rope tightened and inch by inch Yates, feeling as though his arms were being pulled from their sockets, was lifted out of the sucking mud. As soon as he was free of the mud, he was swung out over the river. Hanging onto the rope, he was slowly pulled upward. Then he felt a jar, a jerk and heard a scream of pain. Looking up, he saw that Andy had been slammed against a crossbeam. The foot he used to push himself out and away from the piling was caught and held by a slab of support-iron that had slid as the structure shifted.

"Hold on!" Yates shouted, then hand over hand he began to pull himself up the rope to the hook. Later he was to wonder where he had mustered the strength.

"Oh, God! Oh, God!" Andy's face was twisted in agony. Yates feared that he would pass out and fall off the hook and dangle by the foot caught beneath the iron.

"Hold onto the cable. Don't let go!" Yates grabbed the crossbar, let go of the rope and levered himself up. With all the strength he could muster, he braced himself against the piling and lifted the iron slab enough to free Andy's crushed foot. "Take him up!"

Near fainting from the pain, the man who had saved Yates's life managed to hold on to the cable until hands pulled him up and onto the bridge deck where they lifted him and carefully made their way to solid ground.

Yates hugged the crossbar until his head stopped spin-

ning. Then with his breath coming in gasps, he moved on his hands and knees along the steel girder until he could swing himself down to the muddy bank. He crawled up the slippery slope and sank down. Breathing heavily, he huddled there and listened to the activity around him.

"That was plain, flat-out stupid." The foreman was ranting at the man who lay writhing on the ground.

"Maybe so. I had to give it a try. Is the boy all right?"

"I told you to get off the damn hook. We'd a snaked him out from the side."

"Shit, Mac! That bank was going. If you'd tried that, he'd have been buried alive and you know it."

"So what? You've got a wife and kid at home. He's nothin' but a damn thief."

"Don't give me that shit," the mild-mannered Andy shouted. "He's just a wet-eared kid. And he's been a damn good worker."

"Yeah? You almost got yourself killed for a sorry son-of-a-bitch that wouldn't give you the time of day. If those beams had buckled, you'd a been a goner. A thief ain't worth a good man takin' a risk for." The foreman rolled up a coat and placed it under Andy's head. He continued to mutter. "He could be a murderer, too, for all we know. I didn't know he was a jailbird till after I hired him."

"How bad is it?" Andy lifted his head, trying to see his foot.

"Hell, I don't know. A stretcher is comin'."

"Give the boy some credit, Mac. He got the . . . iron off me. I don't know how the hell he did it. He's been sick with the influenza."

"What the hell!" The foreman reared up and cursed long and loud. "The goddamn bank gave way again. If

you hadn't gone down with the rope, he'd be a dead duck by now. He owes you plenty."

"He don't . . . owe me anythin'—"

"He'll make himself scarce around here. Never thought he had the guts to do a man's work nohow."

"You're a hard ass, Mac."

The foreman yelled, "Harris, back my truck up here and for God's sake stay out of the mud."

"Brin' my wife to the doc's—"

"I'll see to it that she gets there. Hold on, Andy. The boys are here with the stretcher. Hey! Careful or you'll slide down that muddy bank—"

"Tell the boy . . . thanks—"

"Shit! He should be over here kissin' yore ass for what ya done instead of mewin' around like a sick cat. Them damn kids is all alike; sittin' round with their finger up their butts lookin' for handout or somethin' to steal. Ain't a one of 'em worth the powder it'd take to blow 'em up."

Yates, sitting on the ground with his head in his hands, heard the foreman's words. Weak from his recent bout with influenza and shaken from his brush with death, his stomach suddenly rebelled and he became violently sick. He hurried to the woods, wrapped his arms around a young sapling and emptied the contents of his stomach on the ground.

Leona held tightly to Yates's hand while he was talking. When he finished, she gave it an extra squeeze.

"I never saw Andy again until I stopped at the garage for gas. I've always regretted that I didn't hitch a ride to the hospital to see him."

Chapter 15

What made you decide to come back?" Leona felt a closeness to him she'd not felt before. It gave her the courage to ask the question.

He moved her hand, flattened her palm on his thigh and covered it with his. His palm stroked the back of her hand. Leona felt the hammering of her pulse. She turned her face a fraction and looked at him. The moon shed a pale light on his profile. Midnight-black hair, always resentful of a brush, had fallen on his forehead. He looked younger, softer, more vulnerable. His face turned toward her and, if she could believe what she saw in it, it was loneliness, pain.

Inside she trembled.

"I don't really know why I was compelled to come back. It was guilt or that I needed to know how he'd made out. I had heard that he'd lost his foot."

"It was rough on him and Irene for a time. Then he bought the garage. I don't really know, but I think he got help from the bank through Mr. Fleming. The garage is paid for now."

"You're easy to talk to, Leona. Easy to be with."

She lost her breath for an instant, then said, "How old were you . . . when it happened?"

"I'd just turned nineteen—old enough to have some self-confidence. But I had none. I was humiliated and scared. I'd spent a month in jail accused of stealing a man's wallet. I didn't do it. I had money. I didn't need to steal, but no one believed me. The foreman treated me like dirt. I swore, then and there, that never again would anyone talk to or about me the way he did."

"Good for you," she murmured, thinking about the time she'd made up her mind to take no more abuse and had broken out of Virgil's shed.

"The first thing I did was the hardest." He rubbed the palm of her hand along his thigh. She didn't seem to notice. "I went back home and confronted my adopted father and demanded that he give me my inheritance from my mother and grandparents."

"Did he give it to you?"

"Reluctantly." Yates waited until an approaching car had passed before saying anything more. The headlights shone briefly on his face turning his cheeks into dark hollows and his eyes into shadows beneath his black, level brows. His mouth was firm and unsmiling. Now he looked big, tough and hard as stone. "I have to wait until he dies to get the rest of it. I stay away or I'd be tempted to kill him."

Leona wanted to know more about his relationship with his father, but was too polite to ask. She remained silent. He moved his hand from hers to change gears as they passed through Elk City. When they were on the highway again, he blindly searched for the hand she had placed in her lap, found it and laced his fingers through hers.

"Lord, it feels good having you close to me. I like holding your hand," he said softly. "Do you mind?"

"No." She felt as if her heart was going to jump out of her chest.

"It's made the drive between here and the city go fast. It's hard to believe that we're almost home."

His words jarred her back to reality. *It made the drive go fast.* That's all there was to it for him. She had been handy, a good listener and it had made the time go fast. She had foolishly thought that he had told her about himself because he liked her, and had wanted to share with her some of what made him the man he was. She tried to pull her hand from his, but his fingers tightened.

"I've enjoyed the day. Far more than I thought I would." He took his eyes off the road to glance down at her. She had turned her head and was looking out the window. "Leona?"

"Yeah, so have I." After a pause, she rushed into speech. "I wonder what kind of day Deke had, and if we have campers. It was good of Deke to use his Sunday to stay at the garage. People seem to like him. He could talk to a stump."

Yates immediately sensed the change in her and when she tugged on her hand again, he released it. They drove the rest of the way to the garage in silence. He was puzzled by her sudden aloofness. A few minutes ago she seemed not to mind being close to him and he had loved the feel of her soft body against his. Now, she was doing her best to keep from even touching him.

She was thinking that she had been gullible to think that because he held her hand and told her of his past he was interested in her. He was a man who had been places, done things and obviously wasn't short of money. Why would he give a girl like her a second look? She'd better get her head out of the clouds or she'd be in for some dark days ahead. He'd be moving on when Andy came home.

Deke was sitting on the front porch when the car stopped behind the garage. Yates came around and took the sleeping child from Leona's arms.

"We're home, honey," he said when, disturbed, JoBeth whimpered a protest. "You'll be in your bed soon."

"Ya all right, darlin'? Ya look tired." Deke extended his hand and helped Leona out of the car. His homely, familiar face was a welcome sight. She didn't even resent the usual irritating "darlin'."

"Thank you. I'm kind of stiff from sitting so long," she said with a light laugh, grabbed his hand and let him pull her out of the car. "It's been a long day." She opened the back door and shook Ruth Ann's shoulder. "Wake up, Ruthy. We're home."

Holding on to the sleepy girl, Leona led the way into the house. She turned on the light and directed Yates to the bedroom where he placed JoBeth on the bed. Ruth Ann climbed up beside her and was asleep almost as soon as her head hit the pillow.

"Thank you," Leona murmured to Yates as she removed JoBeth's shoes.

"I'll bring in the picnic basket."

Leona undressed the girls, leaving them to sleep in only their underpants, and pulled a sheet over them. She turned out the light and left the room. Yates had placed the picnic basket and the sack of hot tamales on the kitchen table. Hearing the murmur of voices on the porch, she hurried there to thank Deke before he left. The men were sitting on the step. Both stood when she came out onto the porch.

"I just wanted to say thanks, Deke, for staying so we could go see Andy. And thanks for the hot tamales. I'll warm them up and have them tomorrow."

"You're welcome, darlin'. Anytime you want anythin', ya know I'll get it for ya if I can." Without the Stetson hat, he looked like a small boy standing beside Yates.

"I know that, Deke. Goodnight," Leona said and watched the men go down the path to stand beside Yates's car.

"Feller came in on a motorcycle with a girl in a side car. They're camped down there in the woods," Deke said, and screwed his big hat down on his head. "I sized him up as a blow-hard, know-it-all pissant. Wanted to borrow tools. I made him use them here where I could keep an eye on him."

"Did he give you any trouble?"

"Naw. He tried to tell me how great his cycle was. It's a pile of junk. He said he used it to chase down jackrabbits. Shhhh-it! He couldn't catch clap in a whorehouse."

Yates grinned.

"I didn't like the way he talked to his woman. She was a quiet little thing. It didn't seem to me like the two went together. She bein' kinda lady-like, him not bein' fit to shoot."

"You meet all kinds here on the highway."

"Did my girl have a good time?"

"Leona? I think so. She was glad to see Andy."

"Andy's a good man. She ort to marry him."

Yates frowned down on the little man puffing on his cigarette. The brim of his big hat shielded his face.

"I thought she was your girl. Why would you want her to marry another man?"

"She'd not marry me if I asked her. I want her to have a good man who'll take care of her. Andy's a good man. After a while talk about her would simmer down if she married him." Deke dropped his cigarette on the ground and ground it out with the toe of his boot.

"Not as long as Virgil is here to keep it stirred up."

"I just might have to kill that son-of-a-bitch."

Yates wished that he'd kept count of how many times Deke had said that. "Maybe he'll ease off after a while."

"Don't count on it." Deke snorted. "The deputy sheriff was here today nosin' round."

"What'd he want?"

"Wanted to know who you were, where you came from, and if you were living here with Leona while Andy was gone. He hinted that Leona wasn't fit to be raisin' Andy's girls. The mangy polecat's got a nasty mind."

"Andy told me that he and Virgil belonged to that overzealous group in the holy roller church."

"Yeah. My mama goes to that church. Not all of them think like Virgil. He thinks that God put females on this earth for men to use as they see fit."

"Is the deputy an elected official?"

"Appointed by the county sheriff. Course, Sayre is about the only thin' in the county and it's full of those who believes like the deputy does, but maybe not as strong."

"Is the sheriff one of them?"

"Naw, but he pretty much lets Wayne have his way around here. Sheriff McChesney is busy looking for bootleggers."

"Who's the district marshal around here?"

"If there's one, he ain't been around. Don't mess with old Wayne. Give him an inch and he'll plop you in the jail house if he ain't pissin' on the dirt you're layin' under. Then it'd be too late for Sheriff McChesney to do anythin' about it. Wayne'd like nothin' better than to get you out of the way so Virgil can come get Andy's girls."

"Virgil won't get Andy's girls and he won't touch Leona either. I don't care how many lawmen he has with him."

Deke lit another cigarette. "I'd stick around, Yates, but they're hayin' out at the ranch and Mr. Fleming depends on me to keep the machinery goin'."

"We'll be all right. I've got a couple of irons I can pull out of the fire if I have to."

"Just want you to know that you're not alone out here. I'll be by every few days to help ya keep a eye on things. Watch that bird in the campground. I don't like the looks of him."

Deke got into his truck and started the motor. "Thanks for takin' care of my girl today."

Yates watched Deke drive away. He was a strange, likable little cuss. He had no doubt that he'd tear into anyone or anything that was a threat to Leona and fight with all the strength in his small wiry body to protect her. It was a sad, cherishing kind of love since he had to know that she would never be his.

The sound of a motor awakened Leona. She turned over, lay for a few more minutes before she sat up in bed and rubbed the sleep out of her eyes. It was that short period of the morning just before sunup. She rolled out of bed and dressed swiftly. After washing her face and hands, she ran the comb through her hair to smooth out a few of the tangles, then picked up the milk pail and headed for the barn.

"Mornin', MaryLou," she called to the brown cow who was waiting patiently and lowed as she neared her. Leona pulled up an overturned bucket and sat down.

She liked the smell of the barn, the cow, and the warm milk streaming into the pail. Life was so uncomplicated for a cow, she thought as she nudged the udder and squeezed the cow's teats. All MaryLou had to do was stand there and someone would come and give her relief from her aching udder. Milk shot into the bucket Leona held between her feet. She milked steadily for several minutes.

"You're a pretty girl, aren't you?" She spoke softly to the cow and rested her head against her smooth brown side. Strong fingers squeezed and pulled in rhythm until the milk stopped coming. "I'm finished. You can go out and find some nice green grass to chew on."

"Does she ever answer you?"

Yates's voice was close behind her and so startling that

Leona spun around. Her foot kicked the milk pail. She caught the handle just in time to keep it from spilling.

"You scared me."

"Sorry," he said, but he didn't look sorry. His smile softened the hard contours of his face. "I looked in the kitchen. When you weren't there I figured to find you here with MaryLou."

"Yeah, well, MaryLou and I get together every morning for a little chat." The sight of him brought back the memory of sitting close to him in the dark, his hand wrapped tightly around hers, her hip and thigh pressed snugly against his. She could feel the warmth of the blood that rushed into her face.

"I thought you'd sleep in a little later this morning."

"I was tempted." She stood and picked up the pail of milk.

"Are you going to feed us the hot tamales for breakfast?" Yates took the pail from her hand.

"Cold tamales and left-over deviled eggs." She squinted up at him through thick, gold-tipped lashes, then walked ahead of him out into the early morning sunlight. On the way to the house, she stopped to let the chickens out. "Shoo, shoo—"

"There's a girl sitting on a suitcase over in the campground. I think the man she was with has run off and left her." Yates imparted the news when Leona joined him on the back porch.

"My goodness! The poor thing."

"I was opening the garage doors when he roared away on the cycle. Then the girl came running from the outhouse. She looked down the road then went back to where he'd left her suitcase, looked in it, then sat down and cried."

"She's still there?"

"I asked if she wanted to come up to the garage and wait for him to come back. She was crying, but I think she said he wouldn't be back."

"I'll take in the milk then go talk to her."

"If you're making biscuits, I'll start the oven—on the kerosene stove. It's going to be too hot to fire up the cookstove." He had followed her into the kitchen.

"I'd thought to have pancakes with the tamales," she said seriously, but couldn't keep her lips from twitching.

"You're kiddin'. Aren't you?" He reached out with a finger and touched her nose. "You stubborn little dickens. You're determined not to use the kerosene oven." A mischievous light came into his silver eyes. He looked down into her upturned face. She had pulled in her lower lip and held it between her teeth to keep from smiling.

"How did you know?"

"It wasn't hard to figure out. You even fired up the cookstove yesterday morning before we left for the city."

"I don't know how to use that newfangled oven."

"I'll show you."

"While you're at it, you can make the biscuits, too," she teased.

His forefinger went to her nose again. "Oh, no, sweetheart. That's your job."

"I'll make your biscuits, but first I should go see about the girl down in the campground. If it's true that the man's run off and left her, it was a dirty, low-down trick!"

"She may be gone by now," Yates said, holding open the door.

Sweetheart. Even though the endearment was said in a teasing way, it made her feel warm and tingly. Her heart wanted to sing. As they walked side by side down the path to the campground, she felt giddy, light-hearted, unable to think clearly.

The girl was sitting on her suitcase, her elbows on her thighs, her face in her hands. She hastily brushed the tears from her cheeks and stood as they approached her. She was a small, slender girl, with dark blond hair and big brown eyes, watery and swollen from crying. She wore a green-checked gingham dress, no stockings and sturdy shoes. Leona guessed her to be near her own age.

"Good morning. Would you like to come up to the house and wait for your husband to come back?"

"He isn't my husband, ma'am, and he won't be ba . . . ck." She tried to keep the sobs out of her voice.

"Oh? Are you sure?"

"Yes, ma'am. He took my money out of my suitcase while I was . . . at the privy. He won't be back."

"My goodness. He stole your money and left you stranded?"

"Yes, ma'am. I hired him . . . to take me to California." The girl plucked at her skirt with nervous fingers. "He wouldn't give it back even if the law caught him. He'd just say I owed it to him. He threatened to go off without me, but . . . I didn't think he'd be so . . . mean or if he did that he'd take my money."

"How long have you been on the road?"

"Three days. We left from Conway, Missouri."

"Is there anything we can do about getting her money back?" Leona looked up at Yates. He had stood back, not saying a word.

"Not much. He'll be out of the state before the deputy gets his fat . . . butt out of the chair. If he's caught, it's likely he'll say that she paid him to bring her this far."

"I agreed to pay the gas and the food. I had ninety-two dollars in my suitcase." The girl stared off down the highway. Tears were streaming from her eyes, but she didn't make a sound. "I thought it'd be enough to get me to California and keep me till I found a . . . job or—"

"Do you have folks back in Conway who would send you some money?" Yates had never seen anyone cry silently. It made him want to stomp the man who had abandoned her.

She shook her head. "No one that would send me a penny. My granny died and left me a hundred and eighteen dollars. It was my chance to get out of Conway."

"How did you meet up with the fellow on the motorcycle?"

"He was from Springfield. He'd been in Conway all winter because his sister lives there. He came to the café where I worked. He talked about going to California and said I could go with him if I'd pay for the gas and the food. Nobody had anything bad to say about him."

"You took a chance going off with someone you didn't know."

"I knew his sister. She is nice. Her husband owns the feed store."

"Have you had breakfast?" Leona thought the girl had the saddest eyes she'd ever seen. They were large and brown and bleak.

"He didn't want to build a fire and make coffee or . . . anything. He wanted to go to town and eat. I was afraid my money wouldn't last."

"Come on up to the house. You don't have to decide what to do right this minute."

"I don't want to be a bother—" She looked down the road with a worried frown. "Maybe I can hitch a ride to the next town and get a job. I cooked and waited on tables back home in the best restaurant in town."

"The nearest town is Sayre. I don't think you'd have much of a chance finding a job in a restaurant there. There's only one and it's run by a family. Come on up to the house," Leona invited again. "You'll feel better with some breakfast inside you."

"I've got eighty-two cents in my pocket. I'd better not spend it."

"Goodness gracious me! Did you think I'd charge you for breakfast?"

"I'll work for it . . . I'm a good cook. I can weed the garden and do your washin'."

"We'll see. My name is Leona Dawson. This is Mr. Yates. He works in the garage."

"Margie. Margie Kinnard."

Yates tipped his hat and picked up her suitcase.

"There was a little man at the garage yesterday. Ernie wanted to use his tools and when he wouldn't let him use them unless he brought the motorcycle up to the garage, he was madder than all get out. Ernie's got a terrible temper. I was afraid he'd hurt him."

Yates gave Leona a conspiratorial grin when she glanced up at him.

"Ernie might have been the one to get hurt. If he'd messed with that *little man,* Deke would have been all over him like a swarm of hornets."

As Yates followed the women to the house and set the woman's suitcase on the porch, he was totally unaware that he was smiling more and more these days.

Chapter 16

BY MID-MORNING, LEONA FELT AS IF SHE HAD KNOWN MARGIE forever. It was Margie who showed her how to use the kerosene oven while Yates was in the garage with a man who needed a fan belt for his Model A Ford.

Leona and Margie ate breakfast with the girls, then Leona cleared the table and set a place for Yates.

"I usually watch the garage while he eats," she explained to Margie after she told her about Andy being bitten by the skunk and Yates helping out at the garage. "He can eat more biscuits than any man—"

JoBeth interrupted. "He says he could eat a tub full o' Aunt Leona's biscuits. He says they're best. He says—"

"Here we go again." Ruth Ann rolled her eyes toward the ceiling. "She tells everything she knows."

"I do not!"

"Go see if Mr. Yates can come to breakfast," Leona said to JoBeth, and slipped another pan of biscuits in the oven. "This oven is handy as a pocket on a shirt. It's quick and doesn't throw out nearly as much heat as the cookstove," she admitted.

"Mr. Yates told you to use it," Ruth Ann said stiffly. "But you wouldn't because he'd bought it."

"Try to be pleasant this morning. Please . . . honey."

"It's hard to be pleasant when everything is so different round here. Daddy's not . . . here and there's strangers—" The child darted a resentful look at Margie.

"That's enough, Ruth Ann." Leona's voice was gentle, but the look she gave her young niece was not.

"I'll wash the dishes before I go." Margie, looking as if she would cry, poured water from the teakettle into the large granite pan where Leona had stacked the soiled dishes.

"Ruth Ann will help you."

"I can do it alone."

"Ruth Ann will help you," Leona said again, and waited for the girl to get up from the table and take a dry cloth before she went out the door.

Leona met Yates on the path between the house and the garage, Calvin at his heels. He paused in front of her forcing her to stop.

"Whoa. Where are you going so fast?"

"To the garage so you can eat breakfast."

"You didn't fire up the cookstove, did you?"

"No. Margie showed me how to use *your* oven."

"Good. It's going to be a scorcher today. Leona, I've been thinking about the girl. I'll give her a few dollars and take her to town."

"It isn't your place to take care of everyone who stops here . . . like you did the Olivers. You gave them the five dollars."

"You gave them milk and beans from the garden."

"I had plenty. As for Margie, even if she does look like she's a girl, she's at least my age."

"That old?" He lifted his brows; his lips quirked at the corners. "Then she's ancient. Must be about twenty-two or three." He was so charming when he teased that her heart almost jumped out of her chest.

"She doesn't need a walking stick, yet," Leona retorted sassily. She couldn't take her eyes from his face. "I hate to put her out on the road to hitchhike. She seems so nice and . . . trusting."

"Nice and trusting, but foolish to go on a trip with a man she barely knows."

"Maybe he was the lesser threat. She may have a Virgil in her family."

"Did she say so?"

"No. Ruth Ann's nose is out of joint because she's here. The poor child resists any change. She resented you when you first came here."

"If I remember right, she wasn't the only one."

"Well." Leona pressed her lips together to keep from smiling. "You were rather obnoxious."

With his eyelids partially closed, he leaned forward and studied her soft mouth, then asked in a husky whisper, "And now?"

She swallowed hard, but her eyes remained unflinchingly on his. "Some, but not quite so much."

Somehow her hand was caught in his. For a long moment she stood perfectly still. So did Yates. The sounds of cars on the highway filtered into her mind bringing her back to the present.

"I think I'll ask Margie to stay for a few days." She forced herself to speak calmly. "It will give her time to decide what to do and she can help me with the canning."

"It's up to you. Don't forget that you know nothing about her."

"I didn't know anything about you when you came to

stay." The eyes that looked into his brightened with amusement.

"You would bring that up." A smile lifted one corner of his mouth.

"I can use her help. I've got a tub full of beans to can and . . . the tomatoes are coming on. I'll be making chow-chow out of the green ones now and chili sauce later. I usually put up a bushel of peaches, then cucumber pickles." She paused momentarily, enraptured by the curve of his lips, then finished in a rush. "I've got a cellar full of jars to fill up."

"You work too hard."

"My job is to keep house and look after the girls. I don't really consider it a job. It's a privilege."

"I hope Andy knows what a treasure he has here." He squeezed her hand, dropped it and walked away.

Her eyes widened in surprise at his sudden departure. She turned to see him stepping up onto the porch. Calvin, disappointed that Yates was going into the house, dropped down beside the door.

Leona went on to the garage and sat down on the bench in the shade. She pressed a trembling hand to her midriff, hoping pressure would calm the roiling in her insides. A car passed on the highway. Someone waved. She absently waved back.

Careful, she cautioned herself. Yates is a loner. He had as much as told her so. He's staying here to help Andy, and a little flirtation on the side would make the time go faster. She couldn't afford to allow him to worm his way into her heart. He had been moving, drifting for years and would continue to do so. It was the way he wanted it. When Andy returned, he would leave. When that happened, she didn't want to be left with a broken heart.

From now on she had to keep her guard up.

* * *

The day had gone fast. True to Yates's prediction it had been a scorcher. In the late afternoon, the girls, in old cut-off union suits, had gotten into the big tank beside the barn. Margie was watching them, leaving Leona free to make a cobbler for supper using one of the last jars of peaches she had canned last summer.

She was pleased with the day's accomplishments. With Margie's help, the green beans were picked, the tomatoes and cucumber plants watered. Empty jars had been brought up from the cellar and washed for the next day's canning. Margie had milked MaryLou, fed the livestock and gathered the eggs.

"Sit down," Leona had insisted when she brought the basket to the house. "You've been working all day. Sit in the shade and keep an eye on the girls in the tank. I'm afraid to leave them out there alone." Leona covered the crock with a plate where she had placed sliced cucumbers and onions to soak in a vinegar mixture.

Later, when she heard Yates on the front porch, she called, "Come on in."

She was putting the cobbler in the kerosene oven when he strode into the kitchen.

"Now that you know how to use that thing does it mean that we'll have biscuits every night for supper?"

"No, it does not. Sometimes we'll have cornbread. All you think about is your stomach." She gave him a quick teasing smile.

He reached out and slid his hand beneath the damp hair on her neck, his fingers gripping gently. She breathed deeply the scent that was his alone. His clear gray eyes moved warmly over her face. He studied her for a long moment, then said softly, "You're wrong, pretty girl. That isn't all I think about."

His hand suddenly left her neck and he went out the door. *Pretty girl?* He was flirting with her again. She couldn't afford to feel warm and woozy when he touched her. She had to make light of his flattery as she did when Deke called her *his darlin'*.

Leona watched him, tall and lanky, stride toward the tank where the girls were splashing in the water. As he picked up the long tin conduit, he said something to them that made both of them shout and try to throw water on him. He jumped out of the way and began moving the conduit to fill the stock tank.

Oh Lord! It will never be the same around here after he's gone.

The sound of a car horn reached Leona. She looked out the window to see a car at the gas pump. Yates called something to the girls as he trotted around the house on the way to the garage. Several days ago he had attached a sign to the gas pump that read: HONK FOR SERVICE. It worked very well. Leona wondered now why she or Andy hadn't thought of it.

When Yates left, Margie took over the chore of pumping water into the conduit after she had helped the girls out of the tank and they had run for the house. For such a small, slender woman, she had strength and stamina. Tears had flooded her eyes when Leona asked her to stay on and help her.

"Thank you," she had murmured. "I just didn't know what to do."

"Folks come through here on their way to California all the time. Some nice families have camped here. Someone might agree to take you with them."

"I won't . . . do what some of them will want me to."

"Flitter. I hadn't thought of that. Did Ernie try to force you?"

"He didn't force me, but he was madder than a flitter when I wouldn't do . . . it. He said . . . he said I was too skinny to make a good whore anyhow." Margie's heavy blond hair shielded her face when she lowered it. "Now that I think about it, I don't think he ever intended to take me all the way to California. He knew Grandma had left me money and he wanted it."

"The dirty low-down polecat. It would serve him right if his darned old motorcycle broke down while he's in the desert and he was ten miles from a drink of water!" Leona said heatedly.

"I'll be a help to you, ma'am. I swear it." Margie's eyes were wide, and scared, and hoping, when she looked up at Leona.

"No one's ever called me 'ma'am,' Margie. It makes me feel . . . ancient!" Leona said remembering Yates's teasing words only that morning.

She's as alone in the world as I would be if not for Andy. If he hadn't taken me in years ago, I could be walking in her shoes.

While Leona and Margie were getting supper on the table, Yates went to the living room and listened to Lowell Thomas on the radio talk about the 7,000 war veterans who were camped out in Washington, D.C., demanding a war bonus. With sixteen percent of the country unemployed, and the Great Depression showing no signs of letting up, the men had been desperate enough to march on Washington. So far the government had not been sympathetic to their plight.

Yates listened intently when the commentator announced that Herbert Hoover and Charles Curtis had been re-nominated as the Republican candidates for president and vice president. Although the Democratic convention wasn't until next month, Franklin Roosevelt and his promised "new deal" would be the candidate to run against them if he could beat out his nearest rival, Alfred E. Smith.

The other news that caught his attention was that a federal gasoline tax of one cent per gallon would go into effect next week. That meant that Andy would pay a cent per gallon more when he bought a load of gas and would have to pass the cost on to his customers. Folks on the move were bound to feel the pinch.

Democrats in Chicago were pledging to repeal Prohibition and Lou Gehrig had tied the record with four straight home runs in Philadelphia.

Yates was distracted when JoBeth climbed onto the arm of the chair. He pulled the child over onto his lap.

"Is Margie goin' to stay?" she whispered.

"She's going to help your aunt for a while. Is that all right with you?"

"Uh-huh. I like her. Ruth Ann don't."

"Why not?"

"I donno. She's 'fraid she'll sleep in Daddy's bed."

"Your daddy wouldn't mind."

"Ruth Ann don't want her to. She has fleas."

"Really? If she does, she'd better sleep with Calvin."

JoBeth giggled. "Calvin sleeps in the garage with you."

"Sometimes he sleeps under the porch."

"We listened to Orphan Annie today."

"That so? How are Annie and Sandy?"

"I wanted to name our dog Sandy, but he was already named Calvin."

"Calvin's a good name for a dog."

"I like you."

"I like you, too."

"We're ready to eat now," Leona called. "JoBeth, wash your hands."

Yates lifted the child off his lap, but not before he gave her a hug. Damn, it was like nothing he'd ever known before to have a trusting little tyke climb up onto his lap, put her head on his shoulder, giggle and talk to him.

They had just finished eating when they heard the sound of a motorcycle coming into the yard between the house and the garage. Margie was suddenly as alert as a bird with a nest full of eggs and a bluejay circling overhead.

Leona peered out the window. "It's Deke." She waited until he turned off the noisy machine, then called, "Come on in, Deke."

The front screen door slammed, then boot heels sounded on the wooden floor. Deke came into the kitchen, his eyes seeking Leona.

"How's my darlin'?"

"Hello, Deke. Come sit down. We're having peach cobbler."

"Why, thanky, darlin', I will. Ya make the best cobbler in Beckham County, bar none." Deke tossed his hat on the floor beside the door.

" 'Lo, Mr. Bales," JoBeth said.

"Hello, sugarfoot," he replied, then his eyes found Margie. He rocked back on his heels and looked at her. "Hello, ma'am. You . . . you were with—Did that son-of-a—, that bast—," he sputtered, looked quickly at Leona, then said, "Did that stinkin' pile of horse manure run off and leave ya here?"

Margie's face turned a fiery red. Her pleading eyes looked at Leona for help.

"Margie is staying with us for a while, Deke. She's going to help me with the canning."

"You're better off without that smartmouth sucker, sugar. I thought I'd have to whip his hind-end last night when he came up to the garage a-lippin' off. It didn't take long to take his measure and he come up short." Deke took the vacant chair at the end of the table. Completely at home, he reached over to ruffle JoBeth's hair. "How's my girl?"

"Aunt Lee's your girl."

"Yeah she is, but I can have two girls."

Yates felt an emotion he'd seldom felt before. A fierce flood of jealousy washed over him. Shit-fire! He didn't like feeling the outsider. Deke, the homely little weasel, was comfortable with himself and with Leona and the girls and had known them a lot longer than he had.

Watching Leona, he felt a sudden surge of possessiveness. She and the girls were his responsibility. He was here taking care of them, not Deke. He wanted her to be his and only his. And he wanted her to want him. Desperately, he wanted that. He was tired of being alone. The thought hit him like a whirlwind.

Leona was laughing when she placed a dish of cobbler in front of Deke. The little man with the dish-shaped face thanked her, called her his "darlin'" and patted her affectionately on the behind when she turned away.

Yates wanted to kill him.

Chapter 17

DEKE WAITED UNTIL HE AND YATES WERE SEATED on the bench beside the garage before he told him the main reason he had come out here tonight.

"My mama heard at the church that Virgil is going to try and take the girls while Andy is in the hospital. He's got next to Deputy Ham, which ain't hard to do. The pot-bellied hog ain't got the sense God gave a flea. It's a wonder somebody hasn't let a little of the wind out of him with a pig-sticker."

Yates swore. "Because of me being here?"

"That and that this ain't a proper home for 'em. It wasn't proper when Andy was here with Leona as housekeeper, but it's downright indecent, they're sayin', for the housekeeper to be livin' here in sin with another man."

"Hell, I'm not living with them. I live here in the garage and take meals with them."

"I know that. I know Leona. Known her since I was in the fourth grade. She's straight as a string."

"Gawddammit," Yates swore.

"Virgil's tellin' folks that you and Leona are tighter than bark on a tree. You're payin' her bills at White's store, buyin' her a cook oven and a tub to bathe in. He said there ain't no tellin' what all is goin' on out here nights when fellers come in off the road and stop at the campground. He's makin' it sound like she's runnin' a regular whorehouse."

Yates swore long and viciously.

"He's got folks stirred up. Tell ya, Yates. Virgil gets his hands on those girls it'll be hell gettin' them back."

"I'm going to have to bust Virgil's head. I should've ruined that bastard's nuts when I had the chance. He's rotten mean to the bone."

"Speakin' of the rotten, mean to the bone, son-of-a-bitch," Deke said dryly. "That's him with the deputy."

The car that came around the garage and stopped beside the porch was an old topless touring car that had seen better days. The driver wore a white Stetson. Virgil, beside him, was hatless. The deputy, a man with rather short legs, a long body and longer arms, got unhurriedly out of the car when neither Deke nor Yates moved off the bench. Nor did they call out a greeting.

Yates kept his eyes on Virgil, who came around the end of the car and stood leaning against it with his arms folded across his thin chest.

"Howdy." The portly deputy's belt buckle was below his protruding belly. His fat jaws quivered when he spoke. He stared at Yates when he spoke but it was Deke who replied.

"Howdy yoreself, Wayne."

"I'm Deputy Ham." The man's voice was belligerent, his small, squinted eyes still on Yates. He puffed out his chest displaying the large tin star pinned to his shirt.

"Yeah?" Yates bent his leg, rested the heel of one boot on the edge of the bench and wrapped an arm around his leg. "I thought sure you were a salesman for the Star ass-wipe company," he drawled. "They put out a pretty good roll of paper. Never had a finger go through a sheet yet."

The deputy's face reddened. Deke did a poor job of stifling a giggle.

"Trashy-talkin' drifter. Just like I heard ya was."

"Last I heard trash-talking wasn't against the law. What are you doing here?"

Deputy Ham rocked back on his boot heels. "Ya'lI not be so smart-mouthed sittin' in my jail."

"If you're thinking of arresting me, you'd better have a damn good reason."

"Oh, I have one. Yore attack on Mr. Dawson who came out to visit with his sister. I have a witness."

"Ah . . . horsecock, Wayne." Deke snorted. "You know that Abe Patton'd swear that black was white and shit didn't stink if Virgil told him to."

"I'm not talkin' to ya, Deke. Shut yore mouth."

The screendoor slammed. Leona came out onto the porch. Yates hoped that she would stay there, but didn't have much hope that she would. His patience at an end, he stood and towered over the deputy.

"I didn't hurt him as much as I wanted to. If he'd hit his sister like he was going to, you'd have been scraping him up off the ground."

"Ya interfered in a family matter that was no business of yours."

"Damn right I interfered. I'll do it again, only next time he'll leave here with his ass up between his shoulders and his head screwed on backwards. Maybe you'd better explain that to him just in case he doesn't understand."

"Is that a threat?"

"What do you think?"

"Where'er ya from, mister?"

"Here and there."

"Drifter. Just like I thought. Leona," Deputy Ham yelled. "Get out here."

Leona came down the path and stood beside Yates and glared at Virgil.

"I've known ya a long time, Leona. It's my duty—"

"Yore duty?" Deke let out a whoop of laughter. "Yore duty is what's decided at the prayer meetin'. Ain't that right, Wayne? Ever'body knows you kowtow to that bunch of dumb-asses who think women were put here for the use of man and little kids to kick and beat."

Red-faced, the deputy shook his finger at Deke. "Yo're goin' to lip off once too often, and that rich Indian ya work for is goin' to have to find somebody else to tinker with his machines. 'Cause you'll be in my jail."

"*Your* jail, Wayne?" Deke sneered. "Hell fire. I didn't know you'd bought it. I thought it still belonged to Beckham County."

"You're on the edge, Deke. On the edge," the deputy shouted.

"You're a real horse's patoot, Virgil." Her voice was as sharp as the crack of a whip. The smirk of satisfaction on his face stirred the anger in Leona. "I'm glad Mama and Papa aren't here to see that you've gotten so low you'd have to take off your hat to crawl under a snake's belly, and that you're meaner than a cornered cat and got the brains of a pissant. It's the shame of my life to be related to you."

"Hush your mouth!" Virgil lurched forward to stand beside the deputy. "See how she talks, Wayne? She ain't fit to raise little orphan children. They ain't been to church in a month."

"They've got a father. They're not orphans, you stupid toad. I suppose you're fit to raise them? You beat your kids, cram religion and fear down their throats until the little things are so cowed they can't look a person in the eye." Leona finished with a sneer.

"My kids are God-fearin' kids," he shouted. "Yo're goin' to take Abe for yore man. Yo're the shame of the county, is what ya are." He was so angry, his Adam's apple was jumping up and down and he was rocking back and forth on his heels and toes.

"I wasn't until you started spreading dirty lies around about me being out here with Andy."

"All right, all right." Deputy Ham held up his hands. "We came out here to find out about this bird that's stayin' here. Calm down, Virgil. Let the law take its course. We'll get the girls out of here in due time."

"Like hell you will," Leona shouted. Yates put his hand on her shoulder to keep her from getting in the deputy's face.

"See how she swears, Wayne? She's shamed me and the Dawson name since she was old enough to spread her legs for any Tom, Dick or Harry that come along. Even that ugly little runt is after her like a dog after a bitch in heat." He glanced at Deke then dismissed him. "She's got a twitchy twat, is what she's got."

Deke sprang off the bench as if he'd been shot out of a cannon. He dove at Virgil, using his head as a battering ram. It collided with Virgil's genitals with enough force to knock the man off his feet. His scream was cut off when Deke's fists pounded at his mouth. With flying fists and kicking feet, Deke was all over the man on the ground with the speed of an attacking wild cat—stomping, kicking him in the ribs, raining blows on his face.

The deputy grabbed Deke by the belt, pulled him off Virgil and threw him to the ground. Deke sprang to his feet. When the deputy grabbed his shirt front and lifted his fist to hit him, Yates's hand darted out and grabbed his wrist.

"Don't hit him." He spoke with such authority, the deputy dropped his fist.

"I'll kill you! I'll kill you," Deke shouted at Virgil, who was still rolling on the ground. The little man's anger had overcome his good sense. "You lowdown, son-of-a-bitchin' coward! You've knocked her around, talked dirty about her, made her life miserable since she was a little kid. I should've killed you back when we were in school and you whipped her till her back was a bloody mess. Touch her again and I will. I'll swear it on that Bible you're so fond of quotin'."

Virgil, moaning and crying, tried to get to his feet and fell back on his hands and knees.

"You're under arrest, Deke." Deputy Ham reached for the handcuffs attached to his belt.

"Better think about that, Deputy." Yates's voice was loud with authority. "If you arrest him, you'll be biting off more than you can chew. How would the sheriff like to explain your action to the attorney general of the state of Oklahoma? The federal boys are real interested in what is going through Beckham County on Route 66."

"What do you know about it?"

"Plenty. I know how many bootleggers you are letting through and why. I also know who they are," Yates said.

"What's this to you?"

"Use your head, man. Why do you think I'm here? Are you so stupid as to think I dropped in off the road and took a job in this garage? Now pick up that sorry excuse for a man and get the hell out of here."

"You've not heard the last of this."

"I sure as hell hope not."

"He wants his sister's children outta the hands of a wh—of a fallen woman. He's given her to a good man that'll take a soiled woman."

Yates raised his brows. "He can want in one hand and spit in the other, but he'd better not make a move to take them while I'm here or force a man on Leona. It's pretty damn sneaky of him to come around here causing trouble while their daddy is in the hospital."

The deputy didn't answer. He helped Virgil up off the ground and into the car. Yates called a warning.

"Tell that son-of-a-bitch to stay away from here until Andy gets back. The little girls are worried enough about their daddy without having to put up with that crazy bastard trying to take them from their home." Yates stood on spread legs with his arms across his chest.

"I'd be careful if I was you, Yates. You're messin' in somethin' that's none of your business."

"Leona and the girls are my business while Andy is away, and don't you forget it."

The deputy's eyes settled on Deke. "Make one wrong move and you'll be in my jail."

"I'm scared plumb-to-death, Wayne. Mr. Fleming depends on me to keep his machinery goin'. He'll not let me sit in *your* jail while you trump up charges against me. He could eat you for breakfast if he wanted to."

The deputy's lips curled in a sneer. "You can't hide behind that damn redskin forever."

"I'll tell Mr. Fleming you said so."

The car left the yard. Leona stood with her head down, trying to clear the tears of shame from her eyes before she turned to face the men. She felt a hand on her arm. It was Deke, her forever friend.

"Don't let it bother ya, darlin'. Ya know Virgil is as dumb as a stump and meaner than a rattler with his tail tied in a knot. He ain't goin' to get the girls if I have to camp out here with the shotgun. He makes a move and I'll be all over him like stink on a skunk. The man's crazy to think you'd marry Abe Patton."

"It isn't Abe's fault, Deke. He's so dumb he doesn't know enough to come in out of the rain. I'm glad you hurt Virgil. Lordy, he was surprised." She didn't look at Yates for the fear of seeing disgust on his face. "I'd better go in. I told Margie to take the girls to the bedroom and read them a story. Ruth Ann will be upset. Thank you, Yates," she said and headed for the house.

"Leona?" She paused when she heard his voice. He came up behind her. His hands gripped her shoulders. "Don't worry. Things will work out," he said softly, his mouth close to her ear.

She didn't dare speak for fear the sobs would erupt, so she nodded and hurried into the house. She stood inside the door for a moment to get herself under control before she went to the bedroom. JoBeth was listening intently to the story Margie was reading, but Ruth Ann's little face was anxious. She jumped up as soon as Leona appeared in the doorway, ran to her and wrapped her arms around her waist.

"Nothing happened, honey. The deputy wanted to talk to Mr. Yates about what happened the other day. He went away."

"Why did Uncle Virgil come?"

"You know how he is. He's mad at Mr. Yates for hurting him. But the deputy didn't arrest Mr. Yates. He'll be here until your daddy comes back. We don't have anything to worry about."

"Are you sure?"

"Sure as rain. And I think we might get some of that tonight. It was clouding up when I came in."

"Aunt Lee." Ruth Ann reached up to whisper in Leona's ear. "I don't want *her* to sleep in Daddy's bed."

"Why not, honey? She's just a poor girl without anywhere to go and no one to care about her."

"I don't want her to."

"She's got to sleep somewhere."

"She can sleep on your cot. *You* sleep in Daddy's bed."

"Wouldn't you rather I be in the room with you?"

"No. I don't want her in the bed Mama slept in."

"All right, honey. I'll sleep in there."

Leona wandered back out onto the porch after Margie and the girls went to bed. Her nightgown lay on the bed in Andy's room. It had seemed terribly important to Ruth Ann that she sleep there. It would be strange.

She went to the end of the porch, looped her arm around a post and looked toward the southwest. Behind the dark treetops came flashes of lightning followed by a low, throaty growl, like a hungry dog being denied a bone. It faded into a sullen silence, but soon came again.

"We'll have rain before morning." Yates's voice came out of the darkness.

"Oh . . . you scared me."

"I didn't mean to."

"You move around so silently."

"I was hoping you'd come out before you went to bed." He was standing on the ground beside the porch, making her face just a little higher than his. A sprig from the mint plant at the end of the porch was in his mouth. "Are the girls all right?"

"They didn't see or hear anything. Margie took them to the bedroom and read them a story. Ruth Ann knew Virgil came. She doesn't miss much."

"Margie has come in handy already. Does Ruth Ann still resent her?"

"Yes, but she'll come around in time."

"Come sit with me for a while. I need your company."

"JoBeth is afraid of storms. I should stay close. If the thunder wakes her, she'll be scared."

"We'll not be far away."

He pulled her arm from around the porch post and placed it on his shoulder. They stood there for a long tense moment, their faces inches apart. She remained perfectly still. She didn't even blink. The feelings surging through her were all so new. Something powerful moved deep inside her. It was like a warm fountain flowing up from the center of her body to her throat. It was frightening. She didn't want to love this man but she didn't have the strength to resist him. His head was bare. She suppressed the urge to lift her fingers to his hair.

Soon he would be gone. She'd have these memories to cherish.

Yates wrapped his arms around her and lifted her down off the porch, letting her slide against him until her feet were on the ground. His arms continued to hold her. She was too dazed to move away. With one large hand he pressed her head to his shoulder. It was wonderful to lean against his hard strength.

As if reading her mind, he said, "You've not had anyone to lean on, have you? You've had to put up with Virgil's meanness all by yourself." His voice was soft in her ear, his head was bent, his rough cheek pressed tightly to hers, his hand smoothing her hair.

"I've had Andy and . . . Deke."

"You've got me now."

She turned her face to his shoulder. "I'm sorry you were brought into this mess. It was nothing new to Deke. He has always known about it."

"Little bugger is like a buzz saw when he gets going." She could feel the chuckle vibrate in his chest.

"He's fought my battles for most of my life."

"He loves you."

"I know. I love him, too."

"He thinks you should marry Andy."

She raised her head. "He knows I won't do that."

His eyes skimmed over her face illuminated by the jagged streaks of lightning that briefly lit up the swollen, rain-filled clouds. Leona pulled away from him. He caught her hand to keep her with him.

"It'll be a while before it rains. Let's sit on the bench by the garage. I keep forgetting to grease the chains on the porch swing."

"Just for a little while."

They moved down the path together, sat down and leaned back against the wall of the garage.

"I'm going to put my arm around you." Before she could protest, he had pulled her close against him, fitting her shoulder beneath his arm. "Don't pull away. I'd sure hate it if you were afraid of me."

"I'm not afraid . . . I just don't think it's . . . wise."

"Why not? Give me one good reason why we can't sit like this and enjoy each other's company."

"Well . . . you'll think that I . . . that I let every man who comes along put his arms around me."

"I know better than that." His arm tightened around her. "I'm going to kiss you and I don't give a damn if it's wise or not."

"So the time will go fast?" She didn't know why she had said such a dumb thing.

"What do you mean by that?"

"On the way back from the city you said . . . you said

holding my hand made the time go fast." His nearness was making her breathless.

"Yeah, it did. It went too damn fast. I enjoyed having you close to me. I was tempted to drive on to Amarillo."

She pulled back. "I don't want a flirtation . . . not now." Her foolish heart was beating twice as fast as it should be.

"You think too much." Then she felt his breath on her lips. It was warm and moist and flavored with the mint leaf.

He laid his mouth on hers and pressed. He withdrew and pressed again. Each time his mouth touched hers, his lips were parted more. They were warm, urgent, demanding. Her lips opened at his subtle encouragement and all the sensations she had tried so hard to suppress sprang to life. The wanton feelings were strange to her; she was powerless to control them. Instead, they were controlling her, taking over and making her want the physical gratification of his touch, his kisses.

Yates lifted his head and peered down into her face. In a trembling caress, his hands moved over her back and shoulders.

"I've got to tell you—I've wanted to kiss you since the day I came here. I wanted to kiss away the worry and the hurt."

She bent her head and refused to look at him. He lifted her face with a finger beneath her chin and kissed her gently on the lips again. His arms enfolded her and hers went around his waist. Her face found refuge in the curve of his neck.

"I'm just as confused as you are." His voice was close to her ear. "I didn't plan on being attracted to you. But I want to kiss you each time I see you." He laughed a little. "It's a damn nuisance."

Suddenly an ear-splitting crash of thunder rent the

brooding stillness. And then another more frightening thunderclap erupted. It signaled the clouds to open and let fall an unending torrent.

With his arm tightly around her, they raced for the shelter of the porch.

"How long has it been since it's rained here?"

"We had what Andy called a spit-rain about a month ago. I'll not have to water the garden for a while."

"There isn't much wind. I don't think you have to worry about a storm."

At the door Yates bent and kissed her wet lips. "Goodnight," he whispered, and hurried back to the garage.

Chapter 18

I TELL YA GOD AIN'T PLEASED WITH WHAT'S GOIN' ON."

"About the rain?"

"No," Virgil almost shouted. "About Leona shackin' up with that bird out there on the highway."

Virgil paced back and forth across the small room behind the jail where Wayne stayed nights when he wanted to get away from home. The excuse was that he expected the jail would be needed by the federal agents chasing bootleggers. Of course, if it happened Sheriff McChesney took care of it, but his wife wasn't aware of that.

"I ain't pleased 'bout that either, but there ain't much I can do about it now." Deputy Ham pulled open a drawer in an old dresser and took out a package of cigarettes. He took one from the pack, lit it and pulled the smoke deeply into his lungs. He didn't look at Virgil because he knew he would see disapproval on his face.

"Have you backslid, Wayne?"

"No."

"You're smokin'."

"Yeah."

"Does Pastor Muse know?"

"No."

"I'm disappointed in you, Wayne. Smoking is against God's—"

"I know. Don't preach. I tried to quit. I need a smoke once in a while to settle my nerves."

"You could pray. God will calm your nerves."

"I suppose you'll tell the brethren that I'm still smoking."

"If they ask me, I will. God don't expect much of us, Wayne. He expects us to walk in his footsteps. Jesus, when he was here on earth, didn't smoke cigarettes, or go to picture shows and his women didn't rouge their faces or bob their hair."

Virgil's long sad face reminded Wayne of a hound dog he'd once had.

"God won't let a worldly man through the pearly gates, Brother Ham."

Wayne snorted. "They didn't have picture shows back then and *he* didn't have a woman as far as I know."

Virgil clicked his tongue against the roof of his mouth in a gesture of sadness. "God isn't pleased."

"Stop sayin' that!"

"All right, all right. It's between you and—" Virgil cut off his words when a rap sounded on the door. "Put that thing out unless you want it all over the church that you've backslid."

He waited to open the door until after Wayne ground out the cigarette on the floor with the toe of his boot. It was Virgil's turn not to be pleased when he saw his wife, Hazel, standing in the drizzling rain with an old coat over her head.

"What'a you want?"

"Paul is awful sick, Virgil."

"How'd ya know I was here?"

"They told me at the church. Paul is sick," she said again. "I don't know what to do."

"What's the matter with him?"

"He's burning up with a fever and his throat is raw."

"God's punishin' him for sinnin' then lyin' about it."

"He's only eight years old," Hazel said with spirit. "He didn't understand what he did was wrong."

"Are you sassin' me? Get on back home and put a wet cloth on his head. I've got business here."

"I need salve for his back where you whipped him and something to bring his fever down." Hazel seldom stood up to Virgil, and he was shocked to anger.

"I said, go home. I'll call a prayer meeting. If God wants to end his sufferin', he will."

"Virgil, he needs the doctor!"

"You heard me. Go home." He backed away and closed the door. "I don't know what's got into that woman." He turned to face Wayne. "She's been gettin' out of line lately—sassin', talkin' ugly, bein' plumb contrary. I'm goin' to have to take the strop to her butt. It don't do to let the women folk get the bit in their mouth. Ain't no tellin' what they might do."

"Maybe you ought to go home and see about your kid."

"He'll be all right. Sister Blanchard said he thumbed his nose at her little Maudie. He lied about it. I whipped him good. He's just wantin' to be fussed over."

"If you ask me, that's not much to be whipped for," Wayne mumbled.

"I want to know what you're goin' to do 'bout Deke Bales attacking me. Look at my mouth. It's all puffed up."

"That thing 'tween yore legs won't be standin' up for a while." Wayne had to turn away to keep Virgil from seeing the grin on his face. "He hit ya a good one there, too. Between Deke and Yates, your balls has had a rough time lately."

Virgil remembered well the pain both Deke and Yates had delivered to his private parts. He'd not forget that . . . ever! His time would come. It always did.

"Ya got to do something 'bout that bum that's hangin' around Leona."

"I'm thinkin' he ain't no bum. Roy White said he came in and paid off Andy's bill at the store as cool as you please, then peeled off some bills and paid in advance."

"Have ya checked him out? Ain't natural for a feller to be handin' out cash money unless he's a bank robber and it's easy come, easy go."

"Dammit, Virgil. I've got my job to consider. McChesney told me to go soft unless I had somethin' on the fellow. Deke works for Fleming, which makes it hard for me to come down hard on him."

Virgil shook his head and clicked his tongue again. "Swearing. You have backslid, haven't you?"

"Stop preachin' or get out of here," the deputy shouted. Then in a softer tone, "Do you want to file charges against Deke? If you do, it'll come out you're tryin' to take the girls from their pa."

"No. I won't file charges, but I'm goin' to get those two little innocent girls out of that den of iniquity. God told me plain as day. 'Brother Dawson,' he said. 'Let not the sins of the parents corrupt the children.' It's my Christian duty to protect my dead sister's babes."

Wayne looked long and hard at Virgil before he spoke.

"And pay back your other sister for runnin' off and shamin' you, huh?"

"God will punish Leona as he did Irene."

"Stay clear of Deke. He's got Fleming behind him."

"Are you 'fraid of that Indian?"

"Yeah, and you'd better be, too. He's on howdy terms with everyone from the governor on down."

"God will take care of me."

"I'm leery of that other son-of-a-bitch. He could be a fed they've planted here to catch the bootleggers. I want no trouble with the feds. One wrong move would mean my job."

"He ain't no fed. You think the feds set that skunk on Andy to give Yates a reason for bein' here?"

"How do we know that a skunk bit Andy? We only have their word for it. He could've killed Andy and buried him someplace."

"Never thought a that."

"That's why I'm a lawman and you're not." Wayne stood and hitched up his trousers. "One thing is sure, Yates ain't workin' out there for the money."

"That's plain as the nose on yore face. He's got an itch for my slutty sister. Soon as it's scratched good and proper, he'll move on."

"We got to get out of here. McChesney's been in Elk City all day. He's due back."

Virgil opened the door. "It's still rainin'. I been prayin' for rain even though wet wood is hard to saw up. My potato patch needs it. Thank you, God." He raised his eyes to the sky and stepped out into the rain. "Comin', Brother Ham? I'm goin' to the church to pray that God will show me a way to save those poor little girls from bein' ruin't."

"I'll be along in a while."

The deputy closed the door and lit another cigarette. Virgil Dawson was a man he could take only in small doses. He had heard rumors around that he was laying the lash too hard on his kids. It could be that he didn't want the doctor to see his sick kid 'cause he'd discover the marks he'd put on him.

* * *

It was after midnight when Virgil fired up his old truck with the buzz saw mounted on the back. He drove slowly to the square house on the edge of town where he was born, and where he had lived all of his life except for the few years after he married and before his parents passed on.

"Lord, help me. Show me the way," he muttered to himself as he turned off the muddy road into the yard in front of the house. A bright light shone through the window at the back of the house. "Runnin' up the electric bill. That woman's due a whippin'." Virgil pounded his fist on the steering wheel, got out of the truck and slammed the door behind him. "There goes the money for sawin' up old man Peterson's oak tree," he grumbled.

Entering the house, he stomped down the short hall to the back. Standing in the doorway, Virgil surveyed the room crowded with two double beds. Hazel sat between them fanning Paul with a folded newspaper.

"What's the light doin' on? I told you not to turn on the electric." His voice boomed in the quiet room. Paul awakened with a start as did the brother sleeping beside him. The two in the other bed, always alert for their father's footsteps, had roused when he came in the front door, but pretended sleep to keep from drawing his attention.

"Paul is bad sick. His fever is high and he's breathing hard." Hazel's anxious eyes looked up at her husband, then back down at her son.

"All kids get a bellyache. We've not lost one yet."

"It's not his belly. His throat is so sore he can hardly swallow a sip of water."

"He'll be better come morning. Ya ain't leavin' the light on all night cause he's got a tickle in his throat. Mind me and come to bed. I've a need for ya."

"Go on to bed. I'm stayin' here."

Shocked by his wife's defiance, Virgil reached for the light hanging from the ceiling and plunged the room into darkness. Hazel cringed, expecting him to knock her out of the chair.

"Are you denyin' me, Hazel?"

"My child is sick. I'm stayin' here."

Then Virgil's hand came down heavy on his wife's shoulder. "Ya'll come to me, hear? God says a woman shall cleave to her husband and they shall be of one flesh."

"Please turn on the light. I'll come to you as soon as he goes back to sleep."

Virgil kicked the side of the bed where his eleven-year-old son lay. "Isaac, get the kerosene lamp."

"Yes, Pa." The boy sat up, crawled over his brother and scurried out of the room. A few minutes later he returned with the light and stood hesitantly in the doorway.

"Well, brin' it here."

The boy carefully handed the lamp to his father and scrambled over his brother to curl up in the bed. Virgil held the lamp low so that he could look at the sick child.

"He don't look very sick."

"He is sick. Please, won't you go get the doctor?"

"Hush your foolishness. We don't have money to pay a doctor to come out here in the middle of the night."

"I have five dollars Joseph gave me when he came by here after workin' at the CCC camp."

"You have five dollars and didn't tell me?"

"Joseph said to put it back until I really needed it."

"Where is it?"

"Don't take it, Virgil. Let me use it for the doctor."

"Where is it?" he repeated. "Am I the head of this house or not?"

"Yes, you're the head of the house," Hazel said tiredly. "It's under the flour tin."

"I'll bring out Brother Muse in the morning. We'll pray and decide about callin' the doctor. Mind me now and come to bed, Hazel. I've had a hard day, I'll not wait long." He set the lamp on the dresser and left the room.

Hazel's tired eyes followed him from the room. He wouldn't bring the doctor because he didn't want him to see the marks on Paul's back. *Oh, Lord, what could she do?*

Joseph had left home two years ago when he turned sixteen. Peter turned sixteen and left home last year. He had promised Isaac that he'd come back for him when he reached thirteen. Then all she would have left would be the little boys. Thank the good Lord they had never had girls. She wondered if that was the reason Virgil was so obsessed with getting Irene's.

Hazel bowed her head and prayed. *Oh, Lord, please don't take little Paul. He's a good child. He didn't even know what it meant to thumb his nose at Maudie Blanchard. He had seen the other boys do it. Soften Virgil's heart so he will bring the doctor. He'll take the five dollars Joseph gave me, but I'll manage to pay the doctor somehow. . . .*

She dipped the rag in the pail of water beside the bed and placed it on Paul's forehead.

"Mama, I . . . hurt—"

"I know you do, son. I'll get the doctor in the morning."

"Hazel," Virgil bellowed. "Get in here."

"Try to sleep, honey. I'll be back as soon as I can."

Pastor Muse was knocking on the door before the sun was up.

"Deputy Ham said one of your kids was down sick," he

said to Virgil when he came to the door. "I was out this way and thought I'd stop by."

"It's nothin' serious," Virgil said, scratching his head. "Little sore throat. Little fever. Come on in, Brother Muse. Isaac is making coffee."

"Just for a minute or two."

"Hazel," Virgil yelled. "Brother Muse is here."

Hazel came from the back room. Her hair was tousled, her eyes were red from lack of sleep and crying.

"Brother Muse, Paul is bad sick. He's burning up with fever."

"Have you had the doctor?"

Hazel's eyes went to Virgil when he said, "I don't see any need for that yet, Brother. We'll pray."

"I've been prayin' all night, Virgil," Hazel said crossly and earned a frown from her husband. "The Lord says that he helps those who help themselves."

"Watch yourself, Hazel. Don't make a show of yourself in front of Brother Muse."

The pastor was shocked when he looked down on the child. His cheeks were bright red and he was gasping for breath. The other children had left their beds and were sitting around the kitchen table. He placed his hand on Paul's head, closed his eyes and said a prayer. When he finished he laid a comforting hand on Hazel's shoulder and left the room.

"I'll fetch the doctor," he said to Virgil, who was lounging in the doorway.

"I'd be obliged, Brother Muse. I didn't want to leave the woman here alone to go get him."

Eleven-year-old Isaac turned his head to look out the window and curled his lips.

* * *

By noon a red quarantine sign was tacked to the front of the Dawson house. It hadn't taken the doctor long to determine that Paul Dawson was down with diphtheria. There were five other cases of diphtheria in the area, and that many cases, he explained, constituted an epidemic. He injected Paul with an antitoxin and swabbed the throats of the other three boys.

"I'll send the swabs to the health office," he explained to Hazel. "If the germ is found, I'll give them the antitoxin. Keep the other children out of the room, but they are not to leave the house. Do you understand? If they leave the house and mingle with other children you and your husband will be subject to arrest."

Virgil was hasty to assure the doctor. "We'll do whatever you say, Doctor."

"What happened to this child's back?" Doctor Langley knew the child had been whipped, and he wanted the ignorant lout standing in the doorway to know that he knew.

Hazel didn't answer. She left the telling to Virgil.

"Paul's a willful boy, Doc. The Lord says spare the rod and spoil the child. I'm doin' my best to put him on the straight and narrow."

"What did he do? Kill your favorite huntin' dog or swipe a plug of tobacco?" The doctor's voice was heavy with sarcasm, but Virgil didn't notice.

"I don't have huntin' dogs, Doc. And tobacco isn't allowed in the house." Virgil scratched his head in puzzlement over the question.

"Doctor, will he . . . make it?" Hazel asked.

"I'll be truthful, Mrs Dawson. I'm not sure. If I could have gotten to him even twelve hours before and given him the antitoxin, he would have had a chance. Now, I don't know. His throat is coated with crust."

The doctor was looking down at the child and didn't see the look of pure hatred in Hazel's eyes when she looked at her husband lounging in the doorway.

Virgil was allowed to leave after he had scrubbed down and changed clothes.

"Don't come back into the house. If you do, you'll stay until I lift the quarantine."

"My wife will need help, prayers—"

"I think God can hear you out in the road or wherever you use that buzz saw."

The doctor had heard rumors about Virgil Dawson being a man who ruled his family with an iron hand, but he hadn't known how cruel he was in the name of God. His wife and kids were scared to death of him. He wondered if he would have been called at all if not for Pastor Muse. Thank goodness all the Holiness folks were not like Dawson.

"I'll be back in a few hours," he said to Mrs. Dawson as he prepared to leave. "Keep a cold cloth on Paul's head and put ice chips in his mouth."

"We don't have any ice."

"Get some," the doctor said to Virgil as he passed him on the way out. "Leave it on the porch. This young man looks husky enough to get it inside. You can do that and give your mother a hand, can't you, son?"

"Yes, sir."

"That's a good boy." The doctor placed his hand on Isaac's shoulder, and, with an exasperated look at Virgil, stepped off the porch.

Chapter 19

RUTH ANN AWAKENED WITH A START. It was time.

Birds were chirping in the big pecan tree that hung over the house, and it was light enough outside to see the barn. She eased out of bed and sat on the floor beside it to pull on her clothes. After she dressed, she reached under the bed and pulled out the bundle she had hidden there the night before. Peering over the bed she watched to see if Margie had awakened. When several minutes passed and she hadn't stirred, Ruth Ann crept out the back door and hurried across the yard and into the woods.

She had decided to leave last night after Deke came and everyone was laughing and talking. Her eight-year-old mind concluded that she was the only one missing her daddy. She would go ask Mr. Fleming to take her to the city. She would stay with her daddy in the rooming house. By the time they came home the strangers would be gone. It'd just be her, Jo-Beth, her daddy and Aunt Lee again.

Ruth Ann thought, now, as she came out of the woods and walked down the highway toward the turn-off road that led to the Fleming ranch, that she didn't have anything against Margie except that she was there in her mama's house, taking over, using her mama's things. And Mr. Yates might take Aunt Lee when he left. If that happened, she'd take care of JoBeth and her daddy.

It hurt to have strange people in their house. Her mama was gone; her daddy was gone; and Aunt Lee didn't care about her and JoBeth like she used to. She'd let Mr. Yates hold her hand all the way back from Oklahoma City. They thought she was asleep, but she'd heard most of what they'd said. Aunt Lee liked him. She'd never let Deke hold her hand. Maybe she planned for Margie to stay and take care of them, so she could go off with Mr. Yates when their daddy came home.

Tears of self-pity rolled down Ruth Ann's cheeks.

The sun was up and it was getting hot. Several cars whizzed by on the highway. Ruth Ann was careful to stay over to the side of the road, far from the pavement. She was almost to town when a car pulled up beside her and stopped.

"Where you goin', girl?"

"To the Fleming Ranch."

The man behind the wheel studied her for a minute, then it dawned on him who she was. He leaned over and shoved open the door.

"Get in. That's too far for a little girl to walk."

The air was fresh and cool when Leona stepped out onto the back porch on her way to the barn to milk MaryLou. The rain had washed the dust from the bushes and trees, leaving them green and sparkling.

She was tired this morning, having had a hard time falling asleep. Torn between the pleasure she'd had in Yates's arms and the fear that he had expected no resistance because of her reputation, her mind had been tortured. Her heart had pounded as she relived each kiss, each touch, each whispered word. The logical part of her mind told her that a man like Yates who had been to a lot of places and done a lot of things would never be seriously interested in a nobody who hadn't even finished high school. And especially one with her reputation.

Then she had cried herself to sleep.

In the morning light, it was hard for her to believe that Yates had held her and kissed her with such tender possession. She was sure that it meant no more to him than a pleasant passing of time while they waited for the storm to break. She dreaded facing him and had already decided that she would act as if it had not happened and make sure that it never happened again.

When Leona returned to the kitchen, Margie had coffee started on one burner on the kerosene stove and the portable oven heating on the other.

"Mornin'." Leona strived to put a cheerful note in her voice. "It was a nice steady rain we had last night. We'll not have to water the garden for a while."

"Mornin'. I hope Ernie slept in the rain." Margie's smile was a surprise. It made her look young and pretty. "I thought about it while I was snug in that comfortable bed and was half glad he'd run off and left me."

Leona set the milk pail on the counter. "I hope that his old motorcycle got so wet it wouldn't start."

"And he can't find anything to eat. That would kill him 'cause he dearly loves to eat," Margie added, bringing a laugh from Leona. "And he camped in a dry-wash and a flood washed him clear down to Texas."

"My goodness. You're mean as a cornered cat this morning." Leona smiled to take the bite out of her words.

"I woke up with the feeling that my luck started when we camped here. Everything will be all right, now. I'll manage somehow. I'm so grateful that you will let me stay here for a while."

"I'm not doing you a favor. You're working for your keep, and I'm so glad to have your help. I've been looking at that big garden and wondering how I was going to do all that canning by myself. The girls aren't old enough to be much help." Leona spread a cloth over the bucket of fresh milk.

"Give them a couple of years. They are both smart girls."

"I'll make biscuits if you'll slice bacon. We've had eggs every morning. Let's have gravy with the biscuits. Yates won't care. He'll eat anything as long as it doesn't bite him first, and there's biscuits to go with it."

It was while Margie was setting the table that Leona said, "We'll let the girls sleep a while longer this morning. They can eat later."

"Ruth Ann was up when I got up."

"That's odd." Leona put the pan of biscuits in the oven. "I usually have to pry her out of the bed. She's the sleepy head. There's a crock of butter in the icebox. I'll open a jar of plum butter."

"I thought she'd gone to the privy, but I didn't see her."

"She may have gone to the front porch. The breeze is there if there is one."

Leona was carrying hot biscuits to the table when she said, "Would you mind telling Yates breakfast is ready?"

"He's at the water pump. I saw him pass by the window."

"He may come in, but call to him if he doesn't. I'll round up Ruth Ann. As long as she's up she might as well eat with us. I'll save something back for JoBeth."

Leona peeked into the girls' bedroom thinking Ruth Ann might have gone back to bed. JoBeth lay alone, curled up on the top sheet, sound asleep. Passing through the house,

Leona glanced into the front bedroom and the living room before stepping out onto the porch.

"Ruthy," she called toward the garage, then walked down the path and looked in the back door. She called again. When she received no answer, she circled the garage. If she wasn't here she had to be in the privy, the barn or the chicken house.

Leona didn't even have to open the door of the privy to know that Ruth Ann wasn't in there. The door was latched on the outside. She opened it anyway. Irritated, Leona left the privy and headed for the barn. If Ruth Ann was hiding out and sulking because Margie was here, she was going to give her a good scolding.

Irritation turned to sudden panic when, after searching the out-buildings, including the barn and loft, there was no sign of the child. She hurried to the house, jumped up onto the porch and threw open the screendoor.

"I can't find her!"

Yates was standing in the kitchen with a cup of coffee in his hand. He never sat down at the table until Leona and the girls sat down unless the table was set just for him. He saw the panic on her face and set his cup aside.

"Can't find—"

"Ruth Ann. I can't find her." Leona's voice rose to a near hysterical pitch. "She wasn't in bed when Margie got up. She thought she'd gone to the privy. She's not in the garage, not in the barn. Something has happened to her! I just know it—"

Yates reached her in two strides and grabbed her shoulders. "Calm down. If you're thinking Virgil has been here, you're wrong. He couldn't come on the place without me or Calvin knowing it."

"Then where is she?"

"Where have you looked?"

"Barn, chicken house, garage, everywhere—"

"Cellar?"

"She can't lift the door. I can hardly lift it."

"Would she deliberately hide from you?"

"She never has. She was upset last night . . . because of Virgil and . . . other things."

"Upset enough to run off?"

"I don't think so. Surely not."

"I'll take a look around. Wake up JoBeth and see if Ruth Ann said anything to her about running away or hiding."

"I'm scared that Virgil—"

"Don't be scared, honey. We'll find her."

The endearment didn't even register with Leona. She closed her eyes and leaned her forehead against his chest for an instant and thanked God he was here.

"After the rain last night, there may be tracks. Stay on the porch and let me see if I can find anything."

Yates circled the house once, then again in a wider circle. Leona waited on the porch, her heart in her throat. Margie brought JoBeth to her. The bewildered child stood rubbing her eyes. Leona squatted down and put her arms around her.

"Honey, we can't find Ruth Ann. Did she say anything to you about going somewhere?"

"Uh-uh."

"Did you wake up this morning when she got out of the bed?"

"Uh-uh. Where'd she go?"

"We don't know—"

"Leona, come here." Yates called from out past the privy.

"Stay with Margie." Leona stepped off the porch and hurried to where Yates was squatting down.

"Here's a small footprint. Take a look and see if it could be Ruth Ann's."

"It could be," Leona said, after bending and looking at the indention in the dirt. "That's about the size of her shoes."

"She went into the woods."

"By herself?"

"Looks like it. A man would be heavy enough to leave prints." He put his arm across her shoulders and hugged her briefly. "Stop worrying. I could look for more prints, but I doubt I'd find any. There's not much bare ground in the woods. I'm betting she went through the woods and came out onto the road. I'll walk down the highway and see if I can find where she came out.

"I found her tracks," he said a few minutes later. "I'll take the car and go toward town."

"I'll go with you."

"Do you want to leave Margie and JoBeth here alone?" They were walking toward Yates's car, his arm still across her shoulders. "It'll be better if you stay here. Ruth Ann may come back on her own or someone may bring her home. The ice man is due. He may have seen her. If not, you can tell him or anyone else who comes along to keep an eye out."

"I'm so scared. What if she's been picked up on the highway by a kidnapper and . . . and taken away? Oh, poor Andy has already had so much grief."

He shook her gently. "Don't think about that. We'll find her. And if she's hiding I may turn her over my knee and give her a paddling, then give you one for worrying." His attempt to get a smile out of Leona failed. He got into his car. "I'll go into town and if I don't find her, I'll go to the sheriff. Surely he isn't as big an idiot as his deputy."

"If you don't find her, go to the Fleming Ranch and tell Deke and Mr. Fleming."

"Good idea. Deke on his motorcycle could cover a lot of

territory. But I don't think it'll come to that. One little girl can't have gone far."

"Please find her." Leona backed away from the car and watched as Yates turned out onto the highway. "Hurry," she called, knowing that he couldn't hear her, but somehow she needed to say the word.

Yates drove slowly along the highway, his eyes searching the area back from the road on both sides. He hadn't known many children, but Andy's had wriggled their way into his heart. He had thought all little children were happy-go-lucky like JoBeth with an occasional spell of mischief that lasted only a short time.

Ruth Ann was different. He had seen her truly happy on only two occasions—when she was with her daddy and while splashing in the water tank. He was puzzled as to what would cause her to leave the security of her home with the threat of Virgil hanging over the family.

Yates drove slowly into town. The only people who were about were the merchants preparing to open their stores. A few cars were parked around the courthouse square. It didn't take long for him to travel the length of the town and back. On a sudden impulse, he stopped at the courthouse and went into the sheriff's office.

"Howdy." The office door was open. The sheriff was shuffling through papers on his desk. He looked up.

"Mornin'."

"Name's Yates." Yates stepped into the room.

The sheriff stood and held out his hand. "Rex McChesney. What can I do for you?"

The thought passed through Yates's mind that the sheriff was a cut above his deputy. He was tall with a clean-shaven face, dark hair and even rugged features.

"I'm working out at the garage while Andy Connors is in the hospital."

"I've heard about you. How is Andy?"

"Doing all right. His eight-year-old daughter walked away from home this morning. I'm sure that she left on her own. I tracked her into the woods and then found where she came out and walked down the highway. I've looked all over town."

"We'll keep an eye out. She may have gone to a friend or a relative."

"Mornin'." Wayne came into the office. He spoke to the sheriff and scowled at Yates.

"Mornin' to you, too, Deputy," Yates said, in a deliberate attempt to emphasize the man's rudeness.

"What's he doin' here?" Wayne asked.

The sheriff frowned. "Andy Connors's little girl ran off."

"Yeah? What's it to him? He ain't her daddy."

"Wayne, what the hell's wrong with you?"

"Nothin's wrong with me."

"Sorry to bother you, Sheriff, with such a minor thing as a child missing." Yates screwed his hat down on his head. He stepped out of the office and headed for the door.

"Yates," the sheriff called. "If you don't find her by night, come back in and we'll organize a search."

"That's mighty decent of you, Sheriff."

"It's the law. I'm short-handed—"

Yates whirled around and faced him. "I'm warning you, Sheriff. If I find out your fat-assed deputy and that crazy, Bible-thumpin' Virgil Dawson had anything to do with luring Ruth Ann away or keeping her from coming home, I'll have the FBI swarming over this town like a cloud of locusts. Kidnapping is a federal crime, in case you didn't know it."

"Kidnapping? I thought you said she walked away from home this morning."

"She did . . . as far as I know now. Good day, Sheriff. I'll organize my own searching party."

The sheriff watched the tall man go through the courthouse door, then turned back to his office.

"What's between you and that man, Wayne?"

"Nothin' that ain't lawful."

"Well, hell. What did you do that was lawful to get him riled?"

"Virgil Dawson wanted to see his sister and his dead sister's children. This fellow 'bout ruined him. Threw him and Abe Patton off the place."

"Did Virgil sign a complaint?"

"No."

"Then that's the end of it. Don't be messing in a family argument or with that fellow unless you're sure he's broke the law."

"He's either a fed or a bootlegger. I've not decided which."

"What gave you that idea?"

"Does he look or act like a bum off the road who'd take a job in Andy's garage?"

"He doesn't look like a bum, that's sure."

"He says he's Andy's cousin, but I don't believe it. You know as well as I do that Andy couldn't afford to pay him wages. Betcha he's gettin' his pay outta Leona's pants. Virgil says she's got a twitchy twat."

"I don't like that kind of talk, Wayne." The sheriff looked up as the doctor came into the office. "Mornin', Doc."

"Mornin', Rex. We've got a diphtheria epidemic on our hands. I just came from Virgil Dawson's. One of his kids is down with it. I've quarantined the house. I let Virgil out, but if he goes back in, he stays."

"What can I do, Doc?"

"I need to get these cultures to the city." The doctor placed a package on the desk.

"Bus comes through here in about an hour. I'll phone and have a deputy meet the bus."

"Another thing, Sheriff. The sick child has marks all across his little back from a vicious beating with a strop. I'm reporting this to you now, and I'm also going to report it to Mabel Bassett, a woman in Oklahoma City who is heading a drive to make cruelty to a woman or a child a felony."

Sheriff McChesney looked blank for a minute, then said, "Do what you have to do, Doctor."

"That bird better watch himself," Wayne muttered as soon as the doctor left. "He ain't got no business stickin' his nose in when a man takes a rod to his kid."

"He has plenty of business sticking his nose in when a man lays it on a little boy, like he was a mule. I'd like to nail that brainless fool's hide to a barndoor myself." Sheriff McChesney angrily slammed out of the office.

The deputy watched him leave and fervently wished for a cigarette, but didn't dare light one for fear one of the church members would come by. If one of them caught him smoking, it'd be all over the church by noon that he'd backslid.

Yates drove back down the highway, hoping against hope that Ruth Ann would be at the garage when he reached it. He knew that she was not when he saw Leona standing beside the gas pump. She was at the car before he could get out.

"You didn't find her. Where did you look?"

"All over town. I talked to a few people including the

sheriff. He said if she wasn't back by this afternoon, he'd organize a search."

"This afternoon?" Tears that she couldn't hold back flooded her eyes. "She could be a long way by then."

"I know. We won't wait. Give me directions to the Fleming Ranch. I'll get Deke. He knows the country far better than I do."

"I'll go. And I'll ask Mr. Fleming to help. Ruth Ann and his daughter, Marie, are friends."

"Would Ruth Ann have gone out there?"

"It's about seven miles, but . . . she might have gone to ask Mr. Fleming to take her to the city to see Andy. She took her good dress and a pair of white stockings. She wore the dress she wore yesterday."

"Did something happen to upset her . . . more than usual?"

"She didn't like Margie being here. She didn't want her to sleep in her mother's bed, so I slept there and Margie in my bed. Ruth Ann was rude to poor Margie. I had to scold her. She remembers her mother and how it used to be, and she doesn't want any other woman in the house besides me."

"That would make it hard if Andy ever remarried."

"He wouldn't do it if it would make the girls unhappy."

"That's hardly fair to Andy."

"I know, but his children come first. They are all he has left of Irene. I'll take his car and go see if Ruth Ann went to the Flemings'." When Leona turned away, Yates's hand came down lightly on her shoulder.

"I know how worried you are. I'm worried, too, but we must hold onto the belief that she's all right."

Leona allowed him to pull her to him. She wrapped her arms around his waist and leaned her forehead against his shoulder.

"I'm so glad you're here." Yates barely heard the whispered confession.

"So am I, sweetheart. So am I." He bent his head and pressed his lips to her temple. Yates was aware of the blast from a horn as a car passed on the highway. The driver had seen them standing beside the gas pump with their arms around each other.

"I'm afraid. What if we have to tell Andy we've lost her? It'll kill him."

"It won't come to that. We'll find her." He held her away from him so that he could look into her face. It was streaked with tears. He wanted to kiss them away but knew that this wasn't the time or the place. "Take JoBeth with you. I'll lock up the garage and the gas pump and tell Margie to stay in the house and watch in case someone picks Ruth Ann up and brings her back. Bring Andy's car around and let me check it for gas before I lock up the pump."

"What are you going to do?"

"I have a few things in mind. I'll meet you back here at noon."

"Do you think Virgil—?"

"No, honey. I don't think so, but I'm going to make sure."

"Maybe I should do that?"

"No. Let me."

Her hands grasped his arms just above his elbows, and she looked searchingly into the face tilted down toward hers.

"You're like a rock. I don't know what I'd do if you weren't here." The last words were uttered like a cry of pain. She broke loose from him and ran toward the house.

Chapter 20

YATES FOLLOWED LEONA IN ANDY'S CAR until she turned off the highway on the hard-packed dirt road that led to the Fleming Ranch. No other woman had ever stayed in his thoughts the way Leona Dawson stuck there. It seemed to him that he was constantly trying to analyze his feelings for her or hers for him.

One thing he knew without a doubt—he had never felt as possessive about anything as he did about her. He was worried and anxious about Ruth Ann being gone, but he hurt deep in his heart because Leona hurt. He had this terrible desire to shield her, take care of her. He liked to look at her, too, watch her move, hear her laugh. At times he couldn't keep his eyes off her.

Now what the hell did it mean? It means, you fool, that you want to take her to bed.

He hungered for a woman the same as any other man. If she allowed him to make love to her, would that be the end of his interest in her? Would he be able to leave without a backward glance when Andy returned? He didn't think so. He was afraid that he was already in too deeply for that.

On reaching town, Yates's first stop was at the post office.

The man behind the counter wore a visor cap and was sorting mail.

"Howdy. Any mail for H. L. Yates?"

"Yup. How's Andy doing?"

"Pretty good."

"Another letter from San Angelo. Got relatives there?"

"I've got relatives scattered all over Texas." Yates put the letter in his pocket. "I'm looking for Virgil Dawson. Can you tell me where he lives?"

"Sure. Go to the end of the next street"—he raised a pointed finger—"turn right. It's the last house. Sits out there by itself. Years ago it was in the country, but the town is growing out to it. There'll be a red sign on it. The doctor put a quarantine on the house this morning. Virgil's kid got the diphtheria."

"Yeah? Too bad."

"Got six cases in the area. Doc might shut off church meetings and such. It's goin' to put a damper on the Fourth of July celebration."

"That's right. It's coming up in about a week." Yates thought a minute, then asked, "Where's the doctor's office?"

"Upstairs over the bank."

"Thanks."

Yates sat in his car and quickly read the letter from his lawyer in San Angelo. He replayed in his mind the last part of it as he started the car and headed for the telephone office. *My advice to you is, come on down here to San Angelo and wait it out. It won't be long. When it happens, Mrs. Taylor will take everything that isn't nailed down.*

It took almost ten minutes for the call to go through to San Angelo. Ten minutes later he went back to his car and drove to the red-brick bank on the corner. He nodded to the old fellows sitting on the bench in front of the bank, then took the iron steps two at a time up the side of the red-brick building. At the top he paused in front of the frosted glass door before opening it to read: FOREST LANGLEY, M.D.

The office, cooled by a ceiling fan, was empty. He stood for a minute, then rapped on the desk. The door leading to another part of the office opened immediately.

"I'm sorry. I didn't hear you come in." The nurse was a young woman with rosy cheeks and a plump figure. A starched cap with a black stripe was perched on her head.

"Is the doctor in?"

"He is, but he's getting ready to go out. Is there something I can do for you?"

"No, ma'am. I just had a quick question for the doctor."

"He was checking his bag, he'll be out . . . oh, here he is—" She cut off her words when a man came from the back room. He wore wire-rimmed glasses, a white shirt and tie and carried a black bag. He was younger than Yates had expected.

"Doctor, I'll make it fast. I understand you have something near an epidemic on your hands."

"Six cases in this small area *is* an epidemic."

"Ruth Ann Connors is missing. She was troubled over something at home and left this morning. I understand that you put a quarantine sign on Virgil Dawson's house. Did you see the girl there?"

"There wasn't a girl there. I swabbed the throats of three boys. I believe Mrs. Dawson would have told me if there were any other children in the house."

"Was Virgil Dawson quarantined?"

"No. He hadn't spent time with the sick boy and wasn't likely to carry the germ, so I let him go. What are you getting at, Mr.—?"

"Yates. I'm helping at the garage while Andy Connors is

in the hospital getting hydrophobia shots. We stopped here the day he was bitten by a skunk. The nurse told us that you were far out in the country delivering a baby."

"I couldn't have helped him if I'd been here. You did right to get him to the city."

"Virgil Dawson has been out to the house twice since I've been there. He wants to take Andy's girls home and raise them because, according to his beliefs, they're not living in a decent home. I'm checking to see if he has anything to do with Ruth Ann being gone."

The doctor snorted with disgust. "I know Andy Connors. He's a hell of a better father than Virgil Dawson. I'm on my way out there now. I'll look around, but I doubt she's there."

"Thanks, Doctor."

The men went down the steps together. The doctor went to his car, Yates to the grocery store.

"Mr. Yates." The grocer came from behind the meat counter with a friendly greeting.

"Mornin', Mr. White," Yates said politely.

"What can I do for you this fine summer morning? Rain cooled things off a bit. It's sure to help the grassland."

"Ruth Ann Connors, Andy's girl, is missing. I'm offering a twenty-five-dollar reward to the one who brings her home safe and sound. I'm asking you to spread the word to anyone who comes to the store."

"Twenty-five dollars? My, my, that'll get the attention of folks. What happened to the child? Did she run off? I've always feared that no good would come from those children—"

Yates's sharp words cracked like a whip and cut the grocer off in mid-sentence. "Don't say that Ruth Ann is not being raised in a decent home, Mr. White. I'm not in the mood to hear it."

"I didn't mean—"

"I'm sure you did, but we'll let it go for now. Good day, White."

Yates made the rounds of the stores ending at the barber shop. After hearing of Ruth Ann's being missing and the reward being offered for her return, a man getting a haircut spoke.

"First place I'd look would be along the river where the tramps camp out. If those lazy beggars get hold of a little girl, there ain't nothing too nasty for them to do to her."

The barber stopped clipping. "For God's sake, Frank, why'd ya have to say that?"

"It's the bald truth."

"Well, it ain't somethin' a body wants to hear when a kid is missin'."

"So long, gents. I'd appreciate it if you'd spread the word." Yates backed out of the barber shop and headed for his car.

It was in the back of his mind that Ruth Ann could have been picked up on the highway and be out of the state by now. He decided to make another trip to the sheriff's office. He met the sheriff as he was coming out of the courthouse.

"Sheriff, I'm offering a twenty-five-dollar reward for anyone who brings Ruth Ann home. How can I spread the word?"

"I think you're a little hasty offering a reward. She's not been gone eight hours. But the size of the reward should start folks talking. If she's not home by tomorrow we can notify the federal marshal."

"I don't intend to sit on my hands and wait until tomorrow. Where is this place where the hoboes stop when passing through here?"

"Across the railroad tracks and along the road that runs parallel with the river. Wayne checks it out once in a while.

He isn't in now, but I'll find out if he checked it this morning or not."

"Speaking of your deputy, how did you happen to hire such a shithead? He's about as pleasant as a boil on a cowboy's butt."

Sheriff McChesney laughed. "He does strike some folks that way, but he's a dedicated officer."

"He's working with Virgil Dawson to get Andy's girls away from him."

"He and Virgil are friends, but I don't think—"

"I do. And it isn't going to happen. I'll go to the state attorney general if necessary. We'll take it to court, and you might find out some things about both Virgil and your deputy that you don't want to know. Or do you?"

The sheriff pursed his lips, cocked his head and looked into Yates's cold, steel-colored eyes. He said nothing for a few seconds, then, "I heard that you're Andy's cousin."

"I've not been around much, but I owe Andy plenty. I'm going to see that his girls are here when he comes home. You'd better make that plain to your deputy in case he gets a notion to bring crazy Virgil out to the garage again and threaten to take Andy's girls from Miss Dawson."

"When did he do that?"

"Last night. I heard every word of it and will swear to it in court if it comes to that."

"Hmmmm."

"Another thing. If I ever again hear of your deputy referring to Miss Dawson as a whore, I'll go to the state attorney general and have his badge pulled. Then when he's no longer under the umbrella of the law, I'll make him wish he'd been born a jackass instead of acting like one."

"I hope you find that the Connors girl has been hiding somewhere," the sheriff called as Yates walked away.

He liked the sheriff and hoped that he had given him a few things to think about. Yates realized that there wasn't much McChesney could do right now about Ruth Ann. The sheriff probably had had reports of runaway kids every few weeks and most of them had come back home on their own or had gotten in touch with their folks.

Following the directions given him by the postmaster, Yates drove slowly down the road toward Virgil's house. He remembered Deke's telling him that Leona had walked barefoot five miles to where her sister lived at that time after Virgil had given her a beating.

He tamped down his anger, wanting to keep a cool head.

The doctor was driving away as Yates approached the big square house with the wrap-around porch. Yates stopped, and the doctor stopped beside him.

"The girl isn't there. Mrs. Dawson is about to go to pieces worrying about her boy. I'm sure she'd have told me if there was another child in the house."

"How is the boy?"

"I'm afraid he won't make it. I got to him too late. Twelve hours would have made the difference. He was burning up with so high a fever that even the most ignorant fool had to know the boy needed a doctor." The doctor was plainly frustrated. "Too bad Dawson can't be charged with murder."

After the doctor drove on, Yates continued down the road. He paused and looked at the unkempt homestead. Lumber and an assortment of machine parts were piled on the porch. Weeds grew in the yard up to the porch, and holes were punched in some of the window screens.

Yates turned onto a lane running alongside the house and drove to the back where he could see a huge woodpile and a truck with a buzz saw mounted on the bed.

Virgil was working the saw. Abe Patton, the man who

was with him when he came out to torment Leona, was helping him. A pile of cut wood was growing beside a shed. Yates sat and watched him. Virgil continued to work, ignoring Yates, until Yates opened the car door to get out. Leaving the noisy saw going, Virgil walked quickly toward the car. Abe stood silently watching.

"What'd you want here?"

"I just wanted to see where a brainless idiot lived, that's all. Place looks like a pigsty, Virgil. Maybe if you prayed, the Lord would clean it up for you."

"Get off my property."

"And if I don't, you'll call that poor, addle-brained deputy sheriff. What do you have on him, anyway? Are the two of you running booze?"

"The law's the law. This is my property and I want ya off it right now."

"I'll get off when I get damn good and ready. Unless you think you can run me off like I did you when you came out to Andy's."

"I'm a God-fearin' man. Yo're a heathen!"

"Yeah, I know. I'd rather be a heathen than a pious, rotten bastard like you. You're a sorry son-of-a-bitch, Virgil. So are your friends." Yates sent an angry glance at the silent man beside the truck. He had to yell over the noise made by the buzz saw to be heard.

"Go on. Leave." Virgil picked up a stick of wood and made a gesture as if to throw it at the car.

"Throw that and I'll be looking for you some dark night and nail your balls to a tree stump and push you over backward."

Virgil dropped the wood and went back to the buzz saw. Yates watched him and the ignorant lout with him for a minute and wondered for the tenth time how such a stupid, mean bastard could be related to Leona. Finally, he slammed the car door and drove down the lane to the road vowing that someday soon Virgil and he were going to tangle, and he intended to use every trick he'd learned fighting in the tough dives spread along Route 66 from Tulsa to California.

Yates took the highway back to the garage after driving down the river road to take a look at the hobo camp. He tramped amid the bean cans and whiskey bottles and saw no sign of a child having been there. It had been a long shot, anyway. A bum wouldn't have had the means to get a child there without being seen.

Mr. Fleming's big black car was parked in front of the garage, as was Deke's motorcycle, when Yates pulled in off the highway and stopped. Leona, holding JoBeth, jumped up from the bench beside the garage and came to meet him. Her eyes were large, sad and questioning.

"She's not at Virgil's. His boy is bad sick with diphtheria. The house is quarantined. I talked to the doctor, and he said there wasn't a girl in the house."

Yates reached out and took JoBeth from Leona's arms. The child went to him and wrapped her arms around his neck. Together they walked to where Barker Fleming, Deke and several other men were standing. Yates told them where he had been, what he had done and about the diphtheria epidemic.

He finished with, "We'd better keep JoBeth away from other children. There's talk of shutting down church services and other public meetings."

Before Yates finished talking tears were streaming down Leona's face. She knew that she had to get a hold of herself. Crying wouldn't do any good.

"What . . . can we do?" Her tear-filled eyes went first to Yates, then to Deke and Barker Fleming.

"Don't cry, darlin'." Deke threw his cigarette to the ground and stepped on it, before he took Leona's hand and put an arm around her shoulders. "We'll find her. Ya just got to hold on like ya've done before when bad thin's happened."

"A dozen men are coming on horseback," Barker Fleming said. "They can cover a lot of territory." He looked at Yates. "Sheriff McChesney is a good man, but he doesn't have the manpower to spread out and look for a lost child."

"He thinks she ran away and will come back."

"I'm afraid someone picked her up in a car. . . ." Leona clung to Deke's hand.

"Ya better come eat somethin', darlin'. Margie's got a meal ready."

"You all go ahead. I'll stay here . . . in case somebody comes."

"Go eat, Miss Dawson. I'll be here," Barker Fleming said. "Waiting for my men."

It was one of the worst days in Leona's life. The uncertainty of not knowing what had happened to Ruth Ann tore at her and disabled her. She was grateful that Margie, in her quiet way, had taken over the cooking, the chores, and the care of JoBeth when the child wasn't clinging to Leona's or Yates's neck.

The poor child was totally distraught. She crawled up into Leona's lap and patted her cheek.

"Don't cry, Aunt Lee. I'll give Ruth Ann my crayons when she comes back."

Leona hugged her tightly. "That's sweet of you, honey."

"I just feel so bad," Margie said as she dried a glass and placed it on the table alongside a pitcher of iced tea. "She didn't want me here. If I'd gone on, she'd not have run off."

"We don't know that for sure. I'm glad you're here. I don't know what I'd have done without you and . . . Yates."

"I'll leave as soon as she comes back. I've been thinking that maybe if I can get on over into Texas I could get a job cooking on a ranch . . . or something."

"Oh, Margie, I don't want you to leave unless you have something to go to. Have you thought about going back to Conway?"

"I might have to, but I'll just die having . . . everyone know what a fool I'd been going off with Ernie and losing Grandma's money. It'll be hard to face . . . certain people."

As the afternoon wore on, Leona sat dully on the bench in front of the garage. Yates talked to everyone who stopped, asking them to keep an eye out for an eight-year-old blond-haired girl in a blue dress. Deke roared in on his motorcycle to report the Fleming men had searched the area east of the river and were starting on the west side.

"Most of 'em, darlin', are Cherokee—the best trackers there are. Mr. Fleming phoned the sheriff over in Amarillo. I'm goin' to take a swing through the woods over by Virgil's. He could have her hid out somewhere."

As evening approached, Leona's face was haggard with worry. She clutched Yates's hand at every opportunity, needing to feel his strength.

"By tomorrow we'll have to call and tell Andy. It'll kill him if we don't find her."

Yates put an arm around her and drew her close. "We'll worry about that tomorrow."

"He'll come home even if he hasn't had all his shots."

"Of course, he will. So we'll put off telling him as long as we can."

"I've been trying to understand why she ran away. Since her mother died, she's afraid of any change."

"I know. She didn't want me here at first, but I think she's over that now."

"Now it's Margie. Margie feels bad about it."

"Ruth Ann may have a change of heart when she comes home."

"I hope she comes home. I keep thinking what . . . if she doesn't."

Yates put a finger beneath her chin and lifted her face. She knew his eyes were on her, but she kept her eyes glued to his mouth. It was such a beautiful mouth.

"She'll come home. You've got to believe that. Sweet woman, I'd give ten years of my life if I could bring her to you right now."

She raised her eyes to his. "How could I have doubted that . . . you were anything but kind and good."

His mouth quirked into a beguiling grin, and his eyes sparkled with pleasure. "I've not shown you my bad side yet."

"I'm not sure you have one. I'm sorry for the mean things I said."

He laughed. "You weren't mean, just sassy."

"I'm not as trusting as Andy."

"I can't blame you for that. I guess I was pretty high-handed."

"You set my teeth on edge with your closed-mouthed, take-over attitude."

"I was here to do a job, and that's all there was to it until . . . I met you. And you were lippy. It made me like you all the more." He cupped her face with his hands and with his thumbs wiped the tears from beneath her eyes.

"If you'd have known what all you were going to get into when you came here, would you have come?"

"On my knees, if that was the only way I could get here." He bent his head and gently brushed his lips along her forehead.

Chapter 21

AT DUSK ISAAC CAME INTO THE ROOM where his mother had spent the day by Paul's bed, leaving only to get a drink of water. She was fanning him now with a newspaper.

"Ma, Pa's been to the store. He went in the shed with a sack."

"Did he leave ice on the porch?"

"Yes, ma'am. I put it in the box. How's Paul?"

Hazel's work-worn hand smoothed the hair back from her son's flushed face. The child's mouth was open, and he was gasping for every breath. Tears blurred Hazel's vision and ran down her wrinkled, sun-browned cheeks.

She said in a husky voice, "He's bad, Isaac, and there ain't nothin' I can do. I'm losin' him. I'm losin' all my boys."

"I'm here, Mama."

"You'll go like yore brothers when yo're old enough to make it on yore own. I shoulda stood up for all of ya more'n I done. Then maybe Joseph and Peter wouldn't'a left."

"Joseph feared he'd kill Pa if he stayed."

"Ah, he wouldn't of. I shoulda—"

"Ya couldn't a bucked him, Mama?"

"I tried . . . once."

"I remember. Ya couldn't get out of bed for three days," Isaac said bitterly. "Can I get ya somethin' to eat?"

"No, but ya can give the boys somethin'."

"I already did. They've been stayin' on the front porch."

"They're good boys. Have ya been feelin' their heads like I told ya?"

"Yes, ma'am. They ain't hot like Paul was. Pa's been in back sawin' wood all day."

"He's had that blasted saw goin' all day. Most sawin' he's done in a month."

"Sometimes Pa is mean as a ruttin' moose. Why does he whip us so hard? Why'd he whip Paul?"

"He thinks he's doin' the right thin'."

"If that's the right thin', Ma, I ain't ever goin' to church when I leave here."

"Don't talk like that," Hazel said sharply. "God will strike you down."

"Eugene Johnson's pa ain't like him. He doesn't hit Eugene with a strop or make him go to bed without his supper. And they have baseball games out at their house on Sunday afternoons. Why can't Pa be like Mr. Johnson?"

"It's sinful to play games on Sunday. The Bible says to keep the Sabbath holy."

"It also says to forgive yore enemies, Ma. Why can't Pa forgive Aunt Leona for runnin' off? Why does he hate her so much?"

Hazel looked at her son as if seeing him for the first time. Isaac had grown up. He would be leaving soon. Dear Lord, where had the time gone? It seemed only yesterday that he was a baby boy. Now, he was thinking on his own and asking questions.

At that moment one of the boys ran in to say the doctor had arrived.

* * *

The search for Ruth Ann was called off at dark. Mr. Fleming and his riders had met back at the garage and, after making plans to return in the morning, headed back to the ranch. At Barker Fleming's suggestion, Deke stayed. He tended the garage while Yates did the chores. Between the two of them they kept Leona in sight.

The family that pulled off the highway to spend the night in the campground was from Broken Bow, Oklahoma. This was the first night of their journey to California. The four children, although tired, were still excited about the trip and ran around the low-pitched tent playing tag. When Deke told the parents about Ruth Ann's being missing, the father herded his children together, and in a stern voice told them to stay close, then asked if there was anything he could do to help find the child.

"When ya leave tomorrow, keep your eyes open for a eight-year-old, blond, curly-haired little girl in a blue dress."

"We'll sure do that, mister. We sure will. I sure do hope ya find her."

Sheriff McChesney came by to say that if Ruth Ann hadn't come home by morning, he would notify the federal marshals.

"They've already been notified, Sheriff," Yates said. "Barker Fleming called the Texas authorities, and I called Oklahoma City. I didn't see any reason to wait."

The sheriff's face turned red with anger. "A runaway usually comes home within twenty-four hours."

"This is an eight-year-old girl. Damn it, I don't understand this twenty-four-hour shit." Yates was getting more and more agitated. "Were you waiting to give that dumb-ass deputy of yours time to pray her home or to find her and give her to that clabber-brained Virgil Dawson?"

"It's standard procedure to wait twenty-four hours whether you like it or not."

"Well, hell. I don't like it."

"I know you're worried, but I've got a lot more on my plate then one runaway kid." He turned to speak to Leona, who sat on the porch steps with her head down. "The children in town are at risk from diphtheria, Miss Dawson," he said, looking to where JoBeth was clinging to Margie's hand. "Keep the little one away from other children."

With a blank expression on her face, Leona watched the sheriff leave. Her heart felt like a stone in her chest. She sat only until he was on the highway, then jumped up and walked quickly to the edge of the woods.

Deke was worried about Ruth Ann, but he was also worried about Leona. She hadn't eaten or sat down for more than a minute or two at a time. He watched her now prowling from the fence line to the edge of the road and back again. It would be pitch-dark in five more minutes. Would she come back then?

Yates came out of the garage, his eyes on the white blur at the edge of the woods.

"She's goin' to pieces." Deke put the lid back on the can of axle grease he'd used to grease the chains on the porch swing. "Gawd-damm-it, Yates. It tears me up to see her like this."

"Margie is taking it hard, too. She thinks Ruth Ann ran away because of her being here." Yates nodded toward where Margie sat with JoBeth cuddled in her lap. "She says she's leaving as soon as Ruth Ann comes back."

"Lord, she can't no more take care of herself than JoBeth. I hate to see a nice girl like that take her suitcase and walk down the road. Some sidewinder'll pick her up and no tellin' what'll happen to her."

"You could marry her," Yates said, and started across the yard to the woods.

"Ain't but one woman for me, bucko," Deke muttered to Yates's back. "I'm thinkin' ya got yore eye on her. If she takes ya, ya'd better treat her right or ya'll answer to me."

Yates only vaguely heard Deke mumbling to himself; his eyes were on Leona. It seemed to him that she had lost ten pounds today. Already slender as a reed, she now looked as if a stiff wind could blow her over. She had not changed the house dress that swirled around her bare legs since morning. All she had done when she went to the Fleming Ranch had been to whip off her apron.

Yates knew that he had not the words that would comfort her. Angered by his inability, cuss words he hadn't used for years floated through his mind as he realized that all he could do would be to assure her that she didn't have to face this terrible situation alone.

Without saying a word, he walked up to her, took her hand and drew her into his arms. She went willingly into his embrace. Her breasts were soft against his chest, her face fit in the curve of his neck. They stood, in the growing darkness, locked together, his hand caressing her back and pressing her to him.

She moved, mumbled, put her arms around him and snuggled closer. The feeling he had for her now was tenderness, a desire to comfort her.

"Ah . . . honey—" Holding her firmly against him, he kissed the top of her head. "It's going to be all right. We'll get her back."

She lay against him docile and unmoving, lifeless as a rag doll. She was no longer the hard-working, spunky, sassy Leona he'd met that first day, nor was she the one who had ripped into him over the portable oven. The woman he held against him was a mere shell of the Leona who had stood up so staunchly against the brother who had hatefully belittled her.

She mumbled again.

He grasped her shoulders and eased her away from him so he could see her face.

"I . . . should've seen it coming. Ruth Ann wasn't the same after Andy left."

"You couldn't have known what was in her mind. Don't blame yourself."

"What'll we do if we don't find her?" Her voice was a ragged whisper, so sad that it tore at his heart. Utter, complete misery was etched on her face.

"We won't think of that now. Let's think of what we'll do when she comes home. We'll take the girls to a carnival on the Fourth, and to the barnstorming show a couple weeks later. By then Andy will be coming home."

There was a lot he liked about this woman, he thought now as he looked down into her face. He liked the way her dark auburn hair, tangled from the wind, curled about her pale face. He liked her quick mind, the way she looked, smelled and talked. He liked her full expressive mouth, the way the corners tilted up when she smiled. He bent his head to kiss her, but straightened, not wanting to take advantage of her vulnerability.

A shaky, weakening, delicious fear that his life had changed forever spread all through him. She had been in his head day and night since the day he met her. His need for her astonished him.

The pain behind Leona's eyes caused her to close them for a long moment. Yates's face was close to hers when she opened them. He placed a gentle kiss on her trembling lips. The temptation to have someone share her troubles, no matter how fleetingly, was too great. She leaned against him and felt once again his protecting arms around her. Her head pounded, her mind was awash with fear.

She was so tired.

It was dark when Doctor Langley returned to the Dawson house. From the road it appeared to be completely dark. He was glad to see the old truck with the buzz saw mounted on the back was not there. An intense dislike for Virgil Dawson had been building up inside him since he had seen the strop marks on the boy's back.

Isaac let the doctor into the house and led him through the dark rooms to the back where one kerosene lamp was burning. Mrs. Dawson sat beside her son's bed. A bowl of chipped ice was on the table beside her. She moved out of the way to make room for the doctor and watched anxiously as he examined her son.

"Is he any better?" Hazel asked fearfully after the doctor moved back from the bed and began putting his instruments back in his bag.

"I'm afraid not, Mrs. Dawson."

"Is there a hospital or . . . someplace we can take him?"

"No, ma'am," he said gently. "I gave him the antitoxin. It's all I can do. I have another call to make, then I'll come back and sit with you." He placed a comforting hand on her shoulder as he passed her. "I won't be gone long."

Isaac went to the door with the doctor. "Is Paul goin' to die?"

"Yes, son. I'm afraid he is. He would have had a chance if I could have vaccinated him in time."

"It wasn't Ma's fault. Pa wouldn't call you. Ma had five dollars to pay—" Isaac choked back a sob.

"I understand. You've got to keep a stiff upper lip so that you can help your mother. Are the younger boys in bed?"

"Yes, sir. I bedded them down in Pa's bed. I've been feelin' their head to see if they were hot."

The doctor nodded his approval. "Is your electricity not working?"

"Pa turned it off out on the pole. But we've got lots of lamps. I'll light them."

"Do that. Take another one in to your mother, leave one in the kitchen and one in the front room. I'll be back in about an hour."

Isaac stood for a minute after the doctor left. He was ashamed of the tears that filled his eyes and rolled down his cheeks. It had been pounded into him from an early age that it was shameful for boys to cry. But Paul, his little brother who liked to draw and loved going to school, was going to die. He'd never again swing on the sack down by the creek or climb his favorite tree or play with the slingshot Joseph had made for him.

Pa had whipped Paul for thumbing his nose at Maudie. She'd tattled to her mother, and old Sister Blanchard had come storming to Pa Sunday morning. Paul didn't even know what it meant to put his thumb to his nose and wave his fingers—nor did Isaac for that matter. He guessed that it meant something nasty.

In his heart eleven-year-old Isaac vowed his pa would never whip him or the younger boys with the strop again. He didn't know what he would do to prevent it, but he'd do something.

Oh, he wished that Joe and Pete were here, they would know what to do.

* * *

"Ma." Isaac stood in the doorway. "The doc told me to light more lamps. I'd turn the electric on at the pole if I knew how."

"Don't mess with the electric on the pole," Hazel said with a catch in her voice. "Ya could electrocute yoreself."

"I'll have to go to the shed and get more kerosene."

"Then go. Take the lantern from the back porch."

Isaac gathered the lamps he would fill and placed them on the kitchen table, then lit the lantern and went out to the shed. Several pieces of cut wood were piled against the door. He set the lantern down and tossed them aside. Then he pulled open the door and picked up the lantern.

What he saw in the shed was so shocking that he jumped back and slammed into a spade leaning against the wall. It toppled to the floor with a loud bang. A girl in a blue dress lay on an old quilt. A rag was tied around her mouth. Her dress and stockings were dirty. Long, blond curls were tangled with twigs. Her eyes, squinted against the sudden light, were filled with tears.

Isaac stared, blinked, then stared again. "What . . . are you doin' in here?"

Being unable to speak because of the rag in her mouth, she shook her head.

"Are you . . . are you Andy Connors's girl?"

The girl bobbed her head.

"Godalmighty! He took you from . . . Aunt Leona. He said he would. Is your sister here?"

Ruth Ann shook her head.

"Stay here. I've got to go tell Ma. Don't be scared," he said when he saw the panic in her eyes. "I'll leave the lantern."

Noises of protest came from the girl's throat when he left her, but he went out and closed the door, placing a stick against it to keep the light from the lantern from shining out. He raced to the house.

"Ma! Ma!" He skidded to a stop at the bedroom door. "There's a little girl . . . in the shed." His voice broke. "She's . . . she's one of Andy Connors's girls."

"What in the world—a little girl?" Hazel leaped to her feet. "One of Andy's?"

"She's got a rag in her mouth and she's tied up."

"Lord, help us! He took Andy's girl," Hazel said as if she couldn't believe it. "It's all he's talked about since Andy went to the hospital."

"She cryin' and scared, Ma. Can I bring her in the house?"

"No," Hazel said quickly. "She can't come in here. The doctor said no one was to come in. You've got to get her out of there before your pa comes back."

"I can't just put her out. She's just a little girl and she's scared."

"Then take her home. Do you know the way?"

"I know the way, but what if we meet Pa?"

"Go through the woods and stay off the streets. Go now. Your pa'll be ravin' mad when he comes home and finds her gone, but he won't come in the house; and if the doctor asks, I'll let on that you've gone to bed. Bring me the kerosene so I can fill the lamps."

"All right, Ma. Let me put my shoes on."

Back in the shed, Isaac knelt down and pulled the rag from Ruth Ann's mouth and untied her hands and feet.

"We got to hurry before my pa comes back. Can you stand up?"

"I want . . . to go . . . home." Sobs clogged the child's throat.

"Stop bawling. I'll take ya home, but first I got to make it look like ya busted out of here."

With his heavy boot Isaac kicked against a loose board time and again. It finally broke. He continued to kick until he made a hole large enough for the small girl to crawl through. Then, he took her hand and pulled her through the door, closed it and piled the stove-wood against it.

"I'm scared." Ruth Ann continued to cry.

"Hush yore bawlin'! Pa'll hang me to a tree and strip the hide off my back if he finds out I let ya out. How long have ya been in there?"

"Since this mornnn . . . ing."

"Have ya had anything to eat?"

"A bisss . . . cuit."

"We don't have time for me to get ya somethin' to eat. Get a drink at the pump." Isaac quickly blew out the lantern and placed it in its customary place on the porch.

Ruth Ann cupped her hands and drank from them while Isaac worked the pump handle. When she finished, he took her hand and hurried her across the road and into the woods.

"Come on, Ruth Ann. That's yore name ain't it?"

"You know it is."

"I don't know when Pa'll be back, so shake a leg."

"Can't we go on the road? I'm . . . scared in the woods."

"Somebody'd see us on the road. Walk fast. I've got to get ya home and get back. My little brother is goin' to die, and I don't want to leave my ma there by herself."

"My mama d-d-di . . . ed."

"Paul is just a little boy."

"What's he dyin' of?"

"The diphtheria."

"You're Isaac. I've seen you at school."

"Yeah."

"I hate Uncle Virgil."

"Can't blame ya for that."

"It's scary in the woods."

"Don't worry. I won't let anythin' hurt ya. Ya won't tell anyone I took ya home, will ya?"

"Not if you don't want me to."

"All he's talked about was gettin' you and your sister away from Aunt Lee. It'll make him crazy when he finds out you got away. If he knew I helped ya, he'd whip me for sure. Might . . . even kill me."

"I won't tell, I promise."

"Don't tell anyone, not even yore Aunt Leona, where ya've been."

"She wouldn't tell—"

"Don't tell her, I said. I'd have to leave home, and I ought to stay and help Ma."

"All right. I won't tell. I promise. Can we rest a minute? I'm awfully hungry."

"We've got to cross a road up here and go behind some house. Stay here and rest. I'll go see if anyone is out—"

"No. Don't leave me." Ruth Ann clung tightly to Isaac's hand. "Please, Isaac—" she pleaded.

"All right, but ya gotta be quiet. It wouldn't do for someone to see us sneakin' around. They'd go right to the sheriff. And that old Deputy Ham and my pa are thick as fleas on a dog's back."

"The sheriff?" Ruth Ann said fearfully. "I'll be quiet. I promise."

It was near midnight when an exhausted little girl holding tightly to Isaac's hand stood at the edge of the woods near her home. Her feet hurt; her dress was torn and dirty. She was weak from hunger.

The house where she had lived all her life was dark. The only light shone from the dim bulb that burned in front of her daddy's garage. A car with a low white tent pitched beside was parked in the campground. A car passed on the highway, its lights forging a path ahead of it. Then, it was so quiet, she could hear the sound of rustling leaves in the tree limb overhead as a curious squirrel positioned himself to spy on them.

"Go on. I'll wait until yo're in the house."

"I'm scared. Come with me."

"I can't. I've got to get back."

"Please—"

"Don't be a baby!" he said harshly and she began to cry. "Ah . . . stop cryin', Ruth Ann. I said I'd bring ya home and I did, didn't I?"

"You'll stay and . . . watch?"

"I'll watch till yo're on the porch."

"Isaac, I . . . never talked to you at school 'cause I thought you'd be like Uncle Virgil—"

"Well, I'm not. Go on—"

"I don't want you to get a whippin'."

"I won't unless ya tell."

"I won't tell. I promise."

Ruth Ann hesitated. When he said nothing more, she ran toward the house. Isaac watched her until the dog came bounding off the porch, then he took off and ran as if his life depended on it.

Chapter 22

THE DARK SKY WAS STUDDED WITH STARS, and a sliver of moon shone over the treetops. Leona sat in the porch swing with Yates, her heart heavy with dread. The swing moved in response to Yates's foot and was quiet because Deke had greased the chains earlier.

Deke sat on the steps with his back to a porch post, his hand reaching out occasionally to scratch Calvin's ears. The dog, knowing that something was not quite right, had stuck close to the house.

Margie had been a blessing. Moving around quietly, she had made sandwiches and kept a pitcher of iced tea handy. After doing the outdoor chores, she baked a cake in the portable oven and deviled a dozen eggs for tomorrow. She had kept JoBeth occupied all day by telling her stories or cutting strings of paper dolls out of folded newspaper. She showed her how to draw faces and dresses on the paper dolls with her crayons. An hour before she had put JoBeth to bed and stayed with her.

Looking out into the dark night, Leona wondered if Ruth Ann was in the dark somewhere, hungry and scared. Oh, Lord. Would she be able to get the words out when she called Andy in the morning? A moaning sound escaped from her throat. Yates put his arm around her and drew her to his side.

"I don't know how I'm going to tell him," she said, as if the man sitting close to her knew what was in her mind.

"Do you want me to do it?"

"Mr. Fleming said he'd call someone and have him go get Andy and bring him home. I don't want a stranger to tell him."

"We'll go to the telephone company in the morning. You can decide then if you can tell him."

"He'll come home and miss the rest of the shots. He might die. Then, it'd just be me and JoBeth."

"Try to believe that we'll find her tomorrow."

"If she was hiding, she'd have come home at dark."

"Why don't you go in and lie down for a while?"

"No. You and Deke go rest. Deke, you can use Andy's bed. I'll sit here a while."

Neither Yates nor Deke made a move. The three of them sat in silence, each deep in private thoughts. Finally Deke broke the silence.

"I'm thinkin' I'll go see Virgil in the mornin', darlin'. If that bastard's behind this, I'll stomp his guts out if I have to get on a ladder to do it."

"Don't do anything that'll get you in trouble, Deke. If Virgil has taken Ruth Ann, the sheriff will find out about it. I can't believe that even Virgil would take a child into a house quarantined with diphtheria."

"Don't be too sure, darlin'. The man's always had clabber for brains. He's got his mind set on gettin' Andy's girls. He'll keep tryin' till somebody puts the kibosh on him. He's pure mad-dog mean through and through."

Leona's head drooped against Yates's shoulder. His hand stroked her arm from her shoulder to her elbow. She would remember to her dying day the comfort and support he had given her on this dreadful day.

"It's getting late. Why don't you close your eyes and rest a while?"

He shifted so that she would be more comfortable against him and thought of many things he would like to say to her, but they formed no logical order in his mind. To speak of his emotions was not easy for a man like Yates, when the feelings were deep and strong. Besides that, this was not the time nor the place.

The one thought that stood foremost in his mind was that she had needed him, and it had been wonderful to be needed. Surprisingly, he had been happier here in this modest home, tending a run-down garage, than he had been since he was a boy at home on the ranch. Without Leona the future seemed long and lonely.

He gathered his scattered thoughts together and spoke. "Tomorrow will be a busy day, and you'll need your strength."

"I keep thinking the sheriff will drive in with news that someone has found her."

"If he does, I'll wake you up."

"I couldn't sleep."

Calvin stood suddenly and slipped out from under Deke's stroking hand. He went to the end of the porch and stood there stiff-legged, staring off toward the woods. Deke, following Calvin's gaze, could see nothing. Then a low growl began to vibrate from the dog's throat.

"Is someone out there, Calvin?" Deke walked around to the end of the porch.

Yates stopped the swing and got to his feet. He had been around the dog enough to know that Calvin had his eyes on something they couldn't see. Suddenly, Calvin leaped from the porch and raced toward the woods. It was then that Yates's sharp eyes saw a blur of something light running toward the house. Calvin raced past the running figure and dashed into the woods.

"Calvin! Caaal . . . vin! Come back." The shouting voice was Ruth Ann's.

Leona was stunned for a moment, then screamed, "Ruth Ann? Oh, blessed Jesus! Ruth Ann!" Leona pushed past the men to run out into the yard.

"Aunt Lee! Aunt Lee! Make Calvin come back."

Leona reached the child, swung her up in her arms and burst into tears.

"Are you all right? Tell me you're all right." She hugged the child to her.

"I'm all right. Make Calvin come back."

"He's back. He's right here. Oh, honey. We've been so worried."

"I'm hungry, Aunt Lee."

"I'll fix anything you want." Leona kissed her again and again.

Yates reached for the child. "Here, let me have her. She's too heavy for you to carry. Come to me, punkin." Yates lifted Ruth Ann into his arms. She wrapped her arms around his neck. "I was afraid I was going to have to bury your Aunt Lee if you hadn't come back soon."

"Howdy, little sweetheart." Deke's voice was hoarse. "We've been pretty worried 'bout ya."

Yates carried Ruth Ann into the house with Deke and Calvin following along behind. Leona went ahead and turned on the lights.

"Margie, JoBeth," she called out happily. "Ruth Ann's home." Leona sat down on a kitchen chair and Yates set Ruth

Ann on her lap. "Honey, I don't think I'll ever let you out of my sight again."

JoBeth came into the kitchen still in her night clothes. Squinting against the light she saw her sister, ran to her and wrapped her little arms around her.

"You can have my crayons if you won't go off again. You can have the paper dolls Margie cut out for me."

Ruth Ann burst into tears.

Leona stood in the doorway of the bedroom reluctant to take her eyes off the two girls in the bed. She had washed Ruth Ann and dressed her in a clean pair of underdrawers and put her to bed with JoBeth. The child had hardly been able to keep her eyes open while she ate a slice of cake and drank two glasses of milk. She had fallen asleep almost immediately.

Leona had tried to talk to her about where she had been.

"We looked all over and we couldn't find you." She had asked gently, "Where did you go?"

"Ah . . . someplace."

"Can you tell me where?"

"No."

"You don't know where you were?"

"I know, but I can't tell."

"Can't tell your Aunt Lee? Why can't you tell?"

"I promised. I promised not to tell you."

"Oh, I see. Did someone hurt you?"

"Uh-huh. But I'm all right now."

"Oh, honey. I can't stand the thought of someone hurting you."

"Tell me who, sweetheart," Deke said "And your Uncle Deke will take care of him."

"I can't tell. I promised."

"Did someone hurt you and you promised not to tell?" Leona asked.

"Not him. I promised somebody else."

"The one who brought you home?" Yates had squatted down beside the chair.

"Uh-huh." Ruth Ann snuggled against Leona and closed her eyes.

After Leona put the child to bed, she returned to the kitchen and sank down in a chair at the table. Yates was speaking to Deke.

"I was sure someone else was out there when Calvin went dashing into the woods. Whoever found her and brought her home has earned the twenty-five-dollar reward I offered."

"I didn't know you had offered a reward," Leona said.

"I told the sheriff and the storekeepers, thinking it might bring some information out that we'd not get otherwise."

Leona folded her arms on the table and rested her forehead on them. "I'm so thankful that I don't have to call Andy. The suspense of not knowing where Ruth Ann was would have been terrible for him."

Deke stood, came around the table and put his hand on her shoulder.

"You'd better get to bed, darlin'. You've had a hair-raisin' day."

"I'm almost afraid to close my eyes. I'm afraid she'll disappear again."

"Give me a couple of quilts. I'll bed down out on the porch. No use me firin' up that cycle tonight. I'll go back to the ranch in the mornin' and tell Mr. Fleming to call off his searchers."

Leona grabbed his hand. "You've always been there when

I needed you, Deke. I'm proud that you're my friend. Andy will be, too, when I tell him."

"Ya've always been special to me, little darlin'." His fingers stroked her cheek. "I'd crawl over a bed of hot coals to get to ya if ya needed me."

"I know that, Deke. And if you're ever in need, I'll be here for you. You know that, don't you?"

"Yeah, darlin'. I know."

Margie spoke. "I'll get the quilts if you tell me where they are."

"In Andy's room. Take one of the pillows, too."

Yates listened to the exchange between Leona and Deke. He wasn't sure what he was feeling. It couldn't be jealousy. How could he be jealous of this little man and his dogged devotion? Deke loved Leona knowing that he could never have her. She loved him as she loved Ruth Ann and JoBeth. Deke knew that was all he would ever have and was resigned to it.

When they were alone, Yates rose and pulled Leona up to stand beside him.

"You're dead on your feet. You can rest easy tonight. There isn't anything coming or going on this place that either Deke, Calvin or I won't know about."

"Thank you, Yates. You've been the rock that anchored me and kept me sane today."

"It's been my pleasure to be with you and do what I could. Thank God it's over, all except finding out where she's been. *Someone* was holding her, *someone* found her and brought her home. I intend to find out who those two *someones* are."

"Do you think we should still call and tell Andy?"

"Yes, I do. I'm going to talk to the doc here and see if he can give Andy the rest of the shots if we get him the serum. The crucial time has passed. If Andy was going to have a violent reaction to the serum, he would have had it by now."

"Then he could come home?"

"He could come home. It was Barker Fleming's idea. Another thing, honey. We've got to be careful where we take the girls. The doc said he has six cases of diphtheria in the area. The germs travel from child to child."

Looking into silver eyes, which squinted down at her through thick dark lashes, Leona thanked God that Andy had saved his life, and that he had come here and she'd had the chance to know him. She had not imagined there was a man like him and now, in just a few short weeks, he was woven into the very fabric of her life, making her aware of him every minute of the day, making her depend on him.

Making her love him!

She wound her arms tightly around his waist and leaned her head against his shoulder. Fear trickled through her. He would leave when Andy came home. He would take her heart with him.

Would she be able to bear it?

Isaac ran most of the way home. His heart pounded with the fear that his father would discover he had let his cousin out of the shed and had taken her home. He stopped beneath a big pecan tree at the edge of the yard.

Thank goodness his pa's truck was not beside the shed. He almost cried with relief. The doctor's car, however, was parked in the road in front of the house.

Isaac removed his boots when he reached the edge of the porch, tiptoed to the door and eased it open. He moved quickly into the room where his brothers lay in his parents' bed and pulled off his shirt. After waiting a few minutes to calm his breathing, he went to stand in the doorway of the room where his brother lay, rasping sounds coming from his open mouth.

Doctor Langley sat in a chair beside the bed holding Paul's wrist in his hand. Hazel was on the other side of the bed. Tears rolled from her eyes but she made no sound. When she saw Isaac in the doorway, she held her hand out to him and he went to her. She pulled him down onto the bed beside her. He couldn't take his eyes off his brother's face. He would never forget the sight of the small boy gasping for breath.

Minutes turned into an hour and suddenly the rasping sound ceased. The doctor placed Paul's hand on the bed, stood and put his stethoscope to his chest. The room was quiet. Isaac knew his mother was holding her breath. When finally the doctor looked up and shook his head, she let go a long agonizing sob and held Isaac so tightly, he thought his bones would break.

The doctor covered Paul with a sheet, then took Hazel by the arm and led her out of the room. When he left a half hour later, Doctor Langley carried Paul's body wrapped in the sheet and carefully placed it on the backseat of his car.

Isaac stood on the porch with his mother and watched the taillights on the doctor's car fade in the distance.

"Are yore brothers all right?"

"Yes, ma'am. I been feelin' their heads like ya told me."

"Did you take the girl home?"

"Yes, ma'am. She won't tell where she's been. She promised."

"I don't care if she tells," his mother said in a strangely calm voice.

"But, Mama, he'll . . . know I let her out."

"He'll not touch you, Isaac. He'll not touch you and he'll not touch the other boys. I'll kill him first."

He had never heard his mother speak in that tone of voice. In the dim lamplight flowing out onto the porch, he looked at her and realized that she looked old and drawn with grief, but different somehow. Her back was straighter, her head up.

"Why did he want her here, Ma? Folks would know that he took her and the law would be after him, 'cause he has no right to Andy Connors's kids."

"He's always had a strange way of thinkin' about thin's. I don't know why."

Isaac and Hazel sat on the porch, both dreading to go back into the house where Paul had lain for the past three days burning up with fever and gasping for breath. Time passed. The sliver of moon had long ago disappeared from the dark sky. Isaac could not remember ever being up this late or being alone with his ma. Usually the other kids or his pa were here. Tonight she had depended on him. Although he could barely keep his eyes open, he was determined not to leave her alone.

It was long past midnight when the headlights of a car came in sight. Isaac shook with fear. His father was coming home.

"He's comin', Ma."

His mother didn't say anything, as she watched the truck approach. It stopped in the lane beside the house and Virgil got out. He could see them plainly in the light flowing out onto the porch from the window.

"What's all those lights on for? I turned the electric off 'cause I knowed you'd be wastin' it. Now yo're wastin' the kerosene." He stood back from the porch. When Hazel didn't answer, he took a step nearer.

"Don't come any closer," she said. "I don't think I can stand to look at yore face."

Her words shocked Virgil speechless for a moment. Then he said, "What'er ya talkin' about. What's got into ya?"

"Somethin' what should'a got into me long ago. Where've ya been?"

"We're havin' a all-night prayer service for Paul. Folks is a prayin' hard and—"

"Too late."

"Too late? It's never too late for God's—what'a ya mean too late?"

"Just what I said."

"He's gone?"

"Gone." She uttered the word as if it was something nasty in her mouth.

"Gone," he repeated. He stood there with his hands on his hips, then said, "Well, it was God's will."

"Come on, Isaac."

Hazel got to her feet and pulled on her son's hand. When they went into the house, she slammed the door and doused the lamp in the front room, then the ones in the kitchen and bedroom. Still holding to Isaac's hand as if it were a lifeline and she was being washed away in a flood, she went to stand in the kitchen window that looked out toward the shed.

Virgil came to the back porch and lit the lantern, then with a paper sack in his hand he went to the shed and began tossing the stove-wood from in front of the door. He opened the door and stepped inside. Almost immediately he came out. He stood for a minute then came toward the house.

"Hazel," he shouted. "Hazel," he yelled again when he received no answer. He stomped up onto the porch.

Hazel moved quickly to latch the screen. "Shut yore mouth!" she said sharply. "It ain't respectful to be brayin' like a jackass."

Virgil backed off the porch. "Has anybody been around here tonight?"

"The doctor."

"Did he go to the shed?"

"Why'd he go out there for?"

"Did he go out there?" Virgil said, careful to keep his voice down.

"No."

"Get Isaac out here."

"Isaac's gone to bed." Hazel pushed her son toward the bedroom.

"Get him up."

"No."

"No? No? Ya sayin' no to me, woman."

"I'm sayin' no, like ya said no when I wanted the doctor for Paul."

"So that's it. Yo're blamin' me 'cause God saw fit to take him to his heavenly home."

"I'm blamin' ya for that and for whippin' him."

"He needed the whippin'. It was his time to go and there wasn't no mortal man goin' to keep God from takin' him. 'Twas God's will."

"Then it was God's will that ya lost whatever ya had in the shed."

"What'a ya know about what I had in the shed? Ya been out here?"

"I was tendin' a sick boy, whose pa had left strop marks across his little back that he'll take to the grave. A *Christian pa* who wouldn't let me spend the money Joseph gave me to pay for a doctor."

Her words and the venom in her voice angered Virgil, but he knew there wasn't anything he could do about it now.

"I'll go to town and tell the folks to pray for his soul."

"They'd better be prayin' for yours. It's blacker than coal dust."

Hazel slammed the heavy back door and shot the bolt,

locking it. She groped her way in the dark until she reached a kitchen chair where she sat at the table with her head in her arms and cried as she had not done since she was a child. She cried for her little boy who was gone from her forever. She cried for her other two boys who had left home because of their pa. She cried because she had been so stupid as to let it happen.

She didn't even raise her head when she heard the old truck start up, back out and head for town.

Virgil was seething with rage. The boy was dead, and Hazel blamed him for not getting the doctor sooner. It just proved that a woman's mind did not function logically, nor did it have the capacity to fully understand God's word. It was the boy's time to go.

"Receive Paul to thy bosom, O Lord," he prayed aloud as he drove into town. "He was a good boy. I saw to it."

Virgil stopped at the church, got out and looked in the window. There were two people kneeling at the altar; neither one of them was Wayne Ham. In the morning would be time enough to tell them that the boy had already passed over.

He got back into the car and drove around the courthouse. When he didn't see Wayne's car, he drove to the edge of town where the deputy lived in a neat little house with his wife, whose main interest in life was her vegetable and flower gardens. Wayne's car was parked beside the house.

Virgil didn't hesitate. He shut off the motor, walked up to the house and pounded on the door. After a minute or two a light came on in the back of the house. Wayne came to the door in his underwear, saw who it was and stepped out onto the porch. There was enough light for Virgil to see that the deputy was not happy about being roused this time of night.

"What the heck do you want?" Wayne said in a low, raspy voice.

"My kid died." There was the appropriate catch in Virgil's voice.

"I'm sorry about that. When did it happen?"

"Tonight while I was at the prayer meetin'." In the next breath, he said, "The girl's gone."

"Gone? Where'd she go?"

"I don't know. A board was kicked out of the shed and she got out. You gotta help me find her."

"Virgil, I'm not helping you anymore. McChesney will have my job if he finds out what I've already done. They've got searchers out all over the country looking for the girl. There's even a twenty-five-dollar reward to the one who brings her home. That tall-drink-of-water at the garage put it up. I'm not wanting to tangle with him again."

"Fine friend you are. You started it all."

"And I regret it. I found her and took her to a relative. I didn't tell you to lock her up."

"You knew I was goin' to."

"Don't name me in this, Virgil. I'm warnin' you."

"God help you, Brother Ham. You've backslid clear to the bottom of sinners' row. The brothers and sisters at the church are goin' to be disappointed in you. You've been smokin', too. I can smell it."

"What if I have? It's no business of yours."

"It's God's business. I'll pray for you."

"You'd better pray that you find that girl and get her home before something bad happens to her."

"God is tryin' me. He surely is. Hazel blames me 'cause I didn't get the doctor in time for Paul," he whined.

Wayne Ham was silent.

"God was goin' to take him anyhow. Warn't no use spendin' money gettin' a doctor."

"Wayne." The call came from the back of the house. "Are you going out?"

"No. I'll be in in a minute," he called, then to Virgil, "Stop your yammering and go look for the girl. If you find her, take her back to Andy's. As far as I can tell, your sister—"

"Is a whore," Virgil snapped.

"You don't know that."

"I know it! I knew it for God told me to get the little girls out of that den of sin and shame."

"Has anyone told ya she put out for 'em?"

"A man wouldn't tell a thin' like that. Why'd you think them fellers is hangin' round her for? There ain't but one thin' that'd keep that Texan out there—free pussy."

"That's a downright nasty thing to say 'bout your sister! But if she's willin' to screw around with him, it ain't no skin off my nose."

"She's shamin' the Dawson name! Ya know it's what she's doin'."

"She's a grown woman, Virgil. You've got no say in what she does."

"By granny, I've plenty of say. I'm still head of the Dawson family."

"That's between you and her and has nothin' to do with me. Go on, now. My wife will be out here wonderin' what's goin' on."

All Wayne wanted to do was get Virgil off his porch. It would be all right with him if he never saw the bastard again. Lately he'd been nothing but trouble. One thing was sure, if Virgil dragged him into this mess and caused him to lose his job, he'd make him sorry!

Sssh . . . it! He'd give a whole dollar for a cigarette.

Chapter 23

DEKE LEFT AT DAYLIGHT AND, knowing they were in for a hot day, Yates was at the well pumping water into the bathing tank for the girls to splash in when the sheriff's car pulled up beside the house and Rex McChesney got out.

"Morning."

"You're out early. But it isn't necessary. Ruth Ann came home last night."

The sheriff didn't act surprised. "Where had she been?"

"She didn't say."

"Didn't you ask her? Some folks went to a lot of trouble looking for her."

"But not you."

"Hell, I told you she would probably come home. Nine times out of ten a runaway comes back after a day."

Yates adjusted the conduit and continued pumping. "Yeah, ya told me that."

"Well?"

"Well, what? Are you wanting me to tell you how smart you were not to go out and get all sweaty looking for her?"

"You're a real asshole. You know that?"

"I've been told that I was. I'm not convinced."

"Virgil Dawson's boy died last night."

"Diphtheria?"

"Yeah. Six cases in town as of yesterday."

"How do they handle a funeral in a case like this?"

"Only the immediate family at the grave site. Better find out where Andy's girl has been. If she's been anywhere near a sick child she should see the doctor."

"I'll tell Leona."

"You do that." The sheriff turned back to his car.

"Sheriff," Yates called. "If Virgil Dawson comes pestering Miss Dawson and Andy's girls again, I'll have his balls hanging on the clothesline before he can bat an eye. That goes for your deputy, too."

"If that should happen, you'll be in my jail before *you* can bat an eye."

"What about self-defense?" Yates grinned.

"Never heard of it."

Yates continued to work the pump handle as the sheriff's car left the yard. He had finished filling the tank and was pulling away the conduit when Margie came out of the barn, with a full pail of milk.

"Morning." Yates knew that the girl was happy Ruth Ann had come home, but was hurting because she felt responsible for her leaving.

Margie answered with her head down and continued on toward the house. He remembered that she had said she would leave when Ruth Ann came home. He had a sudden memory of being young and homeless and how desolate he had felt having nowhere to go nor anyone to care about him. He'd like to wring the neck of the dirt-clod who had run off with Margie's money.

As soon as he stepped into the kitchen, his eyes sought Leona. She was as perky this morning as a shiny new penny.

"Morning." She ducked her head to put away the pan she used to make biscuits.

"You look chipper this morning. Sleep good?"

"I got up several times in the night to be sure Ruth Ann was in her bed. Otherwise, I slept like a log." Her smiling eyes met his. "I never want to go through such a day again."

"And I hope you never have to." Yates hung his hat on the peg beside the door. "Sheriff McChesney was here."

"I saw him and was going to ask him in for coffee, but he left."

"He said that your brother's little boy died last night of diphtheria."

The smile left Leona's face. "I hate to hear that."

"We should find out if Ruth Ann has been with other children, not only for her sake, but for JoBeth's. Diphtheria is catching and not to be fooled with."

"I'll talk to her when she gets up. She may have been just too tired last night to talk." Leona poured coffee in the thick cup Yates preferred. He always drank at least one cup before he ate his breakfast. "I wish Deke had waited for breakfast."

"He wanted to get out to the ranch and head off the men Fleming would send out this morning." Yates picked up the cup and stepped out of the way so that Margie could set the breakfast table. "I want to go to town this morning and talk to the doctor about bringing Andy home."

He's anxious to bring Andy home so he can leave.

He was gazing at Leona so intently with his silver eyes that she feared he could read her every thought. Those eyes, fixed on hers, were looking into her very soul. Leona turned quickly back to the eggs she was scrambling in the skillet in case the dread she was feeling reflected on her face.

"If he can come, will he take the bus?" Her voice was not quite steady.

"No. I'll go get him before I let him do that. It'd be a long, hot trip on the bus for someone not feeling up to snuff. Fleming offered to bring him home. He has business in the city today or tomorrow."

"May I have a ride to town when you go, Mr. Yates?" Margie stood behind one of the high-backed kitchen chairs, her hand clutching the knobs. Her bald-faced misery was one of the saddest sights Yates had ever seen. "I . . . have my things ready. I'd like to go before the girls get up."

"Margie!" Leona turned to grasp her arm. "I thought you were going to stay and help me fill all those empty jars in the cellar."

"You don't really need me, Leona. It would be best for me to go on and find a permanent way to support myself."

"You can stay here and help me. When Andy comes back he'll not be able to do much in the garage and I'll have to take care of the gas pump."

Yates will be only a sweet memory and my heart will be broken.

"I can't bear to be here knowing that I'm the cause of that child running away. She . . . she could've—something terrible could've happened to her."

"I don't think she ran away just because of you."

"I do. She didn't want me here. She made it plain. I don't blame her. This is her home. She has a right not to want strangers in it."

"Ruth Ann has been very emotional since her mother died two years ago. At first she resented me. She even said that if someone had to die why couldn't it have been me and not her mother. It took her a while to get used to the idea that I was staying on to take care of them as I had done while my sister was sick."

"Better look at the eggs, Leona," Yates said.

"Oh, shoot! They're drier than a bone."

Yates grinned. "They'll be all right. I've never seen an egg I couldn't eat unless it was rotten or raw."

"I was hoping to start canning the green beans today." Leona scraped the eggs into a bowl, then brought the biscuits from the oven. When they were on the table, she sat down so that Yates would.

"The jars are clean and in a tub on the porch. I covered them with a cloth." Margie moved around and eased down in a chair.

"You've been such a help. I don't know what I would have done with JoBeth yesterday, if not for you."

"I've been thinking that I'd like to have a job somewhere in an orphans' home taking care of children . . . at least for a while."

"There isn't one home around here that I know of. Please reconsider and stay. JoBeth is attached to you and I'll talk to Ruth Ann."

Yates planned to stall about going to town to give Leona time to change Margie's mind about leaving. It was clear to him that the girl didn't want to go, that, in fact, she was scared to death. But she was proud and had rather go out into the unknown than be in a place where she wasn't wanted.

"Excuse me, ladies, I have a few things to do." Yates left the table as soon as he finished eating. Then to Margie, "I'll let you know when I'm ready to go. Leona will have to watch the gas pump."

"He's a nice man," Margie said wistfully after the front screen door slammed behind Yates.

"Yes, he is. Although I didn't think so when he first came here." Leona smiled remembering that she had thought him arrogant and high-handed. He was still arrogant, but somehow, now, she didn't mind.

"He likes you."

"I hope so. I'd hate to have someone around that *hated* me. I had that when I lived with my brother."

"I think Yates more than just *likes* you." Margie had to smile at the flood of color that covered Leona's cheeks. "When I worked in the café in Conway, I learned to tell which of the men had a crush on Betty Kay, the other girl who worked there."

"None had a crush on you?"

"Heavens no! Compared to Betty Kay, I was dull as dishwater. Yates may be in love with you."

"You're wrong, wrong, wrong—" *Oh, but I wish that you were right.* "He is just here helping out until Andy comes back. Then he'll hit the road. This diphtheria epidemic scares me." Leona plunged into another topic of conversation. "When I was little there was an epidemic here that killed five or six children. The schools closed and they discontinued church services. My mother kept my sister and me close to the house."

"Do you know the little boy who died?"

"I don't know him. He's my brother's little boy. I wonder which one. He had six boys. Two of them have left home."

"It was Paul. Oh . . . oh—"

Leona turned to see Ruth Ann standing in the doorway in her nightdress, her hand over her mouth.

"Come here, honey." She opened her arms. Ruth Ann ran to her and climbed up onto her lap. "How do you know it was Paul? Were you at Uncle Virgil's?" The child turned her face to Leona's shoulder and wracking sobs shook her. "Don't cry, sweetheart. You're home now."

Leona cuddled Ruth Ann in her arms and stroked the

blond curls back from her wet face until the sobs subsided into an occasional hiccupping.

"Shhh . . . you're here with Aunt Lee . . . and your daddy may be coming home soon. Yates is going to talk to the doctor and maybe he'll even come home tomorrow."

"I . . . was so scared—"

"Of course you were. Anyone would be. Especially a little girl."

"There was a . . . rat—"

"Oh, honey! Can't you tell me where you were?"

"No. I . . . promised." Ruth Ann lifted her head and looked across the table at Margie. "I'm sorry . . . I was mean to you."

"That's all right, honey." Huge tears rolled down Margie's cheeks. "My grandma took care of me when my mother died. I wouldn't have wanted a stranger to come in and make themselves at home."

"But, I was . . . mean. Daddy would . . . be ashamed of me."

"No, he wouldn't." Leona wiped the tears from Ruth Ann's cheeks with the tail of her apron. "He'd tell you that Margie wasn't taking anyone's place. She was going to help me can so that we'd have some good things to eat when winter comes."

"I . . . wish I hadn't . . . run off."

"So many people were worried about you. Yates went to town and offered a reward to anyone who found you and brought you home. Deke came on his motorcycle and went up and down the highway, even up to Elk City. Mr. Fleming brought in riders from his ranch to search for you. It was so lonesome here without you. You're dear to all of us."

"I'm sorry—I was going to Mr. Fleming and—ask him to take me to Daddy."

"You didn't get there, did you?"

"Uh-uh."

"Did someone pick you up?"

"Uh-huh. He said he'd take me to Mr. Fleming."

"But he didn't."

"He . . . he took me someplace else."

"Can you tell me where he took you?"

"I promised, Aunt Lee. You told me I should always keep promises."

"Yes, I did, sweetheart. But sometimes it becomes necessary to break a promise. As of yesterday there were six cases of diphtheria in town. It spreads among children. A lot of them could die from it. The sheriff was here this morning and told us that one of Virgil's little boys had died."

"He . . . said that if I told . . . that *he'd* hang him up and . . . and take the hide off his back—"

"Oh, surely not!"

"Please don't make me tell."

"Honey, I don't want to make you tell, but if you've been near someone with diphtheria we should know about it and take you to the doctor."

"I wasn't near Paul."

"Were you in the house?"

"Uh-uh."

"Were you with someone who had been in the house with Paul?" Ruth Ann turned her face to Leona's shoulder and refused to answer until her aunt prodded. "Tell me, honey. We need to know if you were exposed to the diphtheria for your sake and for JoBeth's. I know that you don't want to bring the germs back to your little sister."

Ruth Ann began to cry again. "He . . . he untied me and took the rag outta my mouth. We came through the woods.

It was dark. He . . . he held on to my hand and told me not to be scared— He's . . . he's not like Uncle Virgil."

"Oh . . . honey—" Leona hugged the child tightly to her. "He was a brave boy." She looked up to see Yates standing in the doorway. She nodded to him, then spoke to Ruth Ann. "Honey, will you sit with Margie while I go out to the garage? I'll not be gone long. Margie was as worried about you as the rest of us. She's afraid you left because of her."

"I . . . I just miss my daddy."

"Come sit on my lap, Ruth Ann, and let me tell you about when I was a little girl. My mother died when I was Jo-Beth's age, and I went to live with my granny. She taught me to sew on buttons, make flour paste and how to cut out paper dolls from folded paper."

With Ruth Ann settled on Margie's lap, Leona quickly left the room and went to the porch where Yates waited.

"Did you hear what she said?"

"Part of it."

"She was tied up someplace and that . . . that low-down, slimy worm put a rag in her mouth." Leona was so angry she neared tears. She gripped Yates's forearms and shook them. "We've got to take her to the doctor. I think one of Virgil's boys brought her home. She won't say that he did, she's afraid he'll be hung up and the hide stripped from his back."

"I heard the last part. What do you want to do?"

"We can't do anything that will cause trouble for the boy after he risked so much to bring her home. What do you think we should do?"

She tilted her head and looked into his face. Yates watched her intently. He didn't answer for such a long while that her eyes wavered beneath the intensity of his. He lifted a finger to her cheek. Every moment he was with her, a medley of emotions passed through him—concern, curiosity and at times anger at himself for being so smitten with her.

Hell, she'd never leave Andy and the girls and, besides, he wouldn't have anything to offer her until his stepfather died and his inheritance came to him.

He had lived the past seven years among rough men, driving the highway, waiting to go back home. He was rough and, at times, brutal. She was soft and sweet. Lord help him, he'd never dreamed of meeting a slip of a girl who could turn him inside out with just a pleading look in her eyes.

"Let's think about it for a while," he said, his eyes still holding hers. "Meantime I'll go in and talk to Doctor Langley about bringing Andy home and tell him about Ruth Ann. Whatever I tell him will go no farther. He'll not want Virgil's boy to be punished."

"You'll tell him that Virgil had her."

"I think I should. He needs to know that Ruth Ann was out there and possibly exposed to diphtheria. Will you be all right here for an hour? The campers have pulled out."

"Of course, we'll be all right. Go ahead and do what you have to do."

"What about Margie?"

"She's staying here."

She's staying and you're going. Oh. Lord. I don't know if I can bear it.

"I won't be gone long. Do you need anything from town?" His hand slid from her arms to her back and he pulled her to him. It was so natural that he wasn't even aware of doing it.

"Two dozen jar lids," she murmured and leaned against him, her eyes closed. She wanted to store away each touch, each caress, to bring out and enjoy during the long lonely years ahead.

"Quart fruit jars?"

"Uh-huh. I'll show you before you go."

She couldn't think of anything except him. Did she feel his lips in her hair or was it just wishful thinking?

The sound of a motorcycle penetrated her haze of happiness. She pulled away from him just as Deke came around the corner of the garage and stopped his cycle beside Yates's car.

"Mornin', darlin'."

"Mornin'." Leona, embarrassed to be caught standing so close to Yates, put her hands on his chest to push herself away. He refused to loosen his arms and let her go. "Have you had breakfast, Deke?"

"Not a crumb, darlin', and I'm hungrier than a starvin' coyote. Mr. Fleming told me to take the day off so I turned around and came right back. He's goin' into the city in the mornin', Yates, and said that he'll stop here on his way."

"I'm glad you're here, Deke. I need to go to town and didn't want to leave the women here alone in case Virgil or that clabber-headed deputy took a notion to come out here."

"Has Ruth Ann said anythin' 'bout where she's been?" Deke removed the handkerchief from around his neck and wiped his face, then ran forked fingers through his thick corn-colored hair.

"We think she was at Virgil's although she didn't come right out and say so."

"One of Virgil's boys brought her home," Leona added. "She promised him she wouldn't tell, so don't let this go any farther. Please, Deke."

"That dirty low-down, rotten bastard! I should of blowed a hole through him a long time ago."

"Ah . . . Deke. If you had, you'd be in jail getting ready to sit in the electric chair. He isn't worth it."

"Come show me the kind of jar lids you need, honey." Yates urged her toward the door with his hand in the small of her back.

Leona glanced quickly at Deke. He was still wiping his face and looking off toward the highway.

Well, she thought, Yates was entitled to call her *honey.* Hadn't Deke been calling her *darlin'* for years?

Chapter 24

HAZEL AND THE THREE BOYS WALKED THE MILE from their home to the cemetery. Virgil and Pastor Muse were waiting beside the open grave when they reached it.

The small group stood apart from Virgil during the service. Hazel's eyes glowed with hostility, her lips tight; she stood rigid beside Isaac and the two younger boys while the grave of her son was being filled with red Oklahoma dirt by two members of the church.

When it was over, Hazel, her black hat sitting squarely on her stiffly held head, and in a black dress much too large for her gaunt frame, stooped and placed a bouquet of iris and yellow daisies on the mound of dirt. She stood for a moment with her head bowed, then turned to Virgil.

"Give me the five dollars Joseph gave me," she demanded.

Virgil glanced quickly at the preacher, then turned sideways and spoke out of the side of his mouth.

"Don't bring shame down on me. I'm warnin' ya."

"I want the five dollars," Hazel said loudly. "I owe it to the doctor."

"Yo're grievin' now, Hazel," Virgil said in a placating tone, loud enough for the preacher to hear. "I'll pay the doctor."

"Give me the five dollars, or I'll start screechin' so loud they'll hear me in town."

Virgil was barely able to control the hand that itched to slap her as he dug into his pocket and produced the bill. After she snatched it from his hand, he turned to the preacher with a mournfully sad expression on his face.

"Poor woman's gone plumb outta her head."

"I ain't gone out of my head, Virgil Dawson. I've just come to my senses. Come on, boys."

"The boys can ride in the back of the truck."

"No. We walked out here. We'll walk back."

"Carl don't have shoes. The sand will be too hot on his bare feet."

Hazel looked her husband in the eye. "Yo're not worried one stinkin' bit 'bout Carl's feet. Yo're worried how it looks to the preacher." She took the hands of the two small boys and started off down the road. Isaac followed closely behind.

With drooping shoulders and a downcast look on his face, Virgil watched his wife and boys walk away. Burning in the back of his mind was the thought that when he got his hands on her, he'd teach her who was head of this family. But when he spoke to the preacher, it was in a gentle tone.

"Hazel ain't herself, Brother Muse. She's acting plumb dozy. She's been like this since Paul took sick."

The preacher avoided Virgil's eyes. "It sets hard with a woman to lose her child, even knowing that he's going to a better place."

"I don't want ya to think hard of her 'cause of how she's actin'."

"Don't worry about that. I understand Sister Dawson's feelings." Pastor Muse turned his back and spoke to the two men with the shovels. "I'll take you back to town."

* * *

Yates parked his car in front of the bank and went up the iron steps to the doctor's office. The nurse, whom Yates had learned was the doctor's wife, was on the telephone and smiled a greeting. When she finished her conversation, she said, "Morning."

Yates nodded, his hat in his hand. "Is the doctor in?"

"He's washing up. He was out most of the night."

"I heard that the little Dawson boy died."

"Yes. Doctor takes it hard when he loses a child. He's been down with the undertaker. The little boy is being buried this morning."

"I'm sure precautions have to be taken when someone dies of an infectious disease."

"That's true. We were relieved to hear that the little girl you were looking for came home. Sheriff McChesney came by this morning and told us."

"We were mighty glad to see her. Her aunt was frightened almost out of her wits."

The nurse went into the other room and came back with Doctor Langley. After a greeting, Yates plunged right in.

"I'll make this as brief as I can, Doctor. I know you're busy."

Fifteen minutes later, Yates walked down the steps with the doctor, who appeared to be bone-tired.

"I'll be out about noon to swab the girls' throats. If Mr. Fleming is going to the city in the morning, I'll ask him to drop the swabs by the clinic."

"The boy, Isaac, deserves the reward I offered. He risked a lot to bring Ruth Ann home."

"You'll have to figure a way to give it to him without his pa knowing."

"I take it you've got somewhat the same opinion of Virgil Dawson that I have."

"I fully intend to pursue the matter of a sick child being brutally whipped."

"Virgil is a religious fanatic. He does what he does in the name of God."

"I know Pastor Muse, and I can't believe that he would approve of such punishment. Nor would he hesitate calling in a doctor for a sick child. I'd not have known about the Dawson boy if he hadn't come for me, and a dozen or more children could have been infected."

"Virgil Dawson may be demented. Taking and keeping Ruth Ann proves that he's gone beyond being fanatical."

"It should be reported to Sheriff McChesney that the girl was held against her will."

"I'm asking you to keep that part of it confidential. Ruth Ann promised that she wouldn't tell who brought her home. She fears that Isaac would be severely punished."

"No doubt he would be." The doctor opened the door of his car and set his bag on the seat. "Tell Mr. Fleming that I'll need written instructions from Dr. Harris about giving Andy the rest of the serum."

"I'll do that and thanks."

"I have two calls to make. I should be out at Andy's about noon."

Yates walked down the street to the grocery store, went inside and tossed the jar lid Leona had given to him on the counter.

"Two dozen of these jar lids."

"Mr. Yates! I was relieved to hear Andy's little girl came home."

"Really?" Yates looked at him, making no pretense to be civil. "I'll take a couple pounds of cheese, box of crackers, two cans of salmon and a couple dozen lemons." Yates flipped open the slanting lid on a jar and brought out a handful of stick candy. He placed it on the counter.

"The lemons came in just this morning." Mr. White, wanting the business, yet resenting the arrogance of Andy's *cousin,* silently began to gather the order, item by item.

"Add a bottle of vanilla flavoring and a can of baking powder." He remembered JoBeth saying her aunt had put the can of baking powder back on the counter before they walked out.

"Have you heard when Andy is coming home?" Mr. White said in an attempt to start a conversation.

"No."

"It must be hard for Andy to be away from his . . . girls."

Yates noticed the slight hesitation and chose to ignore it. "Put all of this on the tab," he said when the last item was placed on the counter. "And give me an account of the credit we have."

Five minutes later, Yates was in his car on his way back to the garage, and Mr. White was kicking himself for his remark about . . . the girls.

"That should get ya by for a while." Deke detached the hand pump from the front tire of an old Model T Ford coupe.

"I'm much obliged, mister. But if ya had just give me a loan of the pump, I'd a done the work."

"Ya got a leak there that's only goin' to get worse. Why don't I take that tire off and put a patch on the tube?"

"I ain't got a dime to my name, mister, and that's the God's truth. Got enough gas, I think, to get us to Erick—that's where our folks live."

"Ya didn't hear me askin' for pay, did ya? Ya'll get a mile and that tire'll be flat as a pancake."

"Is there somethin' I can do for pay? Me and Miz Hayes ain't got but the clothes on our backs."

"How are ya at sharpenin' tools? We got a whetstone and plenty a dull tools."

"Mister, I'll sharpen ever' damn tool ya got if ya fix that tire so I can get my wife on down the road to my brother's place."

"Then pull the car over here in the shade. No need to bake our brains in this hot sun. Tell your woman to walk around to the well if she wants a good drink of water."

After the car was moved into the shade of the big oak tree between the garage and the campground, Hayes got out and opened the door to speak to his wife.

"Get out, honey, stretch and walk for a while."

The woman he carefully helped out of the car was very pregnant. She stood for a minute holding on to him while her legs stiffened. When she turned Deke could see that her dress was stuck to her back with sweat.

"There's a tin cup hangin' on the pump, ma'am."

"Will ya be all right? Ya want me to go with ya?" Hayes was reluctant to allow the thin woman with the huge bulge in front to walk back to the pump on her own.

"I'm fine. Go on and help the man. I'll stand here by the car for a few minutes."

Deke had the car jacked up and was removing the wheel before she ventured toward the pump, her hands holding the small of her back. Hayes sat on the seat and worked the pedals that turned the wheel of the grindstone. Sparks flew from the ax head he was sharpening.

When the woman returned, she was carrying a cup of water for her husband.

The leak in the tube was discovered at once. After it was covered with a patch, tested in the tub of water kept in the garage for that purpose, and the tube stuffed back into the tire, Deke pumped air in the tube. Then he rolled the tire to the car, still resting on the jack, lifted it to the axle, replaced the lugs and tightened them.

He was lowering the car when a motorcycle with a sidecar turned off the highway and slid to a stop in front of the garage doors, stirring up a small cloud of dust. Deke's temper rose when he saw the rider who sat on the seat with booted feet on the ground. Leaving the motor still running, the rider waited for Deke to acknowledge him.

Deke removed the jack from beneath the car, but kept the tire iron he had used as a jack handle in his hand. He hoped the rotten polecat would give him an excuse to hit him.

"Turn off the damn motor on that thing or I'll whack the headlight out with this iron."

The man turned off the motor, flipped down the kickstand and got off the cycle. He was big, bigger than Deke's five feet and one inch, one hundred and ten pounds. Deke had never backed down from size before and wouldn't now.

"Best be careful, little punk, or you'll get stomped into the ground."

"If you think to do it, big man, come on."

"What the hell's the matter with you? I'm not here to pick a fight with a little squirt, I'm looking for my wife. I left her here a few days ago to go into town and got held up."

"I know who ya are. Yore name's Ernie. Ya left her all right. Ya run off with her money, ya low-down, thieving son-of-a-bitch."

"Watch your mouth, you little pissant. All I want to hear from you is—where she went."

"Ya took near a hundred dollars from her. Give it back or ya'll not leave here all in one piece." Deke took off his hat and sailed it out of the way. He stood hunched over, his hair standing up like a straw haystack, the tire iron in his hand.

"Give it back? Ha!" Ernie laughed. "So she's here. The stupid little bitch suckered you in. I'm not surprised. Somethin' like you is all she could get. Where is she? In the house?"

"Stay away from her," Deke shouted.

Ernie ignored him and had taken two steps toward the house when the tire iron hit him on the backs of his knees bringing him to the ground. Roaring with rage, he leaped to his feet and reached for Deke.

"Here now! Here now!" Hayes came from the garage as Deke danced out of Ernie's reach. The motorcyclist was head and shoulders taller and at least fifty pounds heavier. The game little man was using the tire iron as an equalizer. Hayes didn't know what the fuss was about, but he didn't like the odds.

"Come on, ya pile of horseshit," Deke taunted. "I been wantin' to whip hell out of somebody for the past few days. I never thought I'd be lucky enough to run into you again." Then to Mr. Hayes: "Stay out of the way."

"You think you can fight me, you ugly little wart? I'll whip your ass even if you do have a tire iron."

"Then come on and try it."

Ernie charged. A blow from the tire iron landed on his thigh, bringing him down. He yelled. His long arms brought Deke down with him. He endured the blows on his back from the iron until he was able to grab Deke's wrist and wrench the iron from his grasp. He was pounding Deke's face with his fists when Hayes landed on his back.

"Stop that! Get off him!"

"Eldon!" Mrs. Hayes ran toward her husband.

Unhinged by his anger and the pain from being struck by

the tire iron, Ernie bucked to throw the weight off his back. He reached behind him with a ham-like fist, and fastened his fingers in the bodice of Mrs. Hayes's dress, pulled her down and then shoved.

Her scream as she hit the ground was followed closely by the loud boom of a gun.

"Oh, my God! If you've hurt her, I'll kill you!" Hayes released Ernie to go to his wife. The distraught woman broke into a storm of weeping.

"Get off him!" Leona yelled and fired in the air again. "Get off or I'll shoot your damned head off."

"Jesus!" Ernie swore when he felt the gun barrel dig into the back of his neck.

When Yates pulled into the drive in front of the garage, the first thing he saw was Leona with the gun against the neck of a man on top of Deke. Calvin was running in circles around the group, barking at full volume, darting in once in a while to nip at the strange man's pant leg. Yates slammed on his brakes and jumped out of his car.

"What the hell's goin' on?"

Pointing the gun barrel toward the sky, Leona backed out of the way. Yates grabbed the man on top of Deke. No longer feeling the pressure of the gun barrel, Ernie began to fight. Yates lifted him, flung him to the ground and quick as greased lightning, placed his knee on Ernie's head.

"Be still, or I'll grind your damn ear off."

Leona backed off and lowered the gun barrel.

"The woman—he threw her down," Deke gasped. His face was bloody. He rolled over and got to his knees and crawled to where Hayes was cradling his wife in his arms. "Is she all right?"

"I . . . don't know—"

"Who is this? Dammit, I said be still." Yates's knee was still on Ernie's head.

"He's the one . . . who took Margie's money."

"I never took anything that wasn't mine," Ernie gritted out, his face and part of his mouth in the dirt.

"Get a piece of rope out of the garage, honey," Yates said to Leona. "I'll hog-tie this sucker so we can see about the lady."

Leona took the gun to Margie, who stood out of sight at the side of the garage.

Leona said, "Yates will get your money back . . . if he's still got it."

After taking a length of rope to Yates, Leona went to kneel beside the woman, who was being held by her husband.

"Is she hurt? Is it her . . . time?"

"It was the jar, I reckon. She landed on her backside."

"If we can get her into the house, she could lie down on the bed for a while."

"Ma'am, if you'd let us do that, I'll be owin' you for life. Her back's been hurtin' her somethin' fierce all day."

"I saw that . . . bully push her."

"It scared her when I jumped in. Don't know what she thought she could do. Do ya think that ya can stand up, Orah honey?"

With Leona on one side and her husband on the other, they helped Orah to her feet. Her husband lifted her into his arms and carried her toward the house.

"She can rest on Andy's bed," Leona said to Margie when they reached her. "Let the girls help you. It will make them feel important."

"I wonder why he came back. Does he think I have more money?"

"Stay out of sight and let Yates and Deke handle it. You don't have to see him if you don't want to."

"I want to go pull all his hair out, yet I don't want to see him."

"Yates will take care of things."

Leona waited until the man carried his wife into the house, then went back to the garage. She passed Ernie lying in the dirt, his hands tied behind his back. Yates was looping the end of the rope around his ankles. Ernie exploded with every foul word he could think of. Some were even new to Yates, who looked up at Leona and grinned.

"I was hoping he'd fight back so I could get in a few good licks. But he just lay there and let me tie him up." Yates stood and nudged him with the toe of his boot.

Leona went to see about Deke. He had poured a full pail of water on his head and was bathing his face with a wet towel.

"Let me see, Deke. Goodness sake! Your cheek is cut and you're going to have a black eye. At times I think that you don't have a lick of sense. Why in the world didn't you wait? I was coming with the gun."

"I didn't even think about a gun, darlin'. I knew he couldn't hurt my good looks."

"Oh, hush."

"If he hurt that woman, I'll go out there and pound his head to a pulp."

Leona brushed against Calvin, who was still excited over the commotion.

"Why didn't you bite him, Calvin? You had the perfect opportunity. Fine watch dog you are," she scolded.

"Don't be so hard on Calvin. He got in a nip or two." Yates came into the garage. "Hell, Deke, I leave you for a minute or two and you're in trouble."

"He says Margie's his wife," Deke said from behind the wet towel.

"That's a lie!" Leona declared. "He wanted her to sleep with him and she wouldn't. Do you think we can get her money back?"

Deke snorted. "If it's on him we'll get it."

"I like her and hope she stays for a while," Leona said. "I've not had a friend my own age since Irene died."

"I'll let the big, tough boy bake out there in the sun for a while, then I'll haul him down to the sheriff." Yates placed his arm across Leona's shoulders. "You can say one thing about being out here on the Mother Road, sweetheart. There's never a dull moment."

Sweetheart. He says it so casually. I can't believe that he really means it. But, oh, I wish that he did.

Chapter 25

VIRGIL WAS ALMOST BESIDE HIMSELF WITH WORRY. He had been looking over his shoulder all morning expecting to see that big, mean-looking *cousin* of Andy's coming at him. The little puss would have spilled her guts by now. If he could get his hands on her, by golly, she'd tell him who let her out of the shed. One thing she couldn't say was that he'd whipped her, although she had needed it.

He couldn't figure out how the girl had gotten loose from the strips of rag he'd used to tie her, much less kicked out a board in the shed. How had she made her way home without anyone seeing her? If he found out that Hazel had had a hand in it, it wouldn't set well with her. Isaac could have let her out. But he was pretty sure the boy didn't have the nerve to go against him because he knew what would happen to him if he did.

The only person besides him who knew the girl was in the shed was Wayne Ham. Had his deputy friend gotten cold feet and sneaked out there while he was gone? He had to talk to him. He needed to know if the sheriff was going to come out and question him. If that happened, he'd go into that quarantined house and stay there. That would hold off the sheriff while things cooled down.

Virgil had not believed his luck when Wayne drove up behind the shed with the girl. It would be his word against hers that he had kept her there against her will, and, being the good Christian that he was, he was sure he would be believed. *God would forgive him for that small deception.*

The little twit had been mouthy, just like Leona, and he'd been forced to stuff a rag in her mouth to keep Hazel and the boys from hearing her yell. She'd needed the switch, but he'd waited for God to tell him it was time to use the rod. His God was a merciful God and told him nay. It was far more than the sinful little split-tail deserved.

The good Lord had provided him with the opportunity to take the girl, discipline her, and teach her his word so that her immortal soul could be saved. And he had failed him. *Would God's wrath be visited upon him?* He was almost sure the Lord would punish him when he least expected it.

Now, not wanting to go home and sit in the yard, he drove up and down the streets of Sayre hoping to catch Wayne Ham alone. He didn't dare go to the sheriff's office for fear McChesney would be there. He circled the courthouse square, and on the second round, God was with him. The deputy came down the street toward his car. Virgil stopped his truck behind it to keep the deputy's car blocked in.

Wayne came directly to the truck. His face was red, his eyes looked as if he hadn't slept in a week. His fat jowls quivered with anger.

"You're blockin' my car. Get outta the way. I've got a call to make."

"We got to talk, Wayne."

"I said all I'm going to say to you last night. Keep away from me, hear?"

"Don't ya go gettin' high-and-mighty with me, Wayne

Ham. You're into this as deep as I am. You brought the girl out to my place."

"I brought a lost girl to her uncle, you dumb-head! I never told you to tie her up and put her in a shed."

"Ya knew that's what I'd do, and I know why ya brought her to me. Ya didn't want me to tell the brothers at the church that you'd backslid. Ya'd promised God ya'd not smoke cigarettes, use curse words, lust after fast women or take his name in vain, and ya've been doin' it."

"What I promised was between me and God and none of your business. Now get this *damn* pile of junk out of my way. I've got a call."

"See there? Yo're swearin'. God forgive ya, Wayne. The devil's got ya in his evil clutches. I'll have to tell Brother Muse. He'll pray for you. Ya ain't no longer fit to be the Sunday school superintendent, much less a deacon in the church."

"I'm warning you, Virgil. Keep your mouth shut about me or you'll be sorry."

"I ain't goin' to take all the blame for this. We planned to get those two girls and brin' them into the fold. It was God's will."

"If it was God's will, how come he let her get away from you?"

"Can't ya see, Wayne? He's tryin' our faith. We got to hang together on this."

"Move the truck. I can't talk to you now. The sheriff will be out any minute."

"All right, but remember we're in this together; and if I'm asked, I'll have to say ya brought her to me."

The deputy ground his teeth and wished he'd never set eyes on Virgil Dawson. Sheriff McChesney would have his job if he learned he had any part in the girl being held. He would never, ever, wear a badge again. What would he do? How would he make a living for himself and Livy? Livy had warned him about getting too thick with Virgil. He fervently wished that he had listened to her.

All he had done—the deputy reasoned as he drove out of town to check the hobo camp along the railroad track—was pick the girl up off the highway and take her to a relative. But the sheriff would want to know why he hadn't mentioned that when Yates came in asking them to help hunt for her. He would have to have an answer for that. But what?

Virgil followed the deputy's car toward the hobo camp, then turned off to head for home. He parked the truck alongside the shed. It wouldn't be proper for him to saw wood after coming back from burying his kid, even though Paul was just as dead as he was ever going to be. It was the custom for church folks to bring food after a funeral. Some of them might come by and leave food on the porch. He didn't want them to catch him working. He sat for a while, then got out and went to the back door.

"Hazel," he bellowed. "Come out here."

A good five minutes passed. Virgil shouted again.

Hazel appeared behind the screendoor. "Ain't ya got no respect for yore own flesh and blood? Hush yore bellerin'."

"I ain't knowin' what's got into ya, Hazel, but it's comin' to a stop right now. I ain't havin' ya sassin' and talkin' back to me like ya done in front of Pastor Muse. I tried to ease it by sayin' ya was grievin'—"

"I meant ever' word I said. I gave Doctor Langley the address and told him to send Joseph a telegram tellin' about Paul. Joseph's a man now, not a boy ya can cow down with a strop. He'll get Peter and come home. Then things'll change round here."

"Whater ya talkin' about? Them two no-good scutters

ain't welcome in my house. I told 'em when they left they'd never step foot in it again." Virgil's voice rose into an angry shout. His head jutted forward; spit dribbled from the corner of his mouth.

"Joseph and Peter ain't little boys, no more. They'll stand up to ya."

"They're worthless, sinful shidepokes is what they are. They been hangin' round honky-tonks and fast women. I won't have 'em here! Ya hear that, woman? I ain't havin' their sinful ways arubbin' off on my boys."

"You was glad to take the *sinful* five dollars Joseph gave me. Go away, Virgil. Just lookin' at ya makes me want to puke."

Hazel's words, accompanied by the slamming of the kitchen door, left Virgil in shock. After he had taken a few deep breaths, more anger set in. That woman was goin' to get the switchin' of her life, he vowed. He'd not stand by and let her undermine him. He had no doubt that the boys in the house had heard every wicked word she'd said. What an example she had set for them!

Needing to do something to save face, he went to the willow tree that grew near the runoff from the well, and taking his time, took out his pocketknife and cut several long willow switches. He trimmed them carefully before placing the handful of switches in the back of the truck, then sat down in the shade to think and pray.

"Mama." Carl came from the window to where his mother sat at the kitchen table. "Pa's cuttin' switches. Is he goin' to whip us?"

"No, son. He's not goin' to whip us. He just doin' that for show."

"Is he mad at me 'cause I didn't ride with him in the truck?" Carl had a worried look on his small face.

Hazel pulled the boy up onto her lap. "I'm sorry, Carl, that I've let him whip ya so hard." She began to cry. "I told Paul I was sorry, but I don't reckon he heard me."

"He heard ya, Ma." Isaac came to put a comforting hand on his mother's shoulder. "Do you really think that Joseph and Peter will come?"

"I hope so."

"What'll we do when the doc takes that red sign off our house? Will Pa come in then?"

"I'm sure he will, son."

"Can we ask the doc to leave it on till Joe and Pete get here?"

"He said he'd be back after he got word about the swabs he took. We'll ask him how long the quarantine will be on."

"Will . . . the swabs tell him if we're goin' to get sick like Paul?" Luke, the six-year-old, leaned against her.

"The swabs will tell him if he needs to give you vaccine to keep you from getting sick. Remember when we went to the schoolhouse and got vaccinated for smallpox? It'll be like that."

"Pa was mad about that," Isaac said. "But after talkin' to Brother Muse, he got over it."

Luke looked anxious. "Is Pa mad at me, Ma?"

"No, he's just mad at me."

"Will he switch you?"

"He won't!" Isaac declared, and when his mother looked at him, he said again, "He won't. I'll . . . I'll get the gun."

"Hush such talk. It'll not come to that." Hazel felt Luke's head. "If any of ya get a sore throat or feel hot, tell me. I wish to God I'd gone against yore Pa and got the doctor when Paul first got sick."

"Will ya get the doctor if I get sick, Ma?"

"I will, Luke. I promise." Hazel hugged the small boy to her.

Yates untied the rope he'd used to tie Ernie's legs together. He and Deke hauled him to his feet.

"Are you going to walk to the car or do I have to knock you out and drag you?"

"Let me do it, Yates," Deke said. "Let me hit him one more time."

"Yeah, ya ugly little bastard." Ernie snarled. "The only way you can get to me is with my hands tied behind my back."

"From the looks of your mouth, Deke got in a few good licks." Yates opened the back door of his car and pushed Ernie in. He landed on his back. Yates grabbed his feet and twisted the rope around them again. "You look pretty good trussed up like a hog. Smell like one, too!"

"What about my cycle, *Okie?* It better be here when I get back or your ass will be mud."

"Don't worry. I'll take care of the cycle. If you don't have the money you stole from Miss Kinnard, the judge will give her the cycle."

"She's my wife, you stupid shit! The money she had belonged to both of us."

"She says not and I believe her. That woman has too much sense to tie up to a small-caliber dumb-ass like you. Here's a sack from the store, Deke. Take it to Leona and tell her that I'll be back as soon as I can." Yates got into the car. "It'll just be my luck that Virgil will show up while I'm gone and I'll miss out on the fun again."

"If he comes, I won't hurt him until you get here."

Yates drove leisurely into town admiring Deke's courage and entertained by the constant flow of threats and curses coming from the man in the backseat of his car. He stopped on the side of the courthouse that housed the Sheriff's Department and noticed only one police car there. He hoped it was the one Sheriff McChesney used. He didn't have the patience right now to deal with Deputy Ham.

"Don't go away. I'll be right back," Yates said to Ernie when he left the car, obviously enjoying the man's discomfort.

McChesney was standing in the doorway talking to one of the men Yates had seen in the barbershop.

"Thanks for coming in, Gerald. I'll take care of it." The man walked away. McChesney gave Yates an irritated look. "What do you want?"

"That's a fine way to treat a law-abiding citizen who's been doing your work. I've got a customer for you."

"Yeah? Who?"

"Let's sit down and talk about it."

"When are you leaving town, Yates?" The sheriff moved behind his desk and sat down.

"Why does that concern you?" Yates took the round-backed chair and stretched his long legs out in front of him.

"I have the feeling that trouble follows you wherever you go. Are you here to tell me why Andy's girl ran away and where she was hiding out?"

"She wasn't hiding. She was taken and kept against her will."

Sheriff McChesney straightened in his chair. "Who?" he demanded crisply.

"I'm not at liberty to tell you just yet. Someone found her and brought her home. She's all right."

"Then someone collected the reward for bringing her home."

"Not yet, but I'll see that he gets it."

"Are you planning on taking the law in your own hands?"

"Nooo." Yates drew the word out, then added, "Not until I get a few more facts."

"Are you saying that she was kidnapped?"

"I'm not saying anything . . . yet."

"Since the Lindbergh baby, kidnapping is a federal offense."

"Yeah, I heard that."

"Well, dammit, Yates, if you know something, spill it."

"When I know more, you'll be the first to know after I beat the holy shit out of the one who took her."

The sheriff sprang to his feet. "Dammit, Yates! You're a aggravating cuss."

Yates laughed and stood. "Is that all you can say, 'dammit Yates'?"

"If you know who took that girl, I want to know who it was . . . now!"

"I don't know who took her. I've a faint idea where she was and who brought her home, but I'm not saying until I can prove it."

"Have it your way." McChesney sat back down. "If I find out that you're withholding evidence about a kidnapping, I'll do everything in my power to send you to jail."

"Fair enough. I'd expect no less. Now about the *customer* I brought to occupy one of your jail cells. This man is a real horse's patoot. His name's Ernie Harding."

Ten minutes later the sheriff and Yates walked out to his car. Ernie was lying half-on and half-off the seat. He was wet with sweat and mad as a stepped-on snake.

"He thinks he's hot now," Yates taunted and winked at the sheriff. "He'll sweat a bucket full when he's busting rocks at McCalester with the other cons." He untied Ernie's feet and pulled him out of the car.

"Who is filing charges?"

"A girl named Margie Kinnard. He's not only a thief, he's a bully. While he was beating the hockey out of Deke Bales, he took time out to knock a pregnant woman to the ground."

"Was the woman hurt?"

"Don't know yet."

"He's twice the size of Deke."

"And twice the size of the woman he stole from. If I wasn't such a law-abiding citizen, I'd take him out in the country and go through him like a hot chili pepper going through a gringo."

"The little shithead came at me with a tire iron," Ernie snarled.

"Deke's smart enough to know a bull-headed blow-hard when he sees one. This is one big, bad hombre, Sheriff. He steals money from a little slip of a girl and goes on down the highway, leaving her to fend for herself."

"I didn't steal anything, Sheriff. The money belonged to both me and my wife."

"The girl says she isn't married to this buzzard. She agreed to pay gas and food for a ride to California. He stole her money and left her in Andy's campground." Yates's tone was no longer teasing.

"Bring the girl in and I'll take her statement. Meanwhile, I'll put this bird in a cell for safekeeping."

"It may be tomorrow morning before I can bring her in."

"That's all right. Tomorrow, a week from tomorrow. The judge won't hear the case for a week anyhow. I'll give this boy a swatter and put him to work killing flies back in the cells. If he doesn't work, he doesn't eat."

"Do you think he can handle that job?"

"If he can't handle it, I can put him to work cleaning out the septic tank."

"Shit-work. He'd understand that," Yates taunted. "He doesn't know a bee from a bullfoot, Sheriff. He's not got enough brains to hold his ears apart much less aim a fly swatter."

The sheriff had just removed the rope from the prisoner's hands and was putting on the handcuffs when Ernie's temper exploded. He broke loose and dived for Yates, swinging his ham-like fists. He had made only two steps when a rock-hard fist, aimed with precision, slammed into his jaw. He hit the ground like a pole-axed steer.

The sheriff looked down on his prisoner, then up at Yates with disgust. He poked Ernie with his booted foot. Ernie didn't move.

"Dad-burnit, Yates. Why'd you have to do that?"

"I was afraid I'd not get a chance to hit him, but he took the bait." Yates's grin was one of pure pleasure. "Sorry I hit him so hard."

"I don't care that you hit him, but now I've got to drag him to the cell."

"I'll help you. I'll drag him all the way to the Texas line if you'll let me hit him again."

Chapter 26

LEONA AND DEKE WAITED FOR MR. HAYES to get the Ford started. He ground on the starter until Deke feared he'd run down the battery. Then finally it caught.

"Give it a little more gas," Deke yelled. "Don't let it die and don't turn it off till ya get there." They watched as the car crept out onto the highway. Mrs. Hayes waved. Leona waved back.

"Mr. Hayes must love her very much. He was so worried about her he was shaking. Do you think she'll be all right?"

"Didn't the doctor say so, darlin'?"

"After the doctor swabbed the girls' throats, I asked him to look at Mrs. Hayes. He said she could deliver at any time, but she wasn't showing signs of labor yet. He thought they had time to get on down to Erick where Mr. Hayes's brother lives. Mr. Hayes told the doctor right up front that he didn't have money to pay, but as soon as he did, he'd send it."

"He said the same to me, darlin'. The man's poor as dirt, but he's got pride."

"To save his pride, Doctor Langley said that if he'd come out here, especially to see Mrs. Hayes, he would expect pay, but that as long as he was already being paid to make the call, there was no charge."

"That was decent of Doc. Yates said he was an all-right sort of feller."

"You gave Mr. Hayes some money, didn't you?"

"Ya got a eagle eye, darlin'. I gave him a dollar."

"Take it out of the garage money, Deke."

"No. The dollar was for jumpin' in when that feller had me down."

"I saw him on the grinder sharpening tools while his wife was resting."

"Yeah, that was 'cause I put a patch on his tire."

"Deke Bales! You don't want anyone to know it, but you've got a heart of gold."

"My mama likes me." He laughed, obviously pleased by her praise, and went to put gas in a car that had stopped at the pump. "And you do, too, darlin'," he said over his shoulder.

When Yates returned, he talked to Deke for a few minutes, then went to the house.

"Come eat," Leona called when she heard his step on the porch. His eyes drank in the sight of her as he followed her to the kitchen where Margie was putting a bowl of green beans and new potatoes on the table. "It's a good thing we cooked plenty or there wouldn't have been anything left for you. We invited Mr. and Mrs. Hayes to eat with us." Leona took a pan of cornbread from the oven.

"Do you do that often?" he teased, wanting her to look at him.

"Do what often?"

"Take folks in off the road and invite them to dinner."

"We do it every once in a while. Wash up. Margie and I are anxious to hear what happened when you took Ernie to the sheriff."

While he ate, he gleefully told them that Ernie had given him the opportunity to hit him.

"The sheriff had untied him and was putting on the handcuffs when he came at me. My only regret is that I hit him so hard, he didn't wake up until after we'd gotten him in his cell. He's such a mouthy cuss, he'd have given me another chance to tie into him.

"Margie, you'll have to go in and file charges against Ernie in order to get your money back. He had twenty-eight dollars in his pocket when the sheriff searched him."

"Only twenty-eight dollars?" Margie's worried eyes looked away from Yates. "The dirty rat! I wonder what he did with the rest of it."

"My guess is that he got in a card game and lost it. He may have thought you had more money hidden somewhere and came back to find it."

"He played a lot of cards back in Conway. I never told him how much money I had. Did he think I would be foolish enough to go with him again?"

"He thought you'd be glad to see a familiar face." Leona got up to chip more ice for the tea.

"If I could get the twenty-eight dollars back, I'd buy a bus ticket and go back home."

"You'd go back to Conway?" Leona asked.

"I know that I could get a job there. I could start saving up again. And . . . I've got friends."

"But no relatives?"

Margie hesitated. "My . . . daddy is there, but he doesn't have much use for me." She tossed her head, dismissing the subject. "Twenty-eight dollars isn't enough to get me to California and keep me until I find a job, but it's enough to get me back home."

"California isn't a place for a girl alone without friends or relatives," Yates said. "A man works all day in a field for a dollar. You would probably pick half as much and earn two bits."

"I have a half-brother in Bakersville. I don't know him. I wrote to him once, but he didn't answer."

"You could write to him again," Leona said.

"No. He knows that I exist and has never made an attempt to know me. I will not put myself in the embarrassing position of having him turn me away. You've been to California?" Margie asked Yates.

"Yeah, a couple of times."

"Have you been to Hollywood?"

"Just drove through it."

"You have? Did you see any movie stars?"

"I saw Charlie Chaplin and Charles Farrell."

"You did? Did you see Janet Gaynor?"

"Only in *Seventh Heaven*." He smiled at Margie's wide-eyed interest in the movie stars.

"I saw that in Joplin. My favorites are Janet Gaynor, Gloria Swanson and Greta Garbo, who is so beautiful and quiet. She gives me the shivers."

"I like the western movies with Tom Mix or Hoot Gibson." Yates looked at Leona and winked.

"Tom Mix." Margie sighed. "Why didn't you try to get in the movies, Mr. Yates? You're as good-looking as Tom Mix. Oh . . ." Margie's face turned a beet red.

Leona got up to refill his tea glass.

"Me?" Yates let out a whoop of laughter. "I liked California but not enough to stay there. The climate is great for growing things. There are large camps of people out there waiting to pick oranges, lemons or other produce as soon as they're ready."

"Mr. Yates? When do you think I can get my money back from Ernie?"

"The sheriff thought the judge would be back in town tonight or tomorrow. I'll take you in to talk to him."

"Then I'll go back home." She looked quickly at Leona. "But before I go, I'll help you can the beans and put up the pickles."

"It's been nice having you here," Leona said. "Not only for the help, but for company."

"I thank my lucky stars that Ernie didn't dump me some other place."

"Aunt Lee!" Ruth Ann came to lean against Leona. "When will we know if we're going to be sick with diphtheria?"

"The doctor said only a few days. Mr. Fleming will take the swabs to the city tomorrow. Then tomorrow or the next day he'll bring your daddy home."

"Will you be going then, Mr. Yates?"

"Not for a day or two." His eyes went to Leona. "I'll wait until your daddy's on his feet."

"I wish you would stay."

"Thanks, sugarfoot. I never thought I'd hear you say that. I'd better go see if Deke wants to go home."

After Yates left, Ruth Ann lingered, snuggling up to her aunt.

"The doctor said he wouldn't tell about . . . you know. But what if he does?"

"Don't worry, honey. He doesn't want to get Isaac in trouble. He thought it very brave of him to bring you home."

"I don't want Isaac to get diphtheria."

"The doctor will keep an eye on him. Show me the string of paper dolls Margie cut out for you. She said you'd put some pretty dresses on them with your crayons."

* * *

Deke stayed for supper, then left for the Fleming ranch.

"If ya need me, darlin', send Yates and I'll come a flyin'."

Leona was glad Yates wasn't near to hear Deke say that. The idea of her sending him to fetch Deke if she was in trouble was laughable to all but Deke, who didn't have an insincere bone in his body.

"I'll do that, Deke. Thanks for being here the last couple of days."

"Take care, darlin'. I'll be over to see Andy when he gets back. He's goin' to need a hand once in a while after Yates leaves."

Deke crammed his hat in the leather pouch that hung on the side of his cycle and jumped on the start crank. The motor came to life.

Leona watched her faithful friend ride down the highway on his motorcycle, his straw-colored hair waving in the breeze, the sleeves of his shirt puffed out by the wind. He was dear to her and she wished with all her heart that she could have loved him the way he deserved to be loved.

She sat on the bench in front of the garage and watched the cars go by. During the warmest part of summer, some long-distance travelers preferred to travel during the cool part of the day and stop in the afternoon when the car or truck would be more likely to heat up. A few who passed by waved. Leona waved back and silently wished them a safe journey.

Saying that his horse needed exercise, Yates had saddled him; and after giving each of the girls a ride around the yard, he had ridden out across the pasture. Tomorrow or the next day Andy would be home and a few days after that Yates would leave. Lord, she hoped that she wouldn't disgrace herself and cry. She caught her lower lip between her teeth and vowed to do her utmost to send him on his way with her thanks and a smile. *Oh, but it would be hard!*

The wind picked up bringing with it a cloud of dust from the southwest. It crossed Leona's mind that she should go to the house and close the windows. Although they were south of the dust bowl, winds often brought dust from the Texas prairies.

She didn't move and darkness came suddenly. Enjoying this time alone and allowing her face muscles and her shoulders to relax, she leaned back against the wall of the garage. Deep in thought, she did not notice Yates standing beneath the big tree between the garage and the house. She would have been surprised to see the expression in his pale eyes as he watched her.

He was thinking that his life was in danger of being changed, and all because of a slim, spunky woman with dark auburn hair and sky-blue eyes. There was a fastidiousness about her that he liked. She always looked neat and fresh even while milking the cow, working in the garden or a dozen other chores she did during the day. She had been treated badly by family and so-called friends, but it hadn't touched the pure inner core of her. She was sweet and loyal and even handled Deke's unwanted affection for her with compassion for his feelings.

Dammit, he couldn't find a single thing about her to dislike.

When Leona stood, he went toward her, hoping to keep her to himself a while longer. He saw in her intelligence and honor and beauty. God. Just looking at her gave him an erection. Taking off her clothes would be like unwrapping a treasure on Christmas morning.

He remembered the first time he had seen her. She had run out into the yard with the rifle to shoot the skunk. He saw her again when he passed the porch after taking his horse to the barn. His first impression was that she was rather plain. How could he have been so blind?

She didn't appear to be surprised to see him and spoke as if they had been carrying on a conversation.

"If the wind keeps up we'll have a dust storm. I'd better close the windows."

"Margie was closing them when I came by the house. She told me you were out here."

"Just catching my breath after a busy day."

"Sit with me for a while. Margie is with the girls."

"I should go in. There are a hundred things I should be doing."

"Won't it keep until tomorrow? Stay with me. We won't have many more chances like this."

"I know. You'll be going soon." It hurt to say the words aloud.

"Not until the doctor gives Andy the okay to work." He took her hand and pulled her down on the bench beside him. "I told Andy that I'd stay until he's well enough to handle things."

"If you want to go, Deke may be able to come help."

"Trying to get rid of me?" he teased, then said, "Deke is busy with the machinery out at the ranch. It was good of Fleming to spare him the last couple of days."

"Mr. Fleming thinks a lot of Andy. Do you think he'll bring him home tomorrow?"

"If his business keeps him late, he'll bring him the next day." Yates reached for her hand and laced his fingers with hers. They lapsed into silence.

"It's going to be dusty tonight," Leona said, because she couldn't think of anything else to say.

"The wind is high up so maybe it won't be too bad." He

released her hand and put his arm around her. "I like having you close to me. You're soft and sweet."

"And . . . available?" She wished she hadn't said that.

His arm tightened around her; his fingers tilted her face toward him. When she tried to turn it away, he cupped her cheek and held it.

"You don't have a very high opinion of yourself, do you, little sweetheart?"

"Yes, I do. I know what I am and I know what others think of me."

"Do you know what I think of you?"

"I've a pretty good idea. You think I'm a fairly good cook, that I'm good with Andy's girls—"

"Is that all?"

"Well . . . you probably think that I'm a naive country girl who is flattered to be kissed by a man who has been everywhere and done everything."

"I don't think that at all. I think that I'm a man who has been *privileged* to kiss a sweet, pretty woman, who has more integrity in her little finger than most people I know have in their entire bodies."

"You . . . don't know me very well. I can be bitchy, mean and hateful—"

"I've not seen that."

"Maybe it's because I'm so deceitful that I can keep it hidden."

"I don't think so." He laughed and pressed his mouth lightly to hers. His lips felt wonderful and strangely familiar. She let her eyes drift shut. "You're a hatful all right." He kissed her again. "I like to kiss you. I could sit here and kiss you all night long."

"You'd soon get tired."

"You may be right," he murmured between nibbling

kisses. "Kissing you makes me want to do more . . . *intimate* things with you."

Leona was incapable of reply. She gave a tiny sigh against his lips. She was melting against him when she felt him pull away. She knew an instant of disappointment, then realized a big sedan had come to an abrupt stop on the highway and was backing up to turn into the drive.

Chapter 27

YATES WAS INSTANTLY ALERT. "Gas customer." He removed his arm as the car pulled up beside the gas pump and spotlighted them in the headlights. "My rifle is just inside the garage door," he whispered.

Two men got out of the car. "Where's the cripple?" one demanded.

"In the hospital. You want gas?"

"Yeah. That ain't all we want."

"I know. Andy told me. You want gas and you want me to keep my mouth shut."

"Yeah. That's what we want."

Yates was already unlocking the gas pump and working the lever to fill the glass cylinder. When he inserted the nozzle in the gas tank, he noticed the back springs on the sedan were sagging. The car was heavily loaded. Bootleggers.

The man who walked over toward the bench where Leona sat was thick-necked and meaty. She stood as he approached. The driver reached in and switched off the headlights. Yates jerked the nozzle from the tank, stepped over the hose and in quick strides was between the man and Leona.

"She belongs to me. I don't share."

The man laughed. "Just wanted to look at her. I see now that she ain't fancy enough to suit me."

"She suits me just fine." Yates took her hand and brought her along when he went back to the gas pump. He positioned her beside the pump, inserted the nozzle again and spoke to the driver, who came to lean against the car. "How many gallons?"

"Fill it."

The man who had approached Leona came to stand behind the car to watch Yates. He pulled a cigar from his pocket.

"Don't light that," Yates said sharply. "You could blow us to hell and back."

"You don't have to tell me that. I'm no fool."

Yates ignored him and spoke to the driver. "Eleven gallons is all it'll hold." He pulled out the nozzle and screwed the cap on the gas tank. "That'll be a dollar fifty-four."

The man put his hand in his pocket and pulled out a handful of change. Out of it he picked out three fifty-cent pieces and a nickel and put them in Yates's hand.

"You takin' over the cripple's woman?"

"She isn't *Andy's* woman."

"She lives here with him."

"She's his sister. Not that's it's any business of yours."

"Touchy, ain't ya?"

"About her, I am."

"Tell the cripple that Ramsey was here." The driver slid under the wheel and started the motor. After giving Yates a menacing look, the passenger got in and slammed the door.

The car left the drive and Leona sputtered, "I hate it when they call Andy '*cripple*' or '*crip.*' "

"That's the second late bootlegger that's stopped since I've been here." Yates put the lock back on the gas pump.

"You never told me—"

"A few nights ago a truck pulled in about midnight with four guys riding in the truck bed. The driver asked for Andy. He wanted gas and a bulb for his taillight. I figure he'd made a delivery and he'd broken out his taillight to keep from being followed."

"Andy says Prohibition is wrong. All it is doing is making a few men rich. He thinks that what folks do is their own business. He's in the business to sell gas and supplies, and he'll sell them to whomever needs them."

"Has the sheriff ever questioned him?"

"I think he has a time or two."

"I need to wash my hands, honey. I've got gasoline on them."

"Well . . . I was going in anyway. Goodnight."

"Don't go in yet," he said quickly and caught her arm. "I can wash at the pump. Then we can walk, sit or whatever you want to do. Stay with me for a while."

"All right." Her heart thumped wildly. *He wanted to be with her.* Knowing that made her happy even though she was aware that there was heartbreak ahead.

They walked around the house. It was dark except for a light in the bedroom. Through the window, Leona could see Margie on the double bed with a girl on each side of her. She was turning the pages of a *Silver Screen* magazine and telling the girls about the pictures.

"It looks like Margie has won Ruth Ann over." Yates led her back around the house to the porch swing after he washed in the basin on the back porch.

"Margie just eats up anything about movie stars. She told me she saved to go to Hollywood so that she could see some of them in person."

"She'd be lucky to see one or two. They don't mingle

much with the common folk." He sat down beside her. "I'm glad Deke greased these chains." His arm arched over her head and he pulled her close to his side as if it were something he did every day. "Where were we when we were interrupted? Ah, yes. I remember now. Kiss me, sweet woman," his deep voice demanded.

When he bent his head, she blindly obeyed him. His lips were warm and urgent. He had expected her to participate in the kiss and wasn't disappointed. As before, her nerves ignited, and she accepted the stroking of his tongue along her lower lip. With her nose buried against his cheek, the kiss deepened and she leaned into it, floating in a sea of sensuality where everything was softly given and softly received.

His lips eased from hers and moved over her cheek to her ear. His breath was as much a caress as his searching lips.

"Do you still think I'm a rude, arrogant, know-it-all?"

"Uh-huh."

"I don't blame you. You've made me kind of step back and take a look at myself." He caught her hand and brought it to his mouth, planting a hot kiss in the palm. "I took it for granted that you'd want me here."

"I didn't really like you, but—"

"But you like me now. Say it, sweetheart." Without giving her a chance to answer, he kissed her again, with hard, deep kisses. She knew she should tell him to stop, but she had no strength or will to resist him.

When he had drunk his fill of her lips, he moved to her neck. Tremors vibrated through her body. His hand moved up from her waist to her breast and cupped it lightly. His fingertips found the hardening nipple and gently stroked it. His tongue laved her earlobe, then caught it between his teeth and nibbled on it gently.

She never remembered wrapping her arm around his

neck. He captured her mouth again with his and kissed her with reckless abandonment. Her nipple was like a hard pebble in the center of his palm. His relentless caresses sensitized her whole body and made it quake with an unknown desire.

"Oh, God, I want to love you." The soft utterance that came from his throat was a purr of pure pleasure.

His murmured words fought their way through the muddle of her feeling to her foggy brain, where she had ignored the blaring horns that had sounded an alarm. He expanded the kiss with a pressure that sought deeper satisfaction. The fervor of his passion excited her, and she met it with unrestrained response.

Leona felt her mind whirl, and her nerves become acutely sensitized with the almost overwhelming need to melt into him and ease the ache of her aroused body. Caught in the throes of desire, she pressed herself against him, her arms holding him with surprising strength.

Resisting the pressure about his neck, Yates lifted his head to look at her. His breath came quickly and was cool on her lips, made wet by his kiss.

"You are one sweet woman," he confessed in a raspy whisper. Their mouths met and were no longer gentle. They kissed deeply, hungrily. His fingers moved lovingly over the breast he was holding. He cradled her in his arms, and with smoothing motions of his hands caressed up and down her rib cage and over her breasts.

Leona suddenly realized that she was in danger of losing her ability to think rationally. She caught his wrist and moved his hand away from her.

"No! I can't do this!" She turned her face and tried to push away from him. "I can't . . . I can't—"

"You can't kiss me? You just did." His voice was slurred with an obvious effort to control his breathing.

"I can't . . . be just an . . . amusement." Hurt made her voice sharp.

"Amusement? What the hell are you talking about?" Irritation made his equally as sharp.

"Well . . . you've been stuck here for a while and you're bored. I understand your need for a little . . . excitement."

"Bored? There's been so much going on around here that I've not even had time to ride my horse until tonight."

"I doubt that it's been very exciting for you."

"Exciting enough," he said dryly.

"Yates, I'm a girl who has never been on a date, who has never gone to a dance or a picture show with a man. I've never been kissed in a dark car and never before on a front porch. A so-called decent man wouldn't be seen walking down the street with me. I really can't blame you for thinking that I'd be willing to do . . . this . . . to help while away the time until Andy comes home and you can leave." By the time she was finished, tears were on her cheeks.

"Whiling away the time, huh? That's why you think I want to hold you and kiss you?"

"Yes, and so do you, if you'll admit it." She sniffed, trying hard to make it a small one, but he heard anyway.

"You're crying."

"I'm not!"

"Yes, you are." His fingers tried to turn her face to him, and when she held it firmly away, they stroked her cheeks to wipe away the tears. "So you thought I was amusing myself with you?"

"Weren't you?"

"I thought it was mutual. Didn't you enjoy it?"

"You know I did." She looked into his face, and there was

something there that she had dreamed of but never hoped to see. Was it a little like loving concern for her? No, she simply was seeing what she wanted to see.

"Then why did you cry?"

"I don't know. I've cried more lately than I've cried in years." She hesitated, then began again honestly. "You'll be going away. I don't . . . want to fall in love with you. I already have enough grief in my life." She moved out of his embrace and stood for a moment looking at him, then turned to go into the house.

"Don't go in. Let's talk about this, Leona."

"No. I can't think straight when you . . . when I'm with you. Goodnight." She slipped inside the darkened house.

Well, hell.

Yates left the porch and went to stand beside his car and lit a cigarette. For a moment or two, he was ashamed of how much he wanted to bury himself in her and ease his need for physical release. He would see that she enjoyed it, too. He wasn't that selfish. He puffed on his cigarette and thought of how she had responded to his kisses.

Had she expected his confession of undying love? He hadn't planned to *love* any woman. He liked her, liked being with her. She calmed the restlessness in him for now, but that wasn't enough to make him give up his plans and take a wife when he wasn't ready.

Guilt swamped him, even as he told himself he had nothing to feel guilty about. Leona was a grown woman. She could have gotten up off that bench and gone into the house when he'd kissed her the first time. She'd had the perfect excuse when the car came in for gas.

But she'd stayed.

She didn't want to fall in love with him. Well, that was all right with him. He hadn't planned to take a wife for quite a few years and when he did, she didn't have to love him, just like him. She would have her duties, and he would have his. The kids would come as the natural result of her being a good bed mate.

A woman like Leona was exactly the kind of woman he would consider . . . if he were ready to settle down. But he wanted a woman with no strings attached.

Leona was not that woman.

The next phase in his life was to go home and take over his ranch and see what remained after Arnold Taylor and his wife had been in charge of it for the past ten years. That would be most any day now, if his San Angelo lawyer was to be believed.

He dropped his cigarette and ground it into the dirt with the toe of his boot. Then, not liking at all the empty feeling in the pit of his stomach, he went to his cot in the garage. Leona was right. He hadn't taken their petting seriously. He knew the events of her life, but that wasn't the reason he had kissed her. She was pretty and he'd wanted to kiss her. It occurred to him now that he had that urge every time he was with her.

He stared off into the night. Remembering her small waist, rounded hips and soft breast caused his palms to sweat. When her nipple had responded to his touch and became like a pebble against his palm, his erection had become so big and so hard he wasn't sure the buttons on his pants would hold it.

Well, hell.

Leona would never leave Andy and the girls if he did decide that she was the one. He didn't know why he was even thinking of the possibility. Yet, deep in the back of his mind was the disturbing thought that maybe he'd not be able to leave her without looking back.

For all her sassiness, there was a vulnerability about her that tugged at him. It was why he had felt so possessive toward her. Why he'd wanted to kill Virgil for the things he'd said to her and why he resented even Deke touching her. Where had the insane idea come from that she was his?

He felt sorry for her. Yes, that was it. He'd always had a soft spot for *defenseless* creatures. He smiled in the darkness. When riled, she was about as defenseless as a cornered cat. She'd do whatever she had to do to protect herself and those she loved. She was one of the gutsiest women he'd ever met.

Hell, Yates. Who are you trying to fool? You're falling in love with that girl!

Virgil was waiting for Deputy Ham when he parked the police car in front of his house a little after midnight. It was a quiet, dark, moonless night. He came out of the bushes at the side of the house before the deputy reached the porch. Abe was with him, but stayed out of sight.

"Wayne—"

"Jesus Christ! Don't ever come at me like that. I could have shot you."

"I've got to talk to ya."

"It's midnight. I just got off work. Go home, Virgil."

"Did ya hear anythin' about the girl?"

"Only that she's home. I'm worn out. I'm going to bed."

"Hold on, now. That feller, Yates, was in talkin' to the sheriff. What'd he say?"

"How the hell do I know!"

"Ya got to quit that swearin', Wayne, or yo're headin' straight to hell," Virgil wailed.

"You're enough to make a preacher cuss. I've told you all I know. No one has tied you or me to Andy's kid. Now are you satisfied? Keep your mouth shut and you'll be all right."

"I'm losin' control, Wayne." Virgil continued to whine. "Hazel ain't mindin' me no more. She's a talkin' back and sassin'. Next the little boys'll be takin' her lead. She's sent off for the two ungrateful curs that left home. They been off workin' at a CCC camp somewhere. They've done gone to the dogs, a drinkin' and chasin' after loose women."

"Your family problems are not mine, Virgil. If you got to talk about it, talk to Brother Muse. I've got to go in. My wife will have heard the car and wonder who I'm talking to. If she knew it was you, I'd be in deep shit!"

"What's McChesney sayin' 'bout Andy's kid?"

"Not much. If you can believe what Yates says, the girl didn't say where she'd been."

"Why is that, Wayne? There somethin' wrong here—"

"Ya dumb-ass. Course there's something wrong. You shouldn't of tied her up."

"Hazel's got to be the one who let her out. Maybe the kid got home by herself. But she couldn't of got loose and outta that shed by herself."

"I don't want to hear any more about it. I'm going in." Wayne started for the house. Virgil followed.

"You knew when you brought her out to my place that I would put her in the shed. She'll tell the sheriff. She'll tell that Yates feller. I know she will."

"If she does, it's your own fault. You were so all fired determined to get the girls to spite your sister."

"It weren't for spite. It was to save their souls—"

"Holy shit, Virgil. Little kids'd go to heaven anyway. You know that."

"Little kids has got to have a good example set before 'em or they'll grow up wild and sinful. The devil will get them in his clutches and it's hard to get out. Ya ought to know 'bout that. He had a good hold on you, till ya shook him off."

"I'm not going to argue with you, Virgil. Believe what you want to believe. I told you when I took the girl out to your place that you'd better take her home."

"Ya never said nothin' of the kind. All ya said was, 'Here she is. You owe me.' I figured it out, Wayne. Ya wanted me to keep my mouth shut about your smokin' so the brothers wouldn't throw you off the church council."

"It'll be your word against mine, Virgil. Don't drag me into it. I warn you."

"Wayne?" Livy was at the screendoor. "Who's out there? Is something wrong?"

"Nothing's wrong. Just tying up some loose ends from work." Then in a low tone to Virgil, "Stay away from here." He tromped across the porch and went into the house.

Virgil went back across the yard. "Come on, Abe. That bird's gettin' too big for his britches."

Chapter 28

BARKER FLEMING STOPPED AT THE GARAGE on his way to Oklahoma City. He had already picked up the package Doctor Langley wanted him to take to the clinic along with a letter from him to Andy's doctor in the city.

"I'm sorry that I'll not be able to get back tonight," he said to Leona and the girls, who had come out onto the porch when Yates brought Mr. Fleming to the house. "I have business to attend to in the morning at nine o'clock. If everything goes right, I'll be finished with it, and we can leave around noon and be here by supper time."

"Is there a chance the doctor won't let Andy come home?" Leona asked.

"Doctor Langley seems to think that he'll be released and that he'll be able to give him the rest of the shots. Andy will be terribly disappointed if the doctor insists that he stay. He's pretty tired of being up there away from his family."

Barker Fleming patted Ruth Ann on the head. "Marie wants you to come out to the ranch for a day or two before school starts."

"I'll ask Daddy when he gets here. I think he'll let me come."

"He's anxious to get home. He told me how much he misses his girls."

"Mr. Fleming," Leona said. "I didn't get a chance to thank you for your help the other day. It's a comfort to know that we have friends we can call on in times of trouble."

"No thanks are necessary, Miss Dawson. I'm more than glad to help you or Andy whenever I can."

Fleming smiled fondly at Leona, and Yates's suspicious mind suddenly became alert to the fact that the Indian was a good-looking man, rich and a widower. Deke had told him that the mother of Fleming's children had died a few years back. Was he looking to replace her with Leona? He was at least twenty years her senior, but to some women his assets would more than make up for the age difference.

Yates's eyes narrowed and honed in on Leona's face in an attempt to assess her interest in the man. She was gazing at him as if he had just handed her the world!

Dammit to hell! Didn't she have better sense than to flirt with a man of Fleming's obvious experience? Was she willing to take on another family to raise because Fleming was rich? He was part Cherokee. Didn't she know that in his Indian culture a wife would never be an equal partner with a husband?

She deserved more than a second-hand family.

"After Andy gets home I'd like to bring you all out to the ranch for a picnic."

In polished boots, tailor-made fringed jacket and ten-dollar Stetson, Barker Fleming would stand out in any crowd, not only because of his dress, but because of his bearing and self-confidence. Yates had to admit that a woman would be foolish to turn him down.

"Goody, goody!" JoBeth jumped up and down and

clapped her hands. Ruth Ann gave her a quelling glance. "Can Aunt Leona come?" JoBeth asked.

Fleming laughed. "Of course, she can, little tadpole."

"Yates and Daddy will come. What's a tadpole?"

"I'll explain it to you later. Mr. Fleming probably wants to get on the road. It's a long way to the city." Leona smiled up at the man so sweetly that something tightened in the area of Yates's heart.

He waited impatiently while Fleming took his leave, got into his car and pulled out onto the highway. The girls ran back in the house to tell Margie about the picnic. Leona, not wanting to be alone with Yates, opened the door to follow the girls into the house.

"He's too old for you." His crisp voice stopped her in her tracks.

She turned. "Are you talking to me?"

"You know I am. I said he's too old for you."

"Who are you talking about?"

"Fleming, dammit. Marry him and you're taking on another bunch of kids to raise. Kids that aren't yours."

"What in the world? Mr. Fleming is a gentlemen. It's more than I can say for you."

"Yeah, and he's got money. He'd move you out to the ranch where you'd not have to go into town but once or twice a year. When you did, no one would dare turn their noses up at you because of the Fleming influence. That's what you're angling for, isn't it? You want the protection of a man like Fleming, and you'd marry him to get it."

"You . . . are out of your mind. Mr. Fleming is a friend, has been a friend since long before my sister died. He has no more romantic interest in me than he does in JoBeth." Leona's temper was rising as fast as her awareness of what Yates was insinuating.

"No? How about your interest in him? Hooking him would solve all your problems."

"What problems? I'm doing just fine, thank you."

"You're not doing fine! Virgil is still out there doing his level best to make your life miserable. The narrow-minded biddies and fanatics in town will jump on you like flies on a fresh cowpie every time they get the chance. That's why you don't go to town unless you have to. You're not fine! And that's a fact!" His voice was sharp with tension. His silvery eyes glittered angrily.

"I got along here before you came, Mr. Yates, and I'll get along after you go. The problems I have right now, I've had all my life. The only new one is *you.*"

Leona took a deep breath, her pulse thudding like a tom-tom in her head. She had never before seen eyes like his. There was strength and stubbornness there, just as there was in the rest of his face—in all of him for that matter. But it was mostly his eyes, silver light, clear, deep, seeming to know everything about her, that she would remember long after he was gone.

"I didn't realize that you still resented me so much," he said at last.

"Well, I do. I resent your high-handed interference. So there!"

"You enjoyed what we did last night as much as I. You didn't think I was high-handed then."

"Yes, I did," she retorted stubbornly. "I may be a countrified girl from the sticks, but I'm not stupid. I know exactly what you had in mind."

"If you're so smart, tell me."

"I don't have time to argue with you about it now. I need to get the beans canned while Margie is here." She tried to restore a calm facade, hating that she had risen to his baiting and afraid she was going to cry.

"You do it every time. When you get backed into a corner and don't have an answer, you take off like a cat with its tail on fire."

"I do not!" Her features froze into a glare.

"You did last night."

"I was ashamed that . . . that I had let you paw me."

"I can guarantee you'll not be *pawed* again . . . by me," he said tersely, then pulled his hat down on his forehead, spun on his heel and went back down the path to the garage.

Leona didn't know whether to cry or to scream.

By mid-morning, the back of Leona's dress was wet with sweat, and rivulets of it ran down into her eyes from her forehead. She and Margie had carried the kerosene stove to the porch where they were boiling the jars of green beans to preserve them. Yates had brought his fan from the garage to the kitchen and placed it on the table, where the breeze would blow on the girls as they were working to pack the jars.

He had not looked at or spoken to Leona during the brief time it took to set up the fan. While she worked, Leona played over in her mind the conversation they'd had after Mr. Fleming left and wished that she hadn't used the word "pawed," but it was too late now to take it back.

The noon meal of sliced tomatoes, sandwiches made from egg salad, iced tea and canned peaches was eaten on the front porch. Leona insisted that Margie sit down with Yates and the girls while she tended to the jars in the copper boiler.

By late afternoon both women were tired, but proud of

what they had accomplished. Jars of green beans were lined up on the counter ready to go to the cellar.

"Aunt Lee, Aunt Lee. The sheriff is here." JoBeth ran into the kitchen and skidded to a stop. She never walked when she could run. Afraid that she would miss something, she scurried out, slamming the screendoor behind her after she had delivered the message.

Leona handed Margie a towel to wipe the sweat off her face, then followed her out onto the porch. JoBeth had plopped herself in the porch swing. Ruth Ann was on the other end of the porch skipping rope.

The sheriff and Ernie Harding were approaching the house. They stopped as they reached the steps. Margie drew in a strangled breath when she saw the man who had stolen from her. Sheriff McChesney tipped his hat politely.

"Howdy, ladies." Then after both women acknowledged his greeting, he said, "Miss Kinnard, I spoke with the judge this morning and explained your situation. He said Harding was due pay for bringing you from Conway to Sayre and if he gave you the twenty-eight dollars he had in his pocket you wouldn't have a case against him."

"I don't have a case against him?" she echoed. "He stole ninety-two dollars out of my suitcase."

"It's your word against his. He admits to taking forty dollars."

"Forty dollars?" she cried, cramming a fist against her mouth. "It was ninety-two dollars and he knows it." She shot a glance at Ernie. His mouth quirked into an infuriating grin. "And . . . he's giving me back twenty-eight dollars. That's . . . that's not fair!"

"It's out of my hands, ma'am. The judge made his decision."

"Does that dumb old judge think it cost sixty-four dollars to come from Conway to here? I could have gone to California and back a couple times on the bus for that." She continued to glare at Ernie. He stood to the right and slightly back of the sheriff with a smirk on his face.

"It's a hard lesson learned, Miss Kinnard." He took an envelope out of his pocket and handed it to her. "Here's your money. I'm not saying it's fair."

She snatched it angrily from his hand. "Some of the money could be hidden on his motorcycle."

"Yates and I went over it. There's nothing of value on the cycle. We can't even hold it. The judge told him to take it and get out of the county."

"Thank you for getting back this much for me." Margie went back into the house for fear she would cry, and not for the world would she do that in front of Ernie Harding.

Leona waited on the porch and watched as Yates rolled Ernie's motorcycle out of the garage and waited for him to get on it. Words were exchanged, angry words, but she was too far away to hear them. After Ernie rode away, she went back into the house.

Yates was busy in the garage and didn't come in for supper until late. A caravan of four families had stopped to camp. He sent Ruth Ann to tell Leona that he'd not be in for a while. She left his dinner on the table and went out to do the evening chores while Margie watched the girls playing in the water tank. When she returned to the house with the evening milk, she was relieved to see that Yates had eaten and gone back to the garage.

"You're mad at Yates, aren't you?" Margie asked as she and Leona sat in the tank of water.

They had waited for darkness, then before coming out, Margie had asked Yates to keep an eye out in case one of the campers wandered away from the campground. They had slipped out of the dresses they had worn all day, had sunk naked in the water and flipped the dresses onto the side of the tank.

"Why do you say that?"

"You haven't looked at him all day."

"Yes, I have. He's so darn big, I couldn't ignore him if I wanted to." Leona tried to keep the irritation from her voice. She had thought about it for most of the day and still hadn't been able to figure out why he had said the things he did about her flirting with Mr. Fleming.

"You didn't say anything to him."

"I didn't have anything to say."

"He likes you. He kissed you the other night, didn't he?"

"How did you know?"

"I guessed." Margie giggled. "And now you told me."

"Oh, you—"

"You don't meet his kind very often. In the café back home, I must have met every kind of man there is: Good family men, sorry flirty men, fat men, old, young, clean, dirty and those like Ernie who get by on other folks' sweat and tears. If Yates was interested in me, I might even give up my dream of going to Hollywood and ride off into the sunset with him."

"Why don't you set your cap for him? He wanders all over. Maybe he'd take you to Hollywood." Leona could have bitten her tongue. *Oh, Lord. It will be hard enough to see him leave, but with another woman it would be unbearable.*

Margie laughed. "Are you kidding? He's too smitten with you to notice me."

"You're wrong. He just wants to get a woman in his bed and I'm handy." *And he thinks with my reputation I'd be easy.*

"Don't they all?"

"Yates is a mover. He doesn't stay in one place very long. He'll move on as soon as Andy comes home. Maybe even tomorrow or the next day. He likes to be footloose and fancy-free."

"He's going to take me to catch the bus in the morning."

"Oh. When was that decided?"

"While he was eating his supper. I asked him to take me. I hope you don't mind."

"Why should I mind? He's free to do what he wants. I hate to see you go. I've enjoyed your company."

"I'll never be able to pay you for letting me stay here."

"The work you did today was pay enough."

"The sooner I get back to work, the sooner I'll have the money to go to California. Since I was a little girl and saw my first movie, I've wanted to be in the movies. Oh, I know I'm not pretty like Carole Lombard, or Joan Crawford, but there are roles for girls like me. Look at Zazu Pitts and Marie Dressler."

"What makes you think you're not pretty? Heavens! I bet some of the stars aren't all that pretty. They make them up with paint and hair dye and dress them up in beautiful clothes."

Leona didn't want to tell Margie that she'd seen only two picture shows in her life, and the only movie star she remembered in either one of them was a man named William Powell.

"Here's the soap. Are you going to wash your hair?"

"I thought I would and rinse it at the pump. I left a jar of vinegar out there."

They finished bathing, stood in the tank and put their dresses back on. Leona helped Margie rinse her hair at the pump and when she went to the house, she knelt, bowed her head beneath the spout and rinsed the soap from her own.

She was groping for the jar of vinegar water for the final rinse when she felt it taken from her hand and poured slowly over her head. She worked the water through her hair while it hung from the top of her head, then squeezed out the excess.

"Thanks, Margie." She groped for the towel she had hung on the pump handle.

"You're welcome."

At the sound of Yates's voice, she went still, then before she could react the towel was suddenly wrapped around her head, and a hand on her arm was helping her to her feet.

"Thanks." She took a step away from him and turned to go into the house. His hands on the towel stopped her.

"Hold on. I'll help you dry your hair."

"I don't need help. I've been doing it for years."

"I want to."

"I'll get used to having help and the next time Mr. Fleming comes by, I'll ask him to dry my hair."

To her annoyance, he chuckled. "You're still down gravel mad, aren't you? I thought you'd be over it by now."

"Well, I'm not. I don't take insults lightly."

"Insults? I don't remember insulting you."

"I doubt a jackass remembers every time he brays."

"Are you calling me a jackass?" The laughter in his voice infuriated her.

"It fits." She whipped the towel from her head and shook her wet hair, hoping some of it hit him in the face.

"Really, sweetheart. What did I say that was insulting?"

"Don't call me that! Don't you dare call me that!" She tried to break away from him. He put his arm around her waist and drew her back against him. "Let go of me, you . . . whopper-jawed polecat!"

"Not until you tell me what I said that was so insulting."

"You said . . . that I was flirting with Mr. Fleming and . . . trying to hook him to solve my problems. There!"

"I'm sorry I said that. I haven't had a very good day thinking about it. Do you regret saying that I'd pawed you?"

"No! It was true. And I don't care what kind of day you had. Your days here are numbered anyway."

"Will you miss me when I go?" His lips had nudged the wet hair aside and were close to her ear. His hand was moving over her rib cage, his thumb rubbing the underside of her breast. "Leona Dawson! You don't have anything on but this dress."

"You . . . you—"

"Braying jackass?"

"Take your hands off me."

"If I do, will you go put on some clothes and come back out? But not too soon, unless you want to get in the tank with me."

"No, I will not."

"Then I'll have to come in and get you. Do you want me to wake up the girls?"

"Yes. And I'll tell them just what a . . . a—"

"Jackass I am? They won't care. I'm making Ruth Ann a pair of stilts and JoBeth a doll bed. Sweetheart—" He grasped her earlobe between his teeth and worried it.

"I asked you not to call me that," she said very calmly. "Now let me go. I need to go in and get another dry towel."

"All right. But will you come out? We'll just talk. I won't touch you if you don't want me to," he whispered, his lips close to her ear.

"We'll . . . see. . . ." It was something she often said to the girls.

Leona hurried to the house as soon as he released her. Yates stood by the pump and watched her go.

He swore.

He didn't often second-guess himself. He did that now. Why had he teased her? His intention had been to get her alone and apologize for the things he'd said that morning. He had no intention, however, of telling her that jealousy had caused him to speak so thoughtlessly. Sometime during the day he had stopped and realized that what had raised his hackles when he saw her with Fleming was the thought of her being with another man.

Then realization had hit him with the force of a tornado. He was totally, recklessly, helplessly in love for the first time in his life. How in hell had it happened? Last night he had been sure that he only wanted to pet her a little. Enjoy a pleasant interlude. He wouldn't have allowed it to go further.

Shitfire! He had liked women before, been sexually attracted to them and left them without even remembering their names. This was so different that he was scared almost out of his wits.

The feeling he had for this auburn-haired, plucky woman was a protective kind that made him want to be with her day and night. It made him want to kill anyone who would hurt her or snub her. It must be love. It had crept up on him, had sunk deeply into his heart and mind. He wasn't at all sure that he liked having his contentment dependent on her.

Well, hell. The problem was *what was he going to do about it?* Maybe this *love,* he now identified it as such, wasn't as permanent as he thought. Tomorrow Andy would be home. He would see the two of them together. He wouldn't be tied so firmly to the garage and wouldn't be with her so much. Maybe he'd take a few days and go visit the Bluefeathers. Clear his head.

Maybe when you leave, you idiot, it'll be with a hole in your heart, and you'll wish that you'd never come here.

Chapter 29

LEONA AND THE GIRLS BID MARGIE A TEARFUL GOODBYE as she prepared to leave to catch the bus back to Conway, Missouri. Even Ruth Ann hugged her and told her she wished that she wasn't going. Yates put Margie's suitcase in the car, lifted JoBeth up onto the seat, turned to Leona and spoke tersely.

"I'll not be gone long."

"Take your time."

"Do you need anything from town?"

"No. JoBeth, don't wander off, and watch out for cars."

"I'll take care of her." The black look on Yates's face kept her from saying anything more.

Margie thanked Leona for the hundredth time and got into the car. Leona and Ruth Ann stood in front of the garage and waved until the car was out of sight.

She felt a little uneasy about JoBeth going into town without her. Yates had asked the child at breakfast if she wanted to go with him to take Margie to the bus. JoBeth had jumped up onto his lap, wrapped her small arms around his neck and kissed him. Leona didn't have the heart to dampen her pleasure by refusing to let her go. She had no doubt that Yates would take care of her, but she'd had the sole responsibility for the girls for so long that it was difficult to relinquish it to someone else even for a short while.

The campground was empty. All was quiet except for the occasional car that passed on the highway and the caws of crows in the woods eager to make a meal of the small dead animal that lay on the highway. The campers had pulled out at daylight hoping to get some miles behind them before the heat of the day.

"Swing me, Aunt Lee," Ruth Ann coaxed. Yates had fashioned a new board-seat on the rope swing, and the girls had taken a new interest in it.

"Just for a little bit. I'm going to clean house today. I want it to look nice when your daddy comes home."

Leona pushed the child in the swing, but her mind was elsewhere. A few weeks ago she would have been elated that Andy was coming home. She still was glad, but sad, too. Now it meant that Yates would be leaving.

She hadn't gone out last night after he had surprised her at the pump. She had sat on the bed in the darkened room, toweled her hair and waited to see if he would come and get her as he had threatened. He hadn't come.

Long after she had gone to bed, she had heard Yates playing his guitar. She lay curled with her hands beneath her cheek and listened to the hauntingly beautiful music. He played most of the songs he'd played the first night she heard him and then a few more tunes.

When he played "I'll Be Loving You Always," she had let the tears flow even though she knew he was not playing the tune for her. The tunes that followed were well known to her. "I'm Dancing with Tears in My Eyes," "I'm Confessing That I Love You" and "Goodnight, Sweetheart." She wished with all her heart that he was playing for her, but she knew that it was not true. She told herself that she should be grateful that he had come here and for the memories that would have to last a lifetime.

She had gone to sleep with tears on her cheeks.

It was nearly noon when Yates and JoBeth returned. Leona had been watching the clock and was on the verge of being worried, but she reasoned that the bus could have been late.

Ruth Ann had cleaned the back room, and she did the kitchen between the two trips she had made to the gas pump. She was in Andy's bedroom putting fresh sheets on his bed when she heard the sound of Yates's car returning. Shortly after that the front door slammed, and JoBeth burst into the house.

"Aunt Lee! Looky what Mr. Yates bought me." She grasped the skirt of her dress, held it out and looked down at the shiny black shoes with six button straps and shiny red toes and heels. "Mr. Robinson said they're Roman sandals."

Leona was startled speechless for a moment, then said, "For goodness sake!"

"They're a little big," Yates said. "Robinson said if we got them to fit, they'd be too little by Christmas."

Leona looked behind JoBeth, but let her eyes go only as far up as Yates's breast pocket, paused, then met his twinkling ones.

"She likes them." He was grinning like a schoolboy. "She saw them in the store window."

"I got a button hook. See?" JoBeth dug into a bag and brought out the hook. Ruth Ann crowded into the room. "Look at my shoes, Ruth Ann. We got other stuff for you 'cause we didn't know what size you wore. We each got a sack of candy. Here's yours."

"Don't eat the candy until after dinner," Leona cautioned. "I'll get it ready as soon as I finish with your daddy's bed."

"I hope you haven't started anything," Yates said. "We stopped at the store and got a loaf of bread and a jar of the new Skippy peanut butter."

"We got Post Toasties and cookies with icing in the middle and watermelon," JoBeth added happily.

"That must have made Mr. White happy," Leona said dryly. "Our melons won't be ready for a while."

"Guess what, Aunt Lee. We saw Uncle Virgil and that man that he likes," JoBeth said excitedly. "Mr. Yates was awful mad 'cause Uncle Virgil came up and started tellin' me 'bout him being my uncle. Mr. Yates said for him to get the hell away and stay the hell away, or he'd shove a telephone pole up his ass." JoBeth put her hand over her mouth and giggled.

There was utter quiet. Even Ruth Ann was speechless. Leona's eyes flew to Yates. He grinned sheepishly, then with his hand on JoBeth's head tilted her face toward him.

"You weren't supposed to tell that, honey."

"Oh . . . I forgot!"

In spite of her shock at the words that came from the five-year-old, a vision floated before Leona's eyes that forced a giggle. She couldn't have stopped it if it meant her life. Shining eyes met Yates's briefly, before she turned away to keep the girls from seeing her laughter.

"I'll fix your dinner, and you and the girls can eat on the porch. I want to scrub the kitchen floor, then bake a cake. We're going to have Andy's favorite things for supper."

"He likes chicken and cornbread dressing." Ruth Ann was busy with the fistful of ribbons, a card of barrettes, a box of watercolors and a large sketching pad.

"The chicken is ready to be plucked and dressed. I'll do

that as soon as I scrub the kitchen." She wished that Yates would move out of the doorway. "Girls, did you thank Mr. Yates?"

"I did. I kissed him, too." JoBeth smiled up at Yates. "He let me pick out the candy."

"Thank you, Mr. Yates."

"You're welcome, Ruth Ann." Then to Leona, "It looks to me like you've got plenty to do. I'll fix the meal and take it to the porch if you'll come eat with us."

"I can fix it. I'm almost finished here." She gathered up the soiled bedclothes. "Shoo, girls, outta the way."

He followed her through the kitchen and waited, while she went out onto the back porch and placed the linens in a washtub. When she turned to go back into the kitchen, he stood in the doorway.

"Hold on just a minute, Leona." His searching eyes caressed each feature of her face.

"I've work to do." Her voice was low, strained.

His hands grasped her upper arms. "I've got to say this: I'm sorry I accused you of flirting with Fleming."

"All right. I'm sorry I accused you of pawing me. Now we're even." She spoke as calmly as her pumping heart would allow.

"Is there something I can do to help you get ready for Andy's homecoming?" Strong fingers reached out and looped a curl behind her ear.

"Nothing. I have it all planned."

"Honey, don't be mad at me."

"I'm not mad." She shrugged as if what he said meant nothing. "I'll bake the cake, then put the chicken and dressing in your oven on the porch, so the kitchen won't be so hot." She held herself stiffly. She couldn't afford to let him know that his tender words were about to melt her heart.

"You're glad he's coming home?"

"Why, of course, aren't you? You must be eager to get on down the road."

"I'm not leaving for a while. The doctor said Andy should rest while he's taking the shots. I'll stick around until he's back to normal." Then he said, quietly, "Why didn't you come out last night?"

The silver eyes were on her face. Hers were focused on the pocket on his shirt. She had tied her hair back with a piece of frayed black ribbon, her face was sweaty, her dress dirty. She was ashamed of how she looked, but glad, too. He had to think that she didn't care enough to try to make herself pretty for him.

"I was tired and went to bed. I heard you playing your guitar. Why don't you get a job on the radio or with a band? You're better than some I've heard on the *Grand Ole Opry*."

"If you heard me play you didn't go to sleep right away. We could have sat on the porch for a while."

"I didn't think it wise."

"You were afraid I'd *paw* you? I told you I'd not do that. I've not broken my word to you yet, have I?"

"I shouldn't have used the word. I was just as much to blame as you. I had a lapse of judgment, or I would have stopped you." She pushed on his chest. "Now, let me by. I've got a lot to do."

"I'll fix peanut butter sandwiches. I bought bananas to go on them."

"Bananas on a sandwich? I never heard of such a thing."

His smile was boyish and endearing. Leona was sure that she would remember it forever, like the smell of his breath on her face and the touch of his hands on her arms.

"Wait until you try them."

"All right, but don't put a banana on Ruth Ann's sandwich until you ask her. She's a picky eater. And Yates," she said with a sassy grin, "wash your hands first." She suddenly felt light and gay, young and full of happiness.

The meal was ready. The chicken and dressing were being kept warm in the kerosene oven. The table was set with the cloth that was saved for special occasions like Thanksgiving and Christmas. The girls were wearing the dresses they wore to Sunday school. Ruth Ann had pinned one of the new barrettes, as well as a ribbon bow, in her hair.

Leona had hurriedly washed and put on a fresh dress. She slipped a ribbon beneath her hair and tied it in a bow on top. After a thin dusting of powder on her face she applied a touch of Tangee lipstick to her lips. She refused to admit even to herself that she wanted to look nice more for Yates than for Andy.

A truck, with a sturdy stock rack on the back and covered with a tarpaulin, and an old, fully loaded touring car with a mattress strapped to the top were parked in the campground. The two families shared one campfire. The children played together, the men discussed jobs, cars and road conditions, while the women shared stories and prepared a meal. The young folk, if they were of different sexes, eyed each other, as adolescents are wont to do. Most people on the move were friendly and often helped one another out when they came upon a breakdown or an accident.

The Connors girls, waiting for their daddy and Mr. Fleming, were getting impatient. After sitting on the porch for an hour, Ruth Ann came into the house where Leona was emptying the used tea leaves from the strainer.

"He's not coming."

"Of course he is, or Mr. Fleming would have sent word."

"It's supper time."

"Supper time is anywhere from six o'clock to dark in the summer. Where's JoBeth?"

"She's at the garage with Mr. Yates. I think she likes him better than Daddy."

"She likes him in a different way than she likes her daddy."

"When he goes, are you going with him?"

Shocked by the question, Leona made an effort to make her voice light. "Now why would I do that?"

"You like him."

"You and JoBeth like him, but that doesn't mean you'll go with him when he leaves here."

"You like him different," Ruth Ann said stubbornly. "You like him . . . like when you want to marry."

"I don't know where you got that idea, but get it out of your head right now." Leona's voice was stern, and she was immediately sorry when she saw the crestfallen look on the child's face.

"Honey." She put her arms around Ruth Ann, hugged her and rested her cheek on the top of her head. "Are you worried that I'll leave you? Don't be. I've no intentions of leaving you as long as you want me. Maybe when you are grown up and have a home of your own, I'll go somewhere else. But that will be a long time from now."

"Why don't you marry Daddy? You like him."

"That's it, honey. I like him, but your daddy and I don't love each other the way he loved your mother. We are friends and that is all."

"You got cleaned up for him—"

"He's here!"

Ruth Ann broke from Leona when she heard her sister's shout and raced for the door. By the time JoBeth reached the garage, Ruth Ann was behind her. Leona stood on the porch and watched Andy get out of the car and open his arms. The girls ran to him. He hugged them to him, leaning against the car to keep his balance. After kissing each one, he looked toward the house with a broad smile on his face. Leona's eyes filled with tears of thankfulness that he was home. Why couldn't she have fallen in love with this wonderful caring man instead of a man who roamed from one end of the highway to the other? One who, after seven years, would probably never be satisfied to settle in one place and love one woman.

Yates lifted Andy's crutches and the box containing his clothes from the car and stood with Mr. Fleming, while Andy greeted his girls. Leona came down the path from the house. Andy held his hand out to her. The little group huddled close, happy to be together again.

Raw yearning erupted inside of Yates, a yearning to belong to someone who cared for him as Leona and the girls cared for Andy. If ever a man deserved such a family it was this man, who stood so precariously on his wooden peg. Yates's worldly goods far exceeded Andy's, yet Yates knew that Andy was far richer.

He envied him, wanted what he had and felt shame because of it.

Barker Fleming turned down the invitation to stay for supper and, after sincere thanks from Andy and Leona, was soon on his way back to the ranch. Andy went up the path to the house with his family. Yates stayed behind to give them some private time.

"Are you coming?" Leona called.

"As soon as I close the garage."

"Well, hurry it up. I'm putting supper on the table."

* * *

The girls were too excited to eat and Leona was almost too nervous, but Yates and Andy ate heartily. Ruth Ann and JoBeth vied for their father's attention, and Andy listened to what each one of them had to say. They told about Margie being here and about the man who stole her money and about Deke fighting him. JoBeth showed her father her new red-and-black shoes, and Ruth Ann told about her watercolors and how she'd learned to cut out a string of paper dolls. Strangely enough, both stayed away from the story about Ruth Ann running away.

Leona gave them free rein, until JoBeth started to tell about meeting Virgil in town.

"He was goin' to talk to me, and Mr. Yates said, get the—" Leona's hand went over the child's mouth. She shook her head for her to say no more. JoBeth ignored the warning and as soon as Leona removed her hand, continued: "stick a telephone pole—"

"JoBeth!" Leona's hand shot out to cover her mouth again. Yates looked up from his plate trying hard not to laugh. Andy's questioning eyes went from one to the other. "It's your fault," Leona mouthed to Yates over the child's head.

"She wants to say the dirty word Mr. Yates said," Ruth Ann announced in her superior tone. "She blabs everything she hears, 'specially nasty words."

It wasn't until Andy and Yates moved to the porch and Leona was cleaning up after the meal that Yates had the chance to tell Andy about Virgil's visits and the scare Ruth Ann had given them.

"She'll not come right out and say she was at Virgil's, but we're sure that's where she was. I think he picked her up, or someone picked her up and took her to him. She's afraid for the boy who brought her home. He walked her home through the woods. It's got to be two or three miles. They got here around midnight."

"Was she hurt . . . did he—?" Andy asked quietly, leaving the question hanging.

"I'm sure nothing like that occurred, or she would have told Leona. She was worn out and hungry. I'd like to kill the bastard, but our hands are tied if Ruth Ann refuses to accuse him. He's crazy!"

"Mr. Fleming didn't mention that he'd helped search for her. Guess he knew I'd find out as soon as we got here and didn't want me to worry."

Yates told about Virgil trying to take the girls. "I almost twisted his nuts off the first time. I thought that would be enough, but he came back and Deke went after him."

"Good Lord. I've always thought that he was crazy as a bed bug. He's given up on Leona, and now he's after the girls."

"Maybe he thinks he'd not be able to handle Leona."

"I'm going to have to leave here, Yates. I'll be afraid to send the girls to school. I don't know how I'll make a living for them, but they can't live like this."

"Sheriff McChesney is a good man. He'll do what he can."

"Virgil is in tight with the deputy. There are a lot of good people in Sayre but a lot of fanatics like Virgil. I'm sure as hell glad you were here. I'll not be able to thank you enough for taking care of my family."

"You gave me my life, Andy. I'll never forget it. But don't sell Leona short. She was ready to jump right in the middle of Virgil. She's got quite a mouth on her when she's riled."

Andy noticed the pride in Yates's voice. It gave him food for thought. He put it aside for now and said, "Deke would tackle a wild elephant if it was threatening Leona. He's been in love with her since they were little kids."

"Yeah. I discovered that right away. It's a sad kind of love he has for her. He knows that she'll never be his. Leona is protective of his feelings. She cares deeply for him as she cares for Ruth Ann and JoBeth."

"I suppose you know what folks in town think about Leona." Andy smoked his pipe and rocked the swing gently.

"I know, and it makes me madder than a pissed-on polecat."

"I should have insisted that she marry me. Although it would have been like marrying my sister."

"She told me."

The girls came out and kissed Andy goodnight. Yates stood and stretched.

"Now that you're here, I think I'll go into town for a while."

"Go ahead. I'm going to sit for a bit. Don't feel obligated to stay on if you want to hit the road, Yates. With Leona's help, I'll be able to manage most things. Deke will come in on weekends."

"I'm not ready to leave yet, if you don't mind me being here. I told Doc Langley I'd stay for a while to do the hard work. He'll have my scalp if you have a setback."

"By the way, what was JoBeth trying to say about Virgil when Leona hushed her up?"

Yates told about meeting Virgil in town. "I forgot myself in front of JoBeth for a minute or two. When she repeated it to Leona, I thought Leona would throw me out of the house."

Andy laughed. "Kids at that age soak up everything they hear. She's a pistol."

"I've never been around kids before. Kind of makes me want to have some of my own."

Leona came out onto the porch as Yates was driving away. Her heart plummeted. "He's leaving?"

"Going to town for a while. He'll stay on a bit longer. He told me about Virgil coming out here and about Ruth Ann running off. Lord, but I'm glad he came along when he did."

"He was a big help," she said quietly and sat down in the swing beside Andy.

"I'm thinking of leaving here, Leona. What do you think? As long as you and the girls are here, Virgil is going to cause trouble."

"Where would you go?"

"Wherever *we* go, I would hope that you'd go with us."

"You and the girls are all the family I have, Andy. Without you, I would be alone." Much to her shame, she suddenly burst into tears.

"Ah, honey. What's the matter?" Andy put his arm around her.

"I'm sorry. I guess it's just the strain of having you gone and having him here. Ruth Ann running away and . . . all."

Andy was quiet for a long while, then said, "You've fallen in love with Yates, haven't you?"

"Oh, Lord. How did you know?"

"I guessed at supper when you didn't look at him or speak to him unless it was necessary. Does he feel the same about you?"

"Heavens no! He's eager to move on. He'll never settle down. To him, I'm just a country bumpkin he ran across out here on the highway."

"Are you sure?"

"Absolutely sure. You'll not tell him. Please don't tell him."

"Of course, I won't tell him. But Lee, he's a good man. After seeing all the men who have come through here, I know a good one when I see one. Has he led you to believe that he's interested in you?"

"No. It's nothing like that. He's been really good to us . . . after I got used to him. But he's not for me," she said and wiped away the tears with the heels of her hands.

"Did he . . . ah . . . get fresh with you?"

Leona couldn't help but laugh a little. "No. He's done nothing to offend me. I was amusement for him." She patted Andy's hand. "Don't worry. I'll get over it. After he's gone, I'll realize how foolish I was to think a few kisses would mean something to him."

Chapter 30

YATES DROVE DOWN THE HIGHWAY TOWARD TOWN. It wasn't like him to feel lonely, but that was exactly how he felt. In a week he would no longer have a reason to stay on at the garage, and the thought of leaving did not give him a happy feeling.

The past few weeks had been a revelation to him. He'd had time to stop and think of what was missing in his life. It had been eleven years since he'd had a home or even been in one for more than a few days at a time.

He had discovered that he liked sitting at the dinner table with a family sharing the happenings of the day. He liked being the one they depended on for protection. He liked having a little child sit on his lap and kiss his cheek. It was better than winning the pot in a high stakes poker game to hear JoBeth laugh with utter joy as she did when he bought the shoes. He liked sitting in the porch swing in the evening with his arm around a soft, sweet woman, listening to the night sounds and sharing his thoughts with her.

He wanted to belong to someone, to be important to someone.

The big house on the ranch had been his home for the first seventeen years of his life. He'd left it soon after his mother died. He would be going back there soon. The attorney who had been looking after his interest told him that Arnold Taylor was expected to die at any time and, according to his mother's will, the ranch would be his. He tried to visualize the changes after eleven years. The lawyer said that financially the ranch was in fairly good shape, and that some of the same people who had worked for his mother were still there.

Yates had thought that he would be elated when the day came that he could head back to the Yates ranch. He had been to San Angelo several times during the past few years, but had refused to go to the ranch as long as Arnold Taylor and his wife were there.

On the edge of town his eyes caught the colored lightbulbs around the eaves of the PowWow, a night stop that had a small dance floor and sold Oklahoma beer that was only three-point-two percent alcohol. He pulled in beside a motorcycle. It looked like Deke's but could belong to the shithead who stole Margie's money. If it was, he was in the mood for a good knock-down, drag-out, ass-kicking brawl.

"Hey, Yates." Deke yelled at him from a stool at the bar, as soon as he ducked his head and came in the door.

There were no more than a dozen people in the place, some on stools, some at tables that surrounded the postage stamp dance floor. Behind the counter the barkeep was winding a Victrola. He selected a record from the stack on the back-bar. Two couples began to dance to "I'm Confessing That I Love You."

"Howdy, Deke." Yates straddled the stool beside the little man.

"What'll ya have?" The bartender swabbed the bar in front of him.

"Got any Mexican beer?"

"Nope."

"*O-ah-o-ah-swacka,*" Deke said, causing Yates to give him a quizzical look.

The bartender grinned at Deke and nodded. He went to the end of the bar and returned with a tall glass of foaming beer.

"Thanks." Yates placed a silver dollar on the bar. "Give Deke one or two, or whatever that'll pay for."

The barkeep slipped the money in his pocket and went to change the record.

"What was that gibberish all about?"

Deke grinned. "That means *dig out the good stuff; the man's a friend.*"

"Thanks, friend."

"Andy get home?"

"Got there about supper time."

"Bet Leona and the girls were glad to see him."

"Yeah. And he was glad to see them."

"You leavin' now?"

"Not right this minute. Are you trying to get rid of me?"

"Hell, I was going to ask ya to come out to the ranch for a few days. Mr. Fleming's got one of the finest in the country. Ya at least ought to see it."

"How many acres?"

"I don't know. Must be six to ten thousand. He's got some mighty fine horses."

Yates thought it over. His own ranch was probably twice as big. It covered two counties, but then it took a couple acres of grass to feed one steer in that part of the country.

Two men came to straddle the stools at the bar. The one who wore wide suspenders and a broad-brimmed hat spoke to Deke.

"How'er ya doin', Deke?"

"Pretty good, Cowboy. You?"

"Guess I'll live. Hey, Booger, give me a glass of that slop ya call beer."

"Is Virgil's house still quarantined?" Yates asked.

"Was when I come by there tonight. Why? Are you goin' to pay 'em a visit?"

"Just wondering. I'll see you later, Deke."

Yates left the bar and, deep in thought, drove down Sayre's main street, turned around and came back. He took a left at the courthouse square, drove several blocks to the church on the corner. They were having a service, the windows were open, the congregation was singing. Virgil Dawson's old truck with the buzz saw on the back was parked at the side.

Yates made a U-turn at the corner and headed out of town. He drove slowly along the rutted road, and when he reached the Dawson house, he turned in. His lights shone on the red warning sign beside the door. Lamplight came from a side window in the back of the house. As soon as he turned off his lights, the light in the window went out.

Yates got out of the car and walked up onto the porch. Before he could rap, a voice called out.

"What'a ya want? We got diphtheria here."

"Yes, ma'am. I know that. I'm not afraid of the fever. I'd like to speak to Isaac."

"Who'er you?"

"Name's Yates. I've been helping out at the garage while Andy is in the city getting the rabies shots."

"What'a ya want with Isaac?"

"Andy Connors's little girl sent a message."

"Spit it out." The woman came to the screendoor.

"I'd like to see Isaac, ma'am. We know that Isaac brought Ruth Ann home. She told only me and her Aunt Leona. We are grateful to Isaac and don't want him to come to harm because of it."

"She . . . promised—" Isaac crowded in front of his mother.

"She didn't tell until we told her that she would have to be vaccinated for diphtheria if she had been exposed."

"She didn't come in the house."

"She hasn't accused her uncle of keeping her here for fear that she'll get you in trouble, Isaac. When Ruth Ann was missing, I offered a twenty-five-dollar reward to the person who brought her home. The reward is yours."

"You come to give me somethin'?"

"Twenty-five dollars."

Isaac pushed open the screendoor and came out onto the porch. "Will Pa know?"

"Not unless you tell him."

"I took her home 'cause she was little and scared. Ma told me to."

"It took courage to do that." Yates reached into his shirt pocket and handed the boy the bills he'd put there earlier. "Thank you, Isaac."

"You'd better go, mister. Pa'll be home soon. He'd be mad clear through if he caught ya here."

"We sure don't want that to happen. Isaac, you have friends out at Andy's place. Your aunt doesn't blame you or your brothers for the way her brother has treated her. If you're ever in need, go to her. She'll help you if she can." Yates left the porch.

"Thanks, mister."

He stopped and turned back toward the house. The woman's voice had came from inside the screendoor.

"You're welcome, ma'am. The boy earned it."

Yates was a half mile from the house when he passed Virgil going home.

"Ma! Look at all this money!"

"Thank the good Lord. Run and see if the little boys are asleep. If they heard, they might tell your pa about it." Hazel re-lit the lamp she had blown out when the car drove in.

Isaac shoved the bills at his mother, hurried to the back room and peered at his brothers on the bed.

"We ain't asleep, but we won't tell," Carl whispered.

"If ya do, he'll take it and lay the strop on all of us."

"We won't tell. Honest, Isaac."

"All right. We got to hold on till Joe and Pete get here."

"Tell Ma, we won't tell."

By the time Isaac got back to the kitchen, Hazel had rolled up the bills and tied a string around them. After emptying the contents of her Calumet baking powder can in a cream pitcher, she stuffed the bills down in the can, refilled it and set it back on the shelf.

"He's comin' up the road, Ma."

"Blow out the lamp!"

"The doc will let him back in tomorrow."

"Pete and Joe will be here in a day or two. Don't let him catch ya outside alone. He thinks one of us let the girl out of the shed. I don't know what he'd do if he ever found out that ya took her home."

"That man that was here seems a decent sort, Ma. He could've just forgot about payin' out the reward." From the dark kitchen Isaac watched his father pass the house.

"I don't know what he'll tell the sheriff. We just got to trust him I guess." Hazel sat down at the table. "It took Paul's dyin' to make me see that what's been goin' on here ain't right. We ain't livin' that way no more. I'm thinkin' God ain't wantin' us to."

"What can ya do, Ma?"

"I've been thinkin' that when Pete and Joe come I'll see if we can all go away from here. Bless that man that gave ya the reward money."

"The three of us could work and take care of ya and the boys. We could go to Californy in the wagon if Joe and Pete was with us."

"The team is twenty years old. It wouldn't make it to Amarillo. I don't think—"

"Hazel, get out here!" The shout came from the back porch. "I'm tired foolin' with ya."

Hazel jumped. "He's been lookin' in the window."

"He couldn't see us sittin' in here."

"Let him think we're in bed," she whispered.

"Open the door! When I get my hands on ya I'll take the hide right off yore back."

"He's gettin' meaner than a dog passin' chili peppers."

"I hope I ain't mean like that when I grow up."

"He'll go bed down in the truck pretty soon. Then I'll slip out and bring in an armload of wood for the cookstove. I should'a done it while he was gone. Time just got away from me."

The clock ticked the minutes away while Hazel and Isaac sat in the dark at the kitchen table. They talked in whispers.

"Lots of folks is goin' to California, Ma. Reckon we could go there?"

"We'll talk to Joe and Pete about it when they get here."

Isaac listened to the mournful sound of the train whistle and wished that he could hop on that train and see all the places he'd heard about. But even if he were old enough, he reasoned, he couldn't leave his mother and little brothers. They depended on him.

"Go to bed, son. I'll wait a while longer, then go out the front door and around the side of the house to the woodpile."

Isaac lay down on the bed where his brother had died, but he kept his eyes open. He didn't want to sleep until his mother was back in the house.

It was near midnight when Hazel slipped out of the door. The night was dark. Thick clouds hovered overhead. Hugging the side of the house until she reached the end of it, she paused, then went hurriedly to the woodpile.

She had stooped to fill her arm with the stove wood when she heard the shout and felt the pain of the whip, which landed with enough force to lay open a cut on her back and cause her to lurch forward. Her scream pierced the dark night.

"Ya bitch! Someone was here. I saw the car lights. Who was it? Ya told him 'bout the girl in the shed, didn't ya?"

Hazel shrieked and tried to get to her feet. When she turned, the whip came down on the side of her neck. The tip sliced her cheek to the bone and split her lower lip.

"Ya let that girl out! Yo're a devil-lovin' bitch. Clear as day, God told me ya did. He said punish that lowly wretch. Yo're a disgrace to his name!" Virgil shouted over his wife's screams. Slash, slash. The whip came down again and again. "Ya've sinned against God. Yo're a abomination! I'll beat the wickedness outta ya!" Slash, slash. "Praise the Lord! Lord, help me brin' this lowly wretch back into the fold."

He dropped a stick of wood on the back of her knees and put his foot on it to hold her to the ground while he lashed her in a frenzy. Hazel's screams were constant as the whip ripped through the material of her dress and laid fire on her back time and again.

"Ya vowed to cleave to yore husband and whata ya done? Ya sassed me in front of the preacher. Ya shamed me."

Hazel covered her face with her arms and tried to crawl away. Virgil stomped hard on the thick stove wood lying on the backs of her knees. The pain flattened her. He continued to flay her with the short lead-tip buggy whip. The agony was worse than anything she had ever imagined. It went on and on. It was like the hot fires of hell were licking at her back. She prayed to die.

Virgil's rage and religious zeal gave strength to the arm that wielded the whip. He no longer shouted. Incoherent words spewed from his mouth.

The pain was so all consuming that Hazel never knew when her husband stopped striking her. Even as he lay on the ground, his hand still holding the bloody whip, she continued to scream and scream until she sank into a pit of darkness.

Yates's car lights swept the porch when he parked behind the garage. Leona and Andy were in the porch swing. Andy called to him when he got out of the car.

"Come sit a while. There's a nice breeze up here on the porch."

"There are a few thunderheads around, but I don't think they'll amount to much," he said and sank down on the porch step.

"The prairie is dry as a bone between here and the city. I heard a fellow say on the radio that way up in Iowa and Minnesota they're getting dust from the panhandle."

Leona, glad of the darkness, allowed her eyes to look their fill at the man lounging against the porch post and scratching Calvin's ears. How many more times would she see him sitting there, hear his voice, listen to him tease the girls?

"I saw Deke in town."

"I hope he wasn't looking for Ernie," Leona said.

"He was at the PowWow drinking beer and I didn't see Ernie. The judge told him to get out of town."

"What's this about Deke and someone named Ernie? A lot went on out here while I was gone."

Leona remained silent, and Yates told about Margie being left at the campground and Ernie taking her money.

"You should have seen Leona standing over that fellow with the business end of the rifle pressed to his neck. It was plumb scary." There was laughter in Yates's voice.

"He had Deke down. I hit him across the rump and told him to get off, but he wouldn't," she said with a hint of impatience.

"He must have got the message." Yates chuckled. "He was still as a stone when I got to him."

"All of this happened while I was gone. Shoot! I missed it." Andy was laughing as he got to his feet. "Guess I'll turn in. I'm looking forward to sleeping in my own bed."

"Leona." Yates stood quickly. "Will you stay with me for a while?"

"I'm kind of . . . tired."

"You're young. You can't be that tired," Andy said good-naturedly. "Goodnight." He went into the house, leaving Leona feeling as if she had been deserted.

"Come on." Yates took her hand and gently tugged. He led her off the porch and down the path. "Let's go for a ride and cool off. I want to talk to you about something."

"Can't we do it here?"

"We could, but I'd like to take you for a ride."

He opened the car door and she got in. He went to the driver's side; and before she could collect her scattered thoughts, they were on the highway.

"I went out to Virgil's," he said and pulled on her arm until she was sitting close beside him.

He took her hand and placed it palm down on his thigh and covered it with his. Keeping her eyes straight ahead, she was aware that he glanced at her from time to time. Her heart pounded, and she was sure that he could feel it beating through the hand that covered hers.

"Was Virgil there?"

"His truck was at the church. That's why I went out there. I went to give Isaac the reward. I've not told Andy about that. Have you?"

"No. I thought if you wanted him to know it, you'd tell him." Leona thought a moment, then added, "Virgil will find out why you gave Isaac the money and take it. Then the boy will be punished."

"I don't think so. He wanted to know if his pa would know he had it. I told him not unless he told him."

"Did Hazel see you give it to him?"

"She was there."

Leona groaned. "She'll take it and give it to Virgil. She never goes against him."

"Not if she helped the boy get Ruth Ann out of the shed. Ruth Ann said Isaac told her his mother said take her home. As I was leaving she thanked me."

"Then she's had a change of heart. She's always been mousy and followed Virgil like a puppy dog. She'd lick his hand if he told her to." Cynicism curled Leona's lips.

"I think it'll be all right, but if you think I should, I'll get Sheriff McChesney and go out there in the morning."

"I'm worried for Isaac and the other kids."

"Doc says that none of the other Dawson children have come down with diphtheria, and only Isaac has had contact with Ruth Ann. He thinks there is little need to worry that the swabs he sent in would test positive."

"I'm relieved to hear it."

When they reached the top of the hill, Yates turned the car into a clearing back from the highway and stopped.

"It's cool out here. Look at the heat lightning there toward the southwest."

"I'll have to water the garden if it doesn't rain soon. The shower we had the other night didn't do much good."

"I'll be leaving soon." His words dropped into the quiet darkness of the car.

"I know."

"This is the first time we've really been alone. There's always been someone within calling distance. Come here to me, honey." He turned with his back to the door, reached for her and pulled her to him.

"I don't think that's a good idea." She put her hands on his chest to hold herself away from him. "I meant what I said the other night."

"All right." His hands slid down her arms and clasped her hands. "Have you decided that maybe you're in love with Andy after all?"

"No. I love Andy. I'm not in love with him. I've told you that."

"Could you ever love a man like me?" he asked quietly.

Leona tried to control her shivering. She stared at his dark face and took a deep breath.

"I've not met many men like you." She bent her head, unable to meet his piercing eyes. He put his hands on her shoulders and, ignoring her resistance, pulled her hard against him. "I just want to hold you for a while . . . maybe kiss you a little so I'll have something to remember."

She quivered in his arms. He put a hand to her throat and tilted her face up to his. His eyes searched her face as his hand cupped her chin. A wave of helplessness came over her, and a little whimper escaped from her lips. He lowered his mouth to hers. His kiss was sweet and gentle at first, then deepened. She returned his kiss as if he was all that mattered in the world.

"Sweetheart. Your mouth is so sweet—" His husky voice whispered love words to her, and they echoed on the inside of her brain. "Soft and sweet and pretty." He put his nose in her hair. "I can still smell the vinegar." His lips moved over her eyes and back to her mouth.

"I don't understand myself! I keep thinking that . . . I won't do this!" She moved her mouth from his and gasped.

"Stop worrying, love. You like kissing me, don't you?"

"Yes, but—"

"Shh . . . hh—" He pressed his mouth to hers each time she started to speak until their hunger grew, and there was no time for words. He closed his eyes and whispered, "Lee, Lee, sweet Lee."

Whatever it was that made him become aware of her on the day he returned after taking Andy to the hospital had been developing steadily. Now it almost consumed him. She was so open, so giving. Her mouth parted beneath his, yielding and vulnerable to the invasion of his lips and gentle tongue.

Yates's love had been stored away. He'd shared it only with his mother and his grandparents to a certain extent. Now all the love he had to give belonged to this wonderful, beautiful angel of a woman who had come into his life and turned it upside down. He burrowed his face deep into the fragrance of her hair and felt his whole self harden and tremble.

Leona abandoned herself to the heavenly feeling of being in his arms. Her fingers touched his hair, caressed his nape and felt along the hard line of his jawbone. She clung to him, knowing that soon all she would have of him were her memories. She became aware that his hand covered her breast. Her fingers circled his wrist.

Half-laughing, he locked his arms around her more tightly and traced along her face with his lips and gently kissed her trembling mouth. His whisper came against her lips.

"I've been desperate to touch there. The other night when I saw two hard little knots poking against your wet dress I wanted to put my mouth on them. . . . Still do. I'm crazy about you," he said with a touch of desperation.

Leona pulled back and cradled his face with her hands. "I can't let myself believe that what you feel for me is anything but attraction, because we've been together so much. A couple weeks after you leave here you'll not be able to recall my face." Her lips curved into a sad little smile. "I understand how it is with a man like you. You must understand how it is with a woman like me."

A surge of love for her flowed through him like a river. How was it possible that this woman, of all women, with her sweet smile and calm words, could make him feel like he had the world by the tail? It was too early to blurt out his feelings. She would be sure to think it blather to get her into his bed. Not that he didn't want that. He wanted her with a need that made him so hard, he wasn't sure how much longer he could sit still.

So he said, "Will you come out with me again tomorrow night?"

"Are you asking me out on a date?"

"I guess you'd call it that. I've never been on one."

Her smile grew into a throaty little laugh. "I'll have to check my calendar. I've got a date one day this week with President Hoover."

"Smarty." He kissed her with lusty delight and started the engine.

Chapter 31

THERE WAS NOT MUCH TO MARK THIS MORNING as different from other mornings. It was light, but the sun was not yet up when Yates put three gallons of gas in an old touring car. *Another family was on their way to find a better life.* Two small children were asleep on top of the couple's belongings piled in the back. After he mopped the red dirt from the windshield and collected the money for the gas, Yates handed the woman two sticks of candy.

"For the kids . . . later in the day."

"Thank you! Thank you, so much." The smile that transformed her tired face was all the thanks he needed.

Yates watched them leave. He felt good. If he was going to be here much longer he'd buy a tub full of candy sticks and give one to every kid that stopped. He grinned at his foolish thought.

At breakfast he teased Leona that now that Andy was back she had to make twice as many biscuits. Leona replied, as she had done once before, that all he thought of was his stomach. Their eyes caught. He gave her a conspiratorial wink to let her know he remembered his reply that morning. He'd said that his stomach wasn't all he thought about.

After breakfast, Andy came down to the garage. They sat

on the bench in the shade, and Yates told him about his life up to the time Andy had saved it. He told him the terms of his mother's will and that he would be taking possession of his inheritance soon.

"Well, what'a ya know," Andy said and smiled. "Somehow I thought you were a rancher. Certainly not a city man."

"I've been a little bit of everything the past seven years. I've worked in the oil fields, hoed cotton, even picked oranges in California. I worked on a couple big ranches for a time. Getting my feet wet, so to speak. I like ranching. It's in my blood."

A car passed on the highway, and right behind it was the sheriff's car. It pulled in and stopped in front of the garage. Sheriff McChesney and the deputy got out.

"Morning. Glad to see you back, Andy." The sheriff spoke and held out his hand. The deputy said nothing. He leaned against the car, his arms folded over his chest.

"Glad to be back, Rex. There's no place quite like home."

The sheriff turned his attention to Yates. "I heard that you were in town last night."

"Yeah, I was. Is it a crime?"

"Could be. Deke was there, too, wasn't he?"

"Yeah. I had a beer with him at the PowWow."

"Where did you go when you left the PowWow?"

"I had some private business to attend to."

"Tell me about it."

"Not in front of your big-eared, know-it-all deputy."

"Is Miss Dawson here?" The sheriff switched subjects so fast it took Yates a second or two to catch up.

"Why wouldn't she be?"

"Ask her to come over." The sheriff looked at the deputy and jerked his head toward the house. With a smirk, Wayne

Ham left the car where he'd been leaning and headed for the house. Yates got to his feet.

"What's going on? That son of a bitch insults Leona every time he's near her."

Andy stood as quickly as his crutches would allow. "I think you'd better tell us what is going on, Rex. Does it have anything to do with Virgil?"

"Why do you ask, Andy?"

"Well, I know, as you do, that Virgil has a grudge against Leona and that Wayne Ham and Virgil are close as two peas in a pod. He has helped Virgil spread the gossip that's caused folks to think bad about Leona."

The screendoor slammed. Leona and the deputy came down the path.

"Get your hands off me, you pea-brained polecat!" Leona's angry voice carried. Yates started forward, but he stopped at the sheriff's sharp order.

"Let go of her, Wayne. What the hell's the matter with you? I told you to *ask* her to come down."

"You wanted her here. Here she is." The deputy gave Leona a small shove, his small, bright eyes sweeping triumphantly over Yates.

"It's customary to knock before going into someone's house." Leona gave the deputy a look that would have frozen a hot tamale ten feet away. "This ill-mannered lout walked right in and grabbed my arm as if I was about to run out the back door." She went immediately to stand between Yates and Andy.

"I apologize for Wayne's behavior. I didn't want to tell you this at the house because of the children. Your brother was murdered last night."

There was a bewildered silence. Then Leona said in a choked voice, "Virgil?"

"He left the church after the evening service. Several saw his truck heading home. Abe Patton went out this morning and found him out in the yard. His head was bashed in."

"Who did . . . it?" Leona asked.

"That's what I'm trying to find out."

"You think I did?"

"At this stage, I'm not ruling out anyone."

"Leona was here all evening, Rex. I'll swear to it." Andy's face was covered with sweat from the effort to stay upright.

"That's good enough for me. Sit down, Andy."

"What does Hazel say? Did she hear anyone?" Leona asked.

"I talked to Isaac, the oldest boy, through the screendoor. The house is quarantined. He said his mother was sick. I went by the doctor's office, and told Mrs. Langley to have the doc go out. I don't know if a woman her age could catch the diphtheria or not."

"So I'm a suspect." Yates's voice was matter-of-fact.

"No!" The denial burst from Leona. Anger and panic vied for supremacy in her mind.

"Yeah. You and Deke," the sheriff said. "You were both in town last night, and Wayne heard both of you threaten to kill Virgil. I'm going to have to take you in for further questioning, Yates."

"You can't!" Leona cried. "He was here with me . . . and Andy."

"It's all right, honey." Yates put his arm across her shoulders. "The sheriff's got his job to do."

The deputy stepped forward with a pair of handcuffs.

"You'd like for me to resist, wouldn't you?" Yates said with a sneer. "I'll not give you the pleasure now. But one day, before I leave this part of the country, I'm going to knock you on your fat ass and stomp your guts into the ground." He turned and put his hands behind him.

"Sheriff, I'd like to have a private word with Leona and Andy."

"I don't think so." The deputy jerked on the cuffs.

"Let go of him, Wayne," Rex said. "I see no harm in it."

"But . . . the book says—"

"To hell with the book. Go ahead, Yates. We'll be over here by the car."

As soon as the lawmen stepped away, Yates turned his back to them and looked at Leona.

"I didn't do anything but give Isaac the money when I went out to Virgil's last night. On my way back to town, I passed Virgil going home. Tell Andy about the reward money, honey. Don't worry. The sheriff is a square-shooter even if his deputy is a horse's patoot. I'll be back."

JoBeth and Ruth Ann had come through the garage and were crowding behind Leona. Ruth Ann peered out from behind Leona's skirt.

"Why'er they doin' that to Yates?" JoBeth tried to go to him. Leona held out her arm and pulled her close.

"Daddy. Daddy." Ruth Ann shook Andy's arm to get his attention. "I don't like him—"

"Let's go, Yates," the sheriff called.

"Don't go," JoBeth cried.

"I'll be back, honey. Take care of your daddy and Leona while I'm gone."

He bent his head and quickly kissed Leona hard on the mouth. She stood in stunned silence as he turned and went to the car.

"So that's the way the wind blows," the deputy sneered and climbed into the back seat beside Yates. "Figured it'd not take long for you to smell out free pussy."

"Shut up, Wayne!" The sheriff turned and glared at his deputy.

Yates closed his eyes and counted to ten. *I'll not only stomp your guts out, fat boy, I'll string 'em from here to Amarillo.*

Leona watched the car drive away. "What can we do, Andy?"

"Nothing, right now. If they go out and pick up Deke, Mr. Fleming will be in. He'll get to the bottom of it. He thinks the world of Deke."

"Daddy, I don't like that man. He said he'd take me to Mr. Fleming. He took me to Uncle Virgil and . . . put his hand over my mouth and shook me real hard."

"Oh, honey! The sheriff?"

"The other one. . . ."

Doctor Langley parked his car beside the house and walked up onto the porch. As was his duty as county coroner, he'd gone back with the sheriff when they went to get Virgil Dawson's body and bring it to the undertaker. He had intended to take the quarantine sign off the house then, but it had slipped his mind. He was glad now that he hadn't. There wasn't much of a chance that Mrs. Dawson had diphtheria, but nothing was impossible.

When he reached the door, one of the boys was there holding it open.

"Hello. Carl, isn't it? The sheriff said your mother was sick."

"She's bad hurt. Pa done it."

The doctor followed the boy to the kitchen. Mrs. Dawson lay face down on the floor.

"I don't know what to do!" Isaac looked up with tears streaming down his face. He had just laid a wet towel on his mother's back. "Pa . . . whipped her. He thinks she let Ruth Ann out of the shed. I did it. I let her out and took her home."

"Move over, son. Let me have a look." Doctor Langley knelt down, lifted the towel and drew in a deep breath. The woman's back was like raw meat, her dress in shreds. The floor was smeared with blood where she had crawled into the house. During all his years in medicine, he'd never seen anyone who had suffered such a vicious beating.

"Why didn't you tell the sheriff about your mother when he came to the door this morning?"

"Ma said lock the door, don't let anybody in. We didn't know Pa was dead then. He is, ain't he? I ain't sorry."

"What we've got to do now is take care of your mother. Do you think the two of us could get her up onto the bed?"

"I can help," Carl said.

"Good boy. Take her feet. Isaac, take her head and I'll take the middle. Careful now. We'll do it while she's unconscious, and it won't hurt her so much."

When the doctor left two hours later, Hazel's wounds had been washed, dressed with a coat of healing salve and covered with sterile cloth. The cut on her cheek had two stitches. There wasn't much he could do for her split lip. The two boys had helped remove their mother's bloody clothes, carried water for the doctor to wash her and had found a pair of drawers for him to put on her.

Hazel had come to briefly and cried out. Her cries so unnerved the youngest boy that he ran and hid. Doctor Langley gave her a dose of laudanum and waited until she went to sleep.

"I'm taking the quarantine sign off the house, Isaac. I'll go by and speak to Pastor Muse. He'll come and bring someone to help you take care of your mother."

"They took Pa away."

"I know they did. I was here. The sheriff will want to talk to you."

"I ain't talkin' to him."

"That's between the two of you." Doctor Langley picked up his bag. "I'll be back in a few hours. Your mother won't wake up for a while. Find your little brother and tell him that she's going to be all right."

The doctor went out the back door and stood for a long time near the woodpile. Mrs. Dawson had splinters of wood buried in her knees, arms and the front of her thighs. This was where her husband had whipped her. She had lain face down, her arms trying to shield her face and head.

Doctor Langley's eyes searched the ground in a widening circle around the woodpile. In the bushes, ten feet away, he found the bloody buggy whip, two straps of lead-tipped leather. It was a whip that most men would not use on a horse or a mule.

There was a spot of blood on the ground near the woodpile that couldn't have been Mrs. Dawson's. Puzzled, he walked over to where the body had been found a few feet from the truck. It suddenly occurred to him what had happened. Virgil had been struck a blow at the woodpile and another, more vicious blow, near enough to the truck so that blood and brain tissue had splattered on the fender.

Why, the doctor thought, if you were going to strike a man down, would you hit him and wait for him to crawl fifteen feet before you gave the fatal blow?

Well, he told himself, he was a doctor, not a sheriff. But his years as a coroner had made him curious. He put the whip in the car and drove away from the Dawson house with the feeling that with the death of Virgil Dawson, justice had been served.

After stopping at the minister's house and telling him about the vicious beating Virgil had given his wife, he asked him if someone would go out and stay with the boys.

"We would have gone out this morning if not for the quarantine. It's hard for me to believe Virgil would do such a thing. He was a hard taskmaster, but it was for the good of the family."

"When you see that woman, if you still believe that what he did was for the good of the family, your brains are as scrambled as his. I left the quarantine sign up longer than need be to protect the family from him." The doctor's words were short, clipped and angry.

When Doctor Langley left the minister he went directly to the courthouse to see the sheriff. He walked into the office and tossed the whip onto the desk.

"What's this?" Rex looked up with a frown.

"I just came from seeing Mrs. Dawson. She was beaten severely with that out by the woodpile last night. She was lying on the kitchen floor when I got there. How she managed to drag herself that far, I'll never know. I've never seen such a vicious beating." It was plain to the sheriff that the doctor's temper was boiling just below the surface.

"Goda'mighty! Where did you find the whip?"

"In the bushes by the woodpile where someone tossed it. That's where he beat her, judging from the wood splinters I found embedded in her arms, face and legs. The boy said his pa beat her, and he was glad that he was dead. I don't blame him if he had to watch that beating."

"Could the kid have killed his pa?"

"I hardly think so. There's a little pool of blood out from the woodpile that isn't Mrs. Dawson's. Her blood didn't pool. The fatal blows were delivered over near the truck."

"I've got Yates in a cell back there. He had threatened Virgil, and he was in town last night. So was Deke Bales. They were drinking together at the PowWow, but Deke got so drunk a friend took him back to the ranch."

"I suppose you know about Virgil keeping Andy Connors's little girl in the shed, and Isaac getting her out and taking her home. The boy says his pa beat his ma because he thought she had let the child out."

Sheriff McChesney stood. "What the hell are you talking about?"

"Didn't Yates tell you? Guess it doesn't matter now. Virgil can't hurt the boy. I don't know how he got his hands on the girl, but he did and he tied her up and locked her in the shed. The night Paul died, Isaac got her out and took her home. Virgil blamed his wife. Yates was going to try to get the reward to Isaac without his pa knowing about it."

Rex sat back down in his chair. "Why didn't Yates tell me this?"

"If you want my guess, it's because of your deputy. Yates doesn't trust him . . . nor do a lot of folks for that matter."

After the doctor left, the sheriff put the whip in a lower desk drawer and went back to the cell where Yates was lying on a cot.

"It's hotter than a pistol in here, Sheriff. Can you get me a fan?"

"I'd think a fan would be the least of your worries."

"Why is that? My conscience is clear."

"Did you go out to the Dawsons' last night to give Isaac the reward money?"

"Yeah, I did."

"Virgil came home and you killed him."

"No, I didn't," Yates said calmly. "Before I got to town I passed him going home. Then I went on back home and sat on the porch with Andy."

"How about Deke?"

"The last I saw of Deke he was drinking beer with someone called Cowboy."

"Deke's out of the picture. He got so drunk Cowboy took him back to the ranch. His cycle is still at the PowWow. Were you at the Dawsons' before or after Virgil whipped Mrs. Dawson with the buggy whip?"

Yates sat up on the cot. "How do I know? I was there about five minutes."

"Who did you see?"

"I saw Isaac. He came out onto the porch. I can tell you every word that was said." Yates related what had happened when he went to the house. "Isaac didn't want to take the money, but I promised him that his pa wouldn't know unless he told him. I put the money in his hand and walked away. As I was leaving the woman thanked me. That's it."

"She appeared to be all right?"

"I didn't see her, but she sounded all right. Why?"

"Doc says she's in bad shape."

"That old son of a bitch! What now, Sheriff? Are you going to take me before a judge?"

"Hell, Yates, I'm between a rock and a hard place. Folks are up in arms over the murder. You were my best suspect."

"According to your deputy."

"He heard you threaten Virgil. Hell, I don't depend on him for much, but I couldn't disregard that."

"Why do you keep him on?"

"Did you ever hear of the thing called *politics?* He carries a lot of weight with the voters in this county."

"I see what you mean."

"I want to go back out to the Dawsons'. I'll take you with me if you'll swear to God you'll not run. If you do, I'll shoot you. By damn, I will."

"I'll not run. I want to clear my name and get out of here. I've got a date tonight."

"Too bad it wasn't last night," Rex said dryly and unlocked the cell. "You'd of had an alibi."

Rex led the way out of the cell block. As they came into the front office, Wayne jumped up from behind the desk, grabbing for his gun.

"Hit the floor, Rex," he shouted. "I got a bead on him."

"What the hell! Put that damn gun down before you shoot me!" The sheriff put his hands on his hips. "Do it, Wayne, or I'll shoot you myself."

The deputy lowered the gun. "I thought he had a gun on you and was escapin'."

"Hell and damnation! Sit down behind that desk and play sheriff while I'm gone. Come on, Yates."

Outside, Yates said, "I wouldn't trust that guy as far as I could throw a bull by the tail. Are you sure he won't shoot me in the back?"

"I'm not sure of much of anything where he's concerned," the sheriff growled.

On the way out to Virgil's, Rex told about his conversation with Doctor Langley.

"Doc's pretty smart. He found the whip and figured out what happened. I want to look the place over and see if I can get anything out of the boy. He's bound to have heard Virgil whipping his mother. I figure he'll talk to you before he will to me. Something about lawmen scares kids."

The sheriff drove behind the house and parked the police car behind Virgil's truck. Rex pointed to the spot where Virgil's body was found and to the splatter of blood on the fender of the truck.

"Doc's sharp eyes found these blood spots. He thinks Virgil was struck down over by the woodpile. He crawled toward the truck, then was hit several more times while he was on the ground. Why didn't whoever hit him the first time just finish him off there?"

The two men searched the area until they found the pool of blood, dried now, that the doctor had discovered earlier.

"What Doc says makes sense to me." Yates followed the scuff marks in the dirt. "Look here at the specks of blood. His head was still bleeding as he crawled toward the truck."

A young man came out of the house and down off the back stoop with a water bucket in his hand. Yates and the sheriff stood.

"Howdy. I'm Joe Dawson. My brother, Pete, and I came in on the morning freight. We've been working at the CCC camp over near Fort Sill."

The sheriff greeted Joe and offered his hand. He introduced Yates, who also shook Joe's hand.

"Sorry about your mother."

"She hasn't woke up. She doesn't know we're here. A doctor sent us a telegram after our brother Paul died and we came as soon as we could."

Joe Dawson was well muscled from hard work. He was medium height and had thick sandy hair. His eyes reflected the same intelligence that Yates had seen in Isaac's. Nothing about him even remotely resembled Virgil.

"You and your brother will need to make arrangements for your pa's burial."

Joe's eyes went to the sheriff. According to the expression on his face he was holding his anger on a very tight leash.

"After seeing what he did to Ma, you can tie a wire around his neck, drag him off and leave him for the buzzards. I'll not lift a hand to give him a decent buryin'."

"What he did was terrible, but civilized folks bury their dead."

"Let that bunch of fanatics at the church bury him. That includes your deputy, Sheriff. He's cut from the same cloth as the old man."

"I'd like to speak to Isaac." Yates felt it was time to change the subject. "Will you ask him to come out?"

"Are you the fellow who gave him the reward money for taking Andy's little girl home?"

"I put the reward out. He earned it."

"To go against the old man took more guts than you can imagine," Joe said with a bite in his voice.

"I'm sure it did," said Yates.

"I'll get Isaac as soon as I get a bucket of water." He went to the well and dropped in the long tin cylinder to bring up the water.

Chapter 32

YATES AND ISAAC SAT IN THE SHADE on one of the dead-falls Virgil had dragged to the yard to cut up into stove wood. They'd had a dipper of good, cool well water before they sat down.

"I'm sorry about your mother, Isaac. You've sure had your share of trouble lately."

"Ma didn't do nothin' to deserve a whippin'. Pa thought one of us needed whippin' 'bout ever' day."

"I'm sorry to hear that, Isaac."

"Ma waited till she thought he was asleep 'fore she went out to get wood for the mornin' fire. We'd forgot to go get it while he was gone."

"Was that after I left?"

"Yeah. You'd not been gone long when he came. He called for Ma to open the door, but she wouldn't. He seemed to be madder than usual and swore he'd take the hide off her."

"Did you hear your mother when he was whipping her?" Yates asked quietly.

"He was yellin' nasty things at her. She was screamin'. I couldn't stand it." The boy's thin shoulders shook. "I made Carl hold on to Luke and I ran out. He was crazy. I didn't know what to do." Sobs he was trying to keep buried bubbled up out of his throat.

Yates stretched to put a comforting arm across Isaac's shoulders. He ached for the boy who had endured so much.

"He was a man and you a boy, Isaac. There wasn't much you could do."

"I had to make him stop . . . so I hit him with a stick of wood." He said the words fast. "It knocked him out. I grabbed the whip out of his hand and threw it in the bushes."

"You did what you had to do. He might have killed her if you hadn't stopped him."

"She was cryin' somethin' awful. I tried to get her up, but I couldn't. I yelled at the man to come help, but he just stood there."

"A man?" Yates swallowed his surprise. "Where was he standing?"

"Over by the truck. I saw him when I first came out; but I was so scared for Ma, I never looked again, until after I hit Pa. Then when I couldn't get Ma up, I yelled, but he just stood there," he said again.

"Were your brothers on the porch?"

"Carl was. Luke gets scared and hides."

"Did Carl come help you?"

"Yeah, but he ain't very big."

"Did he hear you yelling for the man to help?"

"I don't know. We had to hurry and get Ma in the house 'cause Pa was wakin' up. Ma come to and helped. We got her to the porch. She crawled in and told me to lock the door."

"Did you see your pa after that?"

"I looked out before I shut the door. He was crawling off toward the truck." The boy's shoulders shook with sobs. "I didn't mean for him to die. I just wanted him to stop hittin' Ma."

Yates pulled a handkerchief out of his pocket and put it in the boy's hand.

"I don't think you killed him, Isaac. Can you tell me something about the man you saw by the truck?"

"I think I know who it was. He's been here a lot of times."

"Was there another car here?"

"I didn't see one. I saw the lawman through the crack in the outhouse the day he brought Ruth Ann. Pa was standing by the car. Ruth Ann was inside. He had his hand on her. I didn't see him put her in the shed."

"Your pa would have been arrested for kidnapping if the sheriff had found out about it."

Isaac made a derisive sound. "Him and that lawman was tighter than ticks to a dog's back."

"The sheriff?"

"That other'n. Me and the boys call him 'Piggy.' "

"Deputy Ham?"

"Yeah. Are you goin' to tell the sheriff I hit Pa?"

"No. But if you want my advice, you should tell him yourself. Tell him what you've told me about hitting him and about seeing the other man standing by the truck."

"Will he put me in jail?"

"I'm sure he won't. He'll be grateful for your help."

"I'm scared of the deputy."

"You'd have to tell the whole thing. Your pa is gone, your brothers are here with you. If I think there's a chance Deputy Ham will hurt you, I'll be here, too."

"I told Joe and Pete. Pete didn't think the law would do anythin' to me for killin' Pa. They said I had to tell. I thought if I told you it'd be enough."

"I wish it was, Isaac. I really do. But the sheriff will have to hear it from you. Why don't we go talk to him? He's up there on the porch talking to Joe."

It was late afternoon when Yates and Andy left the sheriff's office. Andy had driven to the courthouse to see what he could do for Yates, then waited to drive him home.

Yates had been with Rex when he brought in Abe Patton for the murder of Virgil Dawson. After a few questions from the sheriff, Abe babbled on and on about being at the church service. His story became wilder and full of inconsistencies the longer he talked.

Finally he trapped himself when he said that Virgil had invited him to come home with him after church. He had said that tonight he was going to drag Hazel out of the house and teach her to obey him and wanted him to see it. He had seen Isaac hit his father while he was whipping his wife.

"Was that why you killed him, Abe?" Rex asked matter-of-factly while shuffling papers on his desk.

"Heck no. Ain't no law against a man whippin' his woman. She'd been sassin' him. She needed it."

"You must have thought you had a good reason for hitting Virgil with that piece of firewood. How many times did you hit him?"

"I don't know. Two or three or four. He promised me I could have Leona," Abe said as he tried to justify the murder. "He gave her to me a long time ago then went back on his word. I been a waitin' and a waitin' while he dilly-dallied around. I told him that other feller'd get to her if he didn't do somethin'. I kept workin' and he kept puttin' me off till I got a craw full of it."

Abe was as calm as if he were talking about the weather. He sat back in the chair, his hands hooked in the bib of his overalls, his heavy brogans crossed at the ankles.

"I told him I wasn't going to stand for it and I didn't."

"You need a lawyer, Abe."

"What I need is a chaw of tobacco."

Wayne was all swagger and full of self-importance when he took Abe back to a cell. On his return Rex confronted the deputy about taking Ruth Ann out to Virgil's. He scoffed and denied it at first, but later admitted only to taking a lost child to a relative.

"I told him to take her home," he declared.

"You were with Virgil when he came out to Andy's," Yates said. "You knew he was trying to take the girls while Andy was away. I heard you tell Virgil to be patient, that he'd get the girls all in good time."

"I was doin' my lawful duty when I come out there, and this isn't any business of yours. What's he doin' here, Rex?"

"Never mind Yates. This has to do with you. Why didn't you speak up when you heard the girl was missing?"

"I took her out there for him to take home. I didn't know he was keeping her in the shed."

"Why didn't you take her home?" Yates asked.

"Keep out of this," Wayne snarled. "It's not your business."

Rex continued in his mild voice. "You knew she was at Virgil's while we were searching for her. You took the child there against her will. You're guilty of kidnapping, Wayne."

"That's . . . bullshit!"

"One of Virgil's boys found her tied up in the shed and took her home. I suspect Ruth Ann will tell that you picked her up on the highway and refused to take her home."

When the sheriff told Wayne to hand over his badge, he became belligerent.

"Goddamn little bastards are lying," he shouted. "You're takin' their word over mine. I'm a lawman. Been one for eight years. That ought to count for something. We never had any trouble till *he* came here." His face had turned a dark red, his jowls quivered. He pointed a finger at Yates. "I should'a shot that son-of-a-bitch the night he put his hand on me. I'd a been in my rights." Wayne was so out of control with rage that he attempted to draw his gun.

Rex sprang forward and slapped the cuffs on his deputy.

"For God's sake, Wayne! All of this will go down hard against you. Come on back to the lockup and simmer down. The district marshal will be here in the morning. He'll straighten it out."

On the way home Andy and Yates agreed not to tell Leona that Abe had killed Virgil because he failed to force her to marry him.

"No use her having to think about that," Andy said.

"I love her. I'm going to marry her, if she'll have me." Yates looked at Andy. "What do you think of that?"

"I'm glad for both of you."

"Will you and the girls come with us to Texas? I want her to be happy, and she wouldn't be without the girls."

"I'm leanin' that way. It would be best for the girls."

The garage doors were closed, and two families were cooking supper in the campground when Andy turned into the drive and stopped beside the garage. Leona and the girls were waiting on the porch.

When he got out of the car, two squealing little girls flew down the path and wrapped their arms around his legs. Leona was not far behind. Yates opened his arms. Without hesitation she went into them. He hugged all three and happily burrowed his face against the warmth of Leona's neck.

Right here was something he thought he'd never have.

His heart pounded with gladness. For the first time in many years, he felt that he'd come home.

The girls talked, or shouted, he couldn't tell which, he was busy kissing the tears from Leona's eyes.

"We were so worried," she was finally able to say. "Andy was determined to go see about you when you didn't come right back. Then we worried when he didn't come back."

"It's been quite a day. One I'll always remember for more reasons than one." He hugged Leona and kissed her hard on the mouth, not caring a whit who saw him.

"You're kissin' Aunt Lee," JoBeth screeched.

"Yeah, and I'm going to kiss you, too." Yates lifted the child until her face was level with his and kissed her soundly on the cheek.

"I saw Isaac, Ruth Ann," he said when he set JoBeth on her feet. "He's all right and told me to tell you hello. Everyone knows that he brought you home and thinks he's a hero."

"I told Daddy about it and 'bout Mr. Ham taking me to Uncle Virgil's."

"We got a good supper," JoBeth announced. "Me'n Ruthy helped Aunt Lee. She let us get in the tank."

"Just what I'm going to do as soon as it gets dark." Yates looked at Andy with a smile of pure pleasure. "You might want to try it, Andy."

"I just might wrestle you for first dibs on it." He chuckled. "Supper sounds good to me right now."

On the way to the house, Yates, holding tightly to Leona's hand, whispered, "Have you forgotten our date tonight?"

"Date? What date?" Her laughing eyes teased his.

"I've thought about it all day. As soon as it's dark and I have a bath, I'm going to carry you off."

"Fiddle," she snorted. "You're pretty high-handed all of a sudden."

"And you've turned into a smarty. I'll have to take you in hand and teach you to have a little respect for your elders."

"Your mind's gone soft, Mr. Yates," she retorted with a sassy grin, her heart going like crazy in her chest.

While Yates washed up for supper, he gave Leona a sketchy account of how they had discovered Abe Patton had killed Virgil. He told about Isaac hitting Virgil so that he would stop beating his mother.

"He's a good boy. I liked the older boys, too. Joe assured me that he and his brother would stay around. They'll have the truck and the buzz saw."

"I'm sorry Virgil is dead, but he was not a good man."

"The funeral will be tomorrow. I'll take you if you want to go."

"No. I'll not go. That part of my life is over."

"The sheriff is holding the deputy for taking Ruth Ann out to Virgil and not telling about it while we were looking for her. I don't know if he'll go to jail, but he'll never be a lawman again."

"That will be the worst possible punishment. He loved that job."

Yates hung up the towel, reached for her and kissed her soundly. "I want to kiss you all the time."

"You'll have to stop sometime." She laughed happily. "Or you'll starve to death."

After supper Yates went to the tank to bathe. Leona tidied up the kitchen, then took a pan of water to the bedroom, washed and put on a fresh dress. She thought about the kisses Yates had given her and the tender teasing words he had said when he returned. He had looked different, younger, happy, like a kid on Christmas morning. Her hand trembled as she dabbed a bit of Evening in Paris perfume behind her ears.

The world could be ending tomorrow, and her only thought would be that she would have tonight with him.

When she heard JoBeth talking to him on the porch, she hurriedly brushed her hair, slipped a ribbon under it and tied it in a bow on top. After slipping her bare feet in her one pair of sandals, she went through the house and paused only briefly at the screendoor before stepping out onto the porch.

Andy was in the swing with the two girls; Yates stood on the steps. When she opened the door, he stepped up onto the porch and held out his hand.

"Ready to go?"

"Where ya goin'? Can I go?" JoBeth tried to slither out of the swing. Andy held on to her.

"You're going to stay here and take care of me, sweet pea," Andy said. "Yates and Leona are going . . . for a ride."

"But . . . I want to go," JoBeth whined.

"Not this time," Andy said. "This is Leona's time to enjoy herself without having to keep an eye on you."

"Aunt Lee won't care if I go."

"Baby!" Ruth Ann said scornfully. "You can't go. They're going out to kiss and stuff."

Yates laughed. "I'm hoping it'll come to that."

Leona was thankful it was dark. She could feel the heat rush to her face.

"Come on. Let's make our getaway while JoBeth thinks that over."

He didn't speak again until they were in the car and out on the highway. He had pulled her close to him and put her hand on his thigh.

"Is there anywhere you'd like to go?"

"There's not a lot to do." Now that she was alone with him she couldn't think of anything to say.

"I want to take you to town and walk up and down the street so everyone will know that you're my girl."

"No! Please, don't. They'll think the worst." *Please, God, don't let anything spoil this time with him.*

"That we've been sleeping together out at Andy's?"

When she didn't answer, he said, "All right, honey, but it makes me mad enough to bite nails. Someday I'm going to take you to the city. We'll go to a spiffy restaurant and to a show, dancing, or even roller skating, if you want to."

"I'd be a bird on roller skates. I've never been on them in my life."

He laughed and hugged her arm to him. "To me when I was about fifteen, heaven was roller skating. I even learned to skate backwards."

"Backwards? Heavens! It's a wonder they didn't put you in a side show. I used to be able to jump a double rope and I was the champion jacks player at school."

"I bet you were cute jumping rope."

"And you skating backwards. Did you ever fall down?"

"Lots of times."

He released her hand and turned off the road onto a lane, then out onto a hilltop where they could see the lights of Sayre in the distance. He turned off the car lights and the motor.

"I've waited as long as I can."

His arms slid around her. He held her tightly against him for a full minute, then with his fingers lifted her chin. A wild, sweet enchantment rippled through her veins as his mouth moved over hers with warm urgency. His kiss was hungry and deep. The sensation was heightened when his tongue caressed her lips, sought entrance and found welcome.

Ignoring the danger signals flashing in her brain, she pushed her fingers through his hair. It was so dark, thick and soft. Her head was spinning helplessly from the torrent of churning desires racking her body. The intensity of these feelings was strange to her.

"Oh, oh," she gasped. "We shouldn't have started this."

"Why not," he whispered. "You wanted it. I wanted it so bad, I'd have kissed you right down on Main Street, Sayre, Oklahoma, and thumbed my nose at the gawkers."

"My head tells me to stay away from you, but I can't seem to help myself," she confessed in a breathless whisper.

"Honey, you're pretty, you're sweet and perfect. I can't seem to help myself either." He kissed her lips, her eyes and nose, then pulled back. "Let's get out. It's damned hot in here."

He got out of the car and held her hand while she slid under the wheel and out. When he closed the car door, it banged loudly in the quiet night.

"There's a breeze up here," he said as they walked to the back of the car. "Honey, I've put a proposition to Andy about coming with me to San Angelo and working on the ranch. He's thinking about it."

"What could he do? He can't . . . do ranch work."

"He knows business. Ranching is business. I'll need a man I can trust. I want him with me. I want you and the girls. I'll have a big old house, and I want to hear kids running up and down the stairs and you yelling at them to get ready for school."

"He's . . . not said anything."

"He hasn't had a chance." He leaned against the car and

pulled her between his spread legs. "Would you be happy being with me forever?"

"Forever?" she echoed. "Well, it would depend—" *Depend on if you loved me.*

He turned her around. His arms encircled her from behind, and warm lips nuzzled the sensitive spot below her ear. His hands moved to cup her breasts, squeezing them gently.

"You're the sweetest woman I've ever known." She closed her eyes thinking only of the soft purr of his words and the feel of his hands. "I think you've bewitched me, sweetheart." One hand moved down to her belly and pulled her hips tightly back against him.

"Sweet Leona, say you care about me. You acted as if you did when I came back today." His ragged whisper was against her ear.

"I don't want to care for you . . . but I do."

"You don't want to love me?" he asked. She could feel his heart hammering against her right shoulder.

"I don't want to hurt when you go away."

"I'm not going anywhere unless you go with me."

Did he mean that he wanted her to come work for him? Keep house? She was afraid to ask.

She stood very still for several seconds as if absorbing his words. His lips moved hotly over her neck to her cheek, in search of hers, found them, and molded them to his in a devastating kiss. Her senses responded with a deep, churning hunger. She turned in his arms and rose on tiptoe, her fingers clinging to his shoulders.

Stirred by an incredible arousal, she met his passion with intimate sensuousness and parted her lips to glide the tip of her tongue across the edge of his teeth.

"God! Sweetheart. Help me . . . to stop this while I can."

"Don't stop." She moved her hips against him in instinctive invitation.

"I'll not be satisfied with . . . just this, sweet woman. It'll be all or nothing," he whispered raggedly and pulled her roughly against his hard arousal, leaving no doubt as to what he meant.

She burrowed her face against his neck. "I know," she whispered back. "Love me—"

In a little corner of her mind, her logic was warring with her desire.

This wanton behavior is what folks expect of you.

You love him. You'll have this to remember.

"Are you sure, honey?"

"Please!"

"Oh, sweetheart . . ."

It took only a couple of seconds for him to snatch a blanket from the backseat of the car and spread it on the grass. He pulled her down, wrapped her in his arms and lay back on the blanket, pulling her on top of him.

"I'm crazy about you. Kiss me." The kiss was long and tender. Afterward with her stretched out on top of him, he pillowed her head on his shoulder. "I'm scared," he whispered. "I've never loved anyone but my mother, and that was different." He stroked her back with his hard palms. "I need to know, sweetheart, if you love me back. If you give yourself to me I want it to be with love, not lust."

For a moment she was still. This big, quiet, sometimes difficult man was saying that he loved *her,* Leona Dawson, harlot of Sayre, Oklahoma. She raised up and looked into his face.

"Say it again." The whispered words caught in her throat.

"That I love you, sweetheart. I'm afraid that you don't love me back. You've not said if you even *like* me."

"Oh . . . oh! Don't be afraid!" She lowered her head and pressed her cheek tightly against his. Her warm breath caressed his ear. "I love you so much that every time I think about you leaving it's like a knife twisting in my guts. I love you so much that at times I feel light and bouncy, say and do foolish things. I love you because you're a bossy know-it-all. There is no one or nothing in the world more important to me than you, H. L. Yates. I'll spend my life telling you how high-handed you are and how much I love you, if you want me."

"Want you? Oh, love, I want you so bad it's been eating the heart out of me." His voice was a hoarse whisper. He pulled her face down to his and kissed her again and again.

"I want to marry you tomorrow or the next day at the latest. I want to hold you, kiss you and love you anytime I want to. I want us to be together from now until we're old and gray." His hands caressed her buttocks and pressed her to him. "I'll take care of you, honey. I swear it. No one will ever say a harsh thing to you again. If they do, I'll tear them apart."

She laughed happily. "I'll have to share you with JoBeth."

"Only in the daytime. At night it will be just you and me." He rolled her onto her back and leaned over her. "I want a dozen kids running up and down the stairs of that old ranch house. That means you've got to give me ten."

He kissed her with such incredible sweetness that a swell of joy washed over her. Her hands went to his lean buttocks and pressed his arousal tightly to her.

"Then we'd better get started, my love. I'm twenty-two years old. We can't afford to lose valuable time."

Epilogue

1933
Route 66
Near Sayre, Oklahoma

THE TRUCK CHUGGED TO THE TOP OF THE HILL; the gas gauge was on empty. The driver turned off the motor and the heavily laden truck rolled slowly down the hill toward the small building set close to the highway. For miles they had been reading the signs: CAR TROUBLE? NEED GAS? DEKE'S GARAGE AHEAD.

The large doors of the small building were folded back, and a single gas pump stood in front. On the peaked roof of the garage were the words: DEKE'S GARAGE—GAS. Before the truck reached the garage there was another sign, yellow with big black letters: SEE THE WORLD'S LARGEST RATTLESNAKE.

The truck made it to the edge of the drive, then refused to move another foot. A man in overalls and four children got out of the truck and pushed it off the highway.

A man came from the garage wiping his hands on a greasy rag. He wore cowboy boots and a big hat. His chin was covered with a healthy growth of whiskers. Even in boots he was not much taller than the eight-year-old boy who gawked at him.

"Howdy folks. Ain't no need to be straining yore guts to push that load. We'll put enough gas in to get ya to the pump. If you've a notion, ya can camp here for the night. Let the kids run a bit and the woman have a rest. Where you folks from?"

"Ringling."

"Ringling? Is that right? Some folks came through the other day from Ringling. Stayed at the campground. Let's see. Seems like the name was Carroll."

"Joe Carroll. They left a few days before we did."

"Pa, can we see the snake?" A small girl a year or two younger than the boy looked expectantly up at her father.

The little man answered. " 'Course ya can, darlin'. The dang thing is ten feet long if it's a inch. I call him Mr. Hoover, 'cause that's what he was, a snake in the grass that got us into this Depression. He's right here in the tank. I'll lift ya up so ya can see. I got a buffalo out back. I call him Mr. Roosevelt, 'cause he's full of . . . ah . . . something nasty, if he thinks the New Deal is going to put men back to work. I've not had time to put up a sign about the buffer yet. A while back I had a chicken with three legs, but the dang thing up and died on me."

Deke held the little girl so she could look down at the huge snake coiled on the red Oklahoma dirt in the bottom of the tank. The other children crowded around.

"Now, darlin'," he said and set the child on her feet. "After I take care of your daddy, I'll tell ya how I come onto that big old ugly snake and wrestled him till I got him in that tank."

"By yourself?" the boy asked.

"Sure. Ain't ya heard? I'm the best snake wrestler between here and California. Now, let's see what we can do to help your pa and I'll tell ya about it."

References

Oklahoma Route 66, by Jim Ross

Here It Is! Route 66 The Map Series, by Jim Ross and Jerry McClanahan

Route 66 Traveler's Guide, by Tom Snyder

Route 66: The Mother Road, by Michael Wallis